"Come now, Princesa. You had the nerve to propose marriage to me. Don't shy away now."

"I…I do not ask for your fidelity or your love, Gabriel. I do not need such delusions in my life. I only ask that you give me…"

Such color filled Eleni's cheeks that Gabriel stared, transfixed. Her lips trembled and she dug her teeth into the lower one. Lust punched him like an invisible blow, and it was all he could do not to tug at that lower lip and taste her himself.

"Eleni?" he prompted, in a harsh voice set on edge by the delectable temptation she made.

"I want a baby. A child of my own. I was in the process of going through adoption agencies when you…you threatened to pull your company out of Drakon. It's not something I'm willing to give up on—for anyone."

Every muscle in his body stiffened. Every instinct he possessed warned him to walk away from this deal with this woman. But even as he processed it, he had to admire her guts.

"A baby? You're bargaining for a baby?"

The Drakon Royals

Royalty has never looked this scandalous!

To the outside world, the Drakon Royals have the world
at their feet. Yet beneath the surface black-hearted
Crown Prince Andreas, his daredevil younger brother
Prince Nikandros and their illegitimate sister Princess
Eleni hide the secrets of their family name…

Until one brush with desire, and then all the Drakons
find themselves at the heart of their very own scandal!

Find out what happens in:

Crowned for the Drakon Legacy
April 2017

The Drakon Baby Bargain
June 2017

Look out for Andreas's story
September 2017

You won't want to miss this outrageously scandalous
new trilogy from Tara Pammi!

THE DRAKON
BABY BARGAIN

BY
TARA PAMMI

MILLS &
BOON

First Published in Great Britain 2017
By Mills & Boon, an imprint of HarperCollins*Publishers*
1 London Bridge Street, London, SE1 9GF

© 2017 Tara Pammi

ISBN: 978-0-263-92526-5

Tara Pammi can't remember a moment when she wasn't lost in a book—especially a romance, which was much more exciting than a mathematics textbook at school. Years later, Tara's wild imagination and love for the written word revealed what she really wanted to do. Now she pairs alpha males who think they know everything with strong women who knock that theory *and* them off their feet!

Books by Tara Pammi

Mills & Boon Modern Romance

The Sheikh's Pregnant Prisoner
The Man to Be Reckoned With
A Deal with Demakis

The Drakon Royals

Crowned for the Drakon Legacy

Brides for Billionaires

Married for the Sheikh's Duty

The Legendary Conti Brothers

The Surpise Conti Child
The Unwanted Conti Bride

Greek Tycoons Tamed

Claimed for His Duty
Bought for Her Innocence

Society Weddings

The Sicilian's Surprise Wife

A Dynasty of Sand and Scandal

The Last Prince of Dahaar
The True King of Dahaar

Visit the Author Profile page
at millsandboon.co.uk for more titles.

CHAPTER ONE

ONE KISS...

Eleni Drakos stood at the outer fringes of the black-and-white-tiled ballroom and peered through her elaborate mask.

One kiss from any man who'd look at her with warmth and desire, a man who could make her forget that a chasm of cutting loneliness was all that stretched ahead in her life.

One kiss because it was her thirtieth birthday and she was quite sick of her stagnant life, of pretending that the sight of her sister-in-law with her swollen belly didn't send a shaft of ache through her, or that she didn't crave a family of her own.

She'd lived her entire life within the rules her father, King Theos, had set, ensuring that her brothers, Andreas and Nikandros, had everything they had ever needed.

What she hadn't foreseen was that in the end, she would be alone. Just as she had been all these years.

She walked aimlessly at the fringes of the vast oval-shaped ballroom, the cut-crystal chandeliers making the resplendently dressed men and women glitter. She wasn't the only one hiding her identity behind the mask. The masquerade ball was an annual tradition of the House of Drakos and yet, with her father Theos's dementia becoming worse, it had not been held in four years.

But because the conservative traditionalists were balking at Andreas's continued absence after their father's death, and they feared that Nikandros and Gabriel Marquez's partnership was a risk to Drakon's economy, Eleni had suggested that they hold the ball again as a way of pacifying them.

And then she'd put the ball together in three weeks.

Scanning the stunningly dressed women and tuxedoed men who were dancing to a slow waltz, satisfaction filled her veins. Her fingers tingled to look through her fabled to-do list and check it off.

The black-and-white mask she'd bought on her trip to Paris last week went particularly well with the dark red lipstick. Piled high in a chignon, wispy tendrils of her usually unruly hair kissed her jaw.

Strapless and snug around her chest, her black-and-red silk ball gown accentuated an hourglass figure no amount of careful dieting could reduce, dipping at her waist and flaring into a full flounce.

The four-inch stilettos she had pushed her feet into boosted her five-two height, flashing her toned leg through the thigh-high slit. She'd been stunned when she'd looked at her reflection in the gold-filigree full-length mirror.

She'd always be plain compared to her half brothers, the Princes of Drakon; the media frequently reminded her by calling her the Plain Princess, but in that moment, she'd thought she had almost looked beautiful.

Good enough for the House of Drakos, her father would have said.

She continued wandering across the ballroom, marveling at the magnificence of the hotel.

It had been a crumbling Victorian-style mansion with out-of-date plumbing and bad interiors, but in three months Marquez Holdings Inc. had renovated it into a world-class destination for the nouveau rich that were pouring into Drakon, thanks to Gabriel Marquez's interest.

The ruthless real estate mogul was a guest of the palace of Drakon, and had been in Drakon for three months to oversee his company's investment in Drakon.

Casinos, luxury resorts that rivaled the King's Palace in style and ambience, mountain escapes, a world-class racing circuit—the map of Drakon was changing under Mr. Marquez's and her brother Nik's deft guidance.

A modern-day Midas, as the media called him, Eleni wouldn't have believed the transformation of the building Gabriel Marquez had wrought if she hadn't visited it herself almost a year ago.

Taking a sip of her chilled champagne, she looked down over the lush gardens. The scent of roses was thick in the air; a clock struck midnight at the old church in the city's main square.

She took a longer sip than was wise, felt the bubbly kiss her throat cold and sighed. It was a sound that seemed to come from the depths of her lonely soul.

The night stretched empty in front of her again.

"Why the long sigh, *querida*?"

The deep, slumberous voice sent a shiver down Eleni's spine that rivaled the tingles in her throat. Heart beating faster, she turned, bracing her hand on the balcony balustrade. "I didn't mean to interrupt your—"

"Stay."

With the one command, he made her spine lock. Even her father, who had been a bossy, hard-to-please man, had never ordered her around like that. "Excuse me?"

"Stay and keep me company," the man repeated, not even a little taken aback by her stiff tone.

With his back to the wall, the man was huge. Like a bouncer at a nightclub, he was tall and powerfully built.

A veneer of power clung to his frame. Unlike the other men at the ball, no mask covered his face. Only shadows.

His blue-black hair framed his face in thick, unruly waves. The fine white dress shirt, unbuttoned at the throat, clung to lean muscle. The breadth of his frame sent tremors through Eleni.

She couldn't stop her gaze from traveling down his length. One foot crossed over the other and stretched the fabric of his trousers, revealing the hard musculature of his thighs.

Eleni swallowed the strange anticipation that seemed to rise in her throat. He pushed off from the wall.

She barely swallowed the soft gasp that rose to her lips.

Roughly chiseled masculine planes, a wide, sensuously cruel mouth and a nose bent in the middle—it was Gabriel Marquez, the very man she'd been mooning over for months. The man who reminded her she was a woman every minute she spent in his company. The desire and need that she'd thought had disappeared with Spiros still burned bright in her.

The ruthlessness that had made Gabriel a legend in boardrooms across Europe screamed from every inch of him.

Her heart pumped faster as she waited for him to recognize her.

His dark slate-gray eyes studied her. He'd never so much as rested his gaze on her in three months of long meetings and numerous requests she'd dealt with. Not once had he shown any awareness that she was a woman.

No, then she was Princess Eleni Drakos, the facilitator for his firm, the grease between his company and the palace. But now she was a masked stranger, and something flared in those depths. Something that made her aware of how thin the silk of her dress was, of how tightly her skin seemed to be stretched.

"Such a wealth of regret and—" he paused while his gaze seared her "—need from a beautiful woman's lips… it feels like a challenge to any man."

"It wasn't…need," she retorted instantly, somehow negating what she had meant to say.

"Come, *querida*, isn't the idea of the masquerade to be open about our innermost desires while we hide our outward selves?" He traced the lower edge of her mask with a finger. Sensation zoomed from the spot. "You're safe behind that mask."

When his finger continued its journey back down and reached the indent over her upper lip, Eleni grabbed his wrist. If he touched her mouth… "Why aren't you wearing one?" she asked, wishing she didn't sound so breathless.

"Because I don't have to hide myself to express what I want. Nor do I need to validate myself by hiding from the world who I am."

Arrogance dripped from his every word. But why not? There wasn't one single woman in the palace who hadn't lost her breath over the sight of him.

"You sound far too sure of your appeal."

He shrugged. "I am Gabriel Marquez, Ms…?"

Eleni racked her brains for a name that had no association with her or the House of Drakos. She'd taken every precaution not to betray her identity at this ball tonight, including arranging it so that she was thought to be still in Paris by her staff and even by her brother Nikandros. Only Mia knew she was here. And the last thing she wanted was for this man to figure out who she was, especially now that he was staring at her with such male interest that she felt heady and drunk.

"You didn't think of a fake name before you decided to come to the ball tonight?"

A taunt in his question brought her gaze to his. Humor lurked in his eyes and Eleni felt something in her loosen at the sight of it. The twitching curve of his bold mouth unraveled a hidden streak she didn't even know she had. "A name was not required for the goal I had in mind."

His gray gaze gleamed with pure delight. "Now you make me more curious. Still, I would like a name to call you as I figure out what specific goals you had in mind for tonight. And how I can help you succeed in achieving them."

Awareness flooded every inch of her body and Eleni stood shaking in its wake. His bold eyes swept over her face, stilling for a second more on her mouth. His nostrils flared and a wave of heat seemed to emanate from him.

He was attracted to her, she realized with a sudden leap of her heart. The man who had never given her a second glance was attracted to her.

"Cinderella," Eleni whispered, after a moment's thought.

His eyes crinkled at the corners and warmth filled his eyes. It was such an unfamiliar, unusual expression on his usually serious face that Eleni stared hungrily. The man was gorgeous, but his smile made him breathtaking. "And is it the cruel stepsisters and stepmother that you're hoping to hide from tonight, Cinderella?"

A smile came to her easily. As easily as the giddy response. She felt like a teenager, bantering and flirting with the boy she'd been sneaking glances at for a few months. Wild and beautiful and wanted, as if she were any one of those women who were even now skillfully laughing and flirting with available men, women who knew the cues and their own worth, women who would spend the night in a lover's arms.

Women who hadn't been waiting their entire life for a man who'd promised the world. Women who had the guts to go after what they wanted instead of mourning a man who was long gone from her life.

She hadn't thought Gabriel Marquez would be the one who'd seek her out, but in her wildest dreams, wasn't this what she wanted? So why not take what she'd come for? Why not live for the moment?

Why not believe in the fantasy that she was beautiful and desirable and confident, and that the fire she saw in his eyes was all for her?

"You were right on the first guess," she said, jumping into the moment with both feet.

A vertical line formed between his brows, his arms coming to the balcony to cage her. "You sound familiar, Cinderella."

Shoulders rigid with tension, Eleni fought to keep her face straight. Was it the way she had said his name? Or was her disguise not enough to hide who she was?

The levity disappeared from his eyes, leaving them stone cold. "Did you come to the ball looking for me, Cinderella?"

That set her back up like nothing else could have. Lifting her chin, she met his gaze square. "You think a lot of yourself, do you not?"

"Women seek favors of me all the time," he said, the taunt back in his tone. "One does become a little jaded."

"It must be nice to believe the world revolves around oneself."

He threw his head back and laughed, sending trails of pleasure whispering over every inch of her skin. The broad shoulders shook with his laughter, which was a deep, masculine sound. Sleek grooves appeared in his rugged face, rendering that hard face a little beautiful.

"The more I listen to you, the more I like you. Tell me truly, have we met before?"

"In passing maybe," she offered, skating the line between truth and lies. "But I'm too much beneath your notice even if you'd seen me."

"I doubt I would forget you." The cage of his hands shrank around her, teasing her nostrils with the scent of him. Sandalwood and musk and something so essentially masculine it made her want to throw caution to the winds and burrow into his skin. "So if it's not a beastly family, who are you hiding from tonight, Ella?"

She flinched at the way he shortened her name and wished fervently that the shadows had hid it from him. Her brother Nik had always called her Ellie and so did Mia. To hear it fall from Gabriel's lips—it was thrilling and dangerous like nothing else.

"A clingy, dumbstruck lover?" Something hard entered his eyes. "Or a disgruntled husband?"

"No, no husband—" she half choked on the word "—and no lover either.

"I'm hiding from myself," she said, giving voice to the sentiment that had been gnawing at her for a while. "For one night, I wanted to be someone else, something else. I wanted to be daring and beautiful and a woman who lived in the moment. I wanted to be anyone but me." She caught the wistfulness in her voice and colored. "I'm sure you could not understand even if you tried."

He smiled and the grooves in his cheeks made his square jaw even more masculine. Straight white teeth gleamed in the silvery light, the lower lip jutting out in its fullness.

Having grown up surrounded by arrogant, unbending men like her father, King Theos, and half brother Andreas should have made her impervious to the aura of power that surrounded Gabriel, should have made her wary of that ruthless quality that pretty much had ruled her life when her father had been alive.

But it didn't.

For some unknown reason, she had always found herself drawn to Gabriel. To his confidence and arrogance.

"What makes you say that?" he ventured softly, as if he really wanted her opinion of him.

"You are Gabriel Marquez. Your reach and power... you own every space you enter, isn't that what they say?"

He shrugged, as if it were all matter of fact. "I have strived all my life to become what I am, to own everything I do today. And, no, I have never wished to wear another's skin."

Gray eyes searched her face. The perusal sent heat rushing to her cheeks. Long fingers drifted lazily onto her hips and every nerve in her body pulsed and stretched taut. As if it were possible to become smaller or less curvy by willing one's body to shrink.

If he noticed her instinctive reaction to his touch, he didn't heed it. Back and forth, his fingers traced the curve of her full hips, like butterfly kisses.

But it was rapt attention that went to her head, as if she had drunk something to make her euphoric. No man had ever looked at Eleni without the consequences of what and who she was.

Either she was an asset or a liability.

Either she was too low because she was illegitimate and held no real position of power in Drakos, or she was too much of a hassle to get involved with because she was close with her powerful brothers, the Princes of Drakon.

She belonged neither with the palace staff, nor on the wall of the East Hall that was graced by centuries of members of the distinguished, blue-blooded House of Drakos.

"Then my disguise, and my attempt at grabbing this moment under it, must seem like a joke to you. Pathetic even."

"You're wrong, *querida*. Even I need escape sometimes. Even I have to face the fact that I cannot control everything. That I cannot control fate and all the games it plays with us."

A thread of something in his tone tugged at her. As if there was something this powerful man needed that she could provide.

"I came…because tonight I cannot escape what tomorrow brings for me. Because tomorrow I face something I dread."

"Gabriel Marquez, afraid of something?"

Those grooves of his winked at her as he smiled again. "Shh...*querida*. You will spill my secrets and ruin my reputation. Now, tell me, what is it that you want tonight?"

The answer to a question had never come so easily before. "A kiss. I want a kiss." She swallowed at the flames of desire that licked at his gray eyes. "From a man who wants me. Not a pity kiss, Gabriel."

Hands on her hips, he swiveled her with masculine ease. Too shocked by the sudden contact, Eleni turned willingly.

A glass pane stood in front of them, reflecting their image. Even though she was wearing four-inch heels, he still easily overpowered her in height. She barely came to his shoulder. And his breadth—he was so overpoweringly male.

She felt like a doll, a fragile doll, compared to him. Not at all a practical, matter-of-fact woman, but a flimsy, fantastic creature of the night.

Even in the moonlight, it was clear that she was turned on. Her eyes glowed with gold flecks; her mouth, painted vivid red, was wide and vulnerable. She looked stunning, a mix of innocence and desire.

"Do you still think I would kiss you out of pity, *querida*?"

"No," she said loudly, the whisper of his touch filling her with a sense of feminine power.

Swiveling in his arms, she vined her arms around his neck.

When his cool lips slid over hers, Eleni jerked at the contact. For a huge man known for his arrogance, Gabriel kissed with a tenderness she couldn't believe. He tasted of whiskey and dark passion, and Eleni pressed into him shamelessly.

As if on cue, his kiss deepened. She gasped and his tongue flicked into her mouth. Stroked over the warm crevices with wicked intent. Tangled with her tongue in an erotic play that had her moaning.

Hard. Hungry. Hot. He kissed her like he wanted to sink into her. Like she offered him that escape he desperately craved.

His kiss rained sensation upon her, set every nerve on fire. Eleni sank into him gratefully while his hands moved over her hips, up to her shoulders, and then clasped her cheeks.

Long thumbs traced the lines of her face, desire painted on his stunning features. He dipped his head again and took her in another stinging kiss.

Her senses in a haze, she barely paid attention to his words. How could she when he nipped at her lower lip as if he meant to devour her?

When he kissed her as though he needed her more than air?

Low and rough, his words sent shivers through her spine.

Cool air hit her eyes and only then did Eleni realize that her mask had loosened.

The warm, male embrace immediately turned into a cold frost. Heat dissipated from her and she had to blink to see.

Her delicate mask dangled from his fingers, and a scowl etched his brow. He stared at the mask in his hands and then at her. Again and again, back and forth, as if he couldn't believe the sight in front of his eyes.

Her lips burned with his kiss, but this was not the same man. He looked at her as if—she searched his expression— as if she had somehow betrayed him.

"What is the meaning of this, Ms. Drakos?" The mask

fell at her feet with a whisper. "What the hell kind of a joke is this?"

She stepped back, the steel in his tone cutting through any foolish delusions she might still be clinging to. "It's not a joke. It's nothing," she whispered and turned away.

Barely had she gone two steps before a vise-like grip had clamped over her upper arm and turned her. "Why are you here tonight? What do you want from me?"

The nerve of the man! "*You* approached *me*. You…you ordered me to stay and keep you company. You…I only spoke the truth."

"So I'm supposed to believe the Plain Princess of Drakon—" he bit out her moniker with such sarcasm that Eleni flinched "—walks around masquerade balls, accosting men for kisses? That this is your nightly routine?"

"I did not accost you at all. And yes…I wanted a kiss. I wanted to feel less lonely for one night. I wanted…" Her voice caught, but she didn't back down. "Which scenario threatens your masculine ego—that a woman could want to kiss a man, or that in your arrogance you think I came here looking to somehow trap you into kissing me?"

"You lied to me, *Princesa*. I asked you straight and you said you didn't know me. Maybe you even got a little power trip from the fact that you knew who I was and I didn't know who you were. Maybe it's a little game you play every night with powerful men."

"You're crossing the line!"

"I'm sick of deceit and lies. If it is a kiss you want, here it is!"

If Eleni had had any sense, she would have slapped his arrogant jaw, hard. But no, when he touched his lips to hers again, she melted. She had no will or control over her body.

When he licked the seam of her lips, she gasped open for him, like a sunflower.

When he plunged his tongue into the cavern of her mouth, she shamelessly pressed against him.

His hands moved to her bottom and he pressed her against him, until she felt the evidence of his arousal. Until the hard planes of his body were stamped onto her soft curves. Until she was moaning, spreading her legs to feel more of him.

The kiss was over before it had begun, and yet it seemed to spin her senses. And the man who had delivered it looked at her as if she had agreed to sell her soul for pennies. "If you're that desperate for a man, maybe ask one of your powerful brothers to set you up with one, *Princesa*," he said mockingly. "The next man you play your little game with might not be as forgiving as me for your duplicity."

Eleni stared at him, shaking from head to toe, burning with the unspent desire that he had aroused in her. Desire, she now realized, he had aroused with the sole intention of punishing her.

"I would not kiss you again if you were the last man on earth, Mr. Marquez," she shouted but he'd already gone.

Try as she might to fight the temptation, she couldn't help but run her fingers over her stinging mouth. Couldn't stop tasting him on her lips.

CHAPTER TWO

Three months later

"I HATE THIS PLACE, I hate that I had to give up all my friends and move here and I hate you."

The loud, blistering announcement exploded inside the conference room like a small detonation, jerking twelve heads toward the twelve-year-old girl standing just inside the room. Face scrunched, eyes brimming with fat tears, his daughter, Angelina, stood glaring at Gabriel Marquez.

A pounding began behind his left eye.

He had made his father's small construction company into a billionaire real estate firm, he owned major chunks of multinational companies, he had palatial residences in nine different cities in the world, but this was one problem, it seemed, for which he had no solution.

Angelina had come to live with him three months ago after her mother had passed away suddenly—a model he had met in New York, years ago.

His own daughter was a stranger, because until the accident that had killed her, Monique hadn't had the decency to tell Gabriel that he had a daughter.

Now Angelina looked at him as if he were a monster, as if he had taken away the one person who had loved her.

He hadn't been able to have one normal conversation with her in all the weeks she had been in Drakon with him.

"Angelina, calm down and wait for my meeting to finish," he gritted out. His jaw hurt with how tightly he had leashed the urge to vent his frustration that he was floundering just as much as she was.

That they were strangers to each other was not his fault.

His board members stared between him and Angie like spectators at a tennis match, ready to feed fuel to the wildly spreading rumors that Gabriel Marquez was an abysmal father.

Anything he did and said was news to the press. But the fact that he'd successfully hidden the existence of a daughter, who'd been born out of wedlock, for twelve years, sent them into a feeding frenzy. That his daughter hated him with every breath and, even worse, didn't know him at all would be the cherry on a very nasty cake.

"If I waited for you to finish one of your unending meetings, I would wait forever. All I want is to—"

Gabriel shot up from his seat, frustration boiling over in his blood. "You behave like a spoiled brat, with no concern for others' time. Has your mother taught you no manners?"

Her flinch fell on him like a poisoned dart, sinking deep. Goddamn it, nothing he said ever worked with Angelina. The tears that she had somehow contained in those big eyes fell onto her round cheeks, drawing paths down to her neck. "I wish you had died instead of Mom. I wish you weren't my father. I wish—"

"Angelina! That's enough," a feminine voice shot out.

Shock traveled through Gabriel as his daughter, who'd barely exchanged one civil word with him in three months, instantly looked contrite. Her round shoulders straightened and something shifted in the planes of her juvenile face, already struggling to show signs of adulthood.

He startled when Eleni Drakos pushed her chair back and walked toward his daughter, her expression one of sternness and yet somehow kindness at the same time.

Gabriel frowned as her pumps click-clacked against

the marble floor. In three months, he hadn't been able to quite put his finger on the woman the media disparagingly called the Plain Princess.

An opinion he didn't agree with anymore.

Unlike her tall, dark brothers, the Princes of Drakon, Eleni Drakos, on first impression, was a mousy woman. Ten years ago, she'd barely ever met his gaze, hiding behind King Theos's fierce temper.

Since he'd arrived in Drakon a few months ago, however, he'd watched the brisk efficiency with which she ordered the palace staff around—and even his staff.

Every time he turned around, there she was, a petite dynamo. Only now, as he saw her reach Angelina, did he realize how much his staff and he had depended on her to smooth out numerous problems between his company and the palace in those first few weeks.

How much the Crown Prince Andreas and the Daredevil Nikandros relied on her.

His frown deepened as her slim hand went around Angelina.

She whispered something and instantly his daughter's expression cleared. A hesitation emerged in her eyes but Angelina wiped her tears, and then to Gabriel's shock, a tentative smile curved her mouth.

A tight ache emerged in the nether regions of Gabriel's heart. Three months with a string of nannies each more expensive and efficient than the next, three months of gifts and presents to make up for twelve birthdays, three months of fighting the urge to tell her that it was not his fault, not once had Angelina looked at him with anything remotely bordering on the affection in her eyes as she looked at Eleni Drakos now.

What magic had the Princess wrought on his child? To what purpose? When had Angelina become acquainted with her?

Shock buffeted him in fresh waves when Eleni softly nudged Angelina toward him.

The wariness in his daughter's eyes dealt a swift kick to his gut more painful and wretched than anything Gabriel had faced before. But for the life of him, he hadn't been able to forge even a tenuous connection between them.

It was as if fate was laughing at him.

He'd willfully become this man who avoided emotional entanglement at any cost. Now, try as he might, it seemed he couldn't connect with his own daughter.

"I'm sorry," Angelina whispered, her eyes bright and big.

She didn't call him Papa but he knew better than to expect a miracle. She turned to the Princess as if waiting for another cue, as if she could only bear to do this small thing—look at him without hatred—for the Princess.

Breath balled up in his throat, for he'd never felt this strange anticipation.

Hands firmly on those small shoulders, the Princess gave his daughter a cue.

Again, something about her smile snagged him while she and Angelina walked toward him. That his daughter, who treated him as if he were plague-ridden, had found someone to connect with should have been a good thing.

Instead, all he felt was a yawning chasm in the pit of his stomach.

"Now, Angelina," the Princess said, and her voice shivered over his spine. The taste of her came to his lips, his hands fisting against the sensation of her curved hips. It was a sensation he hadn't been able to get out of his head in three months, even as he'd become more and more aware of her husky, low-pitched voice, of the way her dress shirts seemed voluptuous on her body, of the tug of her mouth on one side when she was being sarcastic, of her every movement. Of the fact that she'd avoided meeting his eyes since that night at the masquerade ball.

No woman had ever messed with his head quite so much by trying to ignore him.

I just wanted a kiss, Gabriel.

Had she?

And now here she was with a wide smile bestowed on his daughter.

Muddy brown eyes glinted with warmth, the edges of them tilting up, revealing hints of heritage no one, he was sure, knew about.

The smile seemed to spread to her entire body as she looked at Angelina. It snagged his attention, and every other man's attention, he noted with a flare of annoyance.

"Remember what we talked about," she said. "First we express our anger and hurt in a constructive way instead of hurling accusations at someone, however well deserved they may be."

His daughter nodded like an angel, lifting her chin in a show of condescension toward him. That put-upon anger and the skinny shoulders pretending to be so unaffected, caused Gabriel to feel a realization slam into him: hateful words or not, his daughter was very much just a kid.

And he wouldn't have seen it if not for the woman silently glaring at him over Angie's furiously nodding head. Her judgment of him was clear in her deepening frown.

"You went on your trip again. You not only left me with that…horrible nanny, but you also forgot my birthday. Mom would've never…" A choked sound emerged from Angie's throat. "Mom told me you didn't live with us because you were a busy man. Not because you didn't care about me. But now… I know she was lying to protect me. It's clear that you never wanted a daughter."

Pushing away the Princess's hand from her shoulder, Angie ran out of the boardroom, leaving a minefield of silence behind.

No, he'd never wanted a daughter. He hadn't been in a

relationship with her mother, which he thought was why she'd never told him.

And yet when he'd seen Angelina for the first time, Gabriel had known his life had forever changed. To his own surprise, he hadn't felt an ounce of resentment.

He'd only wanted to welcome her into his life.

But Angelina wouldn't give him a chance. Frustration and fury twisted inside him.

He took a few steps in her direction when he heard the soft command.

"Leave her alone, Mr. Marquez." A pregnant pause, as if the Princess couldn't believe her own audacity. "For now. Please. Don't force her to take back those words just because your ego is smarting."

A burning feeling emerged in his throat and Gabriel realized it was shame.

The Princess was right. He was only thinking about how this affected him, how he wanted to fight the tug of failure.

He'd moved mountains and built castles, immersed himself in the world's real estate games, and yet he didn't possess a single thing that would bring his daughter closer to him.

With one nod, he dismissed the meeting. He watched the quick shuffling of papers on the dark mahogany desk, heard the whisper of chairs as if it were all a background score, his attention fixed on the woman he had forced himself to ignore for three months.

And utterly failed.

He didn't want to have anything to do with this woman who'd made it so easy to unburden himself. Who had, for the first time in his adult life, made him question his choices, his very lifestyle. Made him wonder about the depth of love his father had nurtured for his mother, before it had destroyed him.

* * *

She shouldn't have spoken to him like that. She shouldn't have confronted him. She definitely shouldn't have chastised him as if he were a negligent staff member.

Eleni sighed as her hands brushed against her soft leather bag.

Now he'd probably forbid Angelina from even seeing her. And while she'd miss Angelina with an ache, it would be so much worse for the little girl.

Only last week had Angelina started opening up to Eleni, since she'd come to see that Eleni had no hidden agenda that involved her father.

And now, because she couldn't keep her mouth shut, because she couldn't bear to be ignored by Gabriel again, Angelina would lose the only adult she'd come to trust.

The hair on her nape stood in prickles as the room emptied around her.

Vibrating with a tension she couldn't dispel, she straightened from the table. Gabriel Marquez stood at the corner of the room, a silent specter studying her with hair-raising intensity. "You're full of neat little tricks, *Princesa*."

Eleni stiffened. "I have nothing to say to you."

He made his way across the room with soft strides for such a big man. Like a jungle cat. "I would say it was the opposite, judging by the looks you sent my way. I would say you were raring to rip into me."

Eleni tilted her head back, struggling to keep her gaze away from the hard contours of his mouth. His lips had been so soft and demanding against hers. So full of passion and tender warmth. For days afterward, she'd marveled at the paradox of the man's kiss, which matched the man himself—one moment warm and inviting, and the next cold and ruthless.

"Even the board members now know that you were dying to set me down about Angelina."

Heat rushed into her cheeks and she struggled to keep her thoughts and her gaze from straying. "I...was trying to defuse the situation without further breaking her—" she flinched as his gaze became chilly "—heart. Even you must agree that Angelina's feelings are the most important in that scene."

"Even I?" His taunt was voiced in such a low tone that Eleni had to tilt closer to understand. Instantly, she was suffused in his male scent. Tendrils of warmth settled low in her belly as he reached her. "Explain."

Any mortification she felt at her body's alarming re-action to his nearness died at his curt tone. "Don't bark commands at me."

His gray eyes were cold and bleak, like a winter sky. "Maybe you think I'm one of the staff you order around with such brisk efficiency, *Princesa*. It would be in your best interests to remember who I am."

She tried for a laugh, awareness flooding through her. His hands had traced her hips as if she were a precious treasure. His body had been a fortress of warmth. She couldn't stop that rush of sensation so she held herself rigid instead. "Like you let anyone forget. This is ridiculous, Mr. Marquez. If you want to say something, then say it."

He breathed out in a harsh exhale, tension wreathing his features. "Angelina and you have formed a bond."

"Is there a question in that?" she taunted, ignoring the rational voice that said she was pulling the tail of a tiger.

He hesitated and Eleni saw something in those cold eyes that made her hesitate, rethink her opinion of him. Or at least not to condemn him so easily. "How? When?"

"When what?"

"When did you become close? How did you...have so much access to her?" His frown deepened as he searched her face. "It's not like you sit around playing the charming socialite in the palace."

Was he complimenting her or setting her down? Infuriating man! "I...I... The task of setting up quarters and such for the string of nannies you employed for her fell to me. When you disappeared on your long and frequent business trips, the task of making sure they did their job fell to me. I think it was the second one. Or the third. The poor woman couldn't find Angelina one day for hours and raised an alarm.

"You were in... Sydney, I think. Since you brought her to Drakon," she couldn't resist adding, "I noticed that Angelina always drifts toward the stables. I found her there that afternoon, hiding in my mare's stall. Angelina loves horses—did you know that? I invited her to spend some time during the day with me at the stables. And we...we got close," she finished, her face a swath of color.

Somehow, spending time with Angelina had become the high point of her day. Had filled the gaping hole in her life after her father's death and Andreas's uncharacteristic departure.

"But what did you do? And why? I want to know what you did to get so close to her, Ms. Drakos."

He looked so befuddled that Eleni bit back her temper and sighed. "I didn't do it for some nefarious purpose."

He ran his hands through his hair, tight grooves etching around his mouth. "I'm not accusing you," he said, though his tone did just that. "I'm curious as to what you did, what techniques you employed, what...incentives you offered to get close to Angelina."

"She's not a business deal you're trying to close," she burst out, remembering her own confusion at that age.

"I have never lost a business deal in my life."

"That's exactly what I'm saying." She exhaled roughly

and willed herself to be patient. For that twelve-year-old, if not for the arrogant Spaniard in front of her.

For three months, she'd tried to pretend that the kiss hadn't happened. That it hadn't been the most glorious moment of her life, even when he'd pushed her away with such apparent disgust. That her heart didn't speed up every time she laid eyes on him.

That she didn't hope in the farthest corners of her heart that he would look at her with that passion in his eyes again, that he would see her as a woman and not as a part of the palace machinery. That he would kiss her again, just one more time.

But no.

Five layers of makeup, a dress that displayed every curve and a sign around her neck that said she was willing and wanton. And of course, her identity hidden behind a mask.

That was the only way he would want her apparently.

She swallowed away the disappointment as she always did, tired of her own pathetic longing. There were years of his company's work still to be done in Drakon. Was she going to spend the next decade mooning over one kiss that meant nothing to him, like she had mourned the last decade over Spiros and his vows of undying devotion, even after he'd disappeared like mist?

"Angelina, for all that she's been forced to grow up in the past few months, is a little girl. With feelings and emotions. She lost the one person who loved her unconditionally. She's been thrust into an unfamiliar world with a man—"

"It has been eight months since her mother died."

"Eight months is an entire lifetime for her. You can't just…buy her things and expect everything to be all right. You can't just slot into her life and expect her to love you like she did her mother. Not by leaving her with a string of nannies. Not by engaging her in a battle of wills. And definitely not by demanding her affection and love."

"Those nannies came highly recommended with years of experience in dealing with kids."

"But not a single one of them tried to understand her. It was all just schedules and milestones and you can't just ignore…" She swallowed the lump that rose in her throat.

He tucked a finger under her chin and tilted it up. "I can't just ignore what?"

She wished she could hide the expression in her eyes. Erase the hurt from that corner of her heart that never seemed to heal. "You can't fix the loss of her mom by throwing her into the deep end. She's among strangers in a foreign country and she barely sees you. She…she told me last week that she wanted to run away because of what that ghastly girlfriend of yours told her."

If he wasn't holding her chin in his hands, she would have missed his flinch. "She's not my girlfriend. She's an ex. She…said she had experience with kids…that she could help me connect with Angelina."

Now she understood the lineup of exes and "girlfriends" that had been appearing outside his office in the last few weeks. It had taken every ounce of her willpower not to march in there and demand that he send them away. For Angelina's sake.

"Could you not see that they were just using Angelina like some stepping stone toward you?"

She saw it sink in. His jaw tightened. "And you, *Princesa*? You do not have any purpose?"

His gaze promptly fell to her mouth, a languid stroke against her senses. "I told you—I have no designs on you."

"You knew who I was and yet you still kissed me."

"Because my requirements for that night were to kiss a man. You fit the bill. If you hadn't ripped my mask off, I'd have been on my way and no one—"

"If I hadn't ripped the mask off—" his harsh breath purred over her cheeks "—I would have been *inside you*, right on that balcony, with your brother and half the world watching."

Gravelly and low, his words rippled over her skin. Places she shouldn't be thinking of throbbed with need. "Ripping off the mask was the only sensible thing that happened that night."

"I would have—" she licked her lips as if that could stave off the heat pouring through her "—stopped you. It wouldn't have gone that far."

His gaze held hers, amusement and something else glittering there. "Either you're very naive about men or you just like to lie to yourself." A rough exhale left his mouth. "And now I find you, of all the people in my life, bonded with my daughter."

Eleni pushed away from him, needing respite from that overwhelming masculinity. Respite from her own reactions. "Even your conceit can't be that great to think I befriended Angelina with some…underhanded intentions. Sitting in the stables by herself, she reminded me of myself."

"A Princess of Drakon, daughter to King Theos and sister to powerful Andreas and Nikandros—and I'm to believe you understand how Angelina feels? That you have to hide beneath a mask to find a man to kiss you?"

She shrugged, the gleam of interest in his eyes making her heart thud faster. If not for Angelina, he wouldn't have spared her a single glance again, much less a conversation.

"I don't care what you believe about me. Angelina needs to feel like she's important to someone, like there's some constant in her life that won't desert her. She's a sweet girl underneath all that bluster."

"She's sweet with you," he bit out, a vein vibrating in his forehead. "The first time I saw my daughter was at her mother's funeral. It took her a week to understand that I was indeed her father and not some terrifying stranger who was ripping her away from everything familiar. I learned after my ex was in an accident that she had named me as Angelina's father.

"In three months, she hasn't stopped looking at me as if I…were the culprit.

"My own daughter looks at me as if I…" He swallowed hard and looked away. "I've tried to be gentle with her… I've tried gifts. I've tried everything under the sun but not a damn thing works."

Eleni hoped for the little girl's sake that he would learn to express that concern. To show that he cared. But she'd been around too many thickheaded men, and Gabriel Marquez had proved that night that he was the king of arrogant ruthlessness and wouldn't recognize tender emotion if it hit him in that all too gorgeous face.

He'd connected with her that night when he'd thought her a stranger. But as soon as he'd learned her identity, as soon as he'd learned that she knew him, he had shut down. Had closed himself off so fast that for days after she'd wondered if she'd imagined their exchange.

She wanted nothing to do with such a hard man, a man who thought showing his emotions was a weakness.

But for Angelina's sake, she wanted to help. She remembered all too well how alone and frightened she had been growing up in the palace. It was only when her father had married Camille, Nikandros's mother that Eleni had realized that not everyone in the palace resented the illegitimate child that the King had adopted in a fit of uncharacteristic generosity.

Camille had been so busy with Nik's frail health, and yet she'd always had a kind word for Eleni.

"Never let him see a weakness, ma chérie," when Eleni had cowered in the face of her father's rages. *"Never let*

them make you dispensable," when Eleni had, in her innocent ignorance, complained that the Crown Prince Andreas, the older brother she loved so much, didn't care about her either.

So Eleni had taken Camille's advice to heart and made herself indispensable to her father and brothers. She had never imagined becoming the buffer between the three of them.

As she'd observed this father and daughter over the last three months, she'd assumed Gabriel was the same as her own father: controlling, bloated with arrogance, treating his offspring like pawns in his own personal game.

The glittering frustration in Gabriel's eyes gave her hope for Angelina.

"She feels that you've taken her on as a last resort. With me, she knows I love spending time with her. That I don't expect anything in return, that it is not a duty."

Gabriel's gaze moved over her, searching without seeing her. She'd seen that look on her older brother Andreas's face—when he saw people only as a means to an end. When he decided on a course and set upon it, no matter what the cost to others. Her heart thumped in her chest.

"Then you'll teach me how to get through to her," he added softly, utter resolve in his tone, "and you'll help the both of us connect."

"It's not something I can transfer from my head to yours."

"I do not care what you call it, *Princesa*, but you'll teach me how to connect with my daughter." Stubborn resolve made his features look harsher than ever. "And you will do it before it's too late."

"What you're suggesting is…not that simple."

"I will speak to Nikandros about releasing you from all your many unofficial duties. From now on, you'll spend your entire time with Angelina. And me, whenever I'm available." His brow cleared, everything falling into place in his world. Even her soft gasp didn't divert his attention. "I'll try to clear my schedule for a couple of evenings every week and we will dine together. After a month or so, the three of us can take a trip together. I want to find a good school for her and you can accompany us."

The man's nerve! "I'm not your servant to be ordered about. I will not drop everything in my life just for your benefit. I will not..." She couldn't even get the words out at his arrogance. "You insult me with one breath, and then order me around on the next."

Spending months in his company, wishing he would take notice of her, comparing herself to his parade of girlfriends—it would be her personal torture device. "What makes you think I would willingly sign up for anything that concerns you?"

"Because you do not have anything going on in your life. I've been watching you, *Princesa*."

Eleni jerked back, her heart thumping against her rib cage. "Watching me? For what purpose?"

He shrugged, just like she'd done before. And if Eleni hadn't spent an hour with him on a moonlit terrace sharing the depths of her soul, she wouldn't have seen the carefully manufactured gesture. She'd have missed that utterly male gleam in his gaze.

"To figure you out."

"And what have you figured out?"

"You're illegitimate, so you don't rank that high with the traditionalists of the country. You have no boyfriend or lover and no options on the horizon, unless you ask your brothers to set you up. And they are smart enough to keep you around because of course you're sensible and reliable.

"I've seen you with your brothers and the staff. You're a very maternal sort of woman. You know every staff member by name, and you ask after their families. You give hours of your time to children's charities instead of just throwing money at them. And your reckless actions that night prove how desperate you are for your life to change. For it to be more than it is."

Shock robbed Eleni of speech as she stared at him. He'd so efficiently reduced her life to a cold, hard summary, a truthful one. "First I was deceiving, now I'm reckless?"

"Imagine if it had been anyone but me. Imagine if it had been one of the media or a man who could have harmed you in some way. You don't walk around parties advertising you're available, not when you're the bloody Princess of Drakon."

Eleni stared stupefied, the unease in his eyes far too real for her to scoff at. "I...I wouldn't have just walked off with any man."

He raised that arrogant brow and she flushed and looked away.

They both knew she'd have done whatever he wanted of her that night. And that awareness stood between them, taunting her.

"Allowing that you truly care for Angelina, what I suggest would not be a hardship at all. All I ask you is that you spend your time in the lap of luxury with Angelina and me."

"For how long?" she whispered, unable to resist. Unable to walk away from him.

"Until such time as I feel you're not needed anymore."

"So you're offering me a job?"

"Call it whatever you want, Princess. Money, jewels, stocks...you can have whatever you want in return."

A job description with a tenure and conditions. Just another man demanding his due without giving anything back. Just another role for her to play for a limited time. Like she'd always done, filled with the nauseating hope that it would last.

The reliable, responsible daughter to her father.

The buffer between her brothers.

The woman that the man she'd loved had easily and thoroughly forgotten.

The illegitimate but adopted child of the House of Drakos.

All temporary. All meaningless, in the end.

If she accepted his "offer," she would lose a bit of her heart to that little girl, and when she'd served her purpose, Gabriel would calmly remove her from his life. And yet, she wanted to do it. She wanted to spend time with him and Angelina, wanted to help them bridge that gap before it came irreparable.

She wanted to see more of the man she'd talked to that night. Heart thudding dangerously, she admitted that she wanted a chance for him to notice that she was a woman, to remember that he'd kissed her with such abandon.

She jerked in place when he cupped her jaw and tilted her face up to meet his gaze. Slumbering heat glittered there, reminding her of what had happened the last time he'd touched her. Tempting her. Her hesitation was ammunition as he cornered her with a predatory gleam. "Admit it, Princess." Eleni shivered when his hot breath caressed the rim of her ear. "You're tempted."

"Whatever I learned about you that night, I…I kept it to myself. I…trusted that man. But you…you play dirty, Gabriel."

"I play to win, *Princesa*. I always have." His brow rose as he searched her gaze. "It is clear that you truly care for Angelina. And if you agree, maybe I can be persuaded to overlook your deception." His thumb traced the line of her jaw, a featherlight stroke that branded her. The sound of her harsh breaths filled the silence, her body swaying toward him with a will of its own. She raised her gaze, frowning.

"I could even be persuaded to kiss you again, *Princesa*.

I could give you all the excitement you crave, all the daring moments you want. I might even be willing to show you the passion that you desperately want.'

Toes scrunched in her sensible pumps, body thrumming like a tautly stretched string, Eleni stared into his beautiful gray eyes.

His breath caressed her lips, his gaze studying her as if she were the most beautiful woman on earth. She felt drugged, and he hadn't even touched her. "So you're offering me—" somehow she spoke "—an affair in return for looking after your child?"

"We want each other, yes? It's not a big leap from that."

What would happen when she spent days in his company with just a little girl for buffer? What would happen when he didn't stop the next time? When she'd be all twisted and tangled into their lives and he decided he didn't need her anymore?

Where would she land then?

In the same place, with her heart bruised again by another careless man.

Better that she and Angelina cut that cord now before the damage to that young girl was permanent. Before Eleni herself forgot that no man was worth the heartache that she'd already tasted, thanks to Spiros. Thanks to her father.

Love was not for her, whatever silly dreams she wove.

She put her hand on his wrist and pushed it away. Her palm burned at that innocent contact. Her body whimpered silently at the promise in his eyes. "No."

"No what?"

"No to everything you suggested."

"Why not?"

Suddenly, the idea she'd been playing with in her head for a while now was the only lifeline. She would go away. Away from this man and his little girl who already owned a part of Eleni's heart. Away from the unending void that her life had seemed to be lately. "I plan to leave Drakon for a while."

His jaw tightened. From one breath to the next, his gaze became hard, all the heat gone. "How long is a while?"

"Months. Maybe a year." She stepped away, needing the distance. "I've always wanted to see the world and this is my chance."

"And what about Drakon and your duties? What about your precious brothers?"

"Nikandros has convinced me that they'll be here for the rest of our lives. I've never once left Drakon. I've seen nothing of the world beyond this palace and its walls. It is time for me to step out."

Time for her to reach for what she wanted.

Spending all this time with Angelina, nurturing their relationship, seeing the joy that came into the young girl's eyes when she and Eleni spent time together—it gave form to what Eleni herself desperately craved.

She would never love a man. But being a mother to a baby, bringing love into a child's life—someone unwanted, like she'd been—*that* she could do. That was in her hands.

"I wish I could help you, at least for her sake. But I just can't. I can't put my life on hold for anyone. Not anymore."

"When do you plan to leave?"

"In a week maybe. At the most, two. I would like to break it to Angelina with you there. I…I don't care whether you believe me or not, Mr. Marquez, but I do care about her. *So much.* If you care about her, and it seems like you do, then tell her that. Show it with your actions.

"And please, stop letting your ego get in the way of it."

CHAPTER THREE

"Is it true?"

Gabriel sighed and turned toward the figure standing just outside of his suite. As if entering it might force her to concede that he was a presence in her life, his daughter stood at the threshold, staring at him as if he were the enemy.

Somehow, he made his tone even. "Angelina, come inside."

She instantly stiffened, her bony shoulders poking out of her T-shirt like spikes. "I don't want to come inside. I just want to know if it's true."

"What is?"

"Ms. Drakos, is she leaving Drakon?" Damn it, he'd hoped she hadn't heard it yet. "Did she tell you?"

"No," he lied, feeling a hateful powerlessness within. It seemed nothing he offered could induce the Princess to stay. "But I heard one of the staff talking. They said she's going away for a while."

"Will she come back soon?"

His jaw tight, Gabriel shrugged. "It's possible, yes. She...said she might be gone for a month or two. She has her own life, *pequeña*." The Princess had made that very clear. And looking back over their argument, Gabriel cursed. For a businessman who thrived on negotiations and sweet-talking opponents into his camp, he had acted like a fool. Pushed all the wrong buttons.

Just as she did in him.

The sound of a soft whimper from his daughter jerked his head up. Christ, he would welcome the rebellion over this dejection in her eyes.

"Angelina, you will see her again. And even if Ms. Drakos leaves, you will make new friends. And I'll always—"

Tears drew paths over her cheeks as his twelve-year-old leaned against the wall and sobbed silently. Something twisted in his chest and Gabriel fisted his hands.

He reached her and even in the midst of her tears, she shrank from him. He caught the curse that wanted to escape his mouth and waited.

Roughly, and with a self-sufficiency that smacked of someone much older, she wiped at her cheeks and looked up at him. Retreated into herself. "Everyone leaves me. First it was my granddad. Then Mom. Now Ms. Drakos."

"*I* won't, Angelina."

"That's what you say."

"What can I do, Angelina? Tell me."

"You could ask Ms. Drakos not to leave. If you truly care about me, Mr. Marquez," she drawled in her American accent, as if such a thing was an impossibility, "you will somehow make Ms. Drakos stay."

Even the request was made with such resignation, such lack of faith that Gabriel felt winded.

Before he could answer, his daughter turned and walked away, her shoulders dejected. Without once looking back.

"He wants you to be his daughter's nanny?" said her sister-in-law Mia, who was heavily pregnant with twins, on their morning walk around the gardens Nik had had built for Mia.

Eleni nodded. "Wants? More like ordered me. You should've seen him, Mia. He got this look in his eyes, like he wasn't seeing *me* anymore. Just a solution to his problem."

That would make everything right in his world, like all arrogant men expected from those around them.

In the week since Gabriel had made that outrageous offer, she hadn't heard from him. Hopefully, he'd come to his senses. Yet, Eleni continued to feel his considerable power like a shadow over her life.

The gardens were a riot of color, the sky a perfect blue. All in all, it had been one of those perfect Drakon autumn weeks. Everything was ripe and coming to fruition.

She'd made some inquiries into the orphanages in Drakon and submitted her paperwork. It could take months to get through the bureaucratic red tape, but a fierce sense of rightness filled her. And in the meantime, she was planning her trip.

It might not be as long as she'd suggested to Gabriel but it seemed like the perfect thing before she had a child of her own and the responsibility that would go with being a single mother.

"You refused, yes?" Mia probed.

"Of course, I did," she replied, as her gaze shied away from Mia's unbearable concern. Mia knew Eleni was attracted to Gabriel Marquez, that Angelina was coming to mean more and more to her every day. She felt naked, as if all her desperate longing was written on her face for everyone to see.

I could even be persuaded to kiss you again.

Humiliating heat filled her cheeks. She should've slapped the arrogant man.

"I'm worried about you, Ellie." Mia clasped her fingers. "You're getting far too attached to that little girl. I saw how upset she was a few days ago..."

Swallowing the lump in her throat, Eleni tried to sound casual. Angelina's crumpled face wouldn't leave her alone though. She'd been wrong in thinking she could walk out of Angelina's life without hurting her. "I'll be fine, Mia.

If anything, these last few months with Angie have shown me how much I would like a baby of my own."

Mia sent her a stunned glance just as they saw Nikandros walk toward them.

"What the hell is going on between you and Gabriel, Ellie?" Nik said, loudly enough for some of the garden staff to look up curiously.

Eleni frowned. "Just a disagreement about his daughter. Why?"

Nik looked away and back. "He's threatening to pull Marquez Holdings out of Drakon if you don't cooperate with his demand."

"Cooperate? He can't do that!" Eleni's heart sank to her toes. She'd known he was ruthless, but this was beyond belief. "Can he, Nik? I know Andreas had his reservations about Gabriel but I thought we had an ironclad contract."

Nik pushed his hand through his hair, visibly shaking. "We do. Legally, he can't just pull his company out of Drakon. But the last thing we need in this economy is to get into a legal battle with him. He could raise a hundred issues and stall all our projects. He's…everything Andreas said he is when things don't go his way—an utter bastard. He's already canceled two of the investor meetings for no good reason."

Eleni rubbed a hand over her forehead, frustration coiling inside her. Just when she'd finally decided what she wanted in life… "I'll do anything for you and Andreas and… Drakon, Nik." Her daredevil brother had never seemed so anxious. "I'm sorry for—"

"*Christos*, Ellie! I don't blame you for any of this."

Eleni swallowed the lump in her throat. Her brothers did love her. Curse the blasted man for making her doubt it.

"All he keeps saying is that he wants *full access* to you. When I said you were not a resource to be loaned out, he had the gall to say that Andreas and I use you." Nik looked away from her, shame filling his eyes.

"Nik, you can't let him get to you like that." And yet, Gabriel had pinpointed both her own fear and apparently Nik's misgivings like a laser pointer. He rooted out weaknesses and he didn't care what he did with them.

Fury coursed through her veins.

"He didn't say anything I haven't been thinking the last few months. What does he want with you?"

"He wants me to help him forge a connection between him and his daughter. Be…available to them. Make it a priority in my life. When I told him that I was planning to travel, he—" She shivered, remembering the look in his eyes. He hadn't said anything and yet Eleni had known the matter was far from over. "He's desperate and he's pushing back."

"Stop being so damned generous, Ellie."

"I don't like what he's doing any more than you. Given the state Angelina was in when I told her, I…" Tears filled her eyes, frustration coiling inside her. "I feel guilty. I didn't realize how attached she was getting to me. And now, if he walks away from Drakon, it will undo everything Andreas and you are trying to do. There's only one solution."

"I can't let you be his daughter's nanny, Ellie. Haven't you given enough to this family and Drakon?" With another curse, Nikandros pulled her into his arms and Eleni went like a rag doll. The familiar scent of her brother calmed the panic in her tummy.

She knew, just as Nik did, that the ruthless Spaniard had left her no way out. He knew she'd do anything for her brothers. And Angelina too.

Gabriel held all the cards but Eleni had the blood of stubborn warriors in her veins, however tainted her father had thought it.

She didn't intend to let the arrogant Spaniard take anything that she didn't want to give.

She had come to him finally, bristling with righteous fury.

And dressed to kill.

Gabriel watched, transfixed, as Eleni Drakos waited by the steps, awareness jolting him.

The white stone of the restaurant showed off that innate elegance, that quiet grace of hers, reminding him that legitimate or not, she was very much from the illustrious House of Drakos.

The setting sun caught the copper highlights in her shoulder-length hair. Her face didn't have those arresting, stark angles her brothers' did. Nor symmetric features, with her too-proud nose that was clearly inherited from her father. She was neither conventionally beautiful nor had the haughty elegance of a woman born to one of the most distinguished royal houses of the world.

And yet there was a fresh, voluptuous beauty to her form.

The pink fabric of her dress barely kissed her knees and skimmed her lush curves like a lover's hands every time the breeze pressed it against her body. A white metal ring circled her neck, from which the dress flowed down. It bared her rounded shoulders, exposing miles of golden skin.

Up close, the dress was an invitation to sin. A birthmark on her fragile collarbone, the rounded curve of her hip, those long fingers of hers that she used to tuck a stray lock behind her ear—everything about her hit Gabriel like a blow to his solar plexus.

Why had no man stolen her away from under her brothers' control?

What had he been thinking, taunting her with the promise of desire between them?

"You're staring, Mr. Marquez."

Something floral floated toward him. "I've never seen you in a dress, *Princesa*. You look—" he leisurely swept his gaze over her, and saw a rewarding blush steal up through her cheeks "—stunning."

"And of course you're surprised by that," she said dismissively. If he weren't obsessed with every small detail about her, he would have missed the quiver in her voice. The quick flick of her lashes to hide the widening of her eyes.

Was she truly so unused to a man's attentions? Had no man ever wanted her? Touched her? The last thought consumed him. He frowned. "Surprised? What do you mean?"

"You thought I would come here with my tail tucked between my legs, desperate for your promise. Desperate for your—"

The picture she painted made him smile. "If you keep saying it, I promise, *Princesa*. I will begin to like it."

"Like what?"

"You being desperate for me. In any and every way."

She gasped, her eyes voluptuously wide in her lush face before she flicked those thick lashes down.

The lower lip jutted out in a silky pout. Painted a soft pink, her mouth was a lush invitation. "I needed to feel good about myself today, Mr. Marquez. Sort of like being equipped for war."

"This is war for you?"

"Are you saying it isn't? I don't bend to your will like every other being on the planet so you threaten what I hold most dear. The last thing I need is to be riddled by my own insecurities in the midst of it. I have no intention of letting the press coin another—"

"I do not agree with the—"

"You'll find that I'm the most sensible, practical woman

you've ever met and yet you have the…alarming ability to make me lose my faculties."

He stared at her slack-jawed for a few beats before he burst out laughing.

Shoulders rigid, hands fisted, she stood with a patient look.

"Here I assumed you'd dressed up for the simple reason of impressing me. That you were hoping to make *me* lose my faculties."

The tight purse of her lips said it had crossed her mind. "How I dress reflects on my brothers and the House of Drakos, so really, this—" she did a sweeping movement with her hand over her dress, and Gabriel smiled "—has nothing to do with you, Mr. Marquez. You have made the little squabble between us into a national matter. I…could give it no less importance."

Gabriel felt a sting of irritation at the mention of her brothers. He held her elbow and nudged her toward the entrance of the restaurant.

"My daughter's happiness is not a little squabble."

"It isn't." She sighed, her shoulders dropping. "Which is the only reason I'm here to negotiate. Nikandros would rather you sink everything than let me come here, let me bargain with my life. But I can't allow you to go on some macho rampage on Drakon just because you aren't getting your way. Neither can I bear to ignore the fact that I miscalculated."

"Miscalculated what?"

Such raw emotion flickered in her big eyes that Gabriel took a step back. Used to sophisticated, modern women, who, like him, thought emotions were weaknesses, who played games with his head and body, the Princess was a whiplash against his senses.

"How my departure might affect Angelina. I didn't realize how attached she has grown to me, how she could see this also as abandonment." Her mouth trembled, her eyes wide in her face. "The sounds of her tears won't leave me alone."

Gears turned in his head as he evaluated the situation.

There had to be something she wanted that he could provide. Everyone, especially women, wanted something from him. Even his friend Alyssa, who was full of integrity, had needed his backing when she'd first started out.

He was convinced that she would be the best thing for Angelina—she had proved it to him a hundred times over the past two weeks, even as he'd threatened everything she held dear.

A soft gasp from her lush mouth was her only sign that she'd noticed the empty restaurant. They followed the concierge to an intimately laid out dinner on the famed terrace that offered panoramic views of mountains that bracketed Drakon on one side.

The crystal flutes and the champagne bucket glittered in the orange light of the setting sun. He watched the open expressions on her face—awe, a flicker of joy when she saw the mountain peaks followed by dismay and then that practical, nothing-will-efface-me sensibility of hers.

Interesting was an understatement when it came to her.

He held the chair for her. Her usual grace fluttered when she almost slipped. Hand at her elbow, Gabriel straightened her. The slide of her lush curves against him startled an instant reaction from his body. "Thank you," she murmured in a throaty whisper that brought images of her lush limbs beneath him.

Bathed in the setting sun's light, she made a stunning figure. Anyone who saw her now would never call her plain.

Gritting his jaw, he willed his body to calm, his mind to focus on the moment. This was the most important meeting in his life and he didn't intend to fail tonight.

"Champagne?" he asked after they settled down.

The pulse at her throat flickered madly, yet when she raised her gaze to him, it was quite steady. "I'm so stupid," she scoffed, her mouth twisting into a bitter curve.

He frowned, not liking the shutters that fell over her eyes, hiding her from him. He hadn't realized how much of a lure Eleni Drakos's artless honesty was until she shut it away. "I don't know what you mean."

She raised her arms and moved them over the empty restaurant, the gorgeous view of the sunset, the bucket of champagne. "Even after all your threats and insults, I didn't regret…seeing you that night. I held on to the belief that until you ripped off my mask, it had been a genuine moment between us. But you just can't help yourself, can you?"

"Princesa—"

"You will use everything I told you, everything I feel when I see you…to the last drop, to manipulate me to your will."

Something in the curve of her mouth made Gabriel bristle. Guilt was not an emotion he had ever liked nor had any use for. "I do not see why it is such a hardship for you to spend some time with me and Angelina. Not when you claim to truly love her."

"Because my life is not a stopgap measure for you."

"Yet it is for your father, your brothers and even Drakon, is it not? What do I have to do to buy that same loyalty toward Angelina? What is it that I have to do to ensure that you stay in Angelina's life for as long as she needs you, for as long as she and I need to make a connection?"

Her heart fluttered like the wings of a trapped bird. Her fingers shook around the stem and Eleni hid them in her lap. "You might regret making that offer."

"There is no condition of yours that I would *not* meet, *Princesa*. The world will be at your feet if you agree."

She licked her pink lips, and his body tightened. Gabriel swallowed a curse. Really, his attraction to her was becoming a problem. For he knew now that his desire to give her what she'd wanted that night hadn't come solely so that he could bend her to his will. It had come because he'd wanted to explore it with her. And still did. He wanted to taste that lush mouth, he wanted to run his hands and his mouth all over her curves, he wanted to possess her until all the prim propriety that she used as a mask was unraveled, until that self-sufficiency she wielded as a weapon against the world was undone.

Until she was the woman who had kissed him with such hunger that night.

"I want a signed agreement from you that you'll never again put Drakon's economy in jeopardy, ever."

He sat back and took stock of her. Mouth tight with resolve. Eyes glittering with temper. He smiled and took a sip of water just to make her wait for his answer. She fidgeted in her seat, glancing away from him. The woman was good.

"Done," he said finally. "As long as you meet with all my conditions."

"I'm not finished yet."

"Go on."

"I want that agreement as part of a prenuptial contract. I want Drakon and your company bound tightly so that you can't threaten us like this again."

He jerked his gaze from her lovely mouth to her eyes, shock flooding him. "What did you say?"

She pulled her tightly clasped hands out of her lap onto the table, then brought them down again. When she looked at him, resolve filled her features. "I've been over what you want of me a thousand times in my head. Of the number of ways you could hold the threat of Drakon over my head. Of how easily you…you would use what I told you about my life, about me that night for your own advantage. Of how fragile Angelina has been since she heard of my plans."

A soft gasp escaped her mouth, as if this pained her.

"The last thing I want is for her to hate you or blame you when she loses me. The last thing I need is for you to do this to Nikandros all over again because I didn't make her love you in four months. Or whatever ridiculous time frame you think this needs to happen in. I just can't take that chance.

"So I've found a solution that works for all parties and that will not permanently damage the innocent in all of this. I… I want you to marry me. You will use Drakon to ensure Angelina's well-being, and I'm hoping you would think twice about destroying it when it becomes as much her life as it is my own. I want…a chance to do right by myself too."

This time, when he laughed, it was full of sarcasm. Anger fueled him at her outrageous suggestion. "Let me enlighten you, Princess. You will not do right by yourself by hitching your cart to me. I'm incapable of developing romantic feelings for a woman. You'll only be—"

"It will not be a true marriage. I know what I'm bringing to this arrangement and I know what I'll be getting." Eleni would not tie herself to another relationship with yet another man and end up wondering what she lacked all over again. "You would be ensuring that Angelina has a mother who loves her."

"And you would do all this for your precious Drakon? Expect nothing else from me?" Even as he challenged her, her willingness to martyr herself bothered him. Did neither Nikandros nor Andreas care about her future? Was there no one to look after the damned female?

"No, I do want something…"

"Come now, *Princesa*. You had the nerve to propose marriage to me. Don't shy away now."

"I…I do not ask for your fidelity or your love, Gabriel. I…do not need such delusions in my life. I only ask that you give me…" Such color filled her cheeks that Gabriel stared transfixed. Her lips trembled and she dug her teeth into the lower one.

Lust punched him like an invisible blow, and it was all he could do not to tug that lower lip and taste her himself. "Eleni," he prompted in a harsh voice set on edge by the delectable temptation she made.

"I want a baby. A child of my own. I…was in the process of going through adoption agencies when you…you threatened to pull your company out of Drakon. It's not something I'm willing to give up on, for anyone."

Every muscle in his body stiffened. Every instinct he possessed warned him to walk away from this deal with this woman. "A baby? You're bargaining for a baby?" But even as he processed it, he had to admire her guts.

"Yes. As far as the outside world is concerned, as far as Angelina is concerned, we'll be a family. I'll help you forge a connection with her. I'll not make any demands of your time or your emotions. I'd love her as if she were my own. We will lead separate lives except when needed by our children."

"If only the media could see you now… Mad King Theos taught you politics well. Even your brothers I'm sure could not have come up with a better strategy to bind my company to Drakon."

She flinched and shrank back into her seat. She looked down into her lap as if to hide her stricken expression. "You think I *want* this? To marry a man who looks upon me as if I'm trapping him, a man whose affairs are notorious for their short shelf life, a man I have to negotiate with for a child? It will be a marriage of convenience, Gabriel. You will do it for Angelina and I for Drakon."

Any idea that the Princess was manipulating him dissolved at the fury in her eyes.

Gabriel pushed away from the table and went to the empty, glittering bar. Silence stretched in all the spaces between them as he examined his own emotions. That anger he wanted to hold on to was fleeing fast. No one could accuse the Princess of Drakon of being without logic.

He ran a hand through his hair roughly as he heard her movements. Felt the heat from her body stroke his senses. Once she was with him and Angelina, in whatever capacity, he knew that he would have the Princess of Drakon in his bed. The attraction between them was far too consuming.

But for the first time in his life, he could not do as he wanted. He could not take the Princess to his bed and spoil the chance of Angelina having her in her life.

Would an amicable arrangement between them, masquerading as a marriage for the world, for the sake of his own daughter, be so bad? Would binding the Princess to him in the most legal means be the best for his daughter?

"Being a father… It's a role I still haven't settled into, with Angelina. You want me to give you another child knowing that he or she will always look at me and feel as if I've rejected them."

Such ache resonated in those last words that Eleni felt her own heart twist at them. In a matter of seconds, he changed from an arrogant, ruthless businessman to a man familiar with pain. The man she'd met on a moonlit night.

She grabbed his hand with hers on impulse, forcing him to relax his fist. "But you will not be a failure. You will have me to guide you. I know what it feels like to be that child, Gabriel. I know what that kind of a father looks like. I would not expose a child of mine to such a father. You're not that man.

"Your desire to do the right thing by Angelina is what

landed us in this…situation. As much as I hate that you hold the fate of everything I love in your hands, I understand your reasons. We will just be a couple who shares children and who loves them. Successful marriages are built on less."

"And if I say no?" He turned toward her, numerous overhead lights wreathing his hard features with a deceiving softness. "Will you walk away from Angelina? Will you let ruin come to Drakon?"

Eleni forced herself to give him a smile. Or as close to a smile as she could get. Negotiating with Gabriel was like banging glass against a rock. Nik had warned her, outright forbidden her from doing this. But what choice did she have?

Loving that little girl, loving Drakon and her brothers had never felt like a boulder around her neck.

"Yes." Whether she'd be able to withstand it, she didn't know. But she couldn't let him ruin Drakon. Not when she could stop it. "Angelina will hate you for what you're doing. Drakon and its people will suffer. And it will all be on your own head."

Eleni didn't wait for his answer. She'd had enough of the seesawing of her own feelings. Enough of bargaining for the one thing she wanted in her life.

If he didn't agree to this, then he was truly a ruthless bastard, she repeated to herself. A man whose heart was so deeply buried that he might as well not have had one at all.

She'd reached the small courtyard outside the restaurant when she felt his hand on her shoulder. Heart thudding in her chest, she turned around. The black shirt and trousers he wore blended in with the darkness surrounding them, leaving only an outline of the sheer breadth of his shoulders, of his imposing height.

Of his overwhelming masculinity and what she'd boldly demanded of him.

Both his hands landed on her shoulders now and tugged her toward him. As if he too was struggling to see her in the scant moonlight.

His fingers bit into her flesh. "An arrangement then, *Princesa*? No demands, no expectations?"

"Yes," she said, licking her lips. Longing twisted through her when her legs tangled with his. Her hands landed somewhere on his chest, where his heart boldly thudded underneath one palm. Hard muscle and slumbering heat—there was so much of him that Eleni felt suddenly fragile, feminine. "No demands and no expectations."

"No fidelity required?"

"Not after you give me a baby." She tried to sound matter-of-fact but goodness, he was too much man. Her voice sounded husky, uneven instead. "Really, Gabriel. It would not be a bad idea for you to curb your…activities in that area in the short term anyway. Let Angelina see you make her a priority. Not your business, not your love life. But her. Let her see that we love her, and we're in this together, for her. In the meantime, you could…we could…"

His white teeth gleamed, giving her a hint of his feral smile. The sound of his mocking laughter lashed against her senses. She felt utterly drowned in the scents and sounds and feel of him. "So I'm allowed to sleep with my wife until then but no longer?"

"Precisely." Embarrassment burned her and Eleni suddenly thanked the cloak of the night. The devil gleamed in his smile, winked from the glitter of his eyes. Taunted her with the sound of his mockery. "I suspect that by that time whatever novelty I hold for you will have worn off. As long as you're discreet with your affairs, it will not affect the children or me."

He cupped her nape with such possessive intent that Eleni shivered. Rough fingers crawled up into her hair, tilting her head up. "You've got all the little details figured out, haven't you? Princess Eleni Drakos to the rescue, huh?"

She'd no idea whether he was still teasing her or if he was angry. All she could do was feel. Feel the imprint of his fingers on her scalp. Feel the hard contours of his hips against her belly. Feel the hot beat of his breath against her face.

"And you, *Princesa*?" Suddenly, his lips grazed hers, and she jerked at the streak of heat that raced through her. She whimpered when he did it again, never settling his mouth against hers. But teasing and taunting, delighting and declaring the fact that she could have him sign a hundred contracts and check a hundred conditions, but when it came to this fire between them, when it came to the slide of his lips over hers, she bent to his will. "Will you seek out lovers when you want a man in your bed in some later years too?"

She raised a drugged gaze to his, and fierce masculine satisfaction filled Gabriel's every vein. Her finger pads pressed into his chest and he wanted to feel them all over him. He wanted her beneath him, all lush, glorious curves bare, the polite mask she wore unraveled. He wanted that woman from the masquerade ball in his bed. "What?"

The thought of a lover hadn't even entered his mind for months now. How could it, when he was obsessed with the little warrior in front of him? But the thought of her with another man...no, she would not need another man, he promised himself.

If the Princess wanted an amiable arrangement, he would give it to her. But only after he had spoiled her for any other man. "Will you look for a lover, Eleni? When this marriage becomes an arrangement again, when you do not need me?"

"I would never do anything that would harm my kids or damage the reputation of the House of Drakos."

"Right answer, *Princesa*," he whispered, before dipping his mouth to hers.

Shivers passed through her slender frame before she stiffened in his arms. Blood rushing south, he bit that lower lip that always tortured him and with a husky groan, she opened her mouth.

He dipped his tongue inside it, holding her head for his onslaught. She tasted of heat and innocence, her tongue tentatively coming to tangle with his.

If he had had any reservations about her counter-proposal, Gabriel forgot them, lost in the hunger raging through his body.

The Princess in his bed, and a bridge between his daughter and him—maybe this marriage wasn't such a bad idea for the near future.

CHAPTER FOUR

PLAIN PRINCESS SNARES
REAL ESTATE TYCOON!
Love match or convenient arrangement fixed
by her powerful brothers?

ELENI TRIED TO ignore the bald headline she'd seen on a
popular social media site that morning as she walked toward Gabriel's apartments in the palace's west wing.

At six foot three and with a muscular frame, he was sex-
uality incarnate. Add the reach of his name, the sheer confidence that seemed to exude from his very pores, his talent
as one of the foremost architects of their time and his real
estate empire—Gabriel was every woman's dream man.

Yet, he had remained an elusive bachelor for so many
years that the world's gaze had shifted to the woman who
had persuaded him into a momentous commitment. For
the first time in her life, Eleni was the center of attention,
and the limelight only made her uncomfortably aware of
how poorly she measured up to him in the world's view.

When she and Gabriel had broken the news to his
daughter, Angelina had thrown herself into Eleni's arms,
her lanky frame shaking from head to toe. That they were
doing right by the little girl had stopped Eleni from questioning the sanity of it all as the media and the palace had
been thrown into a whirlwind at the news.

The very morning after their deal had been agreed, Gabriel had invited Nikandros and her to a meeting. From the man who kissed her like his life depended on it to the ruthless businessman in the boardroom, the transformation in him was radical. Furious, Nik and his lawyers had pushed to fill every small loophole that Gabriel could use to back out again while he had sat there, calm as you please, dictating the terms of their marriage and sending curious looks her way.

Angelina was already skipping on the front steps, excited about spending the evening with Eleni and her father. Eleni went into the sitting room. Finding it empty, she went into his study.

High windows poured sunlight over the tall, broad form bent over his desk. Sleeves rolled up to his elbows showed corded forearms dusted liberally with dark hair. His pencil and scale looked like tiny implements in his huge hands and yet there was a kind of grace in his movements as he measured and drew on the tabbed white sheet.

Heart palpitating at dangerous speeds, Eleni noted the stretch of his black trousers over his buttocks and thighs, the tight stretch of his shirt over his back muscles.

Jet-black hair fell over his forehead and he pushed it away.

He was immersed in his work—a design for a new resort at the foot of the mountains in Drakon.

And yet, as she stared at the lean fluidity of his powerful body and caught the soft susurrations of the pencil across the paper in the background, all her insecurities came rushing forth.

Had she actually imagined that she would share a bed with him, invite him into her body, and then remain unscathed?

A hundred thoughts crowding her mind, she turned to flee, just as long fingers clamped over her arm.

The scrape of his fingers over her bare arm was a spark

over the ignition. Sensation swirled beneath her skin. Every atom of her being wanted to savor that touch.

"Running away, Eleni?"

His soft taunt raised the small hairs over her neck. "I…" She licked her lips, her mouth utterly parched.

The impact of his touch hit her afresh, the imprint of his hard mouth on hers, the grip of his fingers over her hips… His dress shirt was unbuttoned to his waist, displaying tanned golden skin dotted with sparse black hair. The corded muscles of his throat, the afternoon stubble on his jaw… Eleni closed her eyes to process the devastation he caused to her very equilibrium.

He smelled of cologne and male sweat, an irresistible combination that seemed to fill her senses. Something in the lazy twitch of his mouth reminded her of a tabby cat far too sure of his appeal.

"I was just waiting to see if there would be a break in your focus." Somehow, she managed a steady voice. "My father lost his temper if I so much as bothered him in his office. Even when I had an appointment."

"You needed an appointment to see your father?"

"He was a busy man and, at that time, it wasn't like I was adding any value to the administration."

When he stared at her mutely, she shrugged. He had a way of looking at her that made her feel naked, and not in the physical way. As if she was still the girl who'd been told that the King was her father and that he'd done a great service by acknowledging her as his, let alone adopting her.

To push Gabriel's attention away from her, she said, "Angelina and I have been waiting. For over thirty minutes."

He frowned, and then looked at the big dial on his wrist. "Damn. I completely forgot." Fingers wrapped around the nape of his neck as he studied his work area. In months of working with him and his team, she had never seen him hesitate like this. Never seen him be anything but confident and arrogant, even forceful in his will.

"Is she mad at me?"

"No, she said I was foolish to be surprised that you hadn't shown up," she said, finding her balance again. Talking about Angelina—that she could do. "That much cynicism in one so young, it's not healthy."

"I…was working and forgot." He glanced back at his desk, pushed his hair away from his face. "Maybe it is better if I didn't join you this evening. We're both still reeling from our last disagreement."

Eleni sighed, remembering the staff telling her about the pastries they'd found in the toilet and the pumps that had been shredded to pieces as a result. A thousand-piece puzzle—a map of the United States—was spread out all over the palace. Eleni and Mia had found poor New York in the garden and had laughed nonstop at the girl's imaginative destruction.

The whole palace and its mother knew of the row that had resulted between father and daughter when he'd found out what she'd done.

It seemed Gabriel couldn't stop ordering more and more expensive gifts and Angelina couldn't resist new and imaginative ways to destroy them.

"My daughter and I have matching tempers, *Princesa*. I have learned that it is wise to stay away from each other when we are riled. I might say something that would cause permanent damage. So, it's probably a good idea for you to continue on to whatever entertainment you've planned for tonight."

"For goodness' sake, Gabriel, can't you look beneath her rebellious actions?"

"She shredded the pumps. She threw the diamond earrings in the garbage. I…"

"Because she wanted *you* instead. Gabriel, she doesn't

understand yet that you'll keep her. That you'll be permanent in her life. That you won't abandon her like her mother has done. She keeps rejecting anything you give her."

Eyes like the coldest frost pinned her. "I don't want a lecture, Eleni."

"I don't care what you want. It is my job—" she spanned her hands around them "—to tell you what you're doing wrong. Stop being so manly and bullheaded about it."

"Manly and bullheaded?"

"Yes, like all thickheaded men. Look past your own ego."

"You think me an awful father, *Princesa*, but since I learned of her existence, I have made changes to my life that I have never done for anyone before. I brought her here, I live with her, I've made concessions for her. What else do I need to do?"

"You need to spend time with her, Gabriel. Is that so hard to see?" When he continued to frown, Eleni sighed. "You say you want to bridge the gap between you. You say she is important to you. But in the two weeks that we have agreed on our…deal, you have either postponed, canceled or found an excuse to avoid spending any time with us. *With her.* Angelina sees through your actions and that's the message she gets."

"She seems overjoyed by the fact that you will not be leaving."

"She is."

"Then what else does she need?"

"Did you think I would replace you?" Suddenly, she felt a piece click inside her head. She stared at him. "Something in you resists the effort at forging any real connection with her. Is it any wonder she thinks you don't want her?"

Gabriel stared at the sudden softening of Eleni's eyes and looked away. His jaw gritted, his head hurt at the realization that the Princess was right again. He had done everything his research said he'd have to do, except spend time with his daughter.

He heard the Princess's soft tread, the scent of something floral coiling sinuously around his sore limbs. After his row with Angelina, he'd been working nonstop, burying himself in tasks. Because here, there was no place for failure. Here, there was no place for vulnerability, especially his.

"Gabriel…all your intentions will be for nothing if your actions don't back them up. What is it that you find so hard about this? Please, let me understand."

"There's nothing I find hard, *Princesa*."

Instead of walking away, she put her hand on his arm, a soft tinkling laugh falling from her mouth. "How like a man to say that."

He turned around, intending to set her down. Yet when he looked at her, the soft light of her brown eyes stole through him, loosening up hard places inside him. Making him remember things he'd rather forget. "I had custody of my half sister, Isabella, when I was eighteen while my mother was cleaning up her own act."

"She was engaged to Andreas but she…"

He swallowed the frustration that sat like a lump in his throat. "Had an affair with Nikandros, yes. Isabella was just like my mother, flighty by nature, never settling on one thing. And I think the fact that I resented her only made it worse."

"You resented her?"

"I don't know. I think I did. My mother had her after she deserted my father and got pregnant by her lover. When they came back, she was pregnant with her. My father died a couple of years later and Isabella became my responsibility, I was hardly the loving older brother. At that point, I barely…"

"What, Gabriel?"

"I barely trusted a woman. I…was busy building my empire.

"I always felt guilty that I might have pushed Isabella over the edge with my judgment when she was just an innocent. That, had I been a better brother, she would have had more security. Every time I see Angelina, I remember my treatment of my sister, I guess."

"And you think you'd rather not try than risk failing?"

"Isn't it better that she hates me, that she holds me responsible for everything that happened to her rather than me messing her up even more? What if she sees my resentment of her mother? Won't she be caught between her mother's memory and loyalty to me?" His gaze was far-off, his mouth rigid with tension. "Like you say, maybe I decided it was better this way."

"Then please let me tell you that it is not. Every time you cancel on her, every time you put work or something else before her, you're losing a little more of your daughter, Gabriel. Please, trust me to help you through this. Trust that I will not let you fail. Or else all of this is useless."

Gabriel lifted his gaze to Eleni's, something inside him shifting. He'd never trusted a woman with anything. Of course, he had friends that he liked, even respected, but trusting a woman… He'd lost that ability even before his mom had walked out on him and his father.

He'd lost it when he'd seen her break her promise again and again. He'd lost it when instead of being the adult, she'd filled his ears with her own struggles. He'd lost it when she'd forced him to grow up too fast.

Her brown eyes wide and open, Eleni looked back at him. The lift of her chin, the tilt of her mouth—she radiated a perplexing combination of confidence and innocence that fascinated Gabriel even now.

He glanced down at her fingers moving over his, felt

the fragile pulse at her wrist beneath his fingers. In the week that they had announced to the world their plans, she'd come under close scrutiny by the media.

Every single one of those write-ups had been uncomplimentary toward the Princess, while he had been hailed as the perfect catch. Her background had come under scrutiny—the fact that her mother had been Andreas's nanny and had an affair with the King under the Queen's nose, that her mother had effectively sold Eleni to the King, that since no man had ever shown interest in the Plain Princess this match with Gabriel had been orchestrated by her powerful brothers.

Yet, the Princess had only held her head higher through all the dirt dished by the press, had only carried herself with the dignity that seemed to have been bred into her very bones, while he and Nikandros negotiated their prenup contract in which she gave generously of herself to Drakon.

She'd wanted no accolades, no acknowledgment for what she'd done.

The only time she had interrupted the negotiations had been to ask, with a flush staining her cheeks, that any children they might have would be provided for.

For all her alleged dirty blood, the Princess of Drakon was an asset to the House of Drakos. A woman unlike anyone he'd ever met.

A woman Gabriel didn't quite know what to do with now that she was going to be his. A woman who unnerved Gabriel in how generously she loved his daughter and her brothers.

He took her hand in his and turned it over. Traced his fingers over the dips and highs of her palm. Heard the soft flutter of her breath every time he touched her, which had been mostly accidentally after that searing kiss. Heard her breath hitch into that irregular rhythm.

Her artless, instant reaction goaded the devil within him. "Gabriel?"

He lifted her hand and kissed the center of her palm. Smiling, he let it go when she jerked it back as if scalded. He stood still, used now to the beat of desire in his muscles.

Forced himself to have the patience to wait.

"Fine. I will trust you, *Princesa*. In this, at least."

Any control Eleni thought she had wrested of the situation, of the dynamic between them, disappeared like mist when he held the bottom of his dress shirt and pulled it up over his head in one fluid motion.

Her jaw fell with an audible click. "What...what are you doing?" she croaked out, heat staining her cheeks.

Ropes of leanly defined muscles stretched dark, olive skin. There wasn't an inch of extra flesh on his body. Rubbing a hand over her nape, Eleni was humiliatingly aware of the soft, pillowy cushioning of her own hips and thighs.

Of her unfashionable figure.

Of how her cheeks were plump and her nose far too prominent.

Of how little she had to offer a man like him.

And still, she couldn't unglue her feet from the floor and walk away. Couldn't say "this is off," even to save her pride.

She stared in fascination as he balled up the shirt and threw it into the corner. Heard the splash of water as he went into the adjoining bathroom.

He came out, water running in rivulets over his naked chest, glistening in the light falling from the windows. He dried the front of his chest, under his arms and around his neck with a towel, all the while holding her gaze with a devilish glint in his own.

"You look flushed, Eleni. Are you unwell?"

Eleni licked her suddenly dry lips, could think of no answer.

He threw the towel into the corner where it joined the shirt. Then he pulled on a fresh white shirt and faced her. His chest gleaming golden brown, he stood in front of her.

Eleni breathed compulsively, the scent of male sweat and cologne making her muscles twitch in response. "What is it that you want of me?"

The most unholy twinkle filled his gray eyes. "Button my shirt."

Eleni stared at the ridge of his chest muscles as the shirt flapped in the soft breeze. Sparse hair covered it, narrowing down into a line below his navel and disappearing into his trousers. Her fingers shook at her sides and she balled them.

Finding the sheer will that had, in the end, tamed the ferocious man that her father had been, Eleni looked up into Gabriel's eyes. "I have been celibate for too long, Gabriel. It has to be the only reason for this…almost-violent reaction to you. Once I sleep with you, the power won't be in your hands so much." She started toward the door. "Don't keep your daughter waiting any longer," she threw over her shoulder, without turning.

The mocking laughter that followed her stayed with her for nights to come.

Eleni waited in the courtyard for Gabriel, the evening uncommonly cold for autumn.

A flurry of activities had followed the night after she and Gabriel had taken Angelina to see the musical. Father and daughter didn't say much to each other still, except when they argued, but the fact that Gabriel had been present at dinners and every other evening activity Eleni had suggested for the three of them had not been lost on Angelina.

The girl was as stubborn as her father for she didn't ask him for anything. Yet Eleni had seen the anticipation in her eyes that she struggled to hide, the tilt of her chin when she heard her father's voice.

Just as she had seen Gabriel's gaze lingering on Angelina. He had completely shut Eleni down when she'd asked after his sister again. Still, he had given her a lot to mull over.

It was hard to see a different facet of the arrogant businessman, the gorgeous billionaire who had no soft edges. Yet, the fact that his behavior when he'd barely been an adult weighed on him, spoke of a man who had soft edges. Of a man who felt things deeply.

Eleni herself struggled to keep a little rationality about the upcoming wedding. Spending evenings in his company at myriad activities was all well and good for Angelina but not for her own feeble defenses.

Gabriel, she'd learned in the last two weeks, was a charming companion, a humorous storyteller and when the mood stuck him, which was far too often, the very devil himself.

He taunted her senses relentlessly—soft strokes on her wrist, the graze of his body when he sat too close, the dig of his fingers over her shoulders when they posed for a picture at one of his blasted, endless parties. It was as if he was determined to send her over the edge. As if he was determined to punish her for her comment about resisting him.

Somehow, the attraction between them had become a cat and mouse game, and Eleni was alternately thrilled and overwhelmed at being chased by the most powerful, gorgeous man in the world.

She melted under his caresses, despite knowing it was all a game to him. That she was a novelty.

"Get in, *Princesa*."

They were on their way to another one of his parties—something Gabriel insisted she attend when all she wanted to do was hide from the scrutiny.

Coloring at the obvious amusement in his tone, she stepped into the limo and found herself being thoroughly appraised by the devil in front of her. Heat swamped her as he took in the beige silk cocktail dress she had chosen to match the four-inch stilettos that had gold threads winding around her ankles.

Mouth twitching, he kept his gaze on her ankles. Tingles began in her skin as if he had caressed that part with those rough fingers of his. Eleni uncrossed and crossed her ankles, which made her only doubly aware of the slide of the sensitive skin of her thighs. "What?" she demanded finally, her body a thrum of sensations.

"I thought you didn't like heels."

"How do you know that?"

"Angelina asked you when we went to play in the park the other day and you said you felt like you would fall and break your head every time you tried a pair."

Eleni sat back against the soft leather, struggling to hide her reaction. She had no inkling that Gabriel paid any attention to the things she said. And she couldn't help the warmth that stole through her that he did.

He cleared his throat and looked up, a slight rasp in his throat. "Although I must admit I don't think I've ever seen anything quite so sexy—" his eyes gleamed dark in the intimacy of the limo "—I would prefer my fiancée with her head intact for the wedding." He leaned ahead on the seat, his long legs bracing hers on either side, crowding her with that masculinity of his. "Why, Eleni?"

She shrugged. "I felt like a change."

He arrested her with his hands on her wrists when she would have retreated farther into the leather. "How do you think I will give you what you want if you flinch every time I touch you?"

Eleni forced herself to relax, knowing he was right. "I…I'm just not used to constantly being touched. And I wore the damn heels because I'm tired of feeling so short next to you. As if I could forget it, the media reminds me incessantly of how different I am from your usual type."

"But I like how you feel against me, *Princesa*. So fragile and small. My masculinity feels stroked around you."

She snorted. "Your masculinity hardly needs to be stroked, Gabriel."

He threw his head back and laughed.

Like everything he did, even that was sexy. Crinkles spread out from his gray eyes, which danced with humor. "No, I don't think so. But other parts, yes."

Eleni blushed so profusely she felt like there should be flames coming out of her ears.

"Believe me, Princess. Not a single woman I've ever known could match that lovely blush of yours. This modern world of equality has made me unaware of how attractive a woman's shy blushes and stammering denials are."

"I don't stammer," she burst out, efficiently giving herself away.

Anything else she might have vehemently denied died on her lips when his outstretched hand held a small velvet box.

"Open it, Eleni," he said with an edge of impatience after she'd stared it for several seconds.

Eleni slowly opened it and promptly lost her breath.

A sapphire sat in a princess setting surrounded by tiny diamonds that reflected the sun's rays. It was the most exquisite ring she'd ever seen, and as a member of the House of Drakos, Eleni had seen her share.

It wasn't ostentatious with the stone overpowering the setting. It wasn't a status symbol. It wasn't a ring she'd have expected a man like Gabriel Marquez, a man who proclaimed to the world what and who he was with every breath, to buy for his fiancée.

"You do not like the ring."

Eleni closed her fingers over his wrist just as he was about to shut the box. Breath punched in and out of her throat at the graze of the hair on his wrists against her palm.

"It's the most beautiful ring I've ever seen." Breathless and vulnerable. Desperate and so painfully hopeful. Despite every warning that this was just an arrangement, her heart drummed against her rib cage. "I'm trying to rack my brain as to whether I've ever mentioned to any media outlet that sapphires are my favorite."

"I asked your sister-in-law."

She jerked her gaze to his. "You asked Mia?"

He shrugged. "It was actually Angelina's idea. That I get you something you'd like and appreciate. That women want to be given beautiful things. Apparently, I need relationship advice from my twelve-year-old daughter if I want to keep you happy."

Eleni tried to bat away the warmth that immediately flooded her. "It is good that you two have something to discuss. Finally."

"Oh, believe me, my twelve-year-old daughter is not only chock-full of advice but questions too. Even your brothers, I'd say, are not quite the champions of you that Angelina is."

"What do you mean?"

"She demanded to know why I was marrying you while declaring that you deserve someone far better than an unfeeling, workaholic like me."

When he stared at her pointedly, Eleni shook her head. "As much as I hate your guts sometimes, I would never say such a thing about you in front of her. But..."

"Nikandros has no such reservations and Angelina has such a crush on him that everything he says is the truth to her." Eleni nodded with a smile, and he sighed.

"If you start talking about how she's growing up, I'll...I

think our conversation about you is the first real one we've ever had. The longest too."

"What did you tell her?"

"Angelina's too smart to be deceived. So I told her one version of truth."

"Which is?"

"That I was thirty-six years old and settling down with a wife wasn't a bad idea, especially if it made her feel secure and loved. That a marriage with shared goals is the only one I could tolerate. That your alleged saintly nature made you the best candidate for the position."

"Saintly nature?"

"Apparently, you're not only a wonderful friend, but also a model sister, daughter, a patroness of children's charities and a superb equestrian." His mouth snarled into a cynical curve that twisted the truth of his words. As if she was somehow cheating the world into believing an illusion. "I was hard-pressed to accept that I deserved to marry such a model of righteousness."

"I'm neither dull nor a saint, Gabriel. The urges I feel when I'm with you will attest to that."

"Like wanting to climb atop me right this minute and ravish me with that lush mouth of yours?"

She sputtered and stammered, not getting one lucid word out for a few seconds. The man was such an inveterate rogue. "Like wanting to thump you every time you use the attraction between us to gain the upper hand."

His languid mouth twitching, he took her hand in his and slipped the ring onto her finger. Eleni's throat felt like it was made of glass as the sapphire winked at her in the low lights of the limousine.

It was for show, she told herself, for the world, for the media, for outward appearances. Yet, it was the first time a man had made a commitment to her and the moment stole what breath was left in her lungs. She gathered her buffeted emotions together as he rubbed her knuckle with his finger, a thoughtful look on his face.

She left her hand in his through sheer effort, her heart racing in her chest. "Thank you, Gabriel. The ring…even if it was Angelina's idea, it's very thoughtful. I know that I'm dragging you to the altar."

"In business, we adhere to the strictest standards because customer satisfaction is the primary goal. Not a profit margin, not whether the next contract lands in your pile. I will do everything in my power to give you everything you want and need, and that will ensure that you will do your best with Angelina. Simple common sense. So tell me, are you dragging me, *Princesa*, or am I dragging you to the altar in two weeks?"

"Two weeks? I'm not even sure whether Andreas got the message I sent. I can't marry without him present."

"I'm a businessman first and foremost. I can't let deals wait for anyone. And you do not need Andreas's blessing when you're the one who's saving Drakon from the big bad wolf. I'm aware how much work there is to be done with Angelina and me, and I will not give you a chance to back out. Andreas is busy chasing a ghost. And anyway, once we marry, Angelina will be your priority, not your brothers."

The ring cold on her finger, Eleni stared at him. Why did she keep forgetting that this was a transaction for him, albeit an important one? He didn't think of her as a woman to woo, only a mother for his daughter.

His cold analysis pinched like the tiniest shard of glass stuck in one's hand. "Will I be asked to give you a review once you hold up your end of the deal too? Because I would like some kind of scale and advance notice if I'm to rate your…performance."

This time, his laughter only made her feel cold and alone.

She needed to remember that, despite the soft edges she'd seen in him, Gabriel had as much heart as her cold and controlling father. He saw her only as the means to an end.

If she'd been a romantic, then her hopes and dreams would have turned to so much dust by now. Good thing that between her father's cruelty and Spiros's desertion, Eleni had long ago squashed any such hopes.

CHAPTER FIVE

THEIR WEDDING FEAST was held in the Rose room at the Drakon Palace, hosted by his now brother-in-law, Nikandros, and his wife, Mia.

Gabriel took a champagne flute and raised it in a gesture toward him. Nothing, however, could shake that creeping sense that his life was a little less in his control since he and the Princess had come to their neat little arrangement.

In two weeks, she'd made sure he and Angelina had had dinner every night, forced them to at least look at each other. The Princess herself had, of course, been the perfect buffer.

Angelina still had to be dragged to these dinners, he knew, but at least when she got there, she participated in the conversation, especially if Eleni asked her something.

He, who had never believed in anything that defied logic, had to admit that there was something of magic in his bride's eyes when she joined hands with him and smiled up at him with those beautiful brown eyes.

Something beyond the mundane had touched the mountain air when she'd walked toward him on the path carpeted with rose petals. When she had smiled at Angelina who'd been her flower girl with such love shining in her eyes.

He'd had an event management firm do all the preparations for the ceremony, had ordered them to give his fiancée everything she wanted for the wedding, no matter how expensive or outrageous. Only to be told that his fiancée had a very decided opinion of how she wanted her wedding.

Her love for detail shone through in the smallest of touches.

And still, his commitment to this felt like nothing in the face of hers. Like he was cheapening it with his constant reminders that it was only an arrangement between them, with his continued belief that he was only doing this for Angelina, whereas Eleni, once she had decided on the course, seemed to accept it for what it was.

It felt like a weight he hadn't asked for around his chest, a transaction for which her rewards were vague.

A member of his staff joined Gabriel just as Eleni walked onto the dance floor with Nikandros. He barely heard what the man said. Couldn't shake his gaze from the voluptuous beauty of his wife.

His wife—his to cherish and protect and love. He couldn't do the last, but he could surely do the first two.

The ivory lace of her dress dipped in a graceful curve, only barely hinting at those full breasts that his hands tingled to cup and hold.

The delicate diamond tiara sat atop brown curls that fell around her face in teasing waves. It was a gift from her brother Nikandros, Gabriel knew, for she'd refused any jewelry from him. Had smilingly refused every trinket he'd had the jeweler bring up to her.

Only the rings he had put on her finger and the promise of a child.

Even the settlement that Nikandros had insisted she receive in case they separated, had been arranged in their children's names, if they had any.

She didn't want anything Gabriel could give, or wanted to give her, and it made disquiet bloom in his gut that maybe there wasn't anything he could give this woman to balance what she was giving him.

For a man who had measured the world and the people in it in terms of their worth and the value he could provide them, Eleni left him feeling empty-handed.

So Gabriel had smiled and posed for pictures with her and Angelina, even as his skin prickled.

With repeated instructions—almost step-by-step advice on how to approach Angelina and how to overcome her resistance—he and Angelina had even muddled their way through a dance, something he would have called an impossibility even a month ago.

How the media would laugh if they knew how much his own wedding had moved a hardened cynic like him.

He was about to ask Eleni to dance with him again when he saw a tall, tuxedoed man make a bow in front of her. That wide smile slipped from her mouth. Color fled her cheeks, leaving her eyes glittering with tears in a pale mask.

Gabriel frowned, every muscle urging him into action.

She didn't refuse when the man took her hand in his. In fact, a ghost of a smile dawned slowly, a bit hesitant, a bit nervous. Her gaze searched the man's face furiously, as if she couldn't drink him up fast enough. Her hands went to his shoulders, his face, as if she couldn't believe he was there.

A burst of possessiveness filled Gabriel as the man pulled her onto the dance floor, his hands far too bold and familiar over Eleni's figure. Her slender fingers locked against the man's nape, she tilted her head down to his mouth, as if to hear every word.

That look of distress, of disbelief, never left her eyes, all the while she danced with him. Curiosity ate through him, like flames licking at oil. With a curse, Gabriel walked away.

He wasn't going to hang on to his wife's every movement like a jealous husband. Damn it, she wasn't even going to be his wife in the true sense of the word.

CHAPTER SIX

HER NERVES STRETCHED so taut that she felt she might shatter like a piece of glass, Eleni walked the long corridor to her own apartments rather than return to the Rose room. More than two hours had passed since she had disappeared from her own wedding reception with Spiros.

Surely her absence must have been noted by now. She had spent the past half hour trying to make sense of it all, wandering the palace aimlessly, and she didn't have any more clarity.

Spiros—her friend and confidant from her childhood, the only boy she had kissed until Gabriel, the man who had promised to love her for the rest of their lives—was back. After being gone for ten years with no word, message or a single phone call.

Back in her life, apparently, whatever the hell that meant. Finally free to be with her, he'd said. There was no rhyme or reason to the nonsense he had blurted out at her.

A sob fought through her chest and Eleni swallowed hard to lock it. She didn't know what it was that sat like a lump in her throat.

Was it grief? Anger? Or anxiety at what she had left behind in the reception room?

The palace walls seemed to close in on her as she turned one corner after the other. She should have been furious with him. She had imagined for so many years how she would react if she saw him again.

How she would slap his beautiful face and tell him to go to hell. How she would tell him that he had forever crushed her trust in men, her trust in her own judgment and feelings.

She had done none of those things. Her heart seemed to have lodged in her throat, cutting off any chance of words.

It had been such a beautiful day. Almost as if the universe had conspired to make it grand for her. Perfect for her. She'd begun it with a purpose, with a sense of direction for the first time in so many years. And it had ended with a ghost from her past.

Standing in front of the tilted-edge mirror, clad in her ivory lace gown, every inch polished and poised, with a bouquet of rare orchids that Gabriel had sent over, she had felt like a woman reaching for what she wanted out of life.

With the backdrop of the mountain, the chapel had looked like a magical kingdom. Nikandros had told her she'd looked stunning, a reluctant grin on his lips. Had embraced her in a bear hug when she'd mentioned Andreas.

The air had been crisp and pure and the man waiting for her at the end of the aisle had been the highlight.

Clad in a black tuxedo, his blue-black hair slicked back, he had looked powerful and gorgeous, a most outrageous dream come true. His fingers had been firm on hers, his vows resonating against the very mountain itself.

To protect and honor and cherish he promised in his deep, gravelly voice. She'd wanted to believe every word.

When his lips had touched hers, Eleni had jerked, singed to her very core. Dark brows had drawn down with the same shock she was sure vibrated through her own body.

It was as if their bodies sang to each other, their lips felt that same connection blaze into life even with the barest of contacts.

Her fingers had lingered over his, her face upturned, his for the taking. His mouth had twitched in that satisfied, arrogant way of his and she had blushed to the roots of her hair. But he hadn't deepened the kiss beyond the perfunctory cool slide of his lips over hers.

The ride back to the palace had been filled with chitchat by Angelina. She was a mother in their arrangement, Eleni had reminded herself when Angelina had asked if she could ride with them. Not a proper wife. But even that hadn't dimmed her joy in the day.

Today had been a perfect day she wouldn't soon forget.

Until a suave, smiling Spiros had stood in front of her at the reception, greeting her like a long-lost friend.

Her gut had folded to her feet. She had been so shocked to see him that she had thought him a specter first, a ghost from the past. To remind her of what and who she was, of how naive she could be, how powerful her self-induced delusions if she weren't careful.

When he had taken her arm and pulled her out of the Rose room, she had gone willingly, still grappling with it. When he had held her tight against him, when he had whispered frantic endearments and kissed her hair, she'd frozen into stillness.

Memories she hadn't allowed herself to think of came rushing back, drenching her in pain and sorrow. Spiros had shuddered around her, his greetings shifting to apologies.

And then he'd disappeared as quickly as he had appeared.

Wondering if she was hallucinating, she had roamed the old armory like a wraith, her dress snagging and tearing on a rusted suit.

Her feet hurt like the very devil in her five-inch stilettos.

Leaning against the wall in front of her apartments, she bent and pulled the offending sandals off her feet. All she wanted was to tear her dress off, sink into a bath, and then go to sleep. The sooner morning came, the sooner she could have a bit of her practicality back.

Feet bare, she was pulling at the complicated knot her hair had been twisted into when she saw the shadow of a broad figure saunter into the light of her sitting room.

With the skylights at his back drawing a line around his broad shoulders, Gabriel looked like a devilish creature of the night. A darkly commanding figure. His suit jacket was gone. His white dress shirt unbuttoned and pulled out of his trousers. The edges separated to display a rock-hard chest with olive skin stretched tight.

A glass of scotch, his preferred drink, shone amber in his hands as he filled the doorway, lazily leaning a hip against it. His gaze started at her bare feet that she scrunched against the cold marble, traveled up the tulle skirt, lingered far too long on her hips and breasts and then up her bare neck, toward the hair she had partially pulled free of the knot.

Every inch of her tingled at his lazily possessive perusal. At the banked fire gleaming to life in his gray gaze. Every muscle in her tightened consciously against the onslaught of heat he created with that one long look.

Her sandals fell from her fingers with a quiet thud that resonated with the fierce drumming of her heart. She'd been so consumed with shock over Spiros that she'd even forgotten what tonight meant.

Did he mean to consummate their wedding tonight?

Shock and something more sinuous slowly floated down into her consciousness, setting off tremors in her entire body.

Did she want to refuse him?

No, came her body's resounding answer. Not when she'd been through nervousness, excitement and every other emotion anticipating this one night. Not when it felt like she'd waited for this, for him, her entire life. Would he be gentle or would that hardness she'd sensed in him spill over to their personal intimacies?

But seeing Spiros had sent her on a strange spiral, as if the rug had been pulled from under her feet just when she was finding safe ground. Thoughts and questions about the past filled her to the brim so that her present, this man in front of her, felt like a stinging slap. As if she had brought a shadow into this fresh, new life of theirs.

He took a swig of his drink while she watched and wiped his mouth roughly. "Do you plan to undress right there in the corridor, *querida*?"

Silky as it sounded, Eleni didn't miss the vein of steel beneath his question. "No." When he didn't move, she tried to take stock of her situation. "I…I'm sorry I didn't realize you'd be here tonight." She sounded so lame to her own ears that she cringed.

"Where would a bridegroom be on his wedding night? Or is it not time for me to hold up my side of the bargain yet?"

Eleni gripped her elbows with her hands as if she could ward off the humiliating hurt that pinged through her.

One man had deserted her years ago without a word and one was bent on punishing her for something she hadn't done. Tears made her voice unbearably soft, almost fragile.

"Is my desire for a child so cheap in your eyes, Gabriel? Or is it that you can't force yourself to perform in the bounds of a marriage?"

"I'm not the one who decided to disappear without a word. Imagine my surprise, however, when neither Angelina nor your brother nor I could locate you for well over two hours. Your phone was off, Eleni," he bit out, "and even I know that that thing is almost surgically attached to you."

"I must have left it somewhere in all the rush."

"Even your aide could not locate you."

Her head jerked up as she realized the truth of his hard

mouth, the granite jaw. The deceivingly slumbering stare and the poisonous barbs.

He was angry with her. Blazingly furious. Not even on the night of the masquerade ball had he been like this. A shiver wrapped its fist around her spine. "Gabriel, are you angry with me?"

The question seemed to take him back. As if he hadn't quite realized it himself. "I'm merely confused, *Princesa*. You disappeared from the reception for two hours, and then you appear outside your apartments, close to midnight, your hair unraveled, your dress almost falling apart at the seams and I have to confess to wondering what the mystery is."

Eleni tugged the torn sleeve of her dress against her neck hastily and then realized the futility of the action. He'd drawn his conclusions already.

She pushed her hair from her brow, searching for some suitable story. She couldn't just admit the humiliating truth. Couldn't bear to see the cynicism in his eyes when she told him of how Spiros had disappeared from her life and how she had hung on for years before finally giving up.

The scorn in his eyes at her supposed naïveté.

A stillness claimed him as he correctly read her guilty silence. "I'm waiting for an explanation, *Princesa*."

"I saw an old friend," she said, wanting to stick to the truth as much as possible. "We started catching up and completely lost track of time. I—"

"Is this friend a man?"

Drawing her arms around her neck, she shook her head. "No." The moment the word left her mouth, she wanted to snatch it back. "She...I hadn't seen her in a long time and it was a shock to see her today, that's all."

"You didn't invite...this friend to the wedding?"

"Her sister used to work here at the palace and she decided to surprise me." Lie after lie fell from her mouth and she could not stop them. But what else could she say?

That the man she'd once desperately loved had returned after ten years of being gone on her wedding day? Or that he had held her as if his heart was breaking? Or that he'd promised her in an almost-hysterical whisper that he would never again leave her?

"Why is your dress torn?"

She lifted her chin defiantly, a slow burn of anger washing away the guilt. "What is it that you think I have done, Gabriel?"

"No groom wants to be disenchanted with his bride on their wedding night, does he?" Silken mockery dripped from his every word, making a lie of everything the day had represented.

"I told you before. I'm neither a saint nor as dull as they make me out to be," she snarled back, frustration and guilt coiling into a rope within her.

He shrugged and the movement bared one dark nipple. "Angelina said to say good-night. She insisted on waiting for you, but I finally was able to persuade her to go to bed."

The knot in her stomach twisted some more. She felt like she was on a swing of emotions, going high and low on guilt and regret and anger. All because the one man she'd desperately needed was ten years late, and the man she had promised herself to in his place now stared at her as if she had betrayed him on the very eve of their wedding.

For the rigid set of his mouth and the hard look in his eyes said what he wouldn't voice. "I'm sorry. I completely—"

"Lost track of everything, you said. Despite the fact that Angelina worries unnecessarily when people disappear all of a sudden. You know, after her mother's accident and all."

A mewl of regret fell from her mouth. She knew what

Angelina suffered having seen the panic in her eyes when her dog had been missing one afternoon. "You're beating a dog that's already down," she whispered. "I already said I'm sorry. Nothing is more important to me than the fact that Angelina feels safe and loved."

Gaze intent on her face, he nodded. "And the worry you put me through, *querida*?"

Her gaze jerked to his. He had to be joking.

"You worried about me?"

"Yes. Until now you were just the Princess of Drakon, mostly ignored, working behind the scenes, blending into the palace walls, but now—"

"That's not true," she protested, slow anger burning in her chest.

He pushed off from the wall, dropped his glass onto a side table and neared her. "Now you are Gabriel Marquez's wife. There will be unwanted attention. There will be media curiosity. Whatever you do, there will be someone with a phone or a camera around."

The scent of him filled her nostrils. One long finger reached out and traced the seam of her torn sleeve, drawing a line of fire against her bare shoulder. He radiated such warmth that Eleni thought she would go up in flames. "One chance, *Princesa*. You have one chance to tell me where you were."

Her cheeks flushed with heat but Eleni gazed back at him steadily. "Nothing has happened that warrants this kind of questioning from you."

His head tilted. His disbelief stood between them like the wall of a fortress, crumbling the tenuous connection they had made with each other the past few weeks. He was again that ruthless stranger who didn't trust her at all.

"Now, should I tell you something I have been wanting to say all day to you?"

She nodded, not trusting herself to speak. Not trusting the dangerous glint in his eyes. Not trusting the sharp craving of her own body.

Spine stiff against the wall, she licked her dry lips. His gray gaze zoomed in on the movement. Hands on the wall over her head, he leaned forward until their bodies grazed. Such honed power filled him, such heat emanated from him that she was drawn toward him with every breath, against her own will.

With a flick of his finger, he pushed the torn sleeve aside. Traced the intimate fold of her arm, the rising curve of her pushed-up breast.

Then while he held her gaze with his, he bent and pressed his mouth to the bared flesh.

Eleni gasped low in her throat.

The flick of his tongue sent a molten spark to the flesh between her legs. An ache throbbed into life there and she clenched her thighs tight to hold it off, to stop from falling into the sexual miasma of his presence.

"I have wanted to rip that gown off you from the moment you walked toward me. But since you gave that pleasure to—"

"A suit of old armor did it, Gabriel," she said huskily, desperate for the coldness in his eyes to abate.

"To someone else, I will settle for having you in my bed tonight. I will have to settle with knowing that it will be me moving inside you, *Princesa*."

"I—"

And before she could respond to that sultry statement, he closed his mouth over the flesh he had licked. And sucked it between his teeth.

Head banging hard against the wall, Eleni let out a low sound. Pleasure exploded inside her body. The graze of his lips moved to the upper swell of her breast while his hands molded the dip of her waist, the flare of her hips. "You were made to be loved, *Princesa*. This body, every whimper and moan that comes out of your mouth…they belong to me."

Rough hands rucked her dress up and up until his palm pressed between her clenched thighs. "Let me in, Princess," he uttered roughly.

But her legs were already spreading of their own accord, making a space for him at the innermost core of her.

The slide of his abrasive palms over the tender skin of her inner thighs, the stroke of his hot breath over her neck, the way he had pressed her into the wall with his hard body—Eleni was in heaven and hell.

The sensory input was too much, her body breathing hard to play catch-up.

She wanted to beg him to go slow, to give her a second to get used to the invasive intimacy of his caresses, but she was new to this sharp pleasure, was floating away in it and the required words would not form.

His palm covered her mound and her breath hissed out of her in uneven jerks.

"Your hair glints like burnished gold, *Princesa*. Are you the same here?" Wicked whispers brushed against her swelling flesh, while his fingers boldly opened her up for his exploration. "Shall I kiss you here, Eleni?" One finger dipped inside of her and she arched against him. She had never been so aware of her flesh there, tight and throbbing. Wet and aching.

Then he rubbed a finger over the swollen hood crying for his touch.

Shivers bunched in her muscles making her fevered and achy all over. She tried to reach for him but he was far too strong as he caged her in place with his body. When he flicked that bundle with deft, continual strokes, all breath left Eleni.

"Please, Gabriel…"

His mouth moved over the swell of her breast, toward

the achy center that had hardened into a knot. "I shall make you as crazy as you did me today, Eleni. I shall make you beg."

A sharp cry left her as he tore the bodice and closed his mouth over her nipple. "Oh…" Eleni bit her lip hard. It was the only way to stop herself from begging.

"I warned you, Eleni. I abhor lies and deceit."

The bitter anger in his words barely registered on the sensual haze that filled her mind and body. Stretched taut against the wall, Eleni lost her grip on her will.

Moans and whimpers fell from her mouth, erotic sounds that seemed to fuel her husband's dark demands of her.

His strokes deepened in speed and rhythm until she was riding his hand, grinding her wanton flesh against his palm with a madness she had never known.

His wicked lips pulled at her sensitized nipples while his fingers set a punishing rhythm she couldn't fight. He let the sensitive flesh go with a popping sound that vibrated in tune with the throb at her core. Teeth digging into his shoulder, Eleni sobbed as pleasure splintered in her lower belly and poured through her muscles in deep, clenching spasms.

Turned inside out, she felt raw, utterly spent.

She fell onto him like a rag doll, shattered and bare, tears crowding her throat.

The most intense, earth-shattering experience of her life and he had given it to her in anger. Ice frosted her heart even as tendrils of heat filled her muscles.

While she was still trembling, her heart thundering in her chest, while her muscles were still struggling to return from that heightened state, his hands moved to her thighs and he picked her up, as if she were a china doll.

Pressed against the granite wall of his chest, her breasts felt sore, heavy. Sleep battered her in waves and Eleni struggled to stay afloat.

She'd triggered some emotional reaction in this hard man. Yet the woman in her caved to the man in him, to the masculine possessiveness with which he carried her off. To the deep want etched in the strong planes of his face.

No one had ever wanted her like that. No one had ever shown her a hundredth of the emotion he showed. But even through the lingering waves of her climax, she knew he didn't trust her, that whatever this was between them, it was far from what she'd imagined for them.

When he threw her onto his bed, she tried to move back and tangled her legs in her own dress. When she tried it again, his hand held on to the edge of her skirt. The loud rip of the fabric punctured the sensual web.

Heart thudding, Eleni looked up. "Gabriel?" She said his name, half surrender, half retreat.

Masculine challenge glinting in his eyes, Gabriel leaned his torso toward her. His rough hands crawled up her skirt, on top of it. Knees, thighs, belly, the hollow between her breasts, his broad palm touched her everywhere.

Need coiled deeper and tighter in her again, for this time she knew what he could give her. Her body was desperately eager for another explosion. Somehow Eleni found the sense to still his hands when they reached the bodice.

"Wait, Gabriel," she whispered, the words coming as if through a long tunnel, as if from a rational mind disjointed from the yearning desires of her body.

He sat at her feet, every inch of his rugged face taut and rigid. "Ah…I did not take you for a tease, Eleni."

Sweat beaded her forehead, her body unwilling to let go of him. Through sheer will, Eleni pushed herself onto her elbows. Her dress billowed around her legs as she leaned her forehead against his shoulder.

He stiffened, his fingers pushing at her shoulders.

She clasped his bristly jaw willing him to listen. "I don't

want our first night together to be spent in doubt and mistrust. I don't want a child conceived like this."

"We have nothing but that, *Princesa*. You'll never have a child if you want us to come together in some sort of transcendent emotion that doesn't exist."

"Don't say that."

"All we have is this mindless lust."

"Because I angered you?"

He pressed the heel of his hand to his eyes, and then sighed. Resignation in his gray eyes pierced deeper than his anger. "Because you lied, Eleni. Because you proved that for all the moral pedestal you stand on, you're just like every other woman on the planet. That you're what I thought you that first night."

"What are you talking about?"

He shook a phone in her face. A sick feeling climbed up her throat as he pressed Play. A clip of Spiros and her played like a reel from some ghastly nightmare.

Whoever had shot it should be given a prize, Eleni thought hysterically, for they had shot them from the side. His gaze devouring her, Spiros held her still form in his arms so tight that no one could doubt the meaning of it. He was frantic, almost mad as he ran his hands over her body.

It looked like a lover's caresses, and yet she knew in her heart, he hadn't touched her like that at all.

Bile filled Eleni's mouth as he pressed fevered kisses all over her face all the while muttering things no one could hear. But the shock in her face, that was not visible.

The clip seemed to go on interminably until Eleni grabbed the phone from Gabriel and threw it across the room.

"Gabriel, listen to me. It's not like that at all. Spiros and I—"

Gabriel stood up from the bed, his face set into cold lines. "You had your chance. Now that I have your measure, I feel better about this whole arrangement. To think I felt guilty that you deserved better! That you were being cheated out of everything in this stupid arrangement. Of course you have a nice little lover on the side. Now I see why you were so ready to sacrifice yourself on the altar of Drakon."

Eleni pushed back from him, the depth of his bitterness like a stinging slap against her flesh. "Gabriel, you make me sound positively Machiavellian." A bitter laugh fell from her mouth. "It is no wonder you couldn't forge a bond with Angelina, is it? You have nothing but a stone for a heart. Nothing but poison filling your veins."

Utter frost dawned in his eyes as he stepped away from her. As if she had contaminated him. "I don't give a damn who you cavort with…but one word of it reaches the press, one word of your duplicity reaches Angelina's ears, you will regret the day you walked into my life."

CHAPTER SEVEN

WARM SUNLIGHT KISSED Eleni's face when she opened her eyes. An achy awareness pulsed between her legs. The sheets seemed to caress her very skin; she'd never felt such delicious languor.

The smile fell from her face as the events of the past night came back to her. She ran the back of her hand over her eyes and came away with smudges from her mascara and tears, she was sure. If not for the unfamiliar awareness between her legs, she'd have thought the whole thing a bad dream.

But Spiros had stolen her away from her own wedding reception. And Gabriel had known and been furious about it.

Eleni sat up in her bed and rubbed her eyes with a groan. Thoughts came and went, like pictures in a kaleidoscope. And suddenly she saw things with a clarity that had been lacking last night. How could she have seen clearly when Gabriel's barbs had wounded her so deep?

But why had he been so angry, so irrational? Why, when he'd always seemed so uncaring, so blasé about their impending nuptials?

She'd expected anger, yes, even his derision. But his reaction had been personal, as if she had somehow disappointed him? As if she had hurt him?

She snorted and cursed herself. As if anything she did or didn't do could affect the blasted man.

And the video… Christos, she wanted to slap whoever had shot it and quietly handed it to Gabriel.

In fact, she wanted to give a piece of her mind to all of them—the imbecile who had sneaked up on her and shot it; Spiros, who'd been half-delirious; ending with her husband, who blew hot and cold in the space of a minute.

Was it his ego that had been bruised or had Gabriel truly wanted her with that craving she'd seen in his eyes last night?

Was it her he didn't trust?

Or women in general?

Would she be left in a limbo once again, tied to a man who didn't want her, but now spoken for? Married but never a wife?

Mother to Angelina but not even the possibility of another child?

The darker her thoughts went, the tighter her throat became until she was angry with herself.

Self-pity had never solved anything for her.

She pushed away the duvet and got to her feet. Ordering a coffee, she quickly brushed her teeth, washed up. When breakfast arrived, she ordered it to be arranged on her balcony.

From up here, she had a view of the beautiful gardens that Mia tended to and the riot of color there pushed her spirits up. She grabbed her tablet and began to make a list of things she had to accomplish that day. Nothing was unconquerable as long as she was in action.

First, she'd have to make sure Angelina wasn't still upset over yesterday.

Second, she'd have to see if Mia needed any help.

Then, she'd have to check with Nik and see if he'd heard anything from Andreas.

Sighing, she continued to add items to the list—at this

rate it would be at least a year before she could approach Gabriel again—and finished her coffee.

A staff member brought her a white envelope. Reaching for it, she frowned. "What is it?"

"One of the palace staff said it was given to her by a man and asked to be specifically given to you."

Eleni thanked her and opened the note inside.

Eleni,
I'm sorry for frightening you like that. But seeing you as another man's bride was torture for me, *pethi mou*. I saw the same shock and hope in your eyes.

This time no one will separate us. This time I intend to claim you for my own. Neither your brothers nor your husband scare me. Not anymore.

Wait for me, my love.
Yours,
Spiros

Cold sweat trickled down her nape stealing the warmth of the sun.

Why was Spiros writing to her like this? What the hell did he mean no one could separate them this time? Did he think she was anything but shocked out of her mind to see him?

She needed to talk to him. Find out why he had left her like that last time. Find out why he thought she would welcome him with open arms when he hadn't had the decency to approach her for so many years.

It was only in the past two years that she'd finally looked to the future. Only with Andreas's help, even before her father's death, that she'd realized that she didn't have to spend her life grieving over a man who hadn't looked back.

And just when she had reached for a future, there was Spiros.

The shock of seeing him yesterday now gave way to other questions.

Why now? Why was he writing to her like this? Where had he been and what did he want from her? And why was it all cloaked in such mystery? Annoyed beyond measure, she tore the letter into small pieces. Found a vicious satisfaction in the childish act.

She added "Move On" to her bullet points and sighed. If only it were as easy as that.

A long shadow fell on her tablet blocking her view and Eleni looked up.

"Move on from what?"

His gravelly voice played a chord in that place between her thighs. Steady heat climbed up Eleni's cheeks.

Dressed in black trousers and a long-sleeved gray shirt that made his eyes gleam doubly, Gabriel was watching her. His jaw was clean shaven, his hair wet and slicked back.

Belatedly, Eleni moved her hand over her tablet. "That list is private."

Her breath left her afresh as the breeze carried the scent of soap and skin from him to her.

Ruggedly masculine and gorgeous, he made her mouth dry and her heart ache in her chest. The platinum ring she had placed on his unfamiliar finger gleamed bright in the sun.

A symbol of their relationship, of his commitment to her. She looked down at her own hand and her own ring. The sapphire winked at her, mocking her.

So much for thinking he was much more approachable and easygoing than her father or her older brother, Andreas. "Is there something you needed?" she said, determined to be civil.

His gaze stayed somewhere on her shoulder so she tilted her own head to see what. Her silk robe had slipped off her shoulder, and the morning sun showed the startling bruise his mouth had left on the upper swell of her breast.

Eleni blushed furiously just as his fingers circled her nape and tugged her closer. When the pad of his thumb moved over the purple mark, a sliver of pain made her gasp. A shard of pleasure shot through to her core, making her damp.

Pain and pleasure, he'd given her both yesterday. He hadn't been able to help himself, she realized now, as she felt the solid strength of him surround her. The idea of a helpless Gabriel, a Gabriel who was a slave to his need for her—it unleashed a sense of power that she'd never quite known.

Was she being delusional yet again?

When she leaned into him just so that the tip of her breasts brushed his muscular arm, she felt the faint shudder that traversed his huge body. Mirth bubbled up in her chest.

He was not immune to her, she realized with unabashed curiosity. He didn't trust her, he didn't want to want her, but this gorgeous, powerful man did want her. Suddenly, the dynamic between them was more fluid. Less absolute.

Like she too had a say in where this convenient marriage of theirs went. Was that why his reaction had been so out of character? "Gabriel," she finally said, locking her fingers around his wrist. Tension filled his body, permeating through to her.

"I did that?" he asked, his voice male and low.

Her temper flared. "Yes, just as it was you who put me in a temper, Gabriel. Not the man in the video."

A blank mask fell over the expression in his eyes again. With such thick lashes, no wonder she could never make out what he was thinking. "I apologize."

"For thinking I had gone to bed with another man in the hours between the reception and our wedding night? Or for taking that as a challenge and proving that you could still seduce me? Did it soothe your ego to know that you have that power over me? Is it that old 'I don't want you but my ego will chafe if you so much as look at another man' thing?"

Gabriel blanched, knowing that every word out of her mouth was true. He didn't have an excuse for his behavior.

Even in the corrosive anger that filled him at the thought of that video, he had been a beast to her. He had seduced her, brought her to that raw precipice of pleasure just to prove that she was putty in his hands.

She had called him on it too. The depth of his own bitterness when he'd always breezed through his relationships with women disconcerted him.

Maybe because he'd fallen for the act. Maybe he'd assumed her to be a saint, just because she was such a good mother figure to Angelina.

Maybe the damned woman had got beneath his skin.

Whatever it was, he had never lost control of himself like that. Never had his emotions been in such a riot.

Cheeks flushed with sleep, hair mussed, she looked like a red-blooded male's wet dream. As if all her beauty had needed to bloom into such voluptuousness was a man's touch. His touch.

Even now, all he wanted was to pull her to him and kiss her. To taste her mouth that trembled in such anger. To strip that flimsy robe and nightgown from her body and see the glory of her full curves in sunlight. To mark her again and again until she was covered in the scent of him. Until she forgot every other man.

"I have no excuse for my behavior," he finally said, meeting her soft gaze. "I should not have laid a finger on you last night."

Her shoulders fell on a long exhale. The lines of her face softened and she looked up at him. Her skin glowed with that golden sheen but there were dark shadows under her intelligent eyes. "Since you're determined to be bloody-minded, it falls to me to be the sensible one. To explain."

Gabriel wanted to leave. To not delve further into the woman who was clearly messing with his head. To keep their arrangement strictly platonic, her demands be damned. And yet, he was aware that he would not.

That the identity of that blasted man in that video and what he meant to her would haunt him, leaving him useless for anything else.

"I did give you a chance, *Princesa*. You lied."

Pink filled her sun-kissed cheeks. She licked her lips, looked up and her eyes widened at whatever she saw in his gaze. He didn't care what. A low hum had already begun in his muscles as he took in the silken way her nightgown clung to her curves.

God, she'd been a dream in his hands last night.

"I…I was in shock." She sat down and looked at her fisted hands in her lap. "I hadn't seen him in ten years. For a minute there on the dance floor, I thought him a ghost."

"You had more than two hours for your heartwarming reunion, *Princesa*. Two hours to process it."

"Have you never hidden something humiliating from others, Gabriel? Or were you born like this—invulnerable and hard-hearted?"

"Tell me about him, Eleni. And the truth this time."

A ghost of a smile touched her mouth, as though the memory of him pulled it from her. "Spiros was a ray of light in my life. He…never judged me for my birth. He made me laugh. He told me he loved me for myself, not for what I could mean to him. Or who I was connected to. Before I had formed a bond with Andreas or even Nikandros, Spiros was there, always ready with a laugh and a joke.

"He…used to tell me I was the most genuine person he'd ever met." Another smile. Another thread of that wistfulness in her voice. As if she'd lost something infinitely precious. "That he couldn't help loving me. He was a shoulder to cry on when my father's cruelty was too much to bear. When I felt like I was stuck between Andreas's cold control and Nikandros's impulsive defiance and couldn't lose either. When I felt like nothing I did would ever make me different from who I was. Spiros made me feel wanted. Just for myself."

"What happened then?" he cut in harshly, infuriated that his own heart was racing.

"On my nineteenth birthday, he asked me to marry him. I said yes. He kissed me in the courtyard garden, said he would speak to my father the next day. That's the last I saw of him."

"What do you mean?"

"I mean that I didn't see him again until he appeared at the reception last night. It was like he had disappeared into the night. For years, I thought he had met with some unfortunate accident. Andreas inquired with his family and found out recently that Spiros had just upped and left for the States. They didn't know anything about me or that he'd proposed. I…I just couldn't believe he was back. I went when he asked if we could talk, and I stood there, still in shock, when he hugged me and kissed me.

"When I returned to our suite, there you were. Even if I had told you the truth, you wouldn't have believed me, Gabriel. You already believed the worst."

He had. He did. Until now, he hadn't realized how much his own mother's lies had stayed with him. "Do you love him?"

It was the last question Eleni expected him to ask, this husband of hers who had reminded her again and again that he thought every emotion was a weakness. That he didn't believe in marriage, much less love.

That theirs was a cold, clinical arrangement.

"I loved him years ago. With every breath in me. I believed that he and I…we could be truly happy. Greeting card happy."

"Greeting card happy?" He looked so nauseated that Eleni laughed.

"Like Mia and Nikandros," she said, and looked away.

Suddenly, she felt his fingers under her chin, the rough dig of his thumb onto her jaw. His hard gaze held hers, as if he wanted to plumb the depths of her soul. As if he could will her into giving the answer he wanted. Which was what?

What did Gabriel want? All her confusion about Spiros misted when she gazed into his gray eyes, when she felt his gaze on her.

"You haven't answered my question, *Princesa*. Do you love this man?"

Faint tension filled his frame. Something inside her goaded Eleni, something she'd never felt before. "Would you let me go if I did?"

"No." The word was like a detonation between them, a gauntlet thrown down. Eleni shivered under his touch, aware that his interest in her was personal. She didn't know how but she knew it and it sent a thrill of excitement and fear through her. "If you leave our marriage now, if you turn your back on Angelina, I will—"

"Yes, yes, you will sink Drakon, you will raze the house of Drakos to the ground etc. etc. Really, Gabriel, your threats are becoming tiresome. I have never walked away from a promise I have made."

He continued to stare at her, as if he didn't quite believe her. This matter of trust between them had to be dealt with. Their being at each other's throat like last night could only hurt Angelina, or any other children they had.

He had listened to her—that had to be enough for now.

That he was attracted to her filled her with a rare sense

of feminine power that she'd never known. When he stood up to walk away, she looked up at him. They had crossed some line in their relationship. That awareness tingled in the very air about them.

And Eleni was far too confused by her own reaction to question his right now. Too scared to ask what he wanted of her. "I came to tell you that I'm appointing security personnel to guard you. It's a measure your brothers should have taken long ago."

Hurt splintered through her. "Is that for my protection or for spying on me?"

He shrugged, and for the first time since they had met, he was the one that looked away. Tension tightened around his mouth. "As my wife, you need the protection," he said, and walked away.

Leaving her question about trust unanswered. But at least he'd called her his wife.

Leaving her claimed, even though he hadn't touched her again.

Eleni looked around the huge bedroom with satisfaction. The staff had unpacked most of her stuff and put it away in Gabriel's bedroom. A thrill shot through her as she walked into the stadium-sized closet. When Gabriel had arrived in Drakon, he'd only been a guest of the palace, and yet he'd been given one of the best apartments. His company was a billionaire investor in Drakon, and Nikandros had wanted no deficiency in their hospitality.

Eleni herself had chosen this apartment for him. It afforded a gorgeous view of the mountains in the distance on one side and the ocean on the other. The best of Drakon's views for Gabriel Marquez.

But in seven months, nothing had changed in the suite. No photo frames adorned the side table, not even a picture of Angelina. No keepsakes of his family.

With a frown, she remembered Gabriel hadn't known of the little girl's existence until a few months ago.

She could imagine his wrath that Angelina's mother had hidden such a big truth from him. But beneath that, she wondered now, did he feel betrayal too? Had it perhaps skewed his perception of women? Did he think all women would betray him given the smallest chance?

She had received two more notes from Spiros and she had torn them both up without even opening them. He was in her past; Gabriel was her future.

She'd decided to give him no thought unless he showed himself to her. Unless he stopped playing these silly games with her.

In the meantime, she was determined to sort out her marriage, whatever it took. Gabriel might not want her as his wife but he was attracted to her. They had to move past the impasse they seemed to be at—their relationship was neither the calculated arrangement they initially thought, nor was it going forward.

Beneath the hardness and cold demeanor, there was a man with integrity. A man who loved his daughter, hard though he found it to express it. A man who'd had shown her in three weeks of marriage that he was charming, funny and loyal to those he considered his.

A man who looked at Eleni like she was the tastiest morsel he'd ever seen.

A man who grunted and grumbled when Eleni offered him advice about Angelina but followed it because he wanted his daughter to be happy.

A man who took on Nikandros because he thought she was being taken advantage of by her brothers.

She liked her husband, she realized, running her hands over the sheets. Gabriel's scent—musky and something of the sea—sent acute longing threading through her.

She wanted a proper life with him and Angelina. Even

with his sidelong glances—sometimes fuming, sometimes so hot that she thought she'd sizzle on the spot—the last three weeks had been the happiest she'd known in a long time. Maybe ever.

Throat full, she straightened a few ties in the closet.

It was the sense of belonging he'd given her, she knew. With Gabriel and Angelina, she had a place. Father and daughter—while negotiating a tenuous truce between each other—had made Eleni feel invaluable to them. Made her feel wanted.

She'd do anything to make that permanent.

She'd just have to prove to him that this marriage and this life she shared with him and Angelina was everything to her.

Respect and loyalty and belonging—it was more than she'd ever expected.

She reached for her tablet, opened her to-do list and added an item.

Seducing Gabriel would be more than a bullet point in her list soon.

"Are you and Ellie fighting, Papa?"

The question zoomed out of Angelina's mouth while Gabriel was finishing up the designs for the last mountain resort his company was building in Drakon.

He ripped up the blueprint in front of him and wadded it into a pulp. Restlessness like he'd never known filled him, marring the pleasure he had always found in his work. The pleasure he'd found in making money, or in a sexy woman.

Nothing satisfied him anymore.

Nothing he had done over the last few weeks had distracted his mind from the warm woman he found in his bed every night when he returned to his bedroom.

When he had snarled at Eleni and asked if there wasn't a spare room in the entire damn palace, the minx had looked at him serenely and said she hadn't wanted to give any of the staff a chance to gossip about them.

She'd also pointed out that "wasn't the entire reason he had married her to provide Angelina with a secure, home atmosphere? The security of knowing that there wasn't just one but two people who cared about her?"

Of course, having never shared a suite, much less a bedroom with a woman, Gabriel had no idea what he had signed up for.

Day after day, his damn wife's "stuff" crept all over the apartment, taking up space. If he reached for a shirt, there was her yellow dress that had made her look like a voluptuous sunflower.

If he reached for his cuff links, there was her jewelry case filled with the funky costume jewelry she apparently loved collecting.

If, after a long day at work, he went in for a shower, there she was in the giant tub, filled with frothy bubbles and a hundred candles playing peekaboo with damp, soft flesh he wanted to caress, bare thighs he wanted to kiss.

He was the real estate billionaire and even his bathroom was not his own.

The pocket-sized minx was driving him so insane that any given minute he either wanted to throttle her or kiss her senseless.

The only reason he hadn't stalked out of those apartments was now standing behind him.

Calling him *papa* without even realizing she was doing it.

Whatever torment Eleni was causing his flesh—and he worried he was going to be walking with a permanent hard-on—Gabriel grinned and bore it, for Angelina had bloomed like anything in the last weeks. The sparkle in his daughter's eyes every day, the transformation from a sullen child to a lovely, cheerful girl was amazing.

Clearly, his wife knew what she was talking about.

"If you are busy, Papa," came the tentative voice again, "I'll return later."

"No, stay, *querida*," he replied softly.

Willing the tension in his muscles to ease, swallowing away the urge to snarl, as he'd been doing at everyone else, Gabriel put his pencil down and turned.

Her dark hair bound in a tight braid and clad in a white shirt and jodhpurs, Angelina looked like a little champion. "Had a good riding lesson?" he asked, signaling her to come into his office.

After a reluctant minute, she slowly entered. He smiled for the first time in days. Like him, his daughter was a very calculating sort of person. In every interaction between them, he could almost see her weighing the risks and advantages.

Wondering if he could be trusted. And yet, if Eleni had been present, she wouldn't have hesitated even barging in.

"It was a good lesson, although Ellie didn't join us."

"Oh?" he said, striving to keep his voice casual. For one thing, he hadn't known that Eleni was joining Angelina during her riding lessons, although he couldn't say he was surprised.

Apparently, among all her numerous talents, his wife was a superb equestrian. He hadn't yet seen her ride but Angelina couldn't stop talking about it.

It also hadn't taken him long to realize that Eleni was a very hands-on person, even when it came to matters of Angelina. Nothing was trivial enough—not Angelina's education, not her outfits, not even shopping and ice-cream trips were delegated to a nanny or an assistant. Yet, he was also aware that she'd shed none of her other duties.

Since Nik's wife, Mia, was late into her pregnancy with twins and damn Andreas was still MIA, Eleni was playing hostess for Nikandros for many of the state functions of Drakon.

While he grumbled about her taking up space in his suite, the quiet in those rooms when she was out on the social whirl or some palace affair had become unbearable.

Perversely, it bothered him that she had a full life without him when he should be glad that she hadn't made any demands of him again. That he had acquired a mother for Angelina without having to make any emotional investment.

So why did he feel as though slowly but surely the Princess was winning a game he hadn't even realized they were playing? Why did he sometimes catch her gaze on him with such stark yearning in it, the same deep, visceral need he felt when he found her scrunched up tight on one side of his bed?

She rarely came to bed before him and she was dressed and breakfasting on the veranda with her tablet in hand when he woke up. Gabriel had seen the evidence of her hard work in the bruised shadows under her eyes, in the sunken tightness of her features.

If she didn't slow down, Eleni would work herself into an early grave. Yet the woman had a stubborn will that no one could shake.

"So, tell me, are you two fighting?" Angelina prodded.

"Didn't you ask her the same question?" he said, tugging on her braid.

As had become a habit between them, she swatted his hand away first. But then didn't let go completely.

As if she needed the guise of that slap to touch him.

"You growl and grumble like a grumpy giant, Gabriel. Of course it took her time to become familiar with your... physicality."

"Is that why you flinch every time I touch you?" he'd

asked Eleni, falling into the lure of those wide, fluttering eyes.

"Why don't you touch me now and see?" the minx had taunted him.

The Princess had become bold. Just like his daughter, there was always a sparkle in her eyes, a spring in her step. It was strangely exhilarating to see Eleni come into her own as a mother.

She'd be a fierce lioness, a great mother to any of their children. The errant thought dropped into his head like a small explosive.

With a muffled curse, he ran his fingers through his hair. If he took her, and every cell in his body wanted to, Gabriel knew he was making a deeper commitment. It could never be a convenient arrangement. He already couldn't bear the thought of another man with her, much less touching her or kissing her. And if he did, he couldn't just move on to another woman.

It was not the example he wanted to set for his daughter. And more than that, it was not what the Princess deserved.

So what the hell was he then signing on for? A true marriage? A relationship with respect and loyalty she already had from him, so was this about passion? God forbid, emotion?

"Papa, you're not listening."

Falling to his knees, which he knew she liked, Gabriel made an apologetic face. "Sorry, *Tesoro*."

"Anyway, I wanted to ask Ellie if you and she were fighting. She's been a little quiet this past week and to be honest, I think she's very sad," she said with the stunning perception of a child. "I went to see her yesterday afternoon and she…she wasn't feeling well. So I wanted to ask if you were the reason and to tell you to lay off."

"Lay off?" he said, his mouth twitching at the fierceness of her tone.

"Yes, lay off. I think she's already in shock about her old friend. As strong as Ellie is, it's a lot of people to worry over."

His interest perking up, Gabriel casually said, "Old friend?"

"I heard Nik and her talking about it. She was crying and he held her and said he was sorry. I have never seen her like that."

A jolt went through Gabriel. He couldn't imagine his strong, efficient, smart wife crying. There was a core of steel inside of her, he realized now, an integrity nothing could puncture. She had loved the man who'd deserted her for years, remained loyal to him.

Gabriel had never known anyone to be capable of such depth of feeling.

"Please, Papa. Will you be nice to Ellie and ask after her?"

It was the first time his little girl had asked for something. It was the first time she'd looked at him as if he were capable of something good and positive.

But even if she didn't, nothing could stop him from finding out exactly what his wife was crying over. "Of course," he said, hugging his little girl.

CHAPTER EIGHT

IT TOOK GABRIEL all of two hours to locate his wife.

He looked in the direction in which the groom pointed and came to a standstill at the sight in front of him. With a nod, he dismissed the groom and another staff member, feeling strangely possessive of her.

Without that brisk, matter-of-fact quality to her, she looked fragile and lonely and a rush of protectiveness filled him.

She sat atop a huge pile of hay, her arms around her knees tucked tight against her chest. As if she meant to scrunch herself into nothingness. Shards of sunlight filtered through the wooden slats of the barn, picking out the bronze and gold highlights in her hair. Bathed in the sunlight, she looked like a golden goddess—untouched by cynicism, all soft edges.

"Princesa?"

She looked up, her eyes wide and round in her face. Wariness filled her expression, a sudden tension in the slender set of her shoulders. "Why do you insist on calling me that in that mocking tone? It says you think I'm anything but."

"Does it matter if I think you a princess or not?"

"No," she said, half to herself. "Did you need something? Is Angelina looking for me?"

"I don't need anything, but Angelina's worried for you."

"She's sweet, but I didn't think it was proper for her to see me like this."

"I defer to your superior judgment on that."

"Why are you suddenly being nice to me?" she said, not even looking at him.

"I have been ordered to be nice to you. With the fiercest of threats."

"Ah…now I get it. This is Angelina's doing." As if he did not give a damn about her.

"If I had known you were…unwell, I would have come after you myself."

"Please, all we have is honesty, Gabriel. Don't take that away too."

"Relationships are not my strong point and ours…our relationship hasn't been easy or straightforward from the beginning."

"Because you decided that I deceived you. Because you're incapable of trust."

That kiss had stood between them from the beginning. He had unburdened himself, thinking her a stranger. But what if she'd been telling the truth and all she'd wanted was a simple kiss?

What if the truth was really that simple and that complicated?

Even as she pretended to be happy with her lot, that version of Eleni had been so vulnerably open.

I wanted to be someone else for one night.

And he'd taken it away from her. "I was angry that day. I had just found out what Monique had hidden from me. I came to the ball wanting to be anyone but myself. Women and deceit seemed to go hand in hand in my head that night.

"I knew the Princess of Drakon. Finding out that the enchantress I had just kissed was that princess was a shock. Like nothing was the same or sane in my life anymore. I don't think I even realized how much I had begun to count on you. How much your presence meant."

"You're just saying that now."

"No. There was always a quiet strength about you, even back then. No wonder you were the only one your father listened to, the only one who could calm his rages."

A strange stillness came over her as he closed the door behind him and drenched them in darkness.

With the world and the day shut away, there was a damp chill in the barn. The setting sun sent tendrils of orange light through the rafters. The long line of her neck bared, she looked up at him, the golden flecks in her eyes becoming prominent in the shadows. He saw her swallow as he reached her, saw that flash of yearning before she blinked and shut it away.

Her arms tightened around her. "I came here to be alone." Even when he'd been his snarliest, grumpiest self, she'd never used that tone on him. Like she had no use for him.

"So that you could grieve over…over *him* in private?"

The same thought would have sent him running in the opposite direction even a week ago. Today, he wanted to comfort her.

Gabriel Marquez comforting his wife over the loss of her lover. Surely the world had turned upside down?

"Yes, something like that."

"You're stuck with me, *Princesa*." The words left his mouth and he realized he meant it. In more ways than one.

He lowered his huge body next to her on the same pile of hay and she instantly shifted. But she was limited by the wall on the other side and his thigh pressed against hers.

The sides of their bodies pressed, and then folded against each other, the soft whisper of it amplified in the dark. The scent of hay and damp earth filled his nostrils.

"Eleni…no one is worth your tears."

"He is. I've known him for years. I've loved him for

years. He never looked at me as if I would not measure up. And now I have to say goodbye."

Bitterness mixed with grudging respect filled him. Every atom of his being revolted against having this discussion.

He had the emotional constitution of a car, a lover had once said to him and he'd only laughed and agreed. He'd never been possessive or jealous, for all his relationships had been transient.

Now he couldn't even name the riot of feelings inside of him.

"So you're admitting—" he half choked on the words "—that you're in love with this…man?"

She moved in a blur in front of him, her eyes flashing catlike in the dark. "What? What the hell are you talking about?"

"Angelina told me how much you were grieving over the loss of an old friend. That you had been unbearably sad—"

"Angelina is talking about Black Shadow, my horse of six years."

"Your horse?"

"Yes, my horse, you…you…unfeeling ass. My horse, who I've just found out is terminally ill. My horse who is my closest friend and companion. You actually think I was sitting here crying over some lost lover and that I would tell Angelina about it? What the hell is wrong with you?"

She didn't give him a chance to respond, but came at him like a flash of lightning—dazzling and beautiful in one breath. Her hands thumped him in soft blows. Gabriel put his hands up, afraid of his petite wife hurting herself rather than him. In his overcompensation, he pushed her off the pile and she took him with her.

He landed on top of her on more hay, his heart lighter than it had been in days.

She hadn't been moping over her lover. He wanted to

shout it like a teenage boy who'd found out that the girl he liked liked him back. He felt a lightness he hadn't felt even in his younger, carefree days.

Eleni let out a soft woof as his body pressed her down. "Get off me, you...you unfeeling giant."

He laughed and shifted just enough to ensure he didn't crush her.

She struggled to push him off, as if that were possible, and the slide and shift of her body under his sent his lust into overdrive.

Hell, he liked having her beneath him, all soft and glaring. Another wiggle and her legs separated and straddled him until his hardness nestled against the hottest and softest part of her.

Gabriel let out a filthy oath just as her soft groan filled the air. His hips flexed and rolled in an instinct old as time, his muscles burning with desire. "And if I don't want to move?" He gripped her wrists and pulled them above him, forcing her to look at him. The move forced her upper body to arch toward him, those lush breasts to rub against his chest in the most decadent pleasure. "You have been tormenting me for three weeks, *mia cariña*. Have you any idea what unspent arousal of so many days does to a man?"

It felt as if all the air from the entire world had been ripped out. Leaving only the sensual haze for Eleni to subsist on. Gray eyes watched her as if she were the most delicious dessert that he intended to feast on.

His fingers gripped her wrists in a firm clasp yet gently for a man so big. For days, she had seen him around the suite, in various torturous states of undress, and she knew the power in his muscled frame.

For days and quite a few nights, when he had come to bed and the huge mattress dipped beneath his weight, she had wondered about what it would feel like to be the woman he focused that power on. To be the woman trapped beneath that powerful body.

Shivers had overtaken her at the game she'd been playing every time that gray gaze had swept over her, embers of dark desire in his eyes.

Now she knew.

He didn't quite crush her to the ground but he was a divine, languorous weight on top of her body. Eleni licked her lips, twice, a deep, delicious ache building between her legs. Muscular thighs straddled hers and yet somehow, he kept his lower body away from her, after that first sizzling contact.

Her fingers wound around his upper arms, and she felt the taut clench of his thick muscles. "You're the most aggravating man I've ever met. Tell me, what would you have done if I said yes, Gabriel? If I had truly been moping over my lover?"

He bent his head and the warmth of his breath caressed her trembling lips. She should say no, tell him that she was a real woman with feelings. Not a robot he could use when he needed a mother for his girl, and then ignore.

Holding her gaze, he slanted the angle and pressed his mouth against hers—full flush.

Soft and yet hard, his lips sent a shock that jerked her body into superawareness. Again and again, he did it— moved his lips over hers in a sensual rhythm so visceral that she shivered from the onslaught of it. The world outside the dark barn, the thread of her grief inside, everything fell away under the intense and growing ache within her.

She had waited years, no aeons, it seemed, for the stamp of his body. To be possessed by him.

"I would have reminded you that you promised your body to me, *Princesa*." Only then did he press his hard body into hers. The weight and heat of his erection pressed against her mound and Eleni cried out loud, her body restless in her own skin. Instantly, her thighs created a cradle for him. A satisfied gleam appeared in his gray eyes. "I would have told you that you belonged to me."

Eleni didn't know if she was capable of voicing a question, of asking the same of him, demanding that he promise her the same. He didn't give her the chance to find out. When he finished breathing his guttural promise, he dipped his tongue into her mouth in a long, erotic stroke and Eleni lost the last rational thought in her mind.

"Kiss me back, *Princesa*," he commanded in that same arrogant tone.

Slowly, softly, Eleni opened her mouth and kissed him back.

The raspy slide of their mouths, the heated rush of their breaths, the shiver of hay around them—Eleni had never heard such sensuous sounds in her life. It felt as if every sense of hers was amplified a thousand times over. As if she were nothing but a conduit for sensations.

The strokes of his tongue and lips were maddeningly slow, silky, drawing out the feverish tremors of her body, longer and deeper. The gentleness of his mouth, of his body threw her. It was as if he wanted to savor every stroke of his mouth, hear every gasping hitch of her breath.

As he seduced her mouth with such skill, the barn was drenched in complete darkness. The last fingers of sunlight disappeared and the dark intensified the sensations weaving through her body.

With her hands crawling from his biceps to his shoulders, she dug her fingers into his steel-like shoulders. In answer, he stroked his tongue against hers.

Eleni gasped into his mouth.

She wanted to move; she wanted to touch him everywhere from the torturous prison he created with his own body, but he was so hard and solid over her that she didn't stand a chance. "Gabriel," she whispered, this time it was a plea for more, without doubt.

When he didn't comply, when she could hear the silkily masculine laugh that fell from his mouth, she sank her fingers into his hair and pulled at the thick, rough swaths. Pushed his head toward her with her fingers.

And dug her teeth into his lower lip, driven by an instinct she didn't even know she possessed.

Instantly, he exploded. His kisses became rougher; his tongue plunged deeper and faster into her mouth, imitating the very act of love with such erotic mastery that she was a puddle under him.

The darkness made little of any doubts she would have felt at being naked in front of him when his large hands moved down and, with an economy of movement, undressed her completely.

But when he went to his knees and began pulling his shirt out of his trousers, Eleni wished it weren't so dark in the barn. Her eyes had acclimatized to the shadow and the outline of his body—wide, powerful shoulders, broad chest tapering to narrow hips and the muscular thighs— made her breath go awry.

He was so gorgeously formed—a perfect male and he had chosen her—the short, curvy, diminutive Princess with unruly hair and very little to recommend her.

Was it any wonder the media and the public had such a fascination with their marriage?

When he came back to her and nudged her thighs apart, and then slid his hard body on top of hers, Eleni's head went back in the prickly hay. His skin was like heated velvet, pressing her down.

The rough rasp of hairy thighs against her smooth ones, the press of the hard band of his abdominal muscles against the soft ones in her belly, the silky slide of his chest against her sensitized breasts—a sob flung out of her from the depths of her soul.

Abrasive palms roamed all over her body, learning her curves in the dark. The underside of her arms, the tight dip of her waist, the crease of her thigh—there wasn't an inch of her he didn't worship with his hands. There wasn't an inch of her mouth he didn't devour in long, slow kisses. "Eleni?"

She made some unintelligible sound as his fingers lazily circled her nipple, painfully erect and crying for his attention. Sensations pierced her lower belly, as without any sign, his mouth closed over the hard nub.

A cry that could tear through the rafters rippled out of her as she felt the silky slide of his tongue over her nipple and then the graze of his teeth.

Incomprehensible sounds fell from her mouth as he continued to tease and torment her nipples alternately, as if he couldn't keep his mouth away from them.

A sheen of sweat coated her entire body, her sex damp and swelling. She'd never been so aware of every inch of her body, of every tremor and ripple that shook through her.

"You respond to every touch as if you were an instrument, *Princesa*. You tremble to every touch, you cry in abandon...you have been driving me crazy since that ball."

Her back stiffened when his hand slid down her abdomen. Her cheeks overheated to dangerous levels when his fingers played with the curls there. Masculine demand glittered in every bold stroke, in every invasive touch.

Eleni squeezed her eyes closed, knowing that he watched her. That her pleasure, her moans fueled his own. He took his sweet time, tracing the shape of every fold of her sex intimately, with one finger first and then the next, as if he were memorizing the shape of her down there. As if he had never explored another woman thoroughly before, quite like this.

But of course he had. Every skillful stroke of his, every touch and slide of his lips—he already knew her body better than she did. Better she remember it this time as the most pleasurable, intimate experience of her life, rather than mistake it for emotional closeness.

Rather than delude herself that Gabriel was overtaken by anything other than lust. Afflicted by anything other than a challenge to his pure masculine ego.

Everything she used to convince herself that this was only lust disappeared when he pushed first one and then another finger into her core.

Eleni jerked and locked her hips tight, feeling intensely vulnerable. His fingers were clever as they teased and stroked her, her folds swollen and wet.

"Oh, please," she begged. Was there no part of her he wouldn't discover with intimate knowledge? "Can't you just…I…just want…"

"You just want what, Eleni?"

"I want you inside of me. You don't have to…" His finger hooked inside her wet opening and her eyes rolled back in her head. "Oh, God."

"But I would know your body, *Princesa*. I would know every gasp and moan of yours, I would learn what would drive you mindless with hunger for me, what would send you over the edge…"

Her hands fisted around locks of hay, her entire body thrumming with a new tension. "You're already doing that," she said on the wave of a sob that filled her when his thumb pressed cleverly against the swollen flesh.

Eleni called out and bucked her hips against his touch, desperate for more.

He stopped immediately and she cursed him to hell and damnation, frustration curling her muscles.

"Do you like this, *Princesa*?" he said, while he dragged his finger in and out, making her wetter and crazier.

Again and again, he tortured her while Eleni lost sight of everything but the deep, visceral want of her body. She forgot the number of times he drove her toward release, and then left her, poised and threatening to shatter, on the edge.

She didn't know when, but at some point, she had given up even on begging him. Just when she had decided he was wreaking revenge on her for wicked reasons of his own, he pushed her legs wider apart.

"That was for all the torment you gave me." His voice was husky, low. "I need you desperately, Eleni. But this is the time to stop me if you don't want this, *Princesa*. After this, you won't belong to anyone but me."

She stared into his eyes and clasped his neck. She could only nod, words failing to come. Or the wrong words. Emotional words that she couldn't sift through for her body was drowning in pleasure.

He slid his hand over her hip, down her boneless thigh and opened her wide for him.

Looking down at her, as if he were one of those conquering marauders that had attacked Drakon again and again, he nudged her opening with the head of his shaft.

Blinking, Eleni fought the furious heat that seemed to combust her from within. Giving up any pretense to modesty, she moaned when he rubbed the full length of himself against her, as if to drench himself in her wetness, and then, just when she thought this torture would never end, he entered her in one deep, soul-wrenching thrust that lodged him inside of her so deep that she didn't know where she ended and he began.

She cried out in shock more than pain, just as the intense pressure inside of her finally combusted and she came in a fierce clenching of her inner muscles.

Hands clenched tightly around his naked back, nails

digging into his velvet-rough skin, Eleni tried to make sense of everything that was happening to her.

Her throat felt raw from her cry, her lower belly still clenching and releasing in deep spasms around Gabriel's hard thickness, still getting used to the power and hard heat of him stretching her. Intimate and invasive, being taken by a man with such primitive, possessive need, how was she to keep this in context?

How could she not weave dreams, how could she not tie herself to him forever when he—he did this to her? When it felt like she couldn't breathe again, ever, she couldn't live if he didn't move inside of her? When the thought of him doing all these intimate things with another woman gouged through her very soul?

Pain and pleasure intermingled, her foolish naïveté that she could share his bed, share his life and not lose a part of her splintered, bringing hot, scalding tears to her cheeks.

And in the midst of the emotional and physical storm was the man lying on top of her and staring at her with a thunderstorm in his eyes. "You lied again, *Princesa*."

Eleni bit her lip to puncture the haze around her senses. Her hands roamed over his broad back, traced the deep indent of his spine, as if she couldn't let go of him. A frantic desperation began in her as she realized how deeply Gabriel could hurt her, how enmeshed her life was already with his.

"Stop touching me like that," he said, his voice raised to a storm for the first time against her. The longing in his words resonated in the darkness of the barn, lust etching deep circles around his mouth.

Eleni wriggled under him, trying for succor from the tension in her lower belly, for ease from the continual clenching of her muscles.

"Why didn't you tell me?"

"It was not a question you posed of me when we discussed our marriage. You had very little interest, actually, in anything remotely related to our conjugal life. You barely even kissed me at our wedding."

"You give the impression of a woman who knows her mind, *Princesa*. You said you had been celibate for a long time. You said you loved Spiros."

"You heard what you wanted to hear, Gabriel," she said sounding husky and feeble.

His silence was a deadweight on her chest. "If you're worried that my heart will follow my virginity to you like some kind of bonus offer, please don't. I decided long ago that it would only go to my husband, whoever that was. I couldn't risk the scandal of an affair on top of being illegitimate. Not even for Spiros could I risk the name of the House of Drakos. So my virginity just became another boulder around my neck, another shackle in my fight to be a model daughter for my father."

The bite of his fingers against her hips tightened and she bit back a gasp. Tension thrummed in the hard angles of his face. His skin had a damp sheen, just like hers, and the corded muscles of his neck were so tight that she realized he remained still with a superhuman will.

She sent her hands up his hair-roughened forearms, up his muscled biceps, toward his shoulders. She touched him everywhere and saw the play of tension in his face.

Her heart hammered, waiting for him to push her away, waiting for the explosion she sensed building in him. She didn't know where her boldness came from. But with his hard thickness inside of her, with him poised over her body, Eleni refused to let him go.

She followed the line of his spine down to his buttocks and gripped them. Nudged her body deeper and up toward him.

His snarl sent a spark of sensation down to her pelvis

as did the involuntary, instinctual thrust of his narrow hips. "Hold on to me, *Princesa*." He barely gave her time before his hands slid under her body. Rough fingers tilted her bottom up, and then he slid all the way out, and then thrust back in.

Breath hissed through her mouth as he filled her utterly. He did it again and again, in slow, deep thrusts that had Eleni jerking on the hay, heart pumping double time.

The friction he created in that angle was incredible, her body climbing up toward the peak greedily again. Every time he moved, the heat and pressure intensified until her climax burst upon her, in a shower of pleasure and sparks, stealing her very breath.

She was still clutching the white-hot sensation narrowing down in her pelvis, breathing hard when he thrust faster and deeper.

She felt the moment his own tension broke, the moment when he became as irrational as her in his want, felt his spine stiffen. His snarl of pleasure washed over as he climaxed inside of her.

Her hands ached to hold him, but Eleni kept them by her side. That same sense of vulnerability attacked now that the moment was over. Reality came flooding in the form of hard voices approaching the barn, puncturing the magic of the moment.

Pulling out of her, Gabriel dressed with a calm efficiency that made her skin cold. Or was it because the warmth of his body had deserted her?

"Get dressed, *Princesa*," he said, pulling her to her feet and holding her on her jellied legs before she found her balance.

He picked up her clothes and helped her fasten the zipper on her dress. With the soreness between her legs, it took Eleni a few minutes to find her balance. For her heart to stop thumping loudly in her chest.

For her mind to grasp the fact that they hadn't used protection.

She halted Gabriel when he'd have moved away and tried to find his features in the dark. "Gabriel? I…" Heat scoured her cheeks. "I forgot…we forgot. We didn't use protection."

She felt his shock like a tangible entity in the dark. His distress like a stinging slap against her cheek. "Gabriel," she said, reaching out with her fingers, "say something."

The clasp of his fingers around hers sent breath rushing through her lungs. Her legs tangled with his and she fell against his chest. Strong arms wound around her and held her, even as every cell in her braced for rejection. She felt his fingers slide up her nape into her hair, felt the whisper of his breath against her cheek.

It didn't matter that they were standing in pitch dark. She still felt far too vulnerable. One careless word from him could shatter her.

"Then we will welcome the child. This is what you wanted, yes?"

Shaking from head to toe, Eleni nodded. She had been prepared to be overwhelmed by Gabriel's masculinity, but her imagination didn't even come close to reality.

She felt changed from within.

His mouth touched her temple and then drifted down to take her mouth in a long, deep kiss. Bent over his arm, Eleni gave herself up to the languid strokes of his tongue, to the flutterings of desire even through the soreness of her core. A groan rose from the depths of her. Her legs made a space for him voluntarily, inviting him to do more. Waiting with bated breath for more.

His laughter reverberated against her breasts, a silky, confident, utterly male sound. "I would like nothing more than to take you again, *Princesa*, but you would be sore." Something in the tone of his voice set every hair on her body to alert. His grip tightened in her hair, a strange tenseness in his still frame. "Next time you meet a man in some corner of the palace," he said, and she instantly stiffened against him, "or the next time a man drags you into some corner of the palace and kisses you, scream bloody murder. You'll never see Spiros again. Is that clear, Eleni? You'll not even spare him a thought in your head."

Even after everything they had just shared, it was clear he still didn't trust her.

CHAPTER NINE

WITH GABRIEL IN Barcelona for a fortnight's trip and Angelina busy with her tutor, Eleni spent the afternoons with Black Shadow.

She was avoiding facing the reality that was waiting for her in the form of a pregnancy test. Her breath sped up just at the thought, and Black Shadow whinnied, sensing her anxiety.

Keeping her hands on his thick coat, she soothed him with a whisper. If only she could soothe herself so easily too.

She'd longed for a baby of her own for so long yet the possibility of it now left her with panic.

She wanted this baby, of course, with all her heart. A hundred possibilities, happy ones, crowded her every time she thought of holding a baby in her arms. Her and Gabriel's baby. A younger brother or sister for Angelina.

But with their relationship so fragile, so tenuous, she was scared that it would change him, change the way he saw them.

He'd admitted to them being a real family. But she'd no idea if he'd said that in the heat of the moment or if he'd meant it.

After that evening in the barn, he'd walked her back to her suite and bid her good-night with a lingering kiss. Had told her he had work to catch up on.

When she'd gone to look for him the next morning, he'd

already left the palace. Only a text message informed her that he was already en route to the airport heading to Barcelona on company business.

She'd known as surely as the soreness between her legs that morning, the faint fingerprints on her hips from when he'd held her tightly that he was avoiding her.

She'd been glad for the reprieve too. For she'd have never been able to act normal with him the next morning. If her life depended on it, she couldn't have pretended that their encounter in the barn hadn't changed her.

Until she'd learned that at the same time she was mooning over him, Gabriel was in Barcelona with his ever-present lawyer friend, attending parties and generally making merry.

Of course, the media had reported it.

Has the real estate tycoon already lost interest in his new bride?

It was a wake-up call from the fairy tale she'd begun to weave around them. Whether Gabriel had already gone back to his old habits or not, Eleni needed to face reality. Needed to remember that this was a convenient arrangement.

It was another thing she'd learned about herself.

Making love with Gabriel could never be simple for her. It would mean more, and she'd desperately need for it to mean more to him. For him to never want another woman.

And therein was the problem.

Until she had a handle on her own emotions, she couldn't tell him what she suspected. What she knew to be true in her bones. What she was terrified was in her heart.

Gabriel returned from his trip to Barcelona and went straight to his office to finish signing some documents for his secretary.

Every inch of him was bone tired after dealing with his sister's worries about their mother. Nothing was short of a drama with Isabella. Nothing short of life or death seriousness.

And yet, he was also aware of a mad pulse of excitement inside him. A new awareness of everything around him.

All week, he'd thought of Eleni. Of her crestfallen expression when he'd told her to get dressed in that dismissive tone. Of the way she'd scrunched into herself when he'd warned her that he wanted no lies between them again.

Of the way she'd walked away from him. As if she couldn't bear to be touched even by his shadow.

Setting up the new rules for their relationship, warning her not to give him a reason to doubt her again—he'd needed to do that to wrest control of the situation. Once she understood his rules for their marriage, she would be fine.

Anticipation tightening every muscle, he walked through the maze-like corridors between the wing that housed his office and the residential apartments at the back of the palace. The famed courtyard glittered with its numerous stones in the moonlight, a cool breeze fluttering in from the ocean.

Never had his heart thumped so hard at the prospect of seeing a woman.

Standing under the hot stream of jets in her bathroom, Eleni breathed deeply, trying to rid the anxiety that seemed to swirl in her belly.

It had started the moment Angelina had smilingly whispered that "Papa had returned" this afternoon.

Every cell in her had wanted to leap across the walls of the palace toward him. Every minute of the day that had passed without seeing him had built up the tension inside of her.

Suddenly, the idea of settling herself in Gabriel's bedroom felt like the most naive, most stupid idea she'd ever had. In retrospect, this whole marriage seemed like one, but she couldn't just back out of it.

She needed a to-do list to take control of her emotions, like everything else. Physical distance first, so that she didn't do something stupid like beg him to trust her.

To want her like she did him.

Keeping her dignity would be bullet point two. That way, he'd not know how much he'd hurt her.

That had been her strategy even with her father. Most days, especially in the end, when his dementia had made him vulnerable to attacks of rage and spite, Eleni would pretend that his barbed words didn't hurt. And for a while, at least, she'd bought into her own pretense.

Wresting control over her body and heart—bullet point three.

The water she'd found soothing until it felt far too hot on her tingling skin. With just the thought of Gabriel and what he'd done to her, she felt far too aware of the crease of her sex, the heaviness of her breasts, the ache that came to life between her legs.

She shut the shower off and tapped her forehead against the cold tile. No bullet points would help the longing in her soul.

Thoughts in a whirlpool, she hastily dressed in her pajamas, pulled a robe over top and went back to her old bedroom on the opposite side of the wing.

Dawn was tingeing the sky a delicate pink as she flipped the covers over her bed and looked at it restlessly. She was far too keyed up and anxious for sleep. Far too tired to dress for work already.

She was wandering her bedroom restlessly when there was a loud knock on the door to her suite. She opened the door to find Gabriel standing at the threshold, a thunderous expression in his eyes.

Instinctively, she took a step back and his scowl deepened. He saw the night bag she had packed without thought, her laptop case sitting at the foot of the bed. Her cell phone connected to its charger by her bed.

"What the hell is the meaning of this, *Princesa*?"

"Of what?" she forced herself to say, while her mind, and body, became reacquainted with the sheer breadth of his masculinity.

He moved in with a purposeful stride and banged the door closed behind him. Like he'd done at the barn. He wore an expertly tailored white dress shirt that he unbuttoned roughly. All the while his gaze did a thorough, tormenting sweep of her body.

Alarm chased through her with a follow-up of deep want. "I don't need consoling tonight," she blurted out, feeling as if she was turning inside out.

His fingers stilled on his buttons, his head jerking up. "Excuse me?" He strode toward her, and when she backed away, seemed infuriated. "What did you say?"

Eleni licked her lips and wished she'd kept her mouth shut.

He stood so close that she could scent a thread of his aftershave. Her knees threatened to buckle under her.

"Why have you moved back to your own suite, *Princesa*?" Goodness, he was blazingly furious. Again. "Have you already had enough of this marriage?"

Her cheeks burned with mortification. She craned her neck to see into his eyes. "I needed a little distance," she said defensively. "Also, since you left without a word, didn't even bother to ask after me the next morning, I wasn't sure if you wanted me there."

"Wanted you where?"

"In your bed."

Another step of his toward her, and she backed up a little more. "You didn't ask me the first time if I wanted you there. You lodged yourself in my bedroom as if you were queen of the palace."

"I...I was foolish then. I thought if I dangled myself like a juicy carrot in front of you in close quarters, you'd succumb to temptation."

His mouth twitched but nothing could calm the devilish gleam in his eye. He looked at her the way she looked at a pair of stilettos. With deep, possessive need. "And you succeeded. I fell for the proverbial carrot and devoured you." Her blush rose again and she just gave up fighting it. "Is that the problem?" His face softened, tenderness and something else filling up his eyes. "Did I hurt you?"

He looked so utterly pained by the prospect that Eleni couldn't keep quiet. "It hurt, yes, but...not in a bad way. With our respective sizes, Mia said she figured I would be up for a rough ride." This time she burned with mortification for he laughed outright.

It was the most beautiful sound Eleni had ever heard.

"My point is...it hurt no more than it should for my first time. I think."

He pushed a hand through his hair roughly. And slowly, as if coming out of a fog, Eleni wondered if he had truly worried over her absence in the suite. If she'd just declared defeat without even fighting for their marriage. "Then why are you here, Eleni?"

"You left before I... You left without a single word and you didn't return for a week. Moreover, you stayed with your...lawyer friend, who they say is really close to you. Not everything in this marriage can be your decision, Gabriel. I gave myself whiplash wondering what you were thinking. I wasn't sure if you'd want me in your bed."

"And if I didn't want you, you'd stay out of it, Eleni? Why didn't you do that the first time then?"

This conversation was going nowhere. One of them, Eleni knew, had to take the first step toward the other. Toward honesty in their feelings. In giving more than wanting things in return. In making a leap of faith.

She'd demanded his trust, and yet she hadn't trusted in herself at all. Hadn't believed that she could be his equal, that she could still steer their marriage the way she wanted.

Just like she'd always done with her father. She'd kept her head down, absorbed all his poisonous barbs about her sullied blood, about not being good enough for the House of Drakos with a blind hope that he would come to love her.

God, she'd been such a coward.

But Gabriel meant far more to her than anyone ever had. Then shouldn't she at least fight for him before she gave up?

Hair mussed, shirt hanging open, he'd never looked more gorgeous. Or more out of her reach. Her chest ached with longing. But she had to say her piece. He undid the last button and, mesmerized by the sight of his tanned, perfect chest, Eleni stared mindlessly. "I thought this would be easy. I would look after Angelina, have a baby and you would never threaten Drakon again. But I realized I just can't. I can't—"

"If you're asking for a bloody divorce two months into this marriage, I will—"

"I'm not!" She stared at him, aghast. "Why do you keep assuming the worst about me?"

He sighed. "Then what do you suggest we do, *cariña*? What is it that you want of me?"

"I realized I need more than you'll ever be willing to give, Gabriel. And I...I can't just let you hurt me. Like I let my father all my life. I'm still trying to find a way around that instead of just giving up on us. But infidelity is my last straw. I know what we agreed, but I just can't..."

The tender stroke of his fingers over her cheek made

tears prickle behind her eyes. "I have not touched another woman, nor will I..." Gabriel pushed his hand through his hair, frustration building up inside him. Yet it had nothing on the panic that had swarmed him when he'd found his suite empty of her. She asked for very little. And yet, every word he spoke to her felt like he was giving away parts of himself to her. Permanently.

He still had to try. "I have never slept with two women at the same time in my life, Eleni. With the relentless media focus on Nikandros and Andreas, you have to know that half of it is smoke."

She lifted her chin and met his gaze, as if to assess if he was speaking the truth. "All I care about right now is Angelina. There are enough headaches in my life dealing with you and Angelina, finishing this project in Drakon and to top it all, my mother is getting married again, apparently, and she thinks somehow I will join her and the new chump she's picked out in this celebration. I went to Barcelona to reassure Isabella that I'll look into it. And if my communication and my departure was abrupt, it is because that's how I have lived for thirty-six years. I won't come to you and discuss every filament of feeling or emotion that passes through my head."

"Feeling?"

"Yes. I felt guilty for taking you like that in the barn. For not listening to you about the video. And I don't handle guilt well. I've never—" He cut himself off right there. "I've never been in a relationship with this much hassle." There! That should satisfy her!

No need for the minx to know how possessive he felt about her. Or about the moments of dread when he wondered about the man she'd loved once, the man who was clearly dear to her. Not when the knowledge of him returning, of him offering Eleni the world hung over him like a shadow every waking moment.

But he would deal with it when it came to that.

She was *his* wife now.

She belonged with him and Angelina.

The sexual chemistry between them was off the charts, and when it cooled, they would both come back to earth. They might even have a satisfactory sex life, a relationship with mutual respect and love for Angelina and any other children they might have.

"You went to see your sister, Isabella?" she asked in a small voice, her gaze searching his.

"Yes. Are there any more questions?"

"Your friend…"

"Alyssa has never been my lover and never will be."

This much emotional seesawing was going to make her go up in flames one of these days, Eleni thought, staring at Gabriel's now completely naked, and utterly sexy, chest.

"Your mother lives in Barcelona?" she somehow managed to also ask.

"Yes. We don't speak to each other so Isabella is kind of the go-between. And now I would really like to end our domestic drama and go to bed."

Eleni nodded, feeling her mouth dry completely. Had they resolved anything? She knew now that he would not cheat on her. But he still had deep trust issues. Issues that he wouldn't talk about easily.

Knees feeling like rubber, she walked toward the bed.

One look at the dark blue sheets sent her scuttling back to the sitting area. Did he want to share the bed with her? Did he expect to make love tonight?

Just the thought of it was enough to send her body into a spiral of longing. Could she make the first move?

She had to be the only woman in the world who could command a palace staff of two hundred and yet worry over her husband coming home to bed at night.

Every beat of her heart seemed to take forever as she

heard the shower go on and then off far too soon. In the end, she waited near the window, far too keyed up to sleep.

A towel tied to his waist, his chest still damp from the shower, Gabriel walked out. Any remaining air in her lungs went whoosh.

Dark olive skin stretched over lean muscles. A smattering of dark hair, wetly stuck to his skin now, made a dusky path from his chest to his navel, and then disappeared downward into his towel.

He used another towel to wipe his back, drawing her attention there. Smooth, gleaming skin and broad shoulders... Eleni couldn't stop staring. She only barely remembered to keep breathing.

He plopped onto a chair in front of her and pulled her hands onto his shoulders.

Eleni jerked, the heat of his body singeing her fingertips even through the fabric of his shirt. He was pure steel under her fingers, the span of his shoulders so broad that he encompassed her petite frame. Simply, he took her breath away.

A bird cawed somewhere in the distance. A gentle breeze ruffled in through the French doors. Silence around them thickened until Eleni was sure the thundering of her heart could be heard all around them.

"What...what is it that you expect me to do?"

"I worked for too long in the same pose on the flight. My back aches like hell."

She bristled at the command in his tone. "So?"

Tilting his head to the side, he devoured her with his gaze. "So be a good wife, *Princesa*. Your husband has come home after a long, hard day at work and he needs some attention."

The very devil twinkled in his smile. "Poor Gabriel..."

"This is what marriage is about, you know. Ensuring your husband has everything he needs."

Her mouth twitched, the long-suffering look on his face sending a bubble of laughter up through her throat. "I didn't know you were such an expert on marriage."

He shrugged. "I don't do anything by halves. And *Princesa*?"

Eleni didn't think she'd ever known a moment so filled with utter joy. "What, now?"

"I would have you not work so hard either."

Stunned, she looked down at him. "What?"

"You…are not just the Princess of Drakon anymore, Eleni. You are my wife. You could soak in a diamond-filled tub all day if you wanted. You could give up each and every one of your palace duties. We could…"

"But you accepted my request to stay in Drakon."

"I did. But I still wish for you to make a life outside of the palace. Anything you need, it's yours for the asking, Eleni."

Is your heart available? she wanted to say, but kept the silly question to herself. *One step at a time, Eleni*, she told herself, and right now, all of her energies were consumed by her husband's gloriously naked back.

Pondering his request, she went to work on his muscles. He was right. There were painful knots all over his shoulders and upper back. Even damp, his skin was still warm to her touch.

She kneaded the stiff muscles in silence, working through each knot. Heat flew from her fingers to his skin and back until her own fingers were tingling from it. She didn't know how long she continued like that, but in that small, quiet moment, there was a tenuous connection between them.

The silence went from comfortable to tense, back and forth like the swing of a pendulum. In the next breath, Gabriel turned and lifted her up in his arms.

Eleni could only stare.

He deposited her on the high bed and stood in between her knees. Holding her gaze, he pushed the thin straps of her nightie down, baring her breasts to his slumber-ous gaze.

"I did you a disservice that night."

"How?"

"In the dark, I could only feel and touch. I couldn't wor-ship you with my eyes."

Rough fingers kneaded and played with the bared flesh, setting her nerves on fire. Her spine arched, her upper body leaning toward him of its own accord, demanding he give her that same spine-tingling pleasure.

With a husky laugh, Gabriel complied. His tongue flicked and played with her nipple, until it was painfully sensitive. Sinking her fingers into his hair, Eleni moaned just as he closed his mouth and suckled deeply.

Sensations flew to the apex of her thighs like molten lava. Her silk nightie slithered soundlessly to the floor. Gabriel pressed a reverent kiss to her soft belly, his breath a harsh rhythm in the silence.

"You're the most beautiful woman I've ever seen, *mi princesa*," he whispered, and looking down at her flushed skin, her trembling muscles, Eleni could well believe it.

How could anything that gave her so much pleasure be anything but?

Pushing her back into the bed, his mouth went on a lazy trail from the valley between her breasts to her abdomen.

Eleni stretched on the bed like a cat, the cool sheets doing nothing to help her overheated skin. When he joined her on the bed and pushed a lazy hair-roughened leg be-tween hers, she moaned at the pressure. He pressed at the spot hungering for his touch with his thick muscle and a soft pulse shuddered there.

"You're already damp for me."

Blushing, she turned to him. Bronzed skin gleaming

with vitality, he reminded her again of the marauders that had tried to capture Drakon again and again. She ran her fingers over the spikes of his shoulders, curled them in the crisp smattering of hair on his chest. Heard the hitch of his breath.

She hadn't touched him at all that night. She had only been a receptacle for his mindless caresses. She had waited an entire lifetime for passion like Gabriel had showed her that day, but she'd barely participated.

It had taken her thirty years to take her life into her own hands. It was high time she took the matter of her pleasure into her own hands too. And today, her pleasure was in learning all she could of this hard man who had driven her to the mindless edge that night. Today, she wanted to know what would drive him crazy like he did her.

Today, the Plain Princess of Drakon wanted a little power over her husband.

With a boldness that surprised herself, she pushed him back on to the mattress.

"Eleni?"

She bit her lip, staring at the masculine beauty that was stretched out in front of her. How she wished she'd been a painter like Andreas, so that she could forever memorize the bold, intensely masculine lines of his body. There was such honed strength in him and yet, when he touched her, he was capable of a gentleness she would have never thought possible.

"I want to do this, Gabriel. I want to pleasure you. Will you let me?"

Hands folded behind his head, he raised his brows in a taunt. "I'm all yours, *Princesa.*"

Her eyes darkened, her silky hair falling like a curtain around her face. Candlelight flickered over her lush body, bathing it in a golden glow. She swept that golden gaze over him thoroughly, from his hair to his toes, lingering over the tent the towel made at his groin.

Gabriel had never met a woman quite like his wife. Determined, even in the darkest of times. Never backing down if she thought it right. Reaching for what she wanted, even when he'd behaved like an ass.

And now she stared at him as if he were a delicious feast. He wanted to push her plush body down and thrust into her, and yet, he had already misused her that way.

Today, he would go slowly if it killed him, and with the way she eyed him it probably would.

"You have to unpack me first, *Princesa*," he taunted, and she blushed again.

Fingers swift and sure, she pulled his towel from under him. Her eyes widened, her breath held as she eyed his erection.

Then slowly, gently, she took him in her hands and squeezed. Her grip was tentative but firm as she studied him with such focus that Gabriel turned into stone in her hands.

"I don't know what to do." She licked her lips with a silky innuendo she wasn't even aware of. "Teach me, please."

His eyes closed, a low growl rumbled out of his mouth. "You're going to be the death of me." He closed his hands on top of hers and showed her how to stroke him. How to drive him out of his own skin.

Sweat broke out on his skin, pleasure balling up in his groin as she pumped him with her hands, just as he showed her.

He felt the silky slide of her hair over his chest, teasing his nipples, turning his abdominal muscles into hard rocks. Her tongue licked the shell of his ear and he bit out the filthiest oath he could think of. "What do you want, Gabriel? All you have to do is tell me."

"Take me in your mouth," he growled without hesitation.

When her heated breath fell on his erection, he opened his eyes. Just in time to see her lush, pink mouth close over the head of him.

Eyes rolling back, Gabriel groaned. His hands plunged into her hair, guiding her to take him deeper. Pleasure built up along his spine. With another oath, Gabriel eased her away.

"Gabriel, wait…"

But he was too far gone now. With one flip of his hand, he pulled her on top of him until she was straddling him. He wanted to feast his eyes on her like this—her breasts with those plump nipples moving, her belly contracting, her spine arching, every inch of her lushness only for his eyes.

"Take me inside you, wife," he said in a voice hardly recognizable as his.

The most beautiful smile flared over her face as he nudged her thighs apart. Tension corkscrewed in his pelvis as she edged the tip of his shaft inside her sheath. Hands on her hips, Gabriel waited for her to get used to him again. Fought the urge to ram upward into her slick warmth.

Slowly, she lowered herself into him, her brow tied in focus, her tongue peeking out to lick at her lips.

Beads of perspiration dotted her upper lip.

Inch by inch, she impaled herself on him in slow torture. When she had sheathed him completely, the tightness was incredible, gloving him like a fist. Slow tremors began in his muscles, desire a knife arching through his spine.

He would have bucked his hips up into her. Except the whimper of discomfort that fell from her mouth stayed him.

Somehow, he leashed his own lust, felt the twitch of his hardness inside of her in protest. Gritting his teeth, he looked at her and his heart thudded against his rib cage.

The stiff arch of her spine reminded him that she was new to this. That her body had been untried until only a week ago.

The slow shift of her hips sent a bolt of pure pleasure through his groin. And yet she was still rigid. He molded her hips in his hands, feeling powerless in the face of her hurt. "Does it hurt, Eleni?"

She opened her eyes, her mouth pinched. "Not hurt, but not quite okay." She wriggled her round bottom and gasped again. "It...it feels like you are everywhere, Gabriel, like you have cleaved me in half. And I'm afraid to move." Sudden tears filled her eyes. "I'm sorry for...I just need a few seconds to get used to you."

"It's okay, *Princesa*. We have all night. We have months to learn each other, years to do all the things I want to do with you."

For some blasted reason that he couldn't fathom, that made tears roll down her cheeks.

She wiped at them roughly. "I wanted to be sexy and alluring with you. Not turn up the waterworks."

Had his trysts with other women been anything like this? At that moment, Gabriel couldn't remember another woman's face, much less any sweet words he'd whispered to one after sex.

Sinking his hands in her hair, he pulled her down, uncaring that he slipped out of her warmth. Uncaring that his body coiled tighter with unspent frustration. "You are the most fascinating woman I've ever met, *Princesa*. And it's not your fault. I...didn't quite prepare you. You're tiny and I'm...a big brute."

She laughed against his mouth. "I can't verify that so I have to take your word for it."

He smacked her bottom playfully and nudged her closer to him. "You will, if I have anything to say for it. Don't worry, *querida*. Once we do get used to each other, I'm going to devour you. You're not going to get out of bed for a week."

Eyes wide like saucers looked up at him. "Yes?"

"Yes. Now shut up and kiss me, wife."

Her breasts were lush and a delicious weight, her belly soft as she nuzzled into him. He took her mouth in a soft kiss, tenderness cutting the hard bite of his lust. Using every bit of his skill, he stroked the recesses of her mouth until she was moaning against him.

Slipping his hands in between them, he touched every inch of her—from her taut nipples to the folds of her sex that were silky wet. Only when she was rubbing against him again, only when he could feel her readiness, did he enter her again.

He kept up the pressure of his fingers, brought her to the peak. The moment she leaned forward and kissed him, he thrust up into her. They groaned, their bodies finding an easy rhythm this time.

As if they knew how to create the magic.

They moved together like some wild things, their mouths kissing and licking, their hands clasped together. When he showed her how to move with him, Eleni followed his instruction, arching her back, trusting her body and his, reveling in Gabriel's hoarse grunts of pleasure, the fact that she had brought this powerful, breathtaking man to such undefinable pleasure.

Pleasure burst on them in tandem, and Eleni fell forward on his broad chest. Curling into him, she closed her eyes. Their bodies were damp, their breaths still labored.

The silence was a blanket over them. Yet every beat of her heart said she had irrevocably fallen in love with her husband. Every pulse in her body, every bead of perspiration on her skin wondered at the hard flesh beneath her. The loud thud of the thundering heart beneath her own— she would know it even in the dark, always.

And with the realization flooded in panic. For she knew Gabriel would never give her his heart. Would never love her as she'd love him whether they were together or not. Whether they had a child or not.

For the rest of her life.

CHAPTER TEN

OVER THE NEXT month Drakon celebrated the fact that their beloved Crown Prince Andreas was back from his mysterious expedition.

It was all Gabriel heard from Eleni, whom he barely saw. She was overjoyed that her older brother was back. The one time he had seen Andreas, Gabriel had gotten quite the shock.

Andreas Drakos had always been a hard man, yet it felt as if there was nothing but a fierce, cold rage in his eyes these days. Now Gabriel had information sitting on his desk that he knew Andreas was looking for, information he had acquired because Eleni had begged him to help her brother.

And he was coming to learn he could not deny his wife anything.

Yet, something in the other man's gaze had held Gabriel's hand back.

The Royal siblings appeared everywhere for a few days, Nikandros leaving his pregnant wife's side with the greatest reluctance. Whispers of a great alliance between the House of Drakos and a cabinet minister's daughter abounded but if there was a man who was less suited to be anyone's husband, it was Andreas Drakos.

The portentous niggle that had beset him from the moment Andreas had returned came true when he was informed that the Crown Prince had requested an audience.

Without Eleni's presence.

Gabriel entered Andreas's office after a short knock.

Any civil greeting he had rehearsed disappeared when he spied not only Nikandros but another man in the room.

Spiros Kanellos, if his sources were right. And they always were. The man his wife had once loved. The man who had disappeared from the face of Drakon for close to a decade. The man who had suddenly reappeared the night of their wedding.

Suddenly, everything fell into place. The man's unhindered access to the palace, his outrageous confidence that Eleni would receive him—he was going to throttle Andreas.

Gabriel refused to acknowledge the man's presence. But of course, he couldn't help noticing the defiance in his expression, the perfect symmetry of his features.

Cold fury filled him and beneath that, for the first time in his life, a sense of doom. "What the hell is the meaning of this, Drakos?" he said, refusing to corral his temper.

Andreas didn't even blink at the menace in Gabriel's tone. "From your expression, I gather you know who Spiros is."

"Yes, since he's been scuttling around the palace and sniffing around my wife's skirts, I had to alert my security force that he was a threat to Eleni and that they could shoot him on sight."

The blond man paled while Nikandros muttered, "Damn it, Marquez."

Andreas held Gabriel's gaze, something moving like shadows in his. "Nik, Spirios, leave us."

Muttering something to himself, Nik escorted the man out.

Gabriel waited maybe two seconds before he gave into the rage building inside him and punched Andreas in his jaw.

The celebrated Crown Prince of Drakos clutched his jaw, nary a curse rising to his mouth.

Gabriel shook his hand, savage satisfaction filling him. "Keep your crooked games to yourself, Drakos. She's not your sister anymore. She's my wife. If you don't want me to sink Drakon, if you ever want to see her again, you will stay out of our lives. I will ruin everything before I let you interfere with us."

Andreas continued as if Gabriel hadn't threatened everything dear to him. "She deserves to be loved, Gabriel. She waited for him for eight years. My damn father lied to her all that time. He intended to tie her to a man of his own age, just so that he could have control over her. So that she would be his willing servant for the rest of her life.

"Spiros loves her. He'll give her what she needs. I know you, better than anyone does. In the end, you'll break her heart. You'll crush her. It's not too late, Gabriel."

"She doesn't need love. She entered this marriage with her eyes open," Gabriel protested, yet there was a hollow ache in his gut. "And what she did want out of it, I can damn well give to my wife."

Even though she was busy during the day with Angelina, and their nights were filled with passion that only seemed to grow the more they fed it, Gabriel knew what Eleni craved. Knew the sudden smile she pulled to her mouth when she saw him.

Knew that his inability to love her would one day pain her. Knew that he was forever waiting for the ax to fall on their relationship. Waiting for something to go wrong.

In every word and smile, there was a part of him that held back. That resisted every attempt Eleni made to get close to him. That measured their marriage still as a successful but convenient arrangement.

Andreas homed in on his hesitation and went for the kill. "All her life, Eleni has been pushed around by my father. By me and even Nikandros. By the stain of her birth. By my father's condescending kindness toward her. By being neither daughter nor staff. I'm fixing all the damage he did to us, Gabe. Nikandros is back where he belongs. Eleni deserves to be given a choice in her life, for once. She needs to have a chance at happiness."

Gabriel had never wanted to throttle a man before. Never had he wished that his heart had remained buried. Never had he wished that he'd never met the Princess of Drakon.

If he gave her the chance, would Eleni choose a life with him? Did it matter to him that she chose it, and was not forced into it?

He set his jaw tight. "I have a file on my desk, Andreas. I have the information you're looking for. And you know why? Because Eleni begged me to help you. Because she worries about you and Nik and all of you."

Every inch of Andreas's face hardened, a dark light coming on in his eyes. Outwardly, he was still. But Gabriel knew the rage that was building up inside him. He would separate Gabriel's limbs with his bare hands, but of course he calmed himself. Nothing remained of his hunger for that information except a gleam in his eyes.

Andreas's self-control was legendary.

"You know where she is?" He couldn't quite hide the quiver in his voice, however.

"Yes," Gabriel replied. "I'll give it to you if you make Spiros disappear. I don't ever want to see him."

Andreas rubbed a shaking hand against his eyes, a small betrayal of his inner state. "I can't. You have no idea how tempted I am to play God. But no more. I will not be like the man who raised me. I will not play with other people's lives."

The hard laugh that fell from Gabriel's mouth was hollow. "And the woman in the file?" Despite his determination to stay out of it, he felt a twinge of pity for her. Andreas Drakos was a determined, cold man, made in the mold of his father, King Theos, however much he fought it. "What do you think you're going to do to her, Andreas?"

"She belongs to me, Gabriel. Keep the information. She could go to the ends of the earth, but I would still find her. My sister, however, deserves a choice. Deserves to choose for once how she wants to spend her life. Either you give it to her or I will."

Studiously avoiding the silent bedroom, Gabriel went into the bathroom, stripped and took a much-needed shower. He dressed himself, wandered into the sitting room and poured himself a drink.

Andreas's words went round and round in his head. The sight of the man she had once loved turned the scotch to ash on his tongue.

Did Andreas actually think he would give up his wife, just like that? Did he think he would let Eleni go to some blond fool who hadn't had the guts to fight for her?

But could he live with Eleni knowing that he had forced this on her? Knowing that all she'd ever wanted of this marriage had been a child? Wouldn't he forever wonder if she'd choose him again given a true choice?

He had no more clarity two hours later when the door opened to the suite and Eleni stood at the threshold. Gabriel had never imagined he'd see a sight that would shred him to powerless pieces as did the sight of his wife's tears.

Pale and drawn out, she stared at him with unseeing eyes.

Tenderness filled Gabriel. "Black Shadow?"

She didn't say anything, only nodded. But even in the dark, he could see the sheen of her eyes.

The depth of her pain unmanned him like nothing could. He never wanted to see it again. He opened his arms and she flew into them like she belonged there. Burrowed into him as though he was her everything.

And for the first time in his life, Gabriel wanted to mean something to a woman.

She was tiny, slender against his hard muscles. And yet, there was strength inside this woman.

Squeezing her against him, he left her not even a little space to avoid him. "Tell me about him," he said, in his usual authoritative tone, realizing only after he had spoken that maybe she needed a gentle hand. But he had never been capable of gentleness.

Maybe she wanted a man who would trust without doubt, who could be romantic without ulterior motives in mind, a man who could give words to the tumult inside him. Maybe she wanted Spiros Kanellos back in her life. The thought was like acid, gouging into him.

"Black Shadow was the only gift, the only thing, really, that my father ever gave me. He cost Father some atrocious amount of money and he refused to let any rider tame him. Father had always been proud of my riding talent, my ease with horses. I was a natural since I was a toddler. It proved to him, I think, that I was truly his—that I belonged to the House of Drakos." She spoke as if the fact was still in doubt. As if she had to justify her presence in the royal household again and again.

Was that why she worked so hard for her brothers? Did Eleni still doubt her place as a daughter of the House of Drakos?

Anger filled Gabriel and his arms tightened around her.

"The moment I saw Black Shadow—his coat gleaming, refusing to trust anyone, but needing a tender touch—I fell in love. I think it was mutual," she said with a smile. "He developed a tumor—" her voice caught "—in his belly, and has been deteriorating for a while now. I went to check on him around dawn. I couldn't sleep at all. It was as if he'd been waiting to say goodbye to me."

He felt the sob build through her small frame. Vining her arms around him, she cried as if her heart was breaking.

Ice that he didn't even know had built in his chest thawed. Gabriel ran his hands over her back, up and down, anxious to soothe her, to assuage her grief. Desperate to give her the world if she needed it.

"Shh, *querida*, he must have known how much you love him."

She wiped her face on his shirt and mumbled an apology into his chest. His heart thundered under those questing fingers. Tonight, his mind was reeling, his emotions whirling.

"Eleni, why did you stay in Drakon all these years? Why not leave? Did you love the mad king so much?"

He felt steel return to her spine and smiled to himself. "Please don't refer to him like that. His dementia was real and had far too many consequences."

"What about your mother?" He asked the one question that had always bothered him.

"I don't like to talk about her."

He heard the defensiveness that she couldn't quite hide.

He shrugged, keeping his tone casual, as unfamiliar as he was with painful emotions, even he could see that Eleni hid the pain beneath her acceptance of her position in the Royal household. "As Angelina grows up and asks me about her mother, should I lie and keep the memory she has intact? Or should I tell her the truth?"

A long sigh left her and she tentatively laid her head on his shoulder. He knew she understood what he meant. She understood that Angelina already believed, on some level, that her mother had never told Gabriel about her existence.

Painful or not, the little girl had to live with that fact for the rest of her life.

He didn't know why he pushed Eleni, but he wanted her to share it with him. He wanted to know everything about his wife. He wanted to prove to himself that Eleni was better off with him and Angelina. That she had everything she'd ever need.

"My mother was Andreas's nanny. The Queen apparently had been sick for a long time and she had an affair with Father for years. Things I learned in whispers and rumors from the palace staff. And when she had me, she signed over all rights over me to my father and walked away with a lump of cash. My father might have been controlling, maybe even mad, but he gave me a home. Andreas loved me, in his own way, when he could have hated me for what my mother did to his. Nikandros always told me I was the good one among us. My brothers and my father... they made me feel wanted."

Gabriel searched her face, startled at how innocent she sounded. "How?"

"They needed me. They were always at odds with each other, all three of them, thanks to Father's manipulations. And I was the buffer," she said, as if she hadn't made herself indispensable. As if she hadn't sewn herself into the fabric of their lives.

Did it make her feel useful? Needed? Was that why she'd been so ready to marry him—because she could help with Angelina on one hand and Drakon on the other? The perfect solution for Eleni because her heart already belonged to another?

"In the end, it turned out only I could manage Father. I owe them so much. How could I just walk away? You asked me that night why I wanted to escape who I was.

"Drakon is in my blood as much as it is in Andreas's and Nik's. Even if Andreas found some poor man to marry me—and can you imagine who he would choose?—he wouldn't have understood my attachment to Drakon. He would only marry me as a favor to one of my brothers, or as a business transaction. Even with his cruel taunts, I think my father did a good job of binding me to Drakon, as well as he did my brothers."

"What about love, *Princesa*?"

She looked up at him, her eyes bright with the sheen of tears shed. "What about it?"

"Is it not something every woman wants?"

Lashes flicking down, she hid her expression. "Not me. I...between Spiros and Father and my mother abandoning me, I lost the taste for it, Gabriel." Her voice wavered, a faint tension in her shoulders.

His own breath halted in his throat as Gabriel waited. With every word she said, Andreas's words made more and more sense.

Eleni had never been given the choice to be anything other than what she was, had never had the chance to love herself or anyone else.

"I don't think I even know what love is anymore. If not for Nik's mother and Andreas and Nikandros, I wouldn't even have known what kindness was."

He should have let it go then. Raking up the past would get them nowhere. He was her present. He was her future. For Angelina's sake, he needed to be selfish.

But then who would put *her* first? Clearly, no one ever had. He was beginning to understand that Andreas and Nik tried to, was beginning to see what had led Andreas to play God from behind the curtain.

So he spoke, his own motives unclear, only the need to see into her soul propelling him ahead. "How could a paid employee like your mother, a woman at that, have had any bargaining power with King Theos when he found out that she was pregnant with his child? The whole world knows of his obsession with his progeny, his obsession with the succession of House Drakos. Legitimate or not, you were still his blood and I bet he gave her no choice."

"I would have never given up on a child of mine, under any kind of pressure," Eleni protested. But there was no conviction in her own words.

"He was a ruthless, cruel bastard, *Princesa*." Remembering what Andreas had said, rage shook his voice. "If he gave you a home, Eleni, he did it to stroke his own ego, to cast himself in a better light. Nothing more."

"So I'll never know what she might have wanted," Eleni said through a throat filled with glass. Gabriel's arms tightened around her while her mind whirled.

The small hurts that had amassed over the years, that she had told herself didn't really matter became a wound Eleni couldn't ignore now.

She knew what kind of a man her father had been. How had she never wondered what her mother's situation had been? How had she never questioned his constant condescension toward her?

I gave you a home when she didn't want you, he would say again and again to her until it was all Eleni had heard growing up.

Until her childish mind had been twisted inside out, until pleasing her impossible father had become her life's goal.

A cold sweat drenched her as she thought of the number of times he had reminded her that she should be grateful to him. That she owed it to him, and then to her brothers.

All the times she had internalized that only by becoming indispensable to her father and her brothers did she deserve a place in the palace.

The time he had flown into a rage because she had said she wanted to marry Spiros. Only Andreas's hand had stayed his rage. Andreas, who had stood between her and what would have been marriage to a man thrice her age.

Andreas had tried, she knew, especially in the past few years. He had, again and again, told her to make a life for herself. Told her that she owed neither him nor Nikandros anything. That she had paid for her father's abusive kindness to her a thousand times over.

But the feeling that she alone would never be enough, that she had to earn a place with her brothers, that she had to prove that she belonged with them couldn't be shaken. She dealt with all her relationships the same way.

Numbness filled her very veins as she saw herself clearly for the first time.

The only reason she'd boldly offered to marry Gabriel had been because she could be a mother to Angelina. Oh, she'd demanded so many things of him and yet hid her own self-worth behind her affection for the little girl. Had told herself it was inevitable if she wanted to save Drakon.

It was the same fear that clamped over her heart every time she wanted to tell Gabriel that they were going to have a child—that stole the words from her mouth when she wanted to demand that he love her like she did him. It was that feeling of not being enough that ran through her when she saw the strides Angelina and Gabriel had made toward each other.

Fear that whispered in her ear that soon, very soon, he would not need her anymore. That there would be nothing of value she would be bringing to their relationship.

She hid her face in his chest and waited for the panic to pass. For the knot in her belly to relent. The scent of Gabriel's skin filled her pores and she never wanted to leave his arms again.

But instead of telling him that, Eleni tilted her head back and said, "Gabriel, will you make love to me?"

She saw the fragment of hesitation in his eyes before he

pressed a kiss to her temple. "Princess, there's something we have to talk about."

Eleni straightened in his lap and her hands stole under the opening of his shirt. Warm skin and hard muscles met her palms. The beat of his heart an anchor in her world. His scent sank through her muscles, instantly filling her with a sense of rightness, of goodness.

Gabriel had somehow become the center of her world.

She bent and pressed her mouth to his collarbone. Salt and man—he tasted of heaven. The hitch of his breath, the shift and clench of his muscles, right now, it was all she wanted. Desperately needed. "No, Gabriel," she whispered against his skin. Pulling his shirt open, she trailed her mouth down his chest to his abdomen, until she was on her knees in front of his chair. His thighs were so hard under her hands.

She traced the outline of his erection through his trousers with her knuckles, desire a wild thing inside of her. Looking up, she saw the darkening of those steel-gray eyes, the granite-tight clasp of his jaw, the rigid clamp of his fists against the armrest.

He wanted her. Gabriel Marquez—powerful real estate mogul, gorgeous man, who cloaked his love for his daughter under duty, a man who with harsh words made Eleni see what she could be—this man wanted her.

Slowly she tugged his zipper and began to pull his trousers down.

His fingers on her wrists stayed her, his voice when he spoke, guttural and deep. "*Princesa*, let me love you. You're upset and emotional. You don't have to do this."

Pushing her hair away from her face, Eleni smiled. "No, I don't have to do it, Gabriel. But I want to do it."

In all her life, she had tried to be an exceptional daughter, a good sister, a blameless princess, a friend, a doyenne of charities. All roles she had thought would bring her happiness, would finally earn her a place to belong.

Even when she had married Gabriel, she had done it for Angelina, for Drakon.

But this, this she wanted to do for herself.

The hiss of his breath was a balm to her soul as she took his erection in hand and stroked it. Warmth pooled between her thighs as she licked the soft top, and then the underside.

Hands sank into her hair, guiding her mouth over his hardness. The taste of him was wild, his groans and filthy curses sending shock pulses to her own core. In this moment, in the darkness of this night, in the privacy of their bedroom, she owned this man.

She continued to lave and lick his length, shivering with her own desire.

Rough hands pulled her away from him. When his mouth met hers, it was like a tempest had swirled into the room. As if he wanted to brand her just as she wanted to brand him. As if he wanted to possess her.

His lips nipped and claimed hers in a mad dance, his tongue dipping in and out in an age-old rhythm. Legs falling away to make a place for him, Eleni cried when his erection rubbed against her belly.

Gabriel wanted her. For now that had to be enough. Later, she would make a plan to keep him. With nothing else to offer him, but just her love. Just herself.

Eleni Drakos Marquez, Princess of Drakon.

"You're mine, *Princesa*," he bit out in such a possessive voice that she drowned in it. He pulled the sleeves of her dress down, filling his hands with her breasts. Pinched the taut nipples until Eleni was arching into his body, a slave to his will. "Say it."

"I'm yours, Gabriel," she whispered against his mouth. And he tasted her in another lingering kiss.

When he pushed her onto the bed and rucked up her dress, when he entered her from behind without that tenderness that had marked all the times they had made love,

Eleni exulted in the glorious sensations of being possessed by him. Reveled that she could break his control, bring him to this desperate need.

They moved in perfect rhythm, woman and man, made for this dance, made for each other. When climax burst on them in tandem, Eleni didn't know where she ended and where he began.

When he collapsed on top of her and kissed her temple, she smiled back at him, uncaring of what he saw in her eyes.

Words piled onto her tongue, words she wanted to scream to the world, to him, words she wanted returned. Instead, she poured it all into her kiss.

For now, there was hope and she would grab it with both hands.

CHAPTER ELEVEN

"Ellie, Ellie…where are you?"

Eleni turned away from the mirror, where she'd been examining the faint swell of her belly and pulled down the loose tunic she was wearing.

She had to tell Gabriel soon. But between Andreas returning, the preparations that were in full swing for the coronation, Mia's last weeks of pregnancy and Gabriel traveling more and more, she just hadn't found the right moment.

Or more precisely, she was pooling her courage. And in the process, was overly complicating everything.

Not that the escalating tension between her husband and Andreas helped. Every time Gabriel was back home, and Eleni insisted that they all dine together, a battle of some sort emerged between them.

Neither did it help that she sometimes felt a niggle that Gabriel was slowly pulling away from her. He still laughed with her, teased her about her devotion to all things Drakon, spent his free time with her and Angelina. Made love to her with such possessive passion, drawing it out for so long that she was cursing him, and sometimes with such heartbreaking tenderness that Eleni fell in love with him all over again.

And yet, when they were in bed after he thoroughly exhausted her, when they watched Angelina perform in the local equestrian competition, or when he was away and he called every day to check on Angelina, some sort of tension filled the air.

A distance, an infinitesimal retreat, as if his mind was faraway. Or on something else.

She reminded herself that Gabriel's business consumed his attention, that it was a hard taskmaster. And she was okay with it too, for her hands were full with her own duties. But, still she felt the distance.

Which only made her postpone the truth for a bit longer.

She sighed and turned just as Angelina walked into her bedroom. Her bony arms thrown around Eleni, she hugged her hard. Eleni swallowed and patted her head, her heart full. Soon, she would be holding another baby in her hands.

"You stink of the stables, Angelina," she said with a laugh.

Eyes much like her father's, Angelina smiled back. Her obsession with horses only made Eleni's comment a compliment. "I spoke to Papa this morning. And he's returning this afternoon.

Instantly, her heart raced in her chest. "When?"

"He has a surprise for you. He said I could tell you ahead of time." The girl couldn't stay still for her excitement. "Oh, Ellie, you're going to love it so much." She threw her chest out, her chin lifted. "He asked me for help, you know. So we picked it together."

By now, even Eleni's excitement was boundless. In the last few weeks, Gabriel had been showering her with gifts. Jewelry, couture dresses, a ski lodge in the mountains that they had weekended at once with Angelina, a mansion he was designing himself a few kilometers from the palace—if Eleni ever wanted to leave the palace and live away from her obnoxious brothers, he'd said when she'd laughed and asked what she'd do with a mansion…

The presents were endless, expensive.

"If I didn't know better, I would say you were trying to buy me, Gabriel," she had said with a teasing wink.

But instead of laughing, as he always did when they talked about their relationship, a strange tightness had emerged around his mouth. "Just ensuring that you have everything you could want, *Princesa*."

It had been the perfect moment to tell him that all Eleni could ever want was him. That he'd given her the world and its joys in the form of Angelina and the baby in her womb. That he had given her a sense of herself.

Coward that she was, she had just taken his hand in hers and kissed his palm.

"Ellie, you've got to see it."

"But doesn't he want to give it to me?" she said, playing along with Angelina. Not that she had to fake her excitement.

Angelina laughed, a bubbly, cheerful sound that made Ellie sigh with quiet joy. "This is not something he could give you like that, Ellie. And I bet he won't mind so much if you see it beforehand."

"Okay, fine, you have got me hooked now. Where is it?"

"In the stables. Can I go with you, Ellie, Please?"

Eleni shook her head, knowing how much Angelina was like her father in trying to get her way. "Your math tutor is here, Angelina. How about you and I and your papa can go see it again, once he is back?" When Angelina nodded, she pressed a quick kiss to her cheek. "Please, shower before you see Mr. Stephanapolis," she said, scrunching her nose.

Her heart beat a rapid tattoo as she straightened her hair and pushed her feet into pumps. Angelina would probably have shown more composure in the same situation than her, but somehow she didn't give a damn about propriety right then.

Every time he went away on one of his trips, Eleni felt as if she was losing a limb.

She wanted to ask him to take her and Angelina along. She desperately wanted to tell him that the time he was gone felt like an eternity. She also wanted to tell him that she loved him with all her heart, even when he was his grumpiest and uncommunicative as he'd been the past few weeks.

A nervous sort of quiet reined over the stables when she finally got there.

Sounds from Black Shadow's empty stall sent her heart racing. She hurried over and then leaned against the opposite wall, her knees barely holding her up.

The Thoroughbred was tall, at least sixteen hands, and athletic with a dark brown, gleaming coat. A thing of utter beauty and male perfection, like the man who had bought it for her. Proud and arrogant too, just like Gabriel, in the way he reared his head when she took a step toward him.

Eleni just watched, her breath taken away by his male beauty. Her hands itched to trace those sloping shoulders but he would not like her to. At least not yet.

Like his Arabian ancestor, he would be very high-strung. And yet the very prospect of taming him with correct training, of forming a bond with him sent excitement fizzing through her veins.

When he was hers, his loyalty would be absolute. His love would be forever and unconditional. It was the same thing she craved from Gabriel.

She had no idea when Gabriel had decided on this, or when he and Angelina had even slipped away without Eleni knowing. Father and daughter were slowly building a tenuous bridge toward each other.

After a few minutes of watching him, Eleni turned to walk out of the stables. Excitement fizzed through her at the thought of Gabriel returning. This gift, of all the ones he had showered on her, was so special. It said he knew her; it said he'd wanted to see her happy again, even as he understood that she'd always mourn Black Shadow.

She wanted to thank him personally for such an extraordinary gift. For knowing what would make her laugh again. For simply caring about her.

It was more than she'd expected, more than he had signed on for, she knew.

But the weeks she had spent with him, observing his every interaction with Angelina, learning small things about him, also kindled a flicker of hope.

Contrary to the media's endless stories, she knew now that Gabriel was hardly the love-them-and-leave-them type. She knew that he had a deep core of loyalty toward those he considered his. Despite his initial refusal, he'd agreed to help Andreas in his search for whatever it was he was looking for. Neither of them would tell her what was going on, but she left them to it, used as she was to secrets in the palace and happy to allow Andreas some privacy.

When Monique's mother, Angelina's grandmother, had made a tearful phone call begging to see her granddaughter, Eleni had waited with bated breath. Lies or not, it was clear Monique had loved her daughter. And the thought of Angelina, so much like she'd been at that age, being cut off from another person who loved her, had threatened to slice through Eleni.

To her shock, Gabriel had asked her advice, trusted her to have Angelina's best interests at heart. He'd confessed with a never-before-seen flicker of emotion that every instinct of his wanted to refuse the older woman's request. To cut off his daughter from her mother's family completely.

In the end, he had listened to Eleni's advice that Angelina only benefited from the presence in her life of people who loved her like that.

He'd had Monique's mother chartered to Drakon on his personal jet. However, he had insisted that Eleni accompany Angelina and her grandmother on their day-long tour of Drakon. Had even joined them for dinner that night and had been a charming companion after a satisfactory assessment of Monique's mother.

Her husband, for all his denial of emotions and deep feelings, Eleni realized, felt very deeply when it came to the people he cared about. It was just very rare for anyone to get so close to him as to notice that.

Would he ever consider Eleni one of those? She had no idea. Would they ever share anything beyond the physical connection and their parenting of Angelina?

She had hardly taken another step when she saw a shadow enter the stables.

Her heart thundered that it might be Gabriel. Tucking away a strand of hair from her temple, she stepped into the main corridor between the stalls when she saw who it was.

"Hello, Eleni *mou*."

Eleni's head jerked up.

Hair shining like raw gold, a glorious smile illuminating his beautifully defined face, Spiros stared at her.

Eleni stiffened, her heart beating a thousand miles an hour. She didn't want Gabriel to discover them here. She didn't want the fragile truce they had built to shatter so soon. Not ever.

Would he even believe that she had not planned this? Would he understand that this was a conversation she needed to have?

She could not untangle her complex feelings for Gabriel without saying goodbye to her past forever. She could not even trust herself again until she learned why Spiros had abandoned her.

"Hello, Spiros."

Her reached her and took her hands in his. A pang of familiarity pierced her heart. His face had been so dear to her once. The blond hair, the slender frame, the straight, patrician nose—it was like seeing a much-missed, dear old friend. She was glad that he was okay. That he hadn't died in some unfortunate accident as she'd sometimes feared.

"Are you not happy to see me, Eleni?"

"I…I don't know what to feel, Spiros. Or what to say. You got me in a lot of trouble for the stunt you pulled at my wedding reception. You disappeared without a word, and then you walk back in like you belong here."

"I'm sorry about that." He clasped her cheeks, his gaze reverent. Something inside Eleni—maybe that naive nineteen-year-old—ached at his touch. Couldn't help but soften when she remembered how he'd been her only salvation on the toughest days.

If only he'd never left. If only they'd married back then… She didn't know what the future would have held for her then, but suddenly Eleni knew, as well as the beat of her own heart, that Spiros was too late.

And not just because Eleni had said her vows to Angelina and Drakon.

"It took me forever to get into the palace, and when I did it was to see you in your wedding dress, looking incredibly lovely. I lost my mind right then. I hope that arrogant Spaniard was not cruel to you."

"Gabriel is never cruel." And she had known cruelty at the hands of the mad king. For all his claims to ruthlessness, Gabriel ran his empire with a firm but considerate hand. "Spiros, you left years ago. Without word. Without even a goodbye. Do you honestly expect that nothing has changed in all these years? That I have not changed?"

"But you waited for me, didn't you? You didn't look at another man. You didn't marry until just a few months ago. Andreas told me you didn't. Andreas told me you waited for me, you mourned for me…"

Eleni grabbed the wall behind her, a sick feeling clamping her stomach. Anything that involved her older brother, and the warpath he'd been on since their father's dementia had worsened, did not bode well. For any of them. "What does Andreas have to do with any of this?" And even as she asked the question, things clicked. Andreas asking her about Spiros after their father's death, relentless and incessant. Andreas asking her why she hadn't moved on with her life.

"He's the one who encouraged me to come back to you. He asked me if I still loved you and I said yes. But it was already too late. By the time I sold my business in the States and came back, you were already married to him." Torment flickered across his angelic features while Eleni felt like she had stepped onto a land mine.

When and how had Andreas sought Spiros out? Was this the source of the tension between him and Gabriel?

She could just imagine Gabriel's fury at Andreas's meddling. Familiar fear flew through her veins. She didn't want to lose either of them.

How like Andreas to pull the strings from behind the curtain. She was going to throttle her older brother.

"Say something, Eleni."

"Why did you leave in the first place?" Eleni bit out loudly, frustration coiling through her. "I was so worried about you. I imagined such horrible scenarios. Couldn't you have owned up to my face that we were done? That you never loved me."

"But I did love you, Eleni. Desperately." Spiros's face fell and pity filled Eleni's chest. "It was your father's doing. He said I wasn't good enough for you then. He said I had to grow some balls. When I told him you would run away with me, he threatened my family. You know how much my father and our family depended on the King's goodwill. I let him…convince me to wait. I felt like I had nothing to offer you. He promised that if I made something of myself, he'd consider me again in a few years. But the condition was that I never see you. Never contact you. So I left, Eleni. I traveled the world. I…made something of myself."

Her heart felt like it had received one final blow. "I waited and waited for you…and when you never came back I gave up on you. Then after a while, your family said that you'd gone to America. That you'd met someone there and forgotten all about me."

"I'm sure he made them say that." He moved back and forth in the confined space, his movements restless, angry. "Your father…he was mad. He never meant for you to marry me," he said, coming to the same conclusion Eleni had. "He never meant for you to leave his side, Eleni. I was such a fool to believe him."

Her knees shook with the magnitude of her father's casual cruelty.

Spiros was right. Gabriel had been right. Her father had meant to keep her with him for the rest of his life. Like an unpaid staff member, a companion, forever reminded that she owed him for everything in her life.

He'd not only ruined her life but he'd ruined Spiros's too. "Why did you come back now, Spiros?" She couldn't even muster anger for him. She felt nothing.

"I heard the news of King Theos's death. And I knew you were still…waiting for me."

Eleni didn't bother to correct him even though resentment grew in her.

"As you very well know, I'm a married woman now." She jerked away from Spiros, resignation filling her. Suddenly, she felt immensely tired. "I don't love you, not anymore."

"But *I* love *you*, Eleni. I would wait another ten years if it meant you would be mine." How could she tell him that it would come to nothing? That he should have stayed and fought her father, that he shouldn't have let his insecurities drive him away.

Tears filling her face, Eleni let Spiros fold her into his embrace. Her chest ached for him and for her, for the future they could have had. If not for the machinations of a sick old man.

For her own sanity's sake, she wished she felt something for Spiros. She would never break her vows but at least her heart would remain safe from Gabriel.

But even as Spiros held her tight, even as the man she had once loved promised his eternal love to her, nothing moved in her.

He was not overtly tall. He was not broad in the shoulder and narrow in the hips. He didn't look at her with compelling gray eyes. He did not call her *Princesa* in a mocking way and yet somehow mean it.

He didn't deny feeling any emotions. He didn't fiercely protect everyone he considered his. He didn't threaten her powerful brothers for their supposed neglect of her or even the entire world for insulting her.

He simply was not Gabriel.

"I have already made my vows, Spiros," she said, wanting to do him a kindness. Wanting to alleviate her own guilt at the love she felt for Gabriel. "I have made promises to a little girl and her father. I…I cannot walk away from those. I will not break my word. I'm so sorry. There's no future for you and me. Maybe there never was."

Spiros frowned. His hands digging into her shoulders, he said, "This is not over, Eleni *mou*. I refuse to give you up so easily after all these years. The Spaniard does not love you. He cannot make you happy."

Eleni didn't know how long she stayed in the stall after Spiros left, his dire warnings ringing in her ears.

But it didn't matter.

Gabriel had spoiled her for anyone else.

* * *

I will not walk away from the promises I made. I will not break my word.

Eleni's words to that man haunted Gabriel throughout the day. Damn it, of all the times for him to walk into the stables, of all the things he had to overhear coming from her mouth.

Had he thought her like his mother once? Or like Monique or his sister, Isabella, fickle and full of deceit?

Now he wished she *was* like them. That she didn't care for anyone except her own happiness.

But of course not.

His wife was a bloody saint, forever willing to sacrifice her own happiness on the altars of others' lives.

It was her choice to give up her happiness, something said in his head. A voice that sounded very much like the ruthless, arrogant man he'd been when he'd threatened to sink Drakon if a mere woman didn't cater to his wishes.

He wanted to, God, how he wanted to forget what he had seen in the damn stables.

The pain of a lost future in her eyes, the tears that had fallen when Spiros had told her what her father had done. The way she had folded into that man's arms as if she had no will left.

He would have given anything to un-see it, to carry on like he had been for weeks now. Putting Andreas off, making plans to take Eleni and Angelina away from the cursed palace, reminding himself again and again that Eleni had chosen this marriage, chosen this over some fantastic notion of love.

That she gave everything to it because she wanted to.

Yet the shadow of the man had hung over them. The idea of him waiting forever and Gabriel hiding it from her, crept into all the small spaces between them, until it had become an invisible wall. Until the guilt of it had made him withdraw from her.

Neither had it been missed by her. More than once, Gabriel had seen her hesitate before she said something to him, had seen the stricken look in her eyes when he didn't meet her gaze or avoided spending time with her.

For weeks, he'd existed in a strange limbo, unwilling to let go of her but unable to live with the gift of her choice.

And now—now that he had seen her face, now that he'd heard what she said, he found it unbearable to live like this any longer.

Was this how his father had felt after his mother had come back? Knowing that she still mourned the lover that had abandoned her, yet unable to turn her away? Gabriel had considered it his weakness.

Had his father loved his mother that much then?

Was this how it felt to love someone?

Because he did. Because he wanted Eleni's happiness above all else. He couldn't bear the thought of the future without her but neither could he live with her, knowing that her heart would forever belong to another. Knowing that he had selfishly stolen her happiness from her.

"Gabriel? When did you return?"

He turned to see Eleni walk toward him in the sitting room, a shaky smile on her face. Her eyes looked dull, bruised, the remnants of her tears still on them.

"Just an hour ago. I had to sign some documents for my assistant."

She reached him, and then registering his tense pose, a wariness filled her eyes. "I...I've been waiting to see you."

"Why?" he asked abruptly, his heart crawling into her throat.

She took his hands into hers, turned them over and kissed the knuckles. "I...I wanted to thank you for my gift." When he frowned, she sighed. "The Thoroughbred?

Angelina spilled the beans, and he and I have already become friends. I'm already a little in love with him." She rose up on her toes and kissed his lips. Only he shifted in the last moment and her lips landed on his jaw.

He nodded, then cleared his throat. But for the life of him, he didn't know what to say to her. It was unbearable to be her husband, to steal the intimacy she gave so willingly when in truth she might wish it on another man.

He hated this power she had over him, hated how weak she made him. How she made him want to put his happiness in her hands, how she made the future without her look like an unending abyss.

A nervous laugh fell from her mouth, pulling her attention to him. "Gabriel, is everything all right?"

"Eleni…did you see Spiros again?"

Eleni blinked. "I… Gabriel…"

"Just answer the question, *Princesa*."

The harsh note in his tone made her flinch. But she nodded, dread curling up in her chest. This morning, she'd been planning to pour her heart out to him. Now she was afraid to look into his eyes. Afraid that all she would see were distance and indifference.

"Yes, I did. Just an hour ago, in fact. He… Gabriel, it was a conversation he and I needed to have. I needed to see him one last time." Anger flooded her, a much better emotion than the fear stealing up her throat. "You can't believe that I'm having some supersecret affair with him right under your nose. If you think that, you're a—"

"No, I believe you, *Princesa*. What I want to know is if he told you. What your father had done."

"Yes, he did." Tears filled her eyes again. But she didn't grieve over herself. She felt sad for her father, who had only sought to control and manipulate his children and not love them. She felt sad for Spiros, who was a good man, and who had become a pawn in that game. "But you already made me tough, Gabriel. You already opened my eyes to what he'd been."

"So that's it? You're over him now?"

"It's all in the past, Gabriel. I vowed to be your wife, a mother to Angelina. And I've never broken my promise to anyone. Not to my father, not to Spiros, not to Andreas, and I'll definitely not do that to you or Angelina. For better or worse."

Gabriel had never wanted to hear those damn words out of her mouth ever again. It felt as if he couldn't breathe, as if a part of him was being wrenched away. Like there was already a hole in his chest.

He could not do it anymore. He couldn't live with her knowing that she wanted another man, another future. "There's nothing more in this marriage for either of us, is there?"

"What? What are you talking about?"

"Angelina and I understand each other. But still, I would ask that you not terminate our marriage too soon. I'll leave Drakon within the next day. Angelina will stay here with you."

If she had shown a hint of pain, Gabriel would have taken her in his arms. Would have kept her chained to his side. But his wife's mask was back in place. Only the paleness of her face said he'd just ended their marriage.

Eleni had been taught again and again to place someone else's needs above her own. To keep her word, no matter what.

It would take time but she would see why he had to do this. Why he was ripping out his own heart.

"Why are you doing this?" She ran a hand over her tummy, as if to protect herself. "Gabriel, I don't even understand what you're doing."

"I'm freeing you, *Princesa*, letting you go." He took her face in his hands, unable to resist touching her. "I should never have threatened you in the first place. Never agreed to your counterproposal. You have given me and Angelina enough of your life.

"You're free to pursue whatever, whoever you want. Whatever future you like."

"If this is Andreas's doing, I swear I will rip him apart with my bare hands. Don't do this, Gabriel. This is not right."

"It is right, *Princesa*. The only right thing. The longer we continue this farce, the more I will end up hurting you. How you will convey this to Angelina and not hurt her, I will leave in your capable hands. You see, *Princesa*, I trust you completely. I trust you more than I ever have anyone in my life."

He didn't wait to see what she'd say. He walked out of the Princess of Drakon's life, before she took everything he had.

CHAPTER TWELVE

THE WEEKS FOLLOWING Gabriel's departure were the worst of Eleni's life. Even the cruelest days spent with her father, listening to him rage, struggling to calm him until her arms ached—they were still better than the desolation Gabriel left in his wake.

To the outward world, and thankfully for Angelina, nothing had changed. Somehow, Eleni had convinced the little girl that her father had urgent business that would take months, while leaving the window open for her that she could visit him whenever she wanted.

While Angelina hadn't been completely fooled, she'd decided to play along, for now.

Eleni apparently didn't have the same composure the little girl did. She had confronted Andreas, argued with him, called him names for playing God with her life, sobbed all over him, which had then resulted in a huge row between Nik and Andreas.

It had taken a hugely pregnant Mia to calm her brothers down. And at the end of it, Eleni didn't feel even a little better.

Just that same sense of missing a vital piece of herself.

She was six weeks along now, and hiding it with baggy tunics, she still hadn't told a soul. It was his right to know first and however furious he had made her, she still couldn't take that away from Gabriel.

He called every night to talk to Angelina while Eleni sat

there, pathetically waiting for him to ask for her, pretending to Angelina that she'd already spoken to him. When Spiros had tried to comfort her, she had asked him to leave.

She'd already messed up his life, thanks to her father.

Every cell in her wanted to tell Gabriel about the baby. She knew without a doubt that if anything could bring him back to her, it would be the news of her pregnancy. If he found out that he was going to be a father again, he would bind her to him.

But she didn't want him like that. She didn't want his pity, and neither did she want his duty. She didn't want to be a wife to him if he didn't love her.

Not even for him could she live like that again.

Gabriel walked out onto the acreage behind the stables, looking for his wife.

Stunned, he came to a standstill.

Eleni was riding the huge Thoroughbred, the same beast he had bought for her, astride, through a path cordoned off from the viewing point where he stood. It had been only a few weeks since he had given the horse to her.

Had she already tamed him?

Gabriel's heart jumped into his throat as he saw her urge the horse toward an obstacle course that did not look remotely easy.

His heart stayed in his throat as she jumped each obstacle as if it were a child's game. Not once did she lose her seating on the huge beast. Not once did she lose the focus or the mastery with which she ruled him.

It was almost as if the Thoroughbred and she were soul mates, so easily did the proud beast respond to her. She crouched low over him, whispering commands. Gabriel's pulse sped up dangerously as she crouched low and took the final obstacle with a flourish he had only seen in professional jumpers.

The jumping circuit was clearly a piece of cake for her.

Slowly his heartbeat returned to normal and Gabriel wondered again if he would ever stop being surprised by her. Ever stop wanting her with that soul-wrenching intensity.

Waiting to see what she would do had been torture. After his daughter had told him *Ellie's old friend had left forever*—his daughter had the makings of a spy—waiting in Barcelona to finish dealing with his mother and the aftermath of twenty years of estrangement had been torment.

He waited on the other side of the fence as she jumped off the horse, and then whispered near its ear for long, lingering minutes. If he hadn't seen her take that obstacle course, he wouldn't have believed it now.

The beast seemed huge next to her. She looked fragile, almost breakable, just as she had been in his arms.

He followed a few steps behind her as she led the horse to his stall.

She still hadn't noticed him; she was so immersed in the simple task of grooming the beast. She dismissed the groom, and then filled a trough with oats and water.

Leaning against the opposite stall, Gabriel closed his eyes and let her words, soothing and full of praise, wash over him as she talked to the beast.

Just as she did with Angelina, she took tender care of him. Nothing was beneath her. Nothing was to be hurried.

Her very joy in the simple task suffused the air around them.

She spent almost a half hour brushing the stallion's gleaming coat, all the while telling him what a good boy he was.

The stallion neighed and nuzzled into her face, and again, the same longing rose up inside of Gabriel.

She had reduced him to feeling jealous of a mute animal?

Her amused laughter filled the barn, flew inside the

empty place inside of him he'd never known existed. Something settled there and he refused to question or examine it.

When she stepped out of the stall, he moved out of the shadows and in front of her. Her hair had half flown out of her tight braid, just like Angelina's. Exertion made her skin glow like burnt bronze. Tendrils of flyaway hair stuck to her forehead, coated in sweat.

Her pulse hammering violently at her throat was the only sign that she was affected by his presence. She wore a white shirt and jodhpurs.

The tight pants lovingly delineated the womanly flare of her hips. A bead of sweat ran down her neck as he watched, and disappeared into the lush pillow of her breasts.

Her moans from the long nights they had spent loving each other filled his ears. She had been a revelation in bed, just as she'd been everywhere, willing and wanton in his arms as he taught her new pleasure after new pleasure.

Yet, he'd been the one who was always left breathless, their lovemaking going beyond the physical.

The temptation of her lush body, the scent of her arousal, kicked lust into full gear inside of him. He took a deep breath, trying to corral it now. He never wanted to hurt this woman, through words or actions, he realized.

He needed her warmth, her generous heart, her twisted reasoning, her practical efficiency.

"Hello, *Princesa*."

She lifted her chin in a show of defiance but he had seen the hint of pain in her eyes. Her gaze raked over him with calculated feminine interest that made his body heat up, yet left his heart cold.

"Have you come back to proposition a new arrangement, Gabriel? Because you were right. There's nothing you can offer me anymore." Something about the way she said that sent a coldness unfurling in his gut. "Have you come back only after your little spy told you that I sent Spiros away, that you would not risk anything if you came back now?" He felt the loss of the warmth of her eyes like an ache in his body.

"I wanted you to make a choice, *Princesa*."

"No, you made the choice for me, yet again." Her arms went around herself, her very posture screaming rejection. "Like all the arrogant bastards littered throughout my life. You were no better than my father or Andreas, Gabriel."

He flinched, her words landing like poisonous barbs. "Leaving you was the hardest thing I have ever done."

Tears filled her eyes. "No, Gabriel. Fighting for me, as I have been doing for you all this time, would have been the hardest thing. Putting yourself out there, making yourself vulnerable to me, trusting me with your heart would have been the hardest thing. Christos, you didn't even give me a chance! You just gave up on us as soon as you had no use for me."

How had he not seen how much he was hurting her? Was she right?

Had he hidden his own fear, his own vulnerabilities and called it doing the right thing? Had any woman understood him better than she? "You're right. I…I spent my whole life making myself tough. Not trusting anyone. When I saw you with Spiros, when I heard that I was only a vow to you, I just couldn't bear it. It was as if my worst nightmare had come true."

She scoffed, wiping at the tears on her cheeks roughly. Much like his daughter did when he hurt her with his insensitivity.

"Your word, your loyalty was not enough anymore, *Princesa*."

"What do you mean? What is there that you need that I haven't given you, Gabriel? How have I fallen short, yet again?"

"Your heart," he said, reaching for her, laying his hand on her chest. Her heart thundered under his touch, filling him with such awe that he couldn't speak for several minutes.

She eyed him warily, doubt in her eyes. "Gabriel?"

"I wanted your heart, Eleni. Your generous, kind, loving heart. I didn't want you to be my wife because you made a promise. Or because Angelina needed you. Or because you were programmed to do anything for this damned country. Or worst of all, because we were your only chance at a family of your own. I wanted you to be my wife because your heart belonged to me. Because you belonged with me. Because you couldn't go another day without loving me, just as I couldn't without you."

"Oh, Gabriel," she whispered in such a broken voice that his heart kicked against his chest. Furious tears filled her eyes and sent fear spiraling down his spine.

"Princesa?" he said in such a gentle voice that her tears fell faster. "I cannot give you eight years of your life back. I can't give you back a life with that man. But I would love you with all my heart. I would treasure you every day of our lives. I would give you a brood of children, as many as you want. And I would try to be the best damn husband and father the world has ever seen."

He went on his knees and buried his face in her soft belly. "Give me a chance, Eleni, and you will never regret it."

Eleni sank to her knees and threw herself into his arms. His embrace felt like heaven, the scent of him coiling tight around her like a safe blanket.

He was hers. Her home. Her place of belonging in the world. He was her everything. Didn't the arrogant, thickheaded man not know that?

"I do love you, Gabriel. You saw me more than anyone else in my life has. You made me feel like I mattered even when you grumbled about it. How you could think Spiros meant anything to me after everything we've been together? Why didn't you just talk to me? Why did you leave like that?"

"I had some things to set right. I…I wanted to be a different man for you in the chance that you chose me. Things that were long due."

"What?"

He settled down onto the grass and pulled her into his lap. She felt the shuddering breath he took, burying his face in her hair. His arms were like clamps around her midriff.

Content and delirious with joy, Eleni waited. This man, this husband of hers was worth waiting for.

"My mother was barely eighteen when her father arranged her marriage to my father, against her every protest. Apparently, he was double her age at thirty-seven, much as he had fallen in love with her.

"Within a year, I was born. And she… I think the marriage killed her dreams. She resented her father, then my father. Then me.

"All through my childhood, she…she went off to clubs and parties, made friends with strange men while my father basically waited for her at home. God, I used to think him such a fool. He gave her everything she'd ask for—dresses, expensive jewelry, the latest car.

"I don't know when she started, but she always took me with her to these parties and clubs. Maybe she felt guilty or maybe she used me as a front with my father. But all I remember growing up is lies on top of lies that she told him. I didn't really care back then because she took me with her everywhere.

"This dazzling, beautiful creature, whom everyone loved, who became the light of every party she went to, she was my mother.

"I trusted her, adored her, would have probably killed

my own father if she'd asked me to do it. But then she met this new guy. Until that, I think she was only skating the lines, seeing how far she could go without betraying her vows.

"But this painter came along and she fell for him. I instantly knew she was changing. I begged her not to see him. She promised me she would never leave me behind, that I was 'her little big man,' the love of her life. Only, one night, under the cover of darkness, she left with him."

Her arms went around him and despite the heaviness he felt in his chest every time he talked about his parents, he smiled. He had meant to console her and she had disarmed him yet again.

"In the end, she stayed away for five years. When she came crawling back to him, she was pregnant with my sister."

"Isabella?"

"Yes."

"What did your father do?"

"Against my every argument, he took her back. I despised her for a long time...for putting him through such heartache. To the end, he never looked at another woman, never stopped loving her. She said she was sorry for what she'd done but by then the harm was done. He died a few months later."

"Is that why you...you don't trust women?"

He laughed and she just held on to him. Nothing could ever take away the hollow he felt when he thought of his father, the powerlessness as Gabriel had watched him waste away in the bottle, but how had he thought Eleni would do anything like that?

How had he worried about giving himself over to her?

She was the most generous, most loyal woman he had ever met.

"It's not that I don't trust women, *querida*. I just did not want a committed relationship with one. I promised myself I would never be in his position. Never love so much that even your sense of self-preservation is gone."

"And loving Angelina?"

"Having Angelina has made me rethink everything. On one hand, I can't believe how my mother ever walked out on me. The guilt I think is etched onto her face now.

"On the other, knowing that Angelina will be a woman one day, the idea of her stuck in a marriage to a man double her age…it gives me new perspective.

"For years, my mother wanted to see me. When I heard what your father had done to you…it tore me up. Your pain tore me up.

"And it made me realize what she must have felt. Barely a woman, and saddled with a husband double her age and a son. Caught with no escape or outlet.

"It made me think of how it would have crushed your spirit in a situation like that. I could forgive Andreas anything in the world for stopping your father from doing that to you. When I thought of you, what I had to do became simple, easy."

"What was that?"

"After all these years, I went to see her."

"Oh, Gabriel," Eleni whispered into his neck, love filling her chest. "I wish you had told me this before. I wish I could have been there for you."

"But you were, *Princesa*. You were in my heart. Or else I'd never have understood her pain."

"Was she happy to see you?"

He smiled and there was a depth of joy in it. "She was. She is marrying some guy and I think she thought I wouldn't forgive her for that."

"Are you angry with her again?" Eleni asked, heart aching for him. Because, now she knew, it would only be because he cared. Because he wasn't quite the ruthless man he thought himself to be.

"No. I'm not. I wanted to know more about the guy but I felt it wasn't my place." A hint of his pain, even resentment, maybe, peeked through in his voice. But what he had done was a huge step. Those scars, Eleni knew very well, would take time to heal. "Once I saw her, I couldn't stay away anymore. I couldn't not…see you, *Princesa*.

"Angelina told me you sent Spiros away and I breathed fully for the first time in weeks." He turned toward her and cupped her face. "I love you, *Princesa*. Without fear or reservations. I love you so much that I cannot live without you for a minute."

Heart bursting with happiness, she pressed her mouth to his and sank into his toe-curling kiss. His mouth drifted from her mouth to her nose, to her temple, to her hair, his arms almost crushing the breath from her lungs. In a deft movement, he pulled her up, a sudden urgency to his movements. "Eleni, I know what I promised, but I have a demand to make of our marriage this time."

Laughing, she went on her toes and pressed her mouth to the pulse at his neck. The powerful man shuddered all around her. "Anything, Gabriel."

"I want us to leave the palace, make a home somewhere else. Anywhere in this world that you want to live in. But not here."

Eleni swallowed away the confusion within. "Because of what Andreas did?"

"Because this palace has sad memories for you. It makes you feel as if you were less than the magnificent woman you are, *Princesa*. I would have you happy, Eleni. You and me and Angelina and all the children we will have."

Eleni laughed at that, joy overflowing in her chest. "That was before I met you, Gabriel. Before I…before you showed me what and who I was. Before you challenged all my preconceived notions about myself. But I can't go, Gabriel. Please, not now."

"Why not, *Princesa*?" he said, clasping her cheeks with a tenderness that always snagged her heart.

"I wish I could hate Andreas for his interference, Gabriel. It was just like my father, though I didn't have the heart to tell him that. In those moments when I thought you would never return, when I lay in our bed alone, longing for you…I did hate him then. But he means well. He did it out of love for me. You know that, don't you? He did the right thing, in his own twisted way."

Gabriel nodded.

Only Gabriel's love for Eleni, his respect for everything Nikandros had accomplished in the past year had stopped him from making hell rain on Andreas and his precious Drakon for his interference. Something had happened to Andreas and he felt pity for the woman he was searching for when he found her.

"Andreas made me see I had no choice. Not if I loved you. I hated that he was right, but I had to do it. I had to walk away. But I do not like you anywhere near his controlling influence, *Tesoro*. I do not like him playing with us as if we were pawns."

Tears filled her eyes. "All my life, I've been the buffer between him and Father, him and Nik, Nik and Father. I couldn't take it if you asked me to not see him. If you made me choose between you, I would choose you, yes. But please don't make me.

"He…something's wrong with him. He's possessed, Gabriel. He needs me. He needs us."

Gabriel shook his head, amazed at the generosity of his wife yet again. At her capacity to forgive and forget, at her capacity to love. He took her in his arms again, the sight of her tears unmanning him. In her eyes, in the love she evoked in her hard-hearted brother, Gabriel saw even a chance for Andreas. A slim one. "Andreas doesn't need us, *Princesa*. But yes, until he finds what he does need, we will stay. We will watch over your brother, but not a single day after that."

He kissed her eyes, letting the rush of love and fear flood him. Understanding that loving this fierce woman meant accepting that there would be others who could hurt her. Accepting that she loved everyone without reservations. He pulled her to him and held her tightly. "I will not share you with anyone ever again, *Princesa*. Not with Nikandros, not with Andreas and not with Drakon, yes?"

"You might have to, Gabriel," Eleni whispered against his lips, her heart bursting with happiness.

"What?" he said, scowling.

Eleni pushed a thick lock of hair away from his strong face, her breath stuttering in her throat. She pulled his hand down to her belly and smiled at him.

His gaze flitted up to her face and back down a few times, before it became wary, almost blank. "When would you have told me?" It was a whisper but she heard his growl in it anyway.

"When you decided that you loved me, Gabriel." She clasped his cheeks and forced him to look at her. "If I had told you, you would have taken over my life. You would have made me your wife whether or not—"

"My child and my wife belong with me."

"Whether or not, you loved me? Can't you see? I couldn't take the chance. I couldn't live like that again. I love you, Gabriel. And I will never hide anything from you ever."

Slowly, the anger abated and he kissed her gently. "You better keep that promise, *Princesa*, or you will learn what a grumpy beast I can be."

Eleni laughed. Grumpy beast or not, he was the man who loved her.

EPILOGUE

MARIA DRAKOS MARQUEZ, a tiny bundle that fit in her father's hands, arrived seven months later with a boisterous cry that declared she was no sweet angel.

With thick black hair and gray eyes, she stared out at her father, her cherubic mouth scrunched tight in protest.

His heart had crawled into his throat a few hours ago when his wife's pains had started. Now, as she looked at his baby infant, it seemed as if his heart would never return to his chest.

That life would never cease to amaze him.

And it was all due to his wife.

Gabriel looked at Eleni, an overwhelming tightness in his throat. Each day he spent with his wife and daughter, each moment of joy that touched their lives, he thought couldn't beat another.

And yet, his life seemed to be filled with such glorious moments. With such all-encompassing joy.

"Let me see, Papa," Angelina cooed in his ear, tugging nervously at his arm.

"Slowly, *pequeña*," he whispered, glad to see that his oldest showed no evidence of feeling left out or neglected. Of course, he didn't know who had been more excited about the little girl's arrival—him or Angelina.

Angelina's eyes widened with awe as she traced her little sister's tiny hands in a reverent touch. "She's so tiny, Papa. I…"

He understood exactly how Angelina felt.

He felt both happiness and trepidation that the care and well-being of someone so fragile was in his hands now.

Gabriel carefully handed his precious little baby to his own mother, whose eyes were overflowing with tears. Angelina instantly drifted off toward the baby but before she did, she threw her arms around Eleni, pressed a fierce kiss to her forehead and whispered "I love you, Ellie."

Gabriel smiled as his brothers-in-law, Andreas and Nikandros, crowded around his mama, waiting for their turn to look at his new daughter. His heart thudded in his chest as Andreas took her in his arms and cooed at her. His tone and the slight tremble of his hands belied the fiercely unemotional expression on his face. The hollows of his face became even more pinched as he studied his tiny niece.

Gabriel looked away and took a deep breath.

From Andreas, Maria went to Nik, who carried her with the aplomb and finesse of a new father.

There were so many people who would love Maria. So many who would nurture her and ensure that she was taken care of. And if he made a misstep, his wife would correct him, show him how to love this tiny being.

His lungs expelled in a sudden rush.

"Gabriel?"

The husky, raw tones of his wife made him look up. Sweat pasted thick tendrils of her hair to Eleni's forehead, her eyes sleep-deprived, yet to Gabriel, she had never looked more beautiful.

"Yes, *Princesa*?"

She extended her hand and he took it. Lifting it to his mouth, he pressed a tender kiss to the inside of her wrist. She clasped his jaw, as if she understood the enormity of his emotional reaction to their little daughter.

The wetness behind his eyes slowly abated. To his wife's raised brows, he somehow managed to squeeze himself into the tiny bed and wrapped his arm around her. The others had left the room.

"Was that your mother, Gabriel?"

Nothing went missed by his superefficient wife. "Hmm."

"You asked her to visit?"

"Yes. I…" He nuzzled into her neck, needing the warmth and scent of her. "When you went into labor, I couldn't bear it. I called her and she offered to jump on a plane within minutes. So I sent her my jet and she got here a few minutes before Maria arrived. You've brought me so much love, Eleni, that it seems very hard to hold on to the past, to hold on to anger. There's no place in my heart, it seems, for anything more than love."

"I understand, Gabriel. Loving you has taught me to love myself."

He pushed off a lock of her hair and pressed a kiss to her temple. "*Te amo, Princesa*. With all my heart."

She took his hand and kissed it, her eyelids droopy, her mouth trembling. "Thank you for loving me, Gabriel. Thank you for giving me two wonderful daughters."

"Thank you for making a family with me, *Princesa*," he said.

Within minutes, she was out like a light. When his mother returned a little later and handed him Maria, Gabriel said everything he had to in a kiss on his mother's cheek.

And went back to the bed, sleepy bundle in hand, to wait for his wife to wake up and kiss him again.

Looking at the tight fist that formed around his finger, he realized he was in for a long wait and sighed.

But he didn't care.

The Princess of Drakon and her kisses were worth waiting for.

* * * * *

*If you enjoyed THE DRAKON BABY BARGAIN,
why not read the first installment of Tara Pammi's*
THE DRAKON ROYALS *trilogy?*
*CROWNED FOR THE DRAKON LEGACY
Available now!*

*And look out for Andreas's story,
coming September 2017*

'Then tell me it's not true.' Clasping hold of her wrist, Lukas held it in his grasp.

'Very well.' Callie indignantly tried to snatch back her hand, but Lukas held on. 'I do not have a lover, Lukas.'

'A boyfriend, then? A partner of some description?'

'No, none of those things. Now, kindly let me go.'

'What, then? Tell me. Because I can see it, Calista. I can see it in your eyes.'

Callie hesitated. She could feel the moment closing in on her, weighing down on her with leaden pressure. Suddenly there was no escape.

'I do not have a lover, Lukas.' She summoned the words from deep inside her, where the truth had lain dormant for so long. 'But I do have a child.'

'A child?' He dropped her arm as if it were made of molten metal. 'You have a *child*?'

'Yes.' She watched as the shock that had contorted his handsome features settled into a brutal grimace of stone. 'I have a four-and-a-half-year-old daughter.'

She paused, sucking in a breath as if it might be her last. *This was it.*

'And so, Lukas, do you.'

Secret Heirs of Billionaires

There are some things money can't buy...

Living life at lightning pace, these magnates are no strangers to stakes at their highest. It seems they've got it all... That is until they find out that there's an unplanned item to add to their list of accomplishments!

Achieved:

1. Successful business empire

2. Beautiful women in their bed

3. *An heir to bear their name...?*

Though every billionaire needs to leave his legacy in safe hands, discovering a secret heir shakes up his carefully orchestrated plan in more ways than one!

Uncover their secrets in:

Unwrapping the Castelli Secret by Caitlin Crews

Brunetti's Secret Son by Maya Blake

The Secret to Marrying Marchesi by Amanda Cinelli

Demetriou Demands His Child by Kate Hewitt

The Desert King's Secret Heir by Annie West

The Sheikh's Secret Son by Maggie Cox

The Innocent's Shameful Secret by Sara Craven

Look out for more stories in the
Secret Heirs of Billionaires series coming soon!

THE GREEK'S PLEASURABLE REVENGE

BY

ANDIE BROCK

First Published in Great Britain 2017
By Mills & Boon, an imprint of HarperCollins*Publishers*
1 London Bridge Street, London, SE1 9GF

© 2017 Andrea Brock

ISBN: 978-0-263-92526-5

Andie Brock started inventing imaginary friends around the age of four, and is still doing it today—only now the sparkly fairies have made way for spirited heroines and sexy heroes. Thankfully she now has some real friends, as well as a husband and three children—plus a grumpy but lovable cat. Andie lives in Bristol, and when not actually writing might well be plotting her next passionate romance story.

Books by Andie Brock

Mills & Boon Modern Romance

The Last Heir of Monterrato

Wedlocked!

Bound by His Desert Diamond

One Night With Consequences

The Shock Cassano Baby

Society Weddings

The Sheikh's Wedding Contract

Visit the Author Profile page
at millsandboon.co.uk for more titles.

This one is for Bill. Don't worry,
you don't have to read it! Love M. xx

CHAPTER ONE

'WE DON'T WANT any trouble, Kalanos.'

Lukas roughly shook off the hand on the sleeve of his dark suit, before turning to give its owner a bone-chilling stare.

'Trouble?' He let his eyes travel slowly over the sweating face of the middle-aged man who was trying but failing miserably to square up to him. 'Whatever makes you think I would bring any *trouble*, Yiannis?'

The man took a step away, glancing around for back-up. 'Look, Kalanos, this is my father's funeral—that's all I'm saying. It's a time for respect.'

'Ah, yes, *respect.*' Lukas let the word slide through his teeth like a witch's curse. 'I'm so glad you reminded me. That must be why there are so many people here.' He swept a derisive stare over the sparsely populated grave-side. 'So many people wanting to pay their "respects" to the great man.'

'It's a quiet family funeral. That's all.' Yiannis avoided his eye. 'And you are not wanted here, Lukas.'

'No?' Lukas ground out his reply. 'Well, you know what? That's too bad.'

In point of fact Lukas hadn't wanted to be there. Not yet. Lukas had been far from ready to bury this evil man. He'd had plans for him. The man who had killed his father as surely as if he had driven a blade through his heart. Whose evil machinations had seen Lukas thrown into prison for a crime he hadn't committed. Dark, unspeakable plans that would have seen him begging for mercy and, on realising there was none to be had, pleading for the oblivion of death.

Four and a half years. That was how long Lukas had been incarcerated in one of Athens's toughest jails, with only the dregs of society for company. Plenty of time to go over every detail of his betrayal, and worse—far worse— the betrayal of his father. Years of seething, boiling, melting rage that had solidified inside him until it had become all he was. No longer a man of flesh and blood but hard and cold, hewn from the lava of hatred.

Four and a half years to plot his revenge.

And all for nothing.

Because the object of his hatred, Aristotle Gianopoulous, had died on the very same day that Lukas had been released from prison. Almost as if he had timed it deliberately. Almost as if he had known.

Now Lukas watched the coffin being slowly lowered into the ground as the sonorous voice of the priest bestowing his final blessing filled the air. His cold eyes travelled round the circle of black-clad mourners, moving from one to the next. He let his gaze stay just long enough for his forbidding presence to register, to unsettle them, to shift their focus from the dead man to one who was very much alive. And who wanted them to know it.

Beside him Yiannis Gianopoulous fidgeted nervously, shooting him wary sidelong glances. The son of Aristotle from his second marriage, he was of no interest to Lukas. His brother Christos was here too, scowling at him from the relative safety of the other side of the open grave. There were a couple of old business associates, Aristotle's ancient lawyer, and one of his lady-friends, quietly dabbing at her eyes as if it was expected of her. Slightly to one side stood Petros and Dorcas, Aristotle's last remaining faithful employees, who had worked for him for longer than Lukas could remember. More fool them.

An assorted array of damaged and broken individuals, the detritus of Gianopoulous's life, all brought together under the punishing heat of the midday sun on this beautiful Greek island to bury the man who had doubtless managed to blight all their lives in one way or another. Lukas didn't give a damn about any of them.

All except for one.

Finally he let his eyes rest upon her. The slightly built young woman standing with her head bowed, clutching a single white lily tightly in her hand. Calista Gianopoulous. *Callie.* The offspring of Aristotle's third wife, his youngest child and only daughter. The one good thing Aristotle had produced. Or so Lukas had thought. Until she had betrayed him, too. Playing her part in his downfall in the most treacherous way possible.

Lukas allowed himself a moment to savour her discomfort. He had recognised her immediately, of course, the second he had burst onto this touching scene. Marching through the small graveyard, past the neglected resting place of his own father, he had stormed towards the freshly dug grave, enjoying the palpable wave of alarm that had rippled across the mourners.

And the look of panic that had gripped Calista. He had seen it, even though she was wearing a veil, had witnessed the flash of terror in those green eyes, registered the way her slender body swayed slightly before she had steadied herself and looked down.

Now he watched as she bowed her head still further, pulling at the black lace that covered her glorious red hair as if she could somehow disguise herself, hide from him. But there was no chance of that. No chance at all.

Look at me, Calista.

He found himself willing her to raise her eyes, to meet his searing gaze. He wanted to see her guilt for himself, to witness her shame, to feel it penetrate the solid wall of his contempt.

Or was some small, pathetic part of him still hoping that he'd got it wrong?

But Calista's eyes were firmly fixed on the grave before her, looking for all the world as if she would jump in with her deceased father if it meant she could get away from him. But, no. She would have no such escape. Aristotle might have died before Lukas could exact his revenge, but Calista was here before him—ready for the taking. It would be revenge of a very different kind, but none the less pleasurable for that.

Lukas stared at her through narrowed eyes. The young woman he thought he'd known. How wrong he had been. Over the years they had built up a friendship, or so he had thought, sharing their summers on the island of Thalassa, a private idyll bought jointly by their two fathers when G&K Shipping had made its first million. A symbol of their success and their enduring friendship.

So much for that.

Lukas, eight years Calista's senior, thought back to the lonely little kid whose parents had divorced before she'd barely been out of nappies. Her neurotic screwball of a mother had whisked her back to her homeland of England, but sent her alone to Thalassa for the school holidays. Cutting a forlorn figure, Calista had trailed after whichever half-sibling had happened to be in residence at the sumptuous Gianopoulous residence at the time, her fair skin turning pink in the hot Greek sun, freckles dotting her nose.

She had trailed after Lukas too, seeking him out on his family's side of the island, obstinately settling herself in his boat when he was off one of his fishing trips, or clambering over the rocks to watch him dive into the crystal-clear turquoise waters before pestering him to show her how it was done.

Later she had become Callie the awkward teenager. Motherless by then, she'd been packed off to boarding school, but had still came back to Thalassa for the long summer vacations. Hiding her mop of curly red hair beneath a floppy straw hat and her pretty face behind the fat pages of a blockbuster novel, she'd no longer had any interest in her brothers—nor, seemingly, in Lukas, except for the occasional giveaway glance from those amazing green eyes when she'd thought he wasn't looking, and blushing to the roots of her hair when he caught her out.

Callie, now Calista, who at eighteen, had somehow metamorphosed into the most stunning young woman. *And had tempted him into bed.* Although technically they had never actually made it as far as a bed. Caught up in the moment, the sofa in the living room had served them well enough.

Lukas had known it was wrong at the time—of course he had. But she had been just too alluring, too enticing to resist. He had been surprised, flattered—honoured, even—that she had made a play for him, chosen him to take her virginity. But most of all he had been duped.

And now he was going to make her pay.

Calista felt the ground sway beneath her feet, and the image of the coffin bearing her father blurred through the black lace of her veil.

Oh, please, no.

Not Lukas—not here, not now. But there was no mistaking the figure of the man who was glowering at her from the other side of the grave, or the power of his intensely dark stare as it bored into her. He was broader than she remembered him, and his muscled torso harder, stronger, more imposing, filling the well-cut dark suit like steel poured into a mould of the finest fabric. His sleeves tugged tight against the bulge of his biceps as he stood there with his arms folded across his chest, his feet firmly planted, clearly indicating that he was going nowhere.

All this Calista registered in a flash of panic before lowering her eyes to the grave.

This couldn't be happening.

Lukas Kalanos was in prison—everybody knew that. Serving a long sentence for his part in the disgraceful arms smuggling business that had been masterminded by his father, Stavros—her own father's business partner.

The sheer immorality of the venture had sickened Calista to the core—it still did. The fact that her father's shipping business had gone bust because of it, and her family had been financially ruined, was only of secondary concern. At the age of twenty-three she had already experienced great wealth and great hardship. And she knew which one she preferred.

Which was why five years ago she had walked away, determined to turn her back on her tainted Greek heritage. Away from the collapse of the multi-billion-dollar family business, from her brothers' bickering and back-stabbing. From her father's towering rages and black, alcohol-fuelled depressions.

But most of all she had walked away from Lukas Kalanos—the man whose dark eyes were tearing into her soul right now. The man who had taken her virginity and broken her heart. And who had left her with a very permanent reminder.

At the thought of her little daughter Calista felt her lip start to quiver. Effie was fine—she was safe at home in London, probably running rings around poor Magda, Calista's trusted friend and fellow student nurse, who was in charge until Calista could hurry back. She didn't want to spend any more time here than she had to—she was intending to stay a couple of days at most, to sort through her father's things with her brothers, sign whatever paperwork needed to be signed and then escape from this island for ever.

But suddenly getting away from Thalassa had taken on a new urgency. And getting away from the menacingly dark form of Lukas Kalanos more imperative still.

The burial ceremony was almost over. The priest was inviting them to join him in the last prayer before the mourners tossed flowers and soil onto the top of the coffin, the distinctive sound as they met the polished wood sending a shiver through Calista's slender frame.

'Not cold, surely?' A firm, possessive grip clasped her elbow. 'Or is this a touching display of grief?'

He spoke in faultless English, although Calista's Greek would have been more than good enough to understand his meaning. Using his grasp, he turned her so that now she couldn't escape the full force of him as he loomed over her, glowered down at her. 'If so, I'm sure I don't need to point out that it is seriously misplaced.'

'Lukas, please…' Calista braced herself to meet his searing gaze, her knees almost giving way at the sight of him.

The tangled dark curls had gone, in favour of a close-cropped style that hardened his handsome features, accentuating the uncompromising sweep of his jawline shadowed with designer stubble, the sharp-angled planes of his cheeks. But the eyes were the same—so dark a brown as to be almost black, breathtaking in their intensity.

'I am here to bury my father—not listen to your insults.'

'Oh, believe me, *agapi mou*, in terms of insults I wouldn't know where to start. It would take a lifetime and more to even scratch the surface of the depths of my revulsion for that man.'

Calista swallowed hard. Her father had had his faults—she had no doubt about that. A larger-than-life character, both in temperament and girth, he had treated her mother very badly, and had had a series of affairs that had broken her mother's spirit, albeit already fragile. In turn that had eventually led to her accidental overdose. Calista would never wholly forgive him for that.

But he'd still been her father—the only one she would ever have—and she had always known she would have to return to Thalassa one last time to lay him to rest. And maybe lay some of her demons to rest too.

Little had she known that the biggest demon of all would be present at the graveside, sliding his arm around her waist right now in a blatant show of possessiveness and control.

'I'll thank you not to speak of my father in that way.'

She was grateful to feel her hot-headed temper kicking in to rescue her, colouring her cheeks beneath the veil. Pointedly taking a step to the side to dislodge his hand from her elbow, she pushed back her shoulders and had to stifle a gasp as his arm slid around her waist, the ring of muscled steel burning through the thin fabric of her black dress.

'It is both disrespectful and deeply insulting.' Her voice shook alarmingly. 'Quite aside from which, *you* are hardly in a position to judge anyone.'

'Me, Calista?' Dark brows were raised fractionally in feigned surprise. 'Why would that be?'

'You know perfectly well why.'

'Ah, yes. The heinous crime I committed. That's something I want to talk to you about.'

'Well, I don't want to talk to *you*—about that or anything else.'

Particularly not anything else.

Cold fingers of dread tiptoed down her spine at the thought of what they might end up discussing. If Lukas were to find out that he had a daughter, heaven only knew how he would react. It was too terrifying an idea to contemplate.

Calista had never intended to keep Effie a secret from her father—at least not at first. She had been over five months pregnant before she had even realised it herself, convinced that stress was responsible for the nausea, her lack of periods, her fatigue. Because *no one* got pregnant the very first time they had sex, did they?

Certainly the stress she had been suffering would have felled the strongest spirit, even *before* she'd found out she was expecting Lukas's child. What with Stavros—her father's friend and business partner—dying so suddenly, and then the whole arms smuggling scandal coming out and the shipping business collapsing. And finally making the sickening discovery that Lukas was involved.

By the time she had seen a doctor Lukas had already been awaiting trial for his crime. And on the day she'd gone into labour, a full month earlier than expected, alone and frightened as she pushed her way through the agonising birth with only the midwife's hand to grip for support, Lukas had been in court, with the judge declaring him guilty and sentencing him to eight years in jail.

Effie's first screaming lungful of air had come at the exact moment when the judge had uttered the fateful words, 'Take him down.'

On that day—the day of her daughter's birth—Calista had resolved to wait to tell Lukas of Effie's existence until he was released from jail. Eight years had seemed a lifetime away. Time enough for her and Effie to build their own lives in the UK, to become a strong, independent unit. So the secret had been kept well hidden.

Calista had told no one—not even her father—for fear that if he knew the truth word would spread amongst her Greek family and find its way to Lukas. But if she was honest there was another reason she didn't want her father to know. She didn't want her precious Effie tainted by any association with him.

He would have tried to take control, Calista knew that—both of her and his granddaughter. He would have tried to manipulate them, bend them to his will, use them to his advantage. Calista had worked far too hard to build an independent life to let him do that. Simply not telling him about Effie had been the easiest solution all round.

Now Aristotle would never know he'd had a granddaughter. But Lukas… Calista moved inside the band of his arm, her heart thudding with frantic alarm and something else—something that felt dangerously like excitement. Lukas would have to know that he was a father. That was his right. But not yet. Not until Calista had had a chance to prepare herself—and Effie. Not until she had made sure all her defences were securely in place.

'Calista, people are leaving.' Beside her, but keeping a safe distance from Lukas, Yiannis tried to get her attention. 'They are waiting to speak to us before they go.'

'Leaving so soon?' Lukas gave a derisive sneer. 'Is there to be no wake? No toasting the life of the great man?'

'The boats are waiting to take everyone back to the mainland.' Yiannis wiped the sweat from his brow. 'You'll be on one of them, if you know what's good for you.'

Lukas gave a gruff laugh. 'Funny, I was just thinking the same thing about you.'

'You have brought ruination and disgrace to our family, Kalanos, but Thalassa is the one asset my father managed to protect. You may own half of it now, but not for much longer.'

'Is that right?'

'Yes. We intend to make a claim for your half of the island as compensation for the financial ruin you and your father caused us. Our lawyers are confident we will win the case.' Yiannis struggled to keep his voice firm.

'We?'

'My brother and I. And Calista, of course.'

At the mention of her name Lukas released his arm from her waist, turning to give Calista a stare of such revulsion that it churned her stomach. She had no idea what Yiannis was talking about. She had never agreed to instruct a lawyer to sue for compensation. She wanted nothing to do with Thalassa—even the small share she assumed she'd inherit now, on Aristotle's death. She certainly had no intention of fighting Lukas for his half.

'Well, good luck with that.' Narrowing his eyes, Lukas turned away, seemingly bored with the subject. 'Actually, no.' Turning back, he fixed Yiannis with a punishing stare. 'You might as well know—both of you. The island of Thalassa now belongs to me. *All* of it.'

'Yeah, right.' Christos had joined them, positioning himself between Yiannis and Lukas, sweating profusely. 'Do you take us for idiots, Kalanos?'

Lukas's pursed lips gave an almost imperceptible twitch.

'You are obviously lying.'

'I'm afraid not.' Lukas removed a tiny speck of dust from the sleeve of his immaculate suit. 'I'm only surprised your lawyers didn't tell you. I managed to acquire your father's half of the island some time ago.'

Christos's face turned puce, but it was Yiannis who spoke. 'That can't be true. Aristotle would never have sold to you.'

'He didn't need to. When he and my father bought the island they registered it in their wives' names. A touching gesture, don't you think? Or am I being naive? Perhaps it was simply a tax dodge? Either way, it has proved very convenient. *My* half, of course, came to me upon the death of my mother—God rest her soul. Acquiring *your* half was simply a matter of tracking down Aristotle's first wife and making her an offer she couldn't refuse. I can't tell you how grateful she was. Especially as she had no idea she owned it.'

'But you have been in prison for years. How could you possibly have done this?'

'You'd be surprised. It turns out that you can make some very useful contacts inside. Very useful indeed.' Lukas raised a dark brow. 'I now know just the man for any given job. And I do mean *any.*'

Yiannis visibly paled beneath his swarthy skin. In desperation he turned to Calista, but she only gave a small shrug. She didn't give a damn who owned the island. She just wanted to get off it as fast as she could.

Christos, meanwhile, always blessed with more brawn than brains, had raised his fists in a pathetic show of aggression. 'You don't scare me, Kalanos. I'll take you on any time you like.'

'Didn't I hear you say you had a boat to catch?' With a display of supreme indifference Lukas treated him to an icily withering look.

Christos took a step forward, but Yiannis grabbed hold of his arm, pulling him away to stop him from getting himself into real trouble. As he twisted sideways his feet got caught in the green tarpaulin covering the fresh earth around the grave and they both stumbled, lurching dangerously towards the grave itself, before righting themselves at the last moment.

Yiannis tugged at his brother's arm again, desperate to get him away from humiliation, or a punch on the nose, or both.

'You haven't heard the last of this, Kalanos!' Christos shouted over his shoulder as his brother hastily manoeuvred them away, weaving between the overgrown graves. 'You are going to pay for this.'

Calista watched in surprise as her half-brothers disappeared. Weren't they supposed to have been staying a couple of nights on the island to go through their father's papers and sort out his affairs? Clearly that was no longer happening. Neither did they seem bothered about leaving her behind to deal with Lukas. It was obviously every man for himself—or *her*self.

But it did mean that there was nothing to keep her there any more. Unless she counted the formidably dark figure that was still rooted ominously by her side.

Realising she was still clutching the single lily in her hand, she stepped towards the grave and let it drop, whispering a silent goodbye to her father. A lump lodged in her throat. Not just for her father—her relationship with him had always been too fraught, too blighted by anguish and tragedy for simple grief to sum it up—but because Calista knew she was not just saying goodbye to Aristotle but to Thalassa, her childhood, her Greek heritage. This was the end of an era.

She turned to go, immediately coming up against the solid wall of Lukas's chest. Adjusting the strap of her bag over her shoulder, she went to move past him. 'If you will excuse me I need to be going.'

'Going where, exactly?'

'I'm leaving the island with the others, of course. There is no point in me staying here any longer.'

'Oh, but there is.' With lightning speed Lukas closed his hand around her wrist, bringing her back up against his broad chest. 'You, *agape*, are going nowhere.'

Calista flinched, her whole body going into a kind of panicky meltdown that sent a flood of fear rippling down to her core. Bizarrely, it wasn't an entirely unpleasant sensation.

'What do you mean by that?'

'Just what I say. You and I have unfinished business. And you won't be leaving Thalassa until I say so.'

'So what do you intend to do? Hold me prisoner?'

'If necessary, yes.'

'Don't be ridiculous.'

She hardened her voice as best she could, determined that she would stand up to this new, frighteningly formidable Lukas. Pulling away, she looked pointedly at her wrist until he released it.

'Anyway, what *is* this unfinished business? As far as I'm concerned we have nothing to discuss.'

Her nails dug into her palms at the blatant lie. But he couldn't be talking about Effie. If he had found out about his daughter he would have blown her whole world apart by now.

'Don't tell me you have forgotten, Calista. Because I certainly haven't.'

Dark, dark eyes looked down on her, glittering with intent.

'Let's just say the image of you lying semi-naked on my sofa, your legs wrapped around my back, has stayed with me all these years. I've probably conjured it up more times than I should have. Prison has that effect on you. You have to take your pleasures where you can.'

Callie blushed to the roots of her hair, grateful for the black veil that still partially obscured her mortified face. That was until Lukas gently, almost reverentially, lifted the fine lace and arranged it back over her head. For one bizarre moment she thought he was going to kiss her, as if she were some sort of dark bride.

'There—that's better.'

He stared at her, drinking her in like a man with the fiercest thirst. She held her breath. Each testosterone-fuelled second seemed longer than the last. She shifted beneath his astonishingly powerful scrutiny, her skin prickling, her heart pounding in her ribcage.

'I had forgotten how beautiful you are, Calista.'

Her stifled breath came out as a gasp. She hadn't expected a compliment—not after all the bullying and the veiled threats. Except this was a compliment deliberately tinged with menace.

'I can't tell you how much I am looking forward to renewing our acquaintance. I've been looking forward to it for almost five long years.'

No! Calista choked back a silent cry.

Surely he didn't think she would repeat that catastrophic error? Panic and outrage stiffened her spine.

'If you imagine that I am going to go to bed with you again, Lukas, you are sorely mistaken.'

'Bed...sofa...up against the wall right here in front of your father's grave, if you like. It's all the same to me. I want you, Calista. And I should warn you, when I want something I go all out to make sure that I get it.'

CHAPTER TWO

LUKAS WATCHED THE alarm on Calista's face set her delicate features in stone.

He had been right to declare her beautiful—even if he *had* only meant to say it in his head. She was even more beautiful than he remembered. The intervening years had honed her heart-shaped face, the high cheekbones, the firmly pointed chin. But the small, straight nose was still speckled with a dusting of freckles and her mouth… That was just as he remembered it, wide and full-lipped and deliciously pink—even now, when it was pursed in an attempt at defiance.

How Aristotle had produced such an exquisite creature as this was almost beyond comprehension. Calista obviously took after her mother, Diana, the actress-cum-model whose beauty had ultimately been her downfall. They certainly shared the same colouring, but whereas Diana had been all leggy height and stunning bone structure, which the camera had loved, Calista was petite, with full breasts and a slim waist leading to curvaceous hips that begged to be traced with the flat of his palm. Lukas could feel that urge powering through him right now, and he responded by reaching for her hand, relishing the soft feel of it beneath his own.

'This way.' He started off across the graveyard, pulling Calista behind him, all too aware that he was behaving like some sort of caveman but not caring in the least.

'Lukas—stop this.'

No way. Her feeble protestation only made him all the more determined that she was going to come with him—back to his villa and back to his bed. He had waited far too long for this moment to allow any second thoughts to creep in, or even to let common decency stand in his way. Certainly not her breathless objections.

'Lukas, stop—let me go!'

They had reached the small copse behind the ancient chapel, where he had left his motorbike. Positioning Calista between it and him, Lukas finally let go of her hand.

Calista snatched it back, her eyes flashing with fire. 'Just what the hell do you think you are playing at?'

'Oh, I'm not playing, Calista. This is no game.'

'What, then? What are you trying to prove? Why are you behaving like such a…a horrible bully?'

'Perhaps that's what I've become.' He gave her a casually brutal stare. 'Perhaps that's what four and a half years in prison does to a man.'

Calista's expression tightened. 'I don't even understand why you aren't still there. You were sentenced to *eight* years.'

'Time off for good behaviour.' His eyes glittered coldly. 'You see, I was a very good boy whilst I was in there—as far as the authorities were concerned, that is. Now I intend to make up for it.'

He watched her swallow.

'I do hope my early release hasn't inconvenienced you?'

'It hasn't. I couldn't care less where you are…what you do.'

'Good. Then get on the bike. We are going to Villa Helene.'

'No, we are *not*.' Her hand flew to her chest. 'I'm not going anywhere with you.'

'And there I was, hoping we wouldn't have to do this the hard way.'

Easily spanning her waist with his broad hands, Lukas lifted her off her feet and planted her unceremoniously on the pillion seat of the bike. The thin fabric of her skirt rode up over her thighs, pulling seductively taut, while her breasts heaved with indignation.

Lukas fought down the kick of lust.

'If you don't get me off this thing right now I am going to scream.'

'Feel free.' He smiled darkly. 'It won't make any difference. Your dear brothers, along with the other broken-hearted mourners, are already on their way back to the mainland. No one will hear you.'

He saw the flicker of fear in her eyes but she didn't move. Her pride refused to give him the satisfaction. And for some reason that only increased his admiration—and his arousal. Perched on the leather seat of his bike, she looked like some sort of erotic goddess, her back arched in defiance, her glorious Titian hair tumbling over her shoulders. The mourning veil, he noticed, had fallen to the dry ground at his feet.

'There's Petros…and Dorcas. They're still on the island. Villa Melina is still their home.'

He gave her a telling look. That was something for *him* to decide—not her. Clearly she was forgetting who called the shots around here.

'Look…' She suddenly changed tack, trying for a conciliatory tone. 'What's this all about, anyway?'

'You used to love this bike, Callie, don't you remember?' He deliberately used her shortened name, taking them back to the long hot summers of their shared past. 'You were forever pestering me for a ride.'

They had both loved this motorbike—the sleek black beast that had been Lukas's sixteenth birthday present to himself. He'd had other bikes since, and sports cars, luxury yachts, a helicopter—all the extravagant modes of transport that great wealth could afford. But nothing had surpassed the feeling of straddling this powerful beauty all those years ago, made even better by the feel of Callie's skinny arms clinging to his waist as they had roared off, the sound of her excited squeals in his ear.

Coming across it in the garage this morning, just where he had left it, he had felt as if he were meeting an old friend. One old friend, at least, that hadn't let him down. She had obediently started first time after he had charged the battery.

'I think we've both grown up since then.' Calista tossed back her flame-red hair, all sharp-angled defiance and dignified posturing. 'Or at least *I* have.'

'Indeed…I wouldn't dispute that.' Lukas gave a derisive laugh. 'I seem to remember we engaged in some *very* grown-up activity last time we met.'

Again she flushed, as if she found the memory of what they had done intensely shameful. As well she might.

'Well, that's not something that is going to be repeated, I can assure you. Despite your earlier threats.'

'Not threats, Calista. Think of it more as a promise.'

'You are such an arrogant piece of work, Lukas, you know that?' Emerald eyes flashed with fire. 'I promise you this: what happened between us will *never* happen again.'

'No? You're sure about that, are you?'

'Quite sure.'

'Then coming back to my villa for a couple of hours

won't hurt, will it? Unless you don't trust yourself, of course?'

'I trust myself, Lukas. It's *you* I don't trust.'

'Ah, yes, of course. I keep forgetting that *I'm* the villain of the piece here.'

'Yes, you are!' Calista immediately fired back at him.

He had to hand it to her—her acting skills had improved significantly over the years.

'In that case let me reassure you that nothing will happen between us unless you want it to.'

Was that true? It should be. His well-rehearsed plan had always been to trick her into wanting him, just the way she had him. But if she carried on looking at him the way she was now he wasn't sure he'd be able to hang on to his control.

He studied her from beneath lowered lashes, lazily, slowing himself down. Unless he was very much mistaken there was something else in that fiery look of hers. For all her prim deportment, her expression of outrage, her feisty comebacks, *something* simmered beneath the surface. Something that looked remarkably like sexual arousal. *Yes.* He would have her screaming his name with pleasure before the day was through. And then revenge would be his.

Swinging his leg over the bike, he turned the key in the ignition, gripping the handlebars and feeling the mechanical vibrations rumble through him.

'I'd hang on if I were you.' Speaking over his shoulder he twisted the throttle and the engine roared in reply. 'Let's let this old girl off the leash and see what she can do.'

And with a sudden jolt and a screech they were off.

Calista had no choice but to wrap her arms around Lukas's waist as they sped away from the cemetery, leaving its occupants in blissful peace as Lukas navigated the bike onto the coastal road that wound its way round the island. She leant her body into his, the wind whipping her hair back from her face, drying the breath in her throat as she clung on for dear life.

He was driving deliberately fast, she knew that, trying to frighten her, make her squeal. Well, she wasn't nine years old any more, and she certainly wasn't going to give him the satisfaction of behaving as if she was. In fact as soon as they got to the villa she would show him that she didn't intend to take any more of his bullying ways.

The stunning Greek scenery flashed past, the dramatic coastline with its towering cliffs and secluded coves stretching before them. Screwing up her eyes against the glare of the sun sparkling on the sea, Calista knew it wasn't fear she was feeling anyway. It was exhilaration. She felt alive, invigorated, realising how good it was to be back on Thalassa. More than that, realising how much she had missed it.

She adjusted her position slightly and felt Lukas's body respond, the broad width of his back heating against the crush of her breasts, the muscles of his waist shifting beneath the grip of her hands. A dangerous shudder of pleasure went through her. The island wasn't the only thing she had missed. And she was going to have to be very careful about that.

The twisty road took them past the turning for Villa Melina, *her* family villa, and continued east across the top of the island in the direction of Villa Helene—home to Lukas and his father, Stavros, now deceased.

It was a road Calista knew well—probably a distance of six miles or so. She had cycled it many times as a child, frequently seeking out the company of Lukas and his kindly father in preference to her own curmudgeonly father and boring half-brothers, with whom she'd had absolutely nothing in common. But she'd never paid much attention to the names of the two villas before—Melina, the name of Aristotle's first wife and Helene, Lukas's mother. She hadn't known either woman, but it was obvious now she thought about it that the villas had been named after them.

What she *hadn't* known—what no one had known by the look of it—was that Thalassa had actually belonged to them. No one except Lukas, of course, who had used that information to buy the entire island—presumably as a way of getting back at her family. She had no idea what had happened to the Lukas she had once known. What had become of him…

Turning off the coastal road, Lukas bumped the bike up the dirt track that lead to Villa Helene and pulled up in front of the entrance in a spray of dry dust.

Quickly dismounting, he held out his hand to her, but there was nothing gentlemanly about the gesture. It was done with an aggressively urgent air. Shepherding her before him, he unlocked the front door—an action that surprised Calista in itself. *No one* bothered to lock their doors on the island of Thalassa.

Inside, the villa was just as she remembered it. Even the smell was familiar—somehow both comforting and unsettling. She followed Lukas down the cool hallway until they reached the large living room that ran the entire width of the villa. It was still and dark in there, until Lukas strode over to the bi-fold doors, unlocked them and pushed them wide open, undoing the shutters so that the light streamed in.

Calista blinked. The stunning panoramic view of the Aegean Sea appeared before them, but Calista's focus was solely on the room she now saw so clearly. Or, more specifically, on the sofa in the room. The one she had so recklessly fallen onto with Lukas that evening, in a tangle of fervid, scorching, pumping desire. The one where Effie had been conceived.

'Drink?' Lukas grabbed a couple of glasses from the sideboard and reached for a decanter of whisky.

'No, thank you.' Calista dragged her burning eyes away from the scene of their complete madness.

'Mind if I do?' Pouring himself a generous slug, he knocked it back in one gulp, then poured another.

Clearly he wasn't waiting for her consent.

Averting her eyes from the sheer brutal beauty of him, Calista quickly scanned the rest of the familiar room; the white walls displaying colourful local artwork, the rustic wooden furniture and the travertine marble flooring. She had always loved this villa. More so than her own family's, in fact, which Aristotle had massively extended over the years as a succession of different women had needed to be impressed and the urge to display his wealth had become ever more important.

Villa Helene was more modest, more traditionally Greek, with towering walls affording much needed shade and the exterior woodwork painted that particular Mediterranean blue. Not that it lacked any modern comforts, with its large stainless steel kitchen, a beautiful infinity pool that glistened invitingly through the open doors, five bedrooms, a gymnasium and a library. There was even a helipad where, out of the corner of her eye, Calista had noticed a gleaming helicopter, heating up in the sun as they had walked in. So *that* was how he had got here...

'So, what is this unfinished business?' She decided to take the lead rather than wait for Lukas like a fly in his web. She watched as he set down his glass, swallowing hard as he started towards where she stood in the middle of the room. 'What is it you want to talk about?'

'The talking can wait.' He stopped before her, towering

over her as he gazed down her flushed face. 'Right now I am more interested in action.'

With no warning he reached forward, sliding a hand around the back of her neck, lifting the weight of her hair for a second, before dropping it so that it rippled down her back. 'Right now I want you to kiss me the way you kissed me the last time we were here, *agapi mou*. Do you remember?'

Calista felt herself sway. His hand was branding the back of her neck...his hot, whisky-tinged breath was shooting sharp waves of longing throughout her body. Of course she remembered. She remembered every minuscule, heart-stopping, life-changing detail. She had been living it for the past five years.

It had been her eighteenth birthday party—a gloriously warm June evening. Calista had finished her exams and finally left the boarding school that she had disliked so much, and she'd been intending to soak up a few weeks of Greek sunshine before returning to the UK to start university.

She had been looking forward to the party—not so much to the actual event, the guest list for which had mostly comprised her father's business cronies and their families, rather than her friends, although that had partly been *her* decision. Aristotle had told her to invite as many people as she wanted, offering to pay for their flights from the UK and to put them up at the villa, 'So they can see the sort of wealth you come from.' But she hadn't had that many friends—she'd always been the outsider at school, a motherless red-haired creature with a Greek name—and she hadn't intended to scare off the couple of friends she *had* had by subjecting them to the full force of her father.

Because far from wanting to show off Aristotle's wealth she had been embarrassed by it—or, more precisely, em-barrassed by Aristotle. Over the years he had become ever more boorish, more overbearing, and the large quantities of alcohol he'd consumed, along with the banquet-type meals that he demanded every night, had not helped his general health or his temper. It had seemed the larger he'd got, the more obnoxious he'd become.

But there had been one person Calista *had* wanted to see—Lukas. He had promised her that he would be there, and that alone had been enough to see her struggling to straighten her unruly tumble of red hair, carefully applying some lipstick and eyeliner and easing herself into a short emerald-green silk dress that had hugged her youthful curves in just the right places. Donning a pair of strappy gold sandals, complete with killer heels, she had been ready to go—or, more importantly, ready for Lukas.

Except he hadn't showed up.

The disappointment had been crushing. Calista's fragile hopes had been dashed every time another group of guests had appeared and he hadn't been amongst them. It had seemed as if more and more people had come, spilling out onto the terrace, laughing, drinking, dancing...

Finally Lukas's father Stavros had arrived, bursting onto the terrace in a highly agitated state, seeking out Aristotle and demanding that he go inside with him so that they could talk in private. Calista hadn't even had a chance to ask him where Lukas was.

In the end she had decided to take matters into her own hands. Suddenly she had no longer just wanted to *see* Lukas. Being with him had become an all-consuming compulsion, taking on a frightening urgency that would have seen her do almost anything to achieve her aim.

Which had turned out to be stealing a car. Or rather 'borrowing it' from Stavros, who had left the keys of his SUV in the ignition. Calista had only had a handful of driving lessons—she had certainly never passed her driving test—but such had been her determination to see Lukas that she hadn't been about to let a little thing like that stand in her way.

Somehow she had managed to negotiate the twisty coastal road without tumbling the car off the cliff and then, armed with a bottle of champagne and what she hoped was a winning smile, she had burst into Villa Helene and found Lukas anxiously pacing the floor.

He had looked astonished to see her. 'Callie! What on earth are you doing here?'

'I've come to find you, of course. It's my birthday, in case you've forgotten.'

'No, I've not forgotten. Happy Birthday.'

He'd said the requisite words but there had been none of his usual warmth, no kiss on the cheek or birthday hug.

Instead he had looked distractedly over her shoulder. 'Have you seen my father?'

'Yes, he's at my birthday party. Which is where *you* should be. You promised, Lukas.'

'Did he seem okay?'

'Yes—why?'

'It's just that he left here in a hell of a hurry and refused to tell me what was going on.'

'Well, he seemed fine to me.' It had only been a small lie. Calista could have had no idea of the consequences. 'He was chatting with Papa. He told me to come and get you.'

'He gave you the keys to his car?' Clearly puzzled, Lukas had obviously tried to work out what was going on. But Calista hadn't gone there to talk about Stavros. Right up until that moment she hadn't been entirely sure why she *was* there, but suddenly she had known with an all-consuming certainty.

She wanted Lukas to make love to her.

She still remembered his look of surprise as she had

moved towards him, the way he had finally smiled when she had flung her arms around his neck, the bottle of champagne still in her hand, clunking heavily against his back. He had laughed, telling her to stop being silly, that she must have had too much to drink, but when he had pulled back to look into her eyes he had seen the truth.

That she wasn't a child any more. That she knew what she was doing. *That she wanted him.*

Even so, he had resisted. But as she had shamelessly pressed her body up against his, chucking the bottle of champagne onto a chair so that she could thread her fingers through his dark curls to pull him closer, she had felt him weaken. And when she had finally claimed his lips, when the first split second of panic and insecurity on her part and complete shock on his had vanished, rapidly melting into desire and then into a burning passion that had seen them stumble backwards onto the sofa, there had been no turning back.

And now they were here again—in the exact same spot. And Calista was horrified to find that the pull of his attraction was just as strong…that she still wanted him every bit as much as she had that June night, even knowing what he had done, even having seen the man he had become.

For Lukas was no longer the warm, funny, laid-back guy she had originally fallen in love with. Along with the dark curls, the mischievous twinkle in his eyes had gone, to be replaced by a cruel stare and a grim determination that sent a shiver down her spine.

And yet still she wanted him.

Her whole body thrummed, all but begging to be his. He was too close—far too close—his head bent so that there was no escaping the searing intensity of his eyes.

'Of course I remember.' She dragged up the words from

somewhere, fighting to find some control. 'But, believe me, I won't be making the same mistake again.'

'So it was a *mistake*, was it? That's an interesting choice of word.'

'Yes…yes, it was.' Heat flared in her cheeks.

'Because, you see, *I* don't think it was a mistake at all.' He lowered his head until their lips were only a fraction apart. 'I think it was all very carefully planned.'

'What do you mean?' she whispered hoarsely against the seduction of his mouth.

'And now it's time for my plan to be put into place. My turn to seduce you.'

'No, Lukas, don't be ridiculous!' She tried to pull back but he held her firm.

'And you know what? I have to say I am *very* much looking forward to it.'

Suddenly his mouth was on hers, his hand pushing up through her hair, grasping the back of her head and holding her to him. She was powerless to escape. Even if she had wanted to. Even if she had somehow managed to harness the will-power that had scattered in all directions at the very first touch of his mouth.

His tongue had easily parted her lips and he continued his relentless assault, kissing her with a force driven by need, by hunger and by the dark greed that had clearly overtaken him. It was totally uncompromising, ruthless in its pressure, devastating in its delivery. And impossible to resist.

Because despite everything—despite the whole damned mess of their lives—Calista felt herself melt, dissolve. Molten heat slid through her, unerringly finding its way to her core, where it settled, pulsing hot and deep and hard and relentless. As Lukas continued his skilful assault she found herself leaning in to him, shuddering with pleasure when his hand lowered to the swell of her bottom, tantalisingly skimming over her buttocks before clenching tight in a blatant display of dominance and possession.

She moaned softly, but it was swallowed by Lukas's mouth as he changed the angle of his head so that he could plunder her mouth more deeply, take her completely. His hand flattened, searing into her, pressing her against the thick swell of him. If she had had any resistance before it vanished completely at the shockingly real evidence of his arousal and the deeply carnal response that ricocheted through her body.

He was moving them now, propelling her eager body backwards, one hand still holding her bottom, the other pressed into the small of her back so that he could steer her where he wanted her to go. Together they stumbled as one entwined unit, until Calista felt the wall behind her and realised she had nowhere else to go. Nowhere else she *wanted* to go. Nowhere except into the drugging dark oblivion of Lukas's power.

For a second their eyes met, and Calista felt her breath stall at the darkly savage look that shadowed his handsome face. But then his mouth was on hers again, and she was lost in the rush of sensual need and the burning hunger that shook her entire body.

She felt his hand move to her thigh, lifting her leg over his hip. She wrapped it around him to steady herself, to expose herself more to the pulsing throb of him. She heard his low growl of approval—or maybe it was victory…she didn't have the capacity to tell. His hand pushed up her skirt, his impatient fingers tugging aside the flimsy fabric of her panties so that he could feel her, slide against her, letting out a grunt, a mirthless sort of half-laugh, as he felt her buck against his touch, her shudder of pleasure immediately starting to build and grow.

Quickly pulling away, he released her from his grasp, letting her leg drop to the ground. Feeling in the pocket of his jacket, he took out a condom, ripping open the packet with his teeth at the same time as shrugging off the jacket and unbuttoning his trousers so they fell to the ground. His boxer shorts went next, before he rolled the condom onto himself with one deft movement.

Then he was all hers again, picking up her arms and moving them around his neck, so that when she clung on, holding him as tightly as he knew she would, he was able to lift her off her feet and wait for her legs to wrap around his waist, as he knew they would, her shoes clattering to the floor.

With his free hand he tugged her panties aside again. Only this time it wasn't his finger that nudged against her, it was the head of his arousal—hot and hard and silky and perfectly positioned to sink into her.

It felt like the most erotically glorious promise in the world.

And a second later that promise was delivered.

Suddenly he was inside her, smooth and hard and deep, filling her body and soul, and her every heightened emotion tuned in to nothing except this one incredible moment. Her mew of pleasure turned into a shriek of need, wordlessly commanding him not to stop, to keep going, faster, deeper, to take her to that place she had feared she would never find again.

Which was exactly what he did. Their bodies banged heedlessly against the wall behind them, until Calista could hang on no longer and, screaming out his name, found her shuddering, hollowing release. She felt Lukas stiffen, his body go into a rigid spasm, before he too gave in to the inevitable and roared his surrender into the tangle of her hair.

CHAPTER THREE

PUSHING HIMSELF AWAY from the wall with the palms of his hands, Lukas caged Calista between his locked arms. He wasn't going to give her any more space—not yet. Not while his breath was still heaving in his lungs, his heart hammering in his chest. He stared down at the top of her head, registering the way her slight figure shook, even though she had returned both feet to the floor, rearranging the skirt of her dress as if to pretend nothing had happened.

Well, it had. He had exacted his revenge.

All the hours he had spent plotting and scheming had finally come to fruition. Exactly as he had planned. Exactly on his terms. All done in the name of retribution.

At least that was what he had told himself. But, in truth, lying awake at night and reliving that fateful evening they had spent together had become something of an obsession. And conjuring up Calista's image had not been purely about revenge—far from it. It had become his guilty pleasure. The soft swell of her breasts, the silky touch of her pale skin, her fresh scent, her sweet breath… The memory had transported him from the dismal walls of his cell to a very different place indeed.

He had lost count of the number of times he had travelled the length of her body in his mind, leaving no part of her soft curves untouched by his attentions, and his own body had responded in the most carnal way as he'd listened to the dry snoring of his cellmate in the bunk above him and cursed to hell the situation he had found himself in.

But now he was free. Now he had achieved his goal.

So why wasn't he feeling it? Why wasn't he getting the satisfaction he so badly craved? Why wasn't it enough?

The sex itself had more than lived up to its promise. Just like the first time, there had been something about the connection between them—the chemistry, the fit—that had taken it beyond just sex to another level, as if they had been created solely for the gratification of each other. Not in an easy, comfortable way—not in the way of friends or gentle lovers—but with a wild, dramatic energy.

Like asteroids colliding in the vastness of space, their paths predetermined by a higher being, they had exploded against one another, set each other alight. And ultimately they had blown each other apart.

He could take her again—right here and now—he felt himself harden at the thought of it. In fact he could take her over and over again—keep her here in his villa until he had got her out of his system once and for all. After all, didn't she deserve it after the way she had treated him?

He was halfway to crazily convincing himself it was a good idea when he stopped, looking down at himself. A thirty-one-year-old man, standing there with his pants around his ankles. A man whose desire for the woman in front of him was dangerously close to being out of control.

Perhaps he needed to take a step back to examine his motives. And fast.

Dropping his arms, he wrenched off the condom and quickly disposed of it, then saw to his pants and trousers, buttoning the waistband as he turned away.

'Do you want that drink now?' He spoke over his shoulder, not wanting to look at Calista for fear of what he might see in her eyes. He needed another drink before he could do that.

'Lukas…?'

She whispered his name like a baffled question. The way she might speak to a person she had come across after a very long time—someone who had changed so irrevocably, so much for the worse, that she couldn't be sure it was him. Well, this was him now. And she had better get used to it.

With two glasses of whisky in his hand he turned, bracing himself for what he would see. But still she got to him, those green eyes of hers instantly finding their target, making the glasses clink together in his hand. It was a look of turmoil—of confusion and hurt and something Lukas refused to acknowledge, let alone try to analyse.

He had made her feel bad. But hadn't that been his intention? He refused to let his conscience prick him now.

Striding towards her, he handed her a glass, noticing the way her hand shook as she reached for it, immediately raising it to her lips to take a sip. The whisky seemed to restore her, and the flush of colour in her cheeks lessened from feverish red to a gentle pink.

'Yes, Calista?' He returned her question with the mocking sarcasm built up over five bitter years. He saw her flinch.

'Whatever has happened to you?'

'Let me see…' He pretended to consider. 'Lies, betrayal, deceit, the death of my father, and…oh, yes, four and a half years rotting in an Athens jail.'

He watched as she shook her head. 'I have no idea who you are any more, Lukas. Do you know that?'

'No? Well, maybe that makes two of us.' He took a deep slug of whisky. 'And yet *still* you let me push you up against a wall and have my way with you. Why is that, do you suppose?'

'I…I don't know.'

'*Still* you come apart at the very first touch of my hands, urging me on as if you can't get enough of me, screaming my name as you take what you so badly need from me.'

This felt better—dishing out the punishment he knew she deserved.

'And you are still dressed in black, your dear, departed father scarcely cold in his grave. It's hardly becoming, is it, Calista? It's hardly fitting behaviour for a grieving daughter.'

'No, it's not. It should never have happened. And, believe me, I regret it now.'

'Oh, I'm sure you do. But that doesn't mean it won't happen again.' He closed the space between them with one menacing step. 'Because you and I both know, Calista, that I can have you any time I want, any place I want.'

He watched the way his words inflicted pain, sawed away at her just the way he'd intended them to. But with the pain came adrenalin, swiftly followed by that glorious flash of temper.

'So *that's* what all this is about, is it?' She threw back her shoulders, her hair rippling down her back. 'You have lured me here to prove that you can have sex with me in some sort of pathetic attempt to get your own back?'

'Something like that.'

She opened her mouth, but for a second words failed her. 'You are a despicable, vile creature—do you know that? A lousy piece of—'

'Yeah, yeah.' He shut her down with a bored flick of his wrist. 'I'm sure I'm all that and more. You can call me all the names you want, if it makes you feel better, but it won't change the facts. And do you know what the worst of it is?'

He let his eyes drift lazily over her outraged face.

'You didn't even put up a fight. I had been looking forward to the challenge, the thrill of the chase, to working out how I was going to win you over. But in the end it was so easy it was almost pathetic.'

It was as if he'd punched her. The shock of his words made her fold at the stomach, reach for the back of a chair beside her to stop herself from falling. Raking in a breath, she pulled herself upright. Then, shooting him one last look of utter revulsion, she turned to go.

With lightning speed Lukas reached the doorway before her, easily barring her way. 'Not so fast.'

'I would like you to move, please.' Her voice was brittle with anger and hurt.

'Uh-uh. You will leave when *I* say so.'

'Is this part of your master plan?' She put her hands on her hips, as if to try and anchor herself. 'To hold me against my will? Keep me here as your prisoner so that you can prove just what a detestable macho bully you have become?'

'And supposing I did?' Lukas arrowed her a lethal look. 'You and I both know what would happen. You would be all over me, Calista. Oh, you might pretend to be outraged…put up a display of resistance in the name of decorum. But in truth I would only have to click my fingers and you would be mine. Writhing beneath me, on top of me, down on me, begging for my attentions and then screaming for more. Look how you behaved just now. It's pitiful, really. I should feel sorry for you.'

Slap.

The weight of Calista's palm connected with the side of his jaw with an impressive crack.

He had seen it coming. He could have stopped it. Spending time amongst some of Greece's most notorious criminals had honed his instincts, taught him to read the situation before it happened. Lukas had always had fast reactions—now they were razor-sharp. But for some reason he had let it happen. For some reason he had wanted to feel it—that burn, that most primitive connection—to show that he was alive. To show that he could get to her. And the sting from her palm *had* set his heart racing.

Calista Gianopoulous—the young woman he hadn't been able to get out of his mind, whose betrayal had consumed him so obsessively that it had become part of the fabric of who he was. Now he had her where he wanted her. Now her humiliation was in his grasp. And he could squeeze as tightly as he wished.

He studied her intently, standing there with her chin held high, her breasts heaving seductively beneath the demure black dress, pulling the fabric tight with every gasping, defiant breath. Her eyes flashed with a green so intense, so wild, it was as if she had been stripped of her sanity.

He should be feeling vindicated, triumphant. But he didn't feel either of those things. Instead he was simply consumed with the overwhelming need to possess her body again. His only conscious thought was how utterly magnificent she looked.

He let a second of silence pass and tried to pull himself together, waiting to see what she would do next—almost willing her to strike him again so that this time he could intercept it, grasp her wrist and feel that physical connection between them again, see where it might lead. But instead she let her hand drop by her side, lowering the tawny sweep of her lashes. The pink pout of her lower lip, he noticed, had started to quiver.

'Resorting to violence, Calista?' He gave a derisive laugh. 'I would never have thought it of you.'

'It's no more than you deserve.'

'No? Maybe not. But if we're dishing out home truths, perhaps it's time that you took a look at yourself.'

Her head came up and there was fear in her eyes. 'What do you mean by that?'

'Oh, come on, Calista, let's drop the pretence. You see, I *know*.'

'Kn…know what?'

If Lukas had had any doubt about her part in his downfall it was well and truly dispelled now. Guilt was written all over her pretty face—not just written, but spelled out in big, bold capitals. She positively shook with it, her hands trembling as she raised them to her mouth, her legs looking as if they wouldn't be able to hold her up much longer.

He let out a grim laugh. 'Do you *really* need me to spell it out for you?'

'Lukas…I…'

'Because I will if you want.'

Taking a couple of steps away he then turned, his eyes pinning her to the spot, as if they were in a courtroom.

'Let me take you back to the night of your eighteenth birthday party. The night my father discovered that the police had boarded one of the ships and found it was loaded with arms. While Stavros was over at Villa Melina, trying to find out what the hell was going on, *your* father dispatched you to "entertain" me. And you did a magnificent job—I have to say that.'

He paused, his whole body brittle with seething contempt.

'Aristotle must have been very proud of you. While my father was suffering a heart attack you were in full seduction mode…while people were mobilising a helicopter to get him to the mainland we were in the throes of passion. And by the time they got him there it was too late.'

'*No*, Lukas.' Calista bit down hard on her quivering lip. 'It wasn't like that.'

'Oh, but it *was*, Calista. It was *exactly* like that. Before my father had the chance to confront yours, to defend himself, he conveniently had a heart attack and died. I bet Aristotle couldn't believe his luck.'

'That's…that's an awful thing to say.'

'It was an *awful* deed.' He mocked her use of the totally inadequate word. 'Not only was he profiting from his vile trade in arms, but when he got caught out he set up *my* father to take the blame. He betrayed his oldest friend. It doesn't get much more *awful* than that.'

'No! I don't believe you!' Calista let out a cry of anguish. 'My father had nothing to do with the arms-smuggling. And he would never have betrayed Stavros.'

'And I don't suppose he was responsible for getting me arrested and banged up in jail for four and a half years either?' Lukas gave a harsh laugh.

'No! I don't believe that either. How would that even have been possible?'

'Remarkably easily, as it turned out. It seems your father had villainous friends in remarkably high places. Or should I say *low* places?'

'No! You're making all this up.'

'Don't insult my intelligence by pretending you didn't know.' Lukas ran a hand over his close-cropped hair. 'No doubt you have tried to dress it up over the years—reshape your traitorous actions to ease your conscience, help you sleep at night. But the fact is you betrayed me in the same way your father betrayed *my* father. You traded your innocence for my guilt. I just hope it was a price worth paying.'

Calista turned away from him, stumbling across the room towards the open doors of the terrace. She clearly couldn't face him—well, that was hardly surprising. He stared at her silhouette, dark against the azure blue of the sea meeting the sky. He could feel the thrum of his pulse in his ears, a tightness in his chest that had yet to be released.

He wasn't done with her yet.

'So you see, *agape mou*, this is my little payback. My turn to let you see what it's like to be used. To be taken advantage of. To have your body violated by someone for their own gain.'

Closing the gap between them, he placed a hand on her shoulder, turning her so that she couldn't avoid the hard, dark glitter of his eyes.

'So tell me, Calista. How does it feel?'

Calista tried to swallow past the shock that was blocking her throat. Her heart was thudding wildly in her chest, her palm still stinging from where it had connected with Lukas's jaw. But her brain had gone into slow motion, struggling to process all the terrible things he had said.

Her father had been responsible for the arms-smuggling scandal? He had somehow pinned the blame on Stavros, and then Lukas? And Lukas thought she was part of the conspiracy plot.

It was all too much. She suddenly felt dizzy, clammy. But at least he didn't know about Effie...

Dragging in a breath, Calista made herself focus on the one small speck of relief amid these horrendous revelations.

For one heart-stopping moment she had thought she'd got it wrong—that he had known all along. She had been on the brink of blurting it out—getting in first before he could use it as some sort of weapon against her. Because that was undoubtedly what he wanted to do—hurt her. But hadn't he already done that a thousand times without even trying?

But, no, it wasn't Effie he was talking about. It was all about *her*—how she had betrayed him, used him, somehow been responsible for his downfall. It seemed he had brought her here solely to humiliate her. Setting a trap to lure her into having sex with him as some sort of payback. And she had leapt right in.

The shame of it shuddered through her, right down to her core, which still throbbed where he had been, where she had let him possess her. No, not *let* him—encouraged him, urged, pleaded, begged… She could hear her breathless entreaties as he had taken her, devoured her, driving into her with a raging desire that had consumed them both, obliterating all reason.

Now her reckless words scraped across her skin like sandpaper. It was bad enough that she had fallen so wantonly into his arms. But for it all to have been a trap…? A wave of sickness engulfed her.

She ran a shaky hand over her forehead, pushing back the hair that was sticking to her forehead. She had to get away from here—back to Villa Melina, where she had left her overnight bag, and then across to the mainland so she could catch a flight back to the UK.

She stepped out onto the terrace, squinting against the light, not knowing whether Lukas would try and stop her, no longer having any idea what he was capable of. She could feel his cruel eyes boring into her, following her every movement.

'Nothing to say, Calista?' he called mockingly after her.

'Only that I'm leaving.' She hurled the words over her shoulder.

'No grovelling apology, then? No promises that you will somehow make it up to me?'

'*I* have nothing to apologise for.' She turned on her heel, determined to fire one last parting shot. '*You* are the one who needs to take responsibility for what you did.'

'Have you not understood a word I said?' He was right behind her now, his dark shadow engulfing her. 'Or are the lies so deeply ingrained that you have started to believe them yourself? I had nothing to do with the arms-smuggling. My father had nothing to do with the arms-smuggling. The only person responsible for the whole deadly disgrace was your father—Aristotle Gianopoulous.'

'No!' Calista spun around, focussing on channelling her outrage rather than having to face the awful prospect of letting herself believe it. Because there *was* that niggle of doubt…that worm of suspicion crawling up her spine.

'*Yes*, Calista.'

'But the court case…' Her voice began to crack. 'Stavros was proved to be guilty… You were proved to be implicated.'

'I've told you—it was all a set-up. A couple of corrupt lawyers, someone high up in the police department, a good forger and a few fake witnesses. You'd be amazed what money can buy if you offer enough of it. And at the time Aristotle was positively awash with it—his hands stained red with the blood money that had passed through them. He'd never get away with it now, of course.' He paused for effect. 'Now I too know the right people, and I am fully conversant with the way these things work. But at the time I was naïve enough to think that justice would prevail.'

Calista covered her face with her hands. She desperately didn't want it to be true, desperately wanted to be able to defend her father. But something about the steady look in Lukas's eyes, the flat, leaden tone of his voice, made it impossible not to believe him.

Suddenly the truth of it struck her like a blow to the chest.

'A pretty performance.' Like a big cat stalking its prey, Lukas held himself very still, as if ready to strike with the killer pounce. 'Are you trying to tell me you didn't know?'

'No, Lukas, I didn't know.' Her voice was barely more than a whisper from behind her hands.

'Sadly the evidence doesn't support your claim.' He inched closer. 'What brought you to Villa Helene that night, if not orders to keep me out of the way?'

'I wanted to see you—that's all.' She let her hands fall from her face, looking down at her feet to avoid Lukas's punishing stare.

'Hmm… I'm afraid you're going to have to do better than that. Much better. Because you were a girl on a mission that night, dressed to kill, and I was your unwitting prey. That whole seduction routine was totally out of character. Why exactly *was* that, Calista, unless you were following your father's orders?'

'I'm telling you—my father knew nothing about it. It was my birthday, and I wanted to spend it with you.'

'But *why*, Calista?'

A beat of silence passed before Calista dragged in a breath. She might as well say it. What did it matter any more? What did *any* of it matter?

'Because I was in love with you, of course.' She uttered the words with a quiet, despondent clarity. 'I'd been in love with you ever since I turned thirteen—before that, even.'

Reaching for her chin, Lukas tipped up her face so that he could see into her eyes, searching for the truth. 'But you were just a kid.'

'And that's exactly what I was trying to do.' She blinked against his stare. 'Prove that I wasn't a kid any more.'

She saw his jaw clench as he assimilated this information, his brows lowering into a considering scowl.

'And you expect me to *believe* that?' When he finally spoke his voice was as dark as the night. 'You expect me to believe that it is pure coincidence that you offered yourself to me at the exact same time as my father was confronting Aristotle? In an exchange so heated, so monumental, that the stress of it took my father's life?'

'Do you know what, Lukas?' Calista let out a jagged breath. 'I really don't care what you believe.'

All she could think about was getting away while her legs still had the ability to carry her. Somehow she had to process the shock of her father's guilt, but she couldn't do that here—not on top of the shame of what had just happened with Lukas, not with him standing over her like this, all dark, menacing force.

Turning away, she set off across the terrace, intending to go around the side of the villa and make her way up to the road so she could find her way back to Villa Melina. If she was lucky she might come across Petros in his battered old car. If not she would walk. Anything would be better than staying here to be verbally abused by Lukas.

But she had taken no more than a couple of steps before Lukas had headed her off, blocking her way with the powerful wall of his honed physique.

'Not so fast.' His hair shone blue-black in the sunshine, sharp shadows highlighting the stark angles of his cheeks and jaw. 'I'm not done with you yet.'

'Well, I'm done with *you*. Get out of my way.'

'You didn't really think I would fall for that pathetic *"but I loved you, Lukas"* routine, did you?'

Calista flinched, her body hollowed out by the cruelty of his words. '*Loved,* Lukas. Firmly in the past tense. Now I loathe your guts.'

'Ah, that's more like it. Now we're getting to the truth. And, for the record, I know exactly why you're so desperate to get away, to run back to the cosy little world you have created for yourself in England. *Guilt*, Calista. No matter what you say, how you try and wriggle out of it, your guilt is written all over your face.'

He was right, of course. Calista knew—the guilt he was talking about—she could feel it gripping the muscles of her face, clenching her abdomen. But it wasn't the kind of guilt Lukas thought it was. It had nothing to do with luring him to have sex with her. It was about Effie, and the very real consequences of that fateful night. The fact that Lukas had a daughter he knew nothing about. She knew she would have to tell him. Just not here—not now. Right now she didn't have the strength.

'Perhaps you're mistaking the look on my face.' Still she fought to stand her ground. Because fighting for survival was what she did. What she had always done. 'It's not guilt I feel—it's shame.'

'Guilt, shame—call it whatever you like.' He moved closer, as if scenting a kill. 'Either way I am pleased to see you accepting responsibility for your actions.'

'Oh, I do. I can't ignore what just happened between us—much as I would like to. Because that's the shame I'm talking about, Lukas—the shame I feel for having let you touch me, violate me.'

'Ha!' He let out a cruel laugh. 'So I *violated* you, did I? Was that before or after you wrapped yourself around me, screaming my name in pleasure?'

'I *hate* you, Lukas!'

'Yeah, yeah—so you keep saying. Who are you trying to convince? Me or you? Because you should know that I don't give a damn.'

His eyes narrowed dangerously, glinting as some new idea occurred to him. Calista felt a fresh wave of alarm.

'Or is there another reason you're so desperate to get away, to pin the blame on me?' His voice was as sharp as the edge of a blade. 'Are you seeing someone? Is that it? Do you have a boyfriend, a lover?'

Suddenly the air stilled. The sun that was beating down on them was stiflingly hot. The force of his question felt like a hand around her throat.

'If I did it would be none of your business.' Calista twisted her head as if to dislodge the imaginary grasp, clinging on to her defiance like a shield to protect herself.

'Is *that* why you can't look me in the eye, Calista?' His voice became ever more urgent, more demanding. 'Is *that* why you're so desperate to apportion blame, to make me out to be the bad guy?'

'No. That has nothing to do with it.'

'Then tell me it's not true.'

Clasping hold of her wrist, Lukas held it in his grasp.

'Very well.' She indignantly tried to snatch back her hand, but Lukas held on. 'I do not have a lover, Lukas.'

'A boyfriend, then? A partner of some description?'

'No, none of those things. Now, kindly let me go.'

'What, then? Tell me. Because I can *see* it, Calista. I can see it in your eyes.'

Calista hesitated. She could feel the moment closing in on her, weighing down on her with leaden pressure. Suddenly there was no escape.

'I do not have a lover, Lukas.' She summoned the words from deep inside her, where the truth had lain dormant for so long. 'But I *do* have a child.'

'A child?' He dropped her arm as if it were made of molten metal. 'You have a *child*?'

'Yes.' She watched as the shock that had contorted his handsome features settled into a brutal grimace of stone. 'I have a four-and-a-half-year-old daughter.'

She paused, sucking in a breath as if it might be her last. *This was it.*

'And so, Lukas, do you.'

CHAPTER FOUR

LUKAS STARED AT Calista in frozen, abject horror. No, it couldn't be true. He couldn't *possibly* have fathered a child.

But of course he could. They had had sex—unprotected sex, he recalled with blistering clarity. At the time he had been too astonished, too blown away by the turn of events, even to think about taking precautions. And since that evening he had never given it another thought.

He reined in the emotions that were ricocheting around his head like gunfire and forced himself to think logically. Calista was a scheming, manipulative piece of work—he already knew that. So what was to say she wasn't making this up? Perhaps there was no daughter, or if there were the child wasn't his?

But, much as he wanted to believe either of those versions as fact—any version that meant this was all a pack of lies—the contortion of Calista's face said it all. She looked sick, visibly paling beneath her creamy white skin. She looked as if she wanted to stuff the reckless words back down her throat.

She looked horrified that she had just revealed a deeply hidden truth.

'Sit down.' He pulled out a metal chair, physically lowering her into it before she collapsed in front of him or toppled into the pool, which was only a few feet away.

'So, let me get this straight. You are telling me that I have fathered a child?'

'Yes.'

He saw her painful swallow.

'And you have only just seen fit to tell me about this?'

'You have been in prison, Lukas.'

'Don't you think I *know* that?' Fury roared in his voice…his hands clenched into fists. Calista flinched. 'But that was no reason not to tell me that I was a father.'

'I thought it best to wait…until you were released.'

'Did you, indeed?' Sarcasm ripped through his voice. 'Best for whom, exactly?'

Calista lowered her head.

'So who else knows? Your family? Aristotle? I'm sure he must have enjoyed being a doting grandfather to my child.'

'No, I didn't tell him. I've told no one.'

Lukas hoped this was true—for Calista's sake.

'So what's her name, this daughter of mine?'

'Effie.'

'Effie?' He snarled the name.

'Short for Euphemia.'

'And where is she now?'

'At home in England.'

'Does she know about me?'

He fired the questions at her as they came into his head, not caring in the least about the way they were making Calista wince, shrink into herself.

'I've told her that you live in a different country. Too far away to visit.'

'Well, we will just have to put that right, won't we?'

Raking a hand through his hair, Lukas let his eyes travel over the smooth turquoise water of the pool before swinging them back to Calista's lowered head. His decision was made.

'I want to see her. As soon as possible. I want my daughter brought over here right away—right now.'

'What?' She looked aghast.

'I will have the jet put on standby.' He checked his watch. 'She could be here by this evening.'

'This evening?' Calista gaped. 'You're not seriously expecting me to fly to the UK, pick up Effie and then fly back with her, just like that?'

'No.'

'Well, thank God for that.' Her shoulders dropped.

'*You* are going nowhere. I am keeping you here until I have seen for myself that my orders have been obeyed and the child has been safely delivered to me.'

'Don't be ridiculous!' she shrieked with alarm. 'Effie is four years old. You can't put her on a plane by herself.'

'My staff will take care of her.'

'No, she would be terrified! I won't allow it!'

'I'm not asking for your permission, Calista.' His voice roared around them. 'Your shameful deceit means that I have already missed four and a half years of my daughter's life. I don't intend to miss any more.'

'Well, think of Effie, then.' Real panic clawed at her throat. 'Please! She's never even been on a plane. She would be completely traumatised by having to travel on her own with a group of strangers. You don't know what she's like…how sensitive she is.'

'You are right.' He saw the flicker of relief on her face, savouring the moment before he twisted the knife still further. 'I *don't* know what she's like.' The look of relief vanished as she realised where he was going with this. 'And whose fault is that?'

She lowered her eyes, then suddenly sat up straight

as a thought occurred to her. 'Anyway, Effie can't travel abroad—she doesn't have a passport.'

'Is this another of your lies, Calista? Because if it is…'

'No, it's the truth.'

'Very well.' The synapses in his brain were firing wildly as they adjusted to every new piece of information. 'You and I will fly to England together. That way you can introduce me to my daughter personally.' He met Calista's horrified gaze full-on. 'I will tell my pilot to have the jet ready within the hour.'

Despite his best efforts, by the time they finally pulled up outside Calista's London home dawn was breaking on a new day. The journey had been frustratingly slow. Whisking Calista from Thalassa to the mainland by helicopter hadn't been a problem, but his private jet had had to undergo a series of safety checks before it had been fit to fly.

Apart from a brief period when it had been impounded by the police, before being found legally to belong to Lukas, it had been languishing for years in a hangar at Athens airport, with no one thinking to service it. Lukas had not taken this news well. Now he was out of prison things were going to change—*that* was for sure.

Pulling up outside Calista's house in the car he'd hired from the airport, he craned his neck to take a look. It seemed reasonable enough—a three-storey Victorian terrace on a quiet narrow street.

Beside him Calista was fumbling in her bag for her keys. She had barely spoken to him on the journey here, nor during their long wait at the airport in Athens, or the night flight to London. Not that he cared. He had needed the space to get his head around this astonishing development. To try and work out how to proceed.

Calista had eventually agreed to his suggestion to use

the bedroom on the plane, but by the look of her she hadn't had much sleep. Dark circles shadowed her eyes.

'We need to go in quietly. Effie will still be asleep. And Magda.'

Magda, he had managed to ascertain, was some friend of Calista's who shared the house and helped look after Effie. He would be checking *her* out too, making sure she was a suitable person to be around his daughter. Although it was probably a bit late for that. Bitterness had him clenching his fists.

Calista let them into a hallway that was cluttered with bicycles, a child's scooter and a pile of unwanted post.

'Follow me—we're on the top floor.'

'You don't own the whole house?'

'I don't *own* any of it, Lukas,' she hissed over her shoulder as she climbed the stairs. 'I rent the flat. And I can only afford to do that because I share the cost with Magda.'

Lukas remained silent, straining for the sound of imaginary violins. If she imagined he was going to feel sorry for her she had another thought coming. Besides, he was annoyingly distracted by the sight of her bottom as she climbed the stairs ahead of him. Firm and rounded, it moved seductively beneath the tight jeans that she had changed into when she had collected her stuff from Villa Melina.

'Here we are.'

Inserting the key in the lock, Calista pushed open the door and switched on the light in the narrow corridor. She led him into a kitchen. For a second they stood, staring at each other. Lukas felt too big—out of place in this small but tidy space.

'Cal?' A muffled voice came from down the corridor. 'Is that you?'

'Yes,' Calista answered in a hushed whisper, then turned to Lukas. 'I'm going to speak to Magda. Do you want to make yourself some coffee or something?'

She opened a cupboard and quickly took out a bag of ground coffee, thrusting it into his hands and pointing to the cafetière next to the kettle.

'Do it quietly.'

Lukas filled the kettle, looking out over the London rooftops at the pigeons as he waited for it to boil. Twenty-four hours ago there had been no way he would have expected to find himself here.

'Hello.'

A small but very clear voice had him spinning his head around. A young girl with tousled dark curls and sleepy green eyes was standing in the doorway staring at him.

His daughter.

'Who are you?' She looked at him curiously.

'Lukas. Lukas Kalanos.' Lukas stepped forward with his hand outstretched, then dropped it again, feeling inordinately foolish.

'I'm Effie.'

'Um…yes, I know.'

'That is actually short for Euphemia.' Deciding that this man was clearly no match for her social skills, Effie took the initiative. 'I'm four and a half. How old are you?'

'I'm…er…thirty-one.'

Effie stared at him, as if considering such a great age. 'Mummy is twenty-three and Magda is twenty-three too. But Magda is older than Mummy because her birthday comes first.'

'Right. Um…do you want to go and get your mummy?'

'I can't do that, silly. Mummy has gone to Greece to say goodbye to my grandpa. I've never met him. He's dead. D'you want some juice?'

Dragging over a chair, she climbed up to open the fridge door. She was peering inside when Calista reappeared.

'Effie?'

'*Mummy!*' Slamming the fridge door closed, she launched herself at her mother, winding her skinny legs around Calista's waist and hugging her tight. 'You're back! I've missed you *so* much!'

'I've missed you too, my darling.'

'I have actually been brave, though. You can ask Magda.'

'I'm sure you have.'

Kissing the top of her head, Calista extricated herself from the arms and legs and set her down on the floor, holding on to her hand very tightly.

'I see you've met Lukas.'

'Yes. He's thirty-one.'

'Yes.' Calista shot him a glance. 'I expect you're wondering what he's doing here.'

'Maybe he's lost?' Effie offered helpfully.

'No, Effie, he's not lost. He's come here to meet you.'

'Oh!' Effie looked at him with renewed interest.

'The thing is, Effie…we have something to tell you. Why don't you come here and sit on my lap?'

Scraping back a chair, Calista sat down, bringing Effie with her. Lukas was struck by how close they were—not just physically, although with Effie's arm hooked around her mother's neck and her little pyjama-clad body pressed right up against her a whisper couldn't have got between them—but emotionally. They seemed bonded together, like a single unit.

Under different circumstances it would have been a delight to behold. Now it just made Lukas feel even more of an outsider. Even more incensed by the situation.

'The reason Lukas has come here is because we want to tell you...'

Effie's big green eyes looked from one to the other.

'The thing is... Well, the fact is, what we have to tell you is...'

'I am your father, Euphemia.'

Lukas's voice boomed around the small room, sounding far louder, far more aggressive than he had meant it to. He watched Effie's eyes widen with astonishment before Calista pulled her close, her own eyes blazing with anger.

'*Lukas!*'

'What?' Pushing himself away from the worktop, he drew himself up to his full height. 'The child needs to know.'

In his determination to take control of the situation, not to be painted as the bad guy, it seemed he had managed to do just that. With Effie hugged against her chest Calista started to rock slightly, as if trying and take away the pain. But Effie was struggling to be freed and, finally extricating herself, she stared at him, tucking her hair behind her ear in a gesture that so mimicked Calista it took his breath away.

'Is he telling the truth, Mummy?' Clearly she didn't trust him any more than her mother did.

'Yes—yes, he is, darling. I wish we had broken it to you a little more gently, but Lukas *is* your daddy.'

Sitting up straighter now, Effie reached for the comfort of Calista's hair, twiddling a curl between her fingers. 'Will he be coming to live here with us and Magda?'

'*No!*' Calista and Lukas chorused together.

'Lukas lives in Greece—where I have just been.'

'With my dead grandpa?'

'Well, sort of...'

'Was he very sad that Grandpa died too?'

'Um…tell you what—why don't you run along and get some clothes on? Then we can all have breakfast together and we'll talk about everything. How about that?'

Effie had barely left the room before Calista rounded on Lukas, eyes blazing. 'What the *hell* do you think you were doing?' She snarled under her breath. 'We agreed we were going to break it to her gently and then you go and blurt it out without any warning.'

'*You* agreed. Besides, you were taking too long about it.'

'Too long! I'd barely had two minutes with her!'

'Well, it's done now. She seems fine with it.'

'And you'd *know*, would you?'

'I know she needs to be told the truth. You have deceived her for long enough.'

'It wasn't deceiving her—I was protecting her.'

'Don't give me that. The only person you were protecting was yourself. It's time the child learnt some decent values that don't involve a web of lies.'

'How *dare* you criticise the way I have raised my daughter?'

'*My* daughter too, Calista. Just remember that.'

'Here I am!'

Effie reappeared in the doorway. She was wearing a stripy tee shirt, some sort of skirt made from pink netting and red wellington boots.

'Well done, darling.' Calista turned to smile at her. 'What would you like for breakfast?'

'I've got a better idea.'

Suddenly Lukas was desperate to get out of the stifling atmosphere of this cramped flat.

'Why don't I take us all out for breakfast?'

'Ooh!' Effie's eyes shone with surprise. 'Can I have a doughnut?'

'You certainly can. As many doughnuts as you like.'

Effie looked from him to her mother and back again, not able to believe her luck. When Calista remained silent a huge smile spread across her face.

Lukas puffed out his chest. Round one to him and the doughnut. It might only be a small victory, but it felt good.

'Faster! Faster!'

Calista looked across the small park to where Lukas was pushing Effie on the roundabout. Her daughter had her head thrown back and her eyes closed, her dark curls streaming out behind her. To the casual observer they might look like any father and daughter, enjoying some time together in the sunshine, but Calista could see the hitch in Lukas's shoulders, the tightness in his jaw as he whirled the roundabout round with one strong hand, the other thrust deep into the pocket of trousers.

Breakfast had been taken at the outside seating area of a café in Hyde Park. Effie's choice, as it was close to a children's playground and the boating lake—two of her favourite things. Effie had valiantly fought her way through two and a half doughnuts and Lukas had watched in smug silence, presumably waiting for Calista to react—which she had refused to do.

She wasn't going to get involved in petty point-scoring. Not when there were so many much bigger issues at stake. And besides, if he carried on whizzing Effie round at that speed there was a good chance that nature would score the point for her—preferably all over his immaculate designer suit.

She took another sip of her third cup of coffee. This was so bizarre—it simply didn't feel real. The three of them, here in a London park, with Lukas knowing about Effie and Effie having finally met her father. This enormous guilty secret had been in the back of her mind for so long, gnawing away at her, that it felt like a living part of her.

She had always known that at some point she was going to have to tell them both the truth. It was one of the many things that could keep her awake on those nights when her troubles seemed to pile in and sleep refused to come.

Now it had happened. But as she gazed across at the two of them Calista could feel no sense of relief, no lifting of the burden she had carried for so long. Instead a dark thread of dread wound its way through her, pulling ever tighter as she studied the two of them together.

Lukas had changed so much from the funny, easy-going, generous young man she had fallen in love with. He was a different person now. Cold, calculating, ruthless. A man who would stop at nothing to get what he wanted.

The roundabout slowed to allow a young boy to get on, and Calista saw the boy's mother—or nanny, maybe—eyeing Lukas, moving closer to say something, giving a little laugh and tossing back her head.

She heard Effie's bossy little voice taking command of the situation as the boy scrambled on. 'You will have to hold tight. My daddy's a fast pusher.'

My daddy. Was it really possible that Effie had accepted Lukas just like that? And, if so, why did that only increase Calista's sense of deep unease?

A few minutes later Effie came running back towards her, her eyes shining, the little boy close behind her.

'Can I go on the slide with Noah, please?'

'Yes, that's fine. I'll watch from here.'

The two of them scampered off and Calista raised her eyes to see the woman with Noah looking at her with disappointment. They smiled politely at one another as Lukas came to sit beside her and the woman turned to follow the children.

'More coffee?' Lukas looked round to call the waitress over.

'No, thanks. In fact we should probably be thinking about leaving.'

'Have plans for the day, do you?' He smiled at the waitress as she took his order for another espresso, making her blush prettily. But his words were weighted with sarcasm.

'And what if I do?' Calista leapt to the challenge. 'Effie and I *do* have a life, you know. A good one, in fact. I have made sure of that. I have done everything in my power to ensure that she is happy and secure, that she wants for nothing.'

'Apart from a father, of course.' Lukas stirred sugar into his coffee and raised the cup to his lips.

Calista scowled.

'Luckily I am in a position to be able to rectify that now.'

'Well, that's as may be.' Calista pursed her lips. 'But don't start thinking you can come storming in and take over our lives. Effie is settled—happy. The last thing she needs is a lot of disruption.'

Slowly replacing his cup on the saucer, Lukas raised heavy-lidded eyes. 'The sooner you start to realise who calls the shots around here, the better it will be for all of us.'

'*I* call the shots.' She could feel a flush creeping up her neck—indignation mixed with righteousness and something horribly like panic. 'Where Effie is concerned, *I* make the decisions.'

'Uh-uh. Not any more, *thespinis mou*.'

With her heart thumping painfully in her chest, Calista turned to see Effie waving madly at them from the top of the slide. She waved back and then Effie pointed at Lukas.

'She wants you to wave.' She forced the words through gritted teeth.

Lukas raised a hand and a purposeful Effie launched herself down the slide.

'So what is it, this life you are so determined to protect?' Lukas's all-seeing gaze swung back in her direction.

'I've told you—it's just a normal life, me and Effie.'

'Tell me about it. Do you work? Does Effie go to school?'

'Effie has just finished pre-school. And I'm about to graduate, as a matter of fact.'

'Graduate in what subject?'

'I've been training to be a nurse for the past three years.'

'A *nurse*?' Clearly this had taken him by surprise.

'Yes.' On safer ground now, Calista pushed back her shoulders. She was proud of her achievement. 'It's been hard, trying to fit it around Effie, but luckily I met Magda. She's on the same course as me and she's been such a huge help. I couldn't have done it without her.'

'So you work where? In a hospital?'

'Not yet. I have to wait for my certificate to come through before I can apply for jobs. I'm going to try and co-ordinate it so that I start work in September, when Effie begins full-time school.'

This information was met with narrowed eyes, absorbed, processed and filed away.

'And Greece? Thalassa? You say Effie has never even been there?'

'No.'

'Why *is* that?'

'Because there has been no need. Greece is no longer a part of my life. I would never have gone back myself if it hadn't been for my father's funeral.'

'And yet you gave our daughter a Greek name?'

'Well, yes.' Calista wasn't sure herself why she had done that. Somehow it had just felt right. 'But that's only because it's a pretty name.'

'Nonsense. You are half-Greek… Euphemia is three-quarters Greek. You both have Greek blood running through your veins, pumping in your heart—it makes you who you are. Do you *really* believe you can dismiss it as easily as that?'

'Well, no, but—'

'Greece will always be a part of your life, whether you want it to be or not. And it will certainly be a part of Effie's. *I* intend to see to that.'

A chilling calm settled over his handsome features, pulling the skin taut against his cheekbones, holding his handsome head high.

A trickle of dread seeped into Calista's veins. 'What do you mean by that?'

'I mean that I have no intention of missing any more of my daughter's life. I am going to take Effie back to Thalassa with me.'

'No! No, Lukas, you *can't*…'

'Yes, Calista, I can. Either she comes on her own or you accompany her. The choice is yours. But either way my daughter *will* return to Thalassa with me.'

CHAPTER FIVE

As the helicopter blades whirled to a stop Calista watched Lukas flick off the controls and unbuckle his seatbelt. Less than twenty-four hours had passed and they were back at Villa Helene, just as he had decreed.

He had won.

There was no way she would have let Effie travel to Thalassa without her—the idea was unthinkable. So instead she had tried to reason with him, suggesting they paid a visit at a later date, or that perhaps Lukas could stay in London for a while and get to know his daughter slowly. But Lukas had had none of it. Even Calista's trump card—that Effie didn't have a passport—had been swept aside, and a visit to the passport office had been arranged and completed with scary efficiency.

So there had been nothing for it. Calista had had to agree.

She looked down at Effie, who was sound asleep in her arms. The journey to Thalassa was a long and tiring one when you were only four, and Effie's huge excitement had finally given way to sleep on the final leg of their journey. She had been nestling into her mother's lap and closing her eyes before the helicopter had even left the mainland.

Now Lukas turned to face them, his expression closed, businesslike.

'I have instructed Petros and Dorcas to make the villa

ready for us. I imagine Effie will want to be put straight to bed?'

Calista nodded. 'Yes, she's exhausted.'

Petros and Dorcas. They were working for Lukas now? How had that happened? And what on earth would they make of the fact that she and Lukas had a child together? A child that she had failed to mention when she had been reunited with them on the day of her father's funeral.

Calista had known this lovely couple for ever, Dorcas had served as a surrogate mother for her during the long hot summers on the island, doing a much better job than her own mother had when she was alive and providing a much-needed pair of loving arms after Diana had died.

They had been the only constant members of staff at Villa Melina. Aristotle's irascible nature had meant that over the years employees would come and go with depressing regularity. And latterly it had been just them, his reduced circumstances meaning that Aristotle hadn't been able to afford any more staff even if he had managed to find any. It occurred to Calista that he probably hadn't even been paying them.

But Thalassa was their home—they had moved here at the same time as Aristotle and Stavros. Calista had worried what would happen to them now that Lukas owned Villa Melina, the island…everything. She wouldn't have been surprised to find he had sacked them on the spot, banished them from Thalassa. He was certainly ruthless enough. But it seemed that not only were they still here on the island, they were working for their former enemy.

She extricated herself from the seatbelt that was wrapped around her and Effie, trying not to wake Effie up as Lukas opened the helicopter door on their side.

'Here—hand her down to me.'

Strong arms reached out to take Effie from her, and reluctantly Calista passed her daughter over before clambering down herself. She noticed the trusting way Effie clung onto her father, nuzzling into him in her sleep as he strode purposefully towards the illuminated villa.

The front door opened and there was Dorcas, silhouetted against the light, her hands clasped to her chest at the sight of Lukas with Effie in his arms.

'Come in, come in—you must all be so tired after your long journey.'

'*Kalispera*, Dorcas.' Calista felt decidedly awkward, embarrassed to be turning up like this with a child no one had known about—not even Aristotle, Effie's grandfather.

But as Dorcas flung her arms around her in the warmest of hugs she felt her anxiety evaporate.

'You are a *bad* girl.' Speaking in English, Dorcas repeatedly kissed her cheeks, clearly delighted. 'You never tell me you have a beautiful daughter. And you and Lukas! Whoever would have thought such a thing?'

Ushering them into the villa, she fussed about, issuing instructions to her husband, who was shaking hands with Lukas, peering curiously at the sleeping bundle in his arms. But when Petros turned to Calista she could see that he too had a broad grin on his face.

'We have made one bedroom into a nursery for little Effie. Petros has painted the walls pink for her—haven't you, Petros?—so that she will love it.'

Petros nodded proudly. But Calista felt an increasing unease. *A nursery?* This was all starting to sound alarmingly permanent.

'Well, thank you, Petros.' Squashing down her fear, Calista reached to take Effie from Lukas's arms. 'If you show me which room it is, I'll put her straight to bed.'

'Of course. Follow me.'

Bustling ahead, Dorcas led the way, opening the door

into a room that stopped Calista in her tracks. It had been transformed from what she remembered as a relatively spartan guest room into a pretty nursery, with white-painted furniture, pink and white striped curtains, a child-sized bed, even pictures on the walls of fairies and Disney princesses.

'You like it?' Dorcas whispered expectantly.

'It's lovely, Dorcas. But how did you get it all done so quickly?'

'Lukas say there is no time to waste. It must be done by the time you arrive. So Petros engage a small team of decorators from the mainland. Lukas want everything to be perfect for his daughter.'

Did he indeed?

Her unease was rapidly turning into something more like alarm.

Together she and Dorcas undressed Effie and gently lowered her into the pristine bed, pulling the covers over her and tucking her beloved teddy in beside her. All the time Dorcas was exclaiming in hushed whispers, saying what a beautiful little girl she was, as pretty as her mummy but with her daddy's dark curls. Closing the shutters, Calista almost had to pull her out of the darkened room, leaving the door slightly ajar behind them.

'So are you working *here* now, Dorcas? You and Petros?' Calista was still having trouble figuring this out. She wanted to know what the arrangement was before they rejoined the men.

'Yes. Lukas say he would like us to work for him now.'

'And you are okay with that? I mean after everything that has happened?'

'More than okay, *agapite mou*. Petros and I, we have known Lukas for a very long time, ever since he was a baby. We never believed him to be guilty of such a crime.'

'Really?' Calista stared into the time worn face of kindly woman. 'Then my father... does that mean... did you have suspicions about him, about his involvement?'

'It is not our place to have suspicions, my dear. Now that the Lord has taken the judgement is in His hands.'

Calista swallowed the lump in her throat. 'So, are you living here now? At Villa Helene?'

'No—this is the wonderful thing. Lukas say we can stay at Villa Melina for as long as we want. For ever, even.' The relief was obvious in her voice. 'He say the place is ours.' She turned to look at Calista, suddenly upset. 'I am sorry, Calista—this is your home I talk about. I say to Lukas, *Are you sure you don't want to make Villa Melina your family home?* But he say no—that you will live here, in Villa Helene.'

Now the blood in her veins turned to ice. 'He said *what*, Dorcas? *Who* will live in Villa Helene?'

'All of you—you, Lukas, and dear little Effie, of course. Petros and I couldn't be happier for you. To have a family here on Thalassa again—not just any family, but a Kalanos and a Gianopoulous, joined together like this. Well, it is a dream come true, it really is. To think that Effie will be growing up...'

But Calista could no longer hear Dorcas over the roaring of blood in her ears. A wave of sickness was threatening to knock her legs from under her.

This wasn't just a visit for her and Effie—a few days' stay on Thalassa, even the couple of weeks that Calista had just about been prepared to agree to. Lukas intended that they should stay here *for ever*. No, not *they*—Effie. He had made it quite clear that Calista could do whatever she liked. That she was of no interest to him. It was Effie he wanted. He had as good as kidnapped her.

Well, they would see about that.

Marching back into the living room, Calista squared her shoulders, ready for a fight.

But Lukas met her fierce gaze with infuriating calm. 'Everything all right?'

'No.' Calista spat the word at him. 'Everything is most certainly *not* all right.'

Behind Lukas, Petros was laying the table in front of the window. He looked up with the cutlery in his hand. 'Excuse me? You do not like the room?'

'No—yes. Petros, it's not that. I *love* the room.'

'Your little girl? She no like it?'

'Effie is sound asleep. But I'm sure she will love it when she wakes in the morning.'

'That is good.' Petros went back to laying the table.

'I think what Calista is *trying* to say, Petros, is thank you very much—to you and Dorcas—for doing such a fantastic job in such a short time.'

All relaxed reasonableness, Lukas quirked a dark brow at Calista.

Calista could have hit him—could have cheerfully wiped that smug, supercilious smirk off his face with a hard slap. Except, of course, she had already tried that and it had achieved absolutely nothing. Apart from exposing her lack of control and somehow reinforcing *his* control.

'It was our pleasure, wasn't it, Petros?' Dorcas came bustling through from the kitchen with a casserole dish in her hands. 'Now, come and sit down, both of you. I'm sure you must be very hungry.'

Calista looked from Dorcas to Lukas and back again, suddenly panicky at the idea of being left alone with him. 'Are you and Petros not joining us?'

'Me and Petros? Goodness, no! Whatever are you thinking, Miss Calista?' Dorcas laughed at her. 'I make this especially for you and Lukas. Your first meal here together as a couple…a family.'

'Thank you, Dorcas. I'm sure it will be delicious.' Lukas interjected smoothly. 'Now, you and Petros must go—you have already done far too much for us. Calista and I will be fine from now on. Won't we, Calista?'

'Fine.' Calista spoke the word through clenched teeth. But the door had hardly closed behind them before she launched into her attack. 'Would you like to tell me what the *hell* is going on?'

Pulling the cork from a bottle of wine, Lukas glanced at her briefly before casually pouring two glasses and handing one to her.

'Going on…?' Now he was serving up the meal—dolloping moussaka onto two plates and placing one before her. 'I wasn't aware that anything was "going on". Please—do sit down.'

Calista thumped into her seat. 'Why do Dorcas and Petros seem to think we will all be living here, as a family? What have you said to them?'

He took a forkful of moussaka, chewing and then swallowing before deigning to reply. 'I suppose Dorcas may have got ahead of herself. She has a rather excitable nature.'

'I'll say she has. You need to put her straight, Lukas. Tell her that Effie and I are only here for a short holiday. That we're returning to the UK.'

'I was actually referring more to our situation—me and you. It would seem that Dorcas has got it into her head that we are a couple. An understandable mistake, I suppose, especially for an old romantic like her.'

'Well, yes—obviously she's got that wrong as well.'

'Aren't you going to eat anything?' Lukas waved at her plate with his fork. 'It's really very good. I can see now how your father got so fat, with Dorcas cooking for him.'

Sticks and stones. Calista refused to rise to the bait.

'So are you going to tell her or shall I? That we're not staying, I mean.'

'You can tell her what you like, Calista. You can *do* what you like. Neither thing is of any interest to me. But Effie will be staying here, with me. For as long as I say.'

'No!'

'Yes, Calista.'

'But that's not what we said. It was to be a short holiday—a fortnight at the most. You agreed.'

'Did I?' Lukas continued to eat his supper, totally unperturbed. 'Perhaps that was a small deception. And don't bother to look so surprised. You are hardly a stranger to deceit yourself.'

'That's not fair!'

'None of this is *fair*, Calista. Having my father die from a heart attack wasn't fair, being thrown into prison for four and a half years wasn't fair, and not being told I have a daughter wasn't fair. But now I intend to redress the balance. From now on things are going to be done *my* way. Starting with Effie staying here on Thalassa with me.'

'No! You can't take your grudge against me and my father out on Effie.'

'I have no intention of taking *anything* out on Effie. Quite the reverse. I look forward to building a relationship with her, being a part of her life.'

'But you can't just *keep* her here!'

'I think you will find that I can. Oh, we can do it the hard way, if you like—lawyers, courts, injunctions—but I would advise against it if I were you. Because I *will* win. I can assure you of that. I'm sure I don't need to remind you that we are on Greek soil and Effie is three-quarters Greek.'

'And *I'm* sure I don't need to remind *you* that you have been in prison for arms-smuggling!'

Calista regretted the words before they had left her mouth. The look of thunderous fury on Lukas's face curdled the contents of her stomach.

'No, Calista.' His voice was a low, mean drawl. 'You do *not* need to remind me. And, believe me, I intend to clear my name. But in the meantime I have money and I have contacts. To try and fight me would be very foolish indeed. I am confident the Greek authorities would look favourably on my custody application.'

'Custody application?' Calista thought she might pass out. 'You intend to fight for *custody* of Effie?'

'Maybe… I'm not sure yet.' Lukas picked up his glass and swilled the wine around. 'That all depends.'

'On what?' She could hear the panic in her voice, strangling her vocal cords.

'On you. On how you behave. If you persist in being difficult, obstructing me, fighting me every step of the way, then you will leave me no alternative.'

'So what do you expect me to do? Hand over my daughter to you? Agree to all your terms and conditions without question? Roll over and let you do whatever you want?'

'Well…' The air between them suddenly thickened like syrup. 'If you're offering…'

'I am not offering *anything*.'

'No?' A lazy smile curved his lips. 'That's a shame. Because if you were to roll over and let me do whatever I wanted, I guarantee you would enjoy it.'

'Stop this, Lukas.'

'As would I, of course. Because despite everything you've done, despite who you are, I find that I still want you.'

'Well, I don't want *you*.' She threw the words back at him far too fast, and with far too much passion. And they elicited totally the wrong response—a low, primal groan of amusement.

'No? Of course you don't.' His arrogant smirk belied his words.

Calista looked away, refusing to dignify his facetious comment by attempting to challenge it. Besides, there was a danger she would only dig herself a deeper hole.

'So, you see, how we proceed is up to you. You allow Effie to stay here, accept that she has just as much right to be with me as she does with you, and we can keep everything amicable. No court cases, no custody battles—at least for the time being. Just a civilised arrangement between the two of us.'

Calista bit down on her trembling lip. She felt anything *but* civilised. She felt like a wild, raging beast. One that would do anything to protect its young. But she also knew that to try and fight Lukas on this would be extremely dangerous. She had no doubt that he would carry out his threat to take her to court for custody of Effie. And that he would most likely win.

'It seems that I have no choice.' Her heart thumped heavily in her chest.

Lukas shrugged.

'But I'm not leaving Effie here on her own. If she stays, I stay too.'

'As you wish.'

'Very well.' She sucked in a breath. 'I will agree to Effie remaining here, to us both remaining here, at least for the time being. But this is not for ever, Lukas. Effie starts school in September. Obviously we need to be back in the UK by then.'

'I'm very glad that you have decided to see sense.'

Lukas's eyes slowly travelled over her heated face, down her throat and across her chest, lingering on the swell of her breasts beneath the pale blue tee shirt. Instantly Calista felt her nipples harden, and she folded her arms to cover them up. Lukas responded with the quirk of a dark eyebrow.

'And who knows?' he drawled idly. 'Maybe it doesn't have to be so bad. Maybe we can find some interesting ways to keep each other entertained.'

'I am here strictly for Effie. That's all. Do I make myself clear?'

'Crystal-clear. But, unfortunately for you, like crystal I can see right through you.' His lips twitched with a deadly smile. 'And do you know what I see? A woman fighting her sexual desires. A woman who already knows it's a losing battle because deep down she wants me. Much more that she will ever admit.'

'You are *wrong*, Lukas Kalanos. You are nothing but conceited, arrogant and delusional.'

'Am I, indeed?' Lukas put his head on one side, his eyes glittering as dark as the night. 'Well, it takes one to know one.'

Lukas watched his fiery companion through narrowed eyes. She might be fooling herself, he thought complacently, but she wasn't fooling him. Despite the hot-headed rant, her determination to take him to task, the abject denial that he meant anything to her, Calista's body had given her away. And what was more she knew it. The way those rounded breasts had hitched beneath the tight tee shirt, her nipples hardening at his provocative words, had infuriated her as much as it had delighted him.

Lukas had never had any trouble attracting women. The combination of his dark good looks and easy charm had made him a magnet for members of the female sex ever since he'd hit puberty. Even during his time in prison the few women who had worked there had been putty in his hands—the social workers, the prison librarian, the cooks.

It had been well known that the Kalanos charm bought special privileges, and rather than complain about it the wiser inmates had kept in with him in the hope of picking up the scraps.

But something about Calista's obvious arousal was special. Maybe it was because of the way she tried to deny it, or because it showed he had some power over her.

Or maybe it was just because it was her.

He had always known that she would never leave Effie alone with him. They came as a pair—that much was obvious. Telling Calista that he didn't care whether she stayed or not had been a bluff he'd been sure of winning. Because he *did* care. He was beginning to realise that he cared too much. He felt a creeping sort of awareness that she was somehow invading his thought processes, influencing his judgement.

It did nothing to improve his temper, and at the same time sent his libido soaring off the scale.

He picked up the wine bottle, gesturing towards Calista's glass but only refilling his own when she shook her head. His eyes travelled to the wall behind them—the scene of their crazed lovemaking session only a couple of days before. No, they hadn't made love—they had had sex. Fast, furious, frantic sex.

At the time he had been too riddled with lust to examine what he was doing, but afterwards he hadn't experienced any of the sense of satisfaction he had expected to feel. Instead he'd been left with a vague feeling of distaste.

Not for Calista, or for what they had done—never that. Far from regretting their coupling it had just made him want more…much more. Far from dulling the hunger that clawed inside him, it had turned it into a dangerously powerful craving. The distaste was for the way he had behaved. His motives, his twisted reasoning…

Lukas took a gulp of wine, searching his brain to try and find some justification for this unwanted attack of conscience. All those years without a woman in his bed was bound to have messed with his head. Especially when he considered the lifestyle he had enjoyed prior to walking into Ms Gianopoulous's trap.

As a young man in his twenties he had enjoyed himself, making the most of his looks, his wealth and his power. He'd loved woman, and women had loved him—as the string of beauties who had graced his bed would be able to testify. He fully intended to pick up where he left off... make up for lost time. But first he had to get this infuriating woman out of his system.

Plus there was the fact that he was now a father. Perhaps bedding a succession of women was no longer appropriate. Perhaps it was time to be more responsible. He certainly wouldn't want his daughter faced with a variety of different lovers over the breakfast table. Not that that had *ever* been his way. He had always preferred the anonymity of a hotel room—valued the freedom of being able to close the door and walk away. He'd believed in keeping his private life private.

Unlike Aristotle, of course.

Lukas looked across at Calista, who was pushing her food around her plate, her cheeks still flaming with resentment. Aristotle had had no qualms about parading his latest conquests around in front of his daughter—or anyone else, for that matter.

That was if you could call the succession of increasingly greedy and desperate women that he'd taken to his bed 'conquests'. The older he'd got, the more obese he'd become—and the more obvious it had been what those women were after. And it certainly hadn't been his body. Or his bonhomie or his grace.

He had never been faithful to any of his three wives. Each marriage had ended in misery or, in the case of Calista's mother, tragedy. And Calista had grown up with that. A different woman in residence every time she returned to Thalassa for the holidays…sometimes more than one. She had witnessed the terrible destruction Aristotle had wreaked on her own mother, ending in her death. And yet still she had been prepared to do his bidding—prepared to debase herself and betray Lukas. Still she had stood by Aristotle's grave with a single lily in her hand, the dutiful daughter to the end.

Frowning, Lukas put down his fork. None of it made any sense to him. Unless, of course, Calista was telling the truth about that fateful night. Unless it really *had* been pure coincidence that she had come to him—not to trap him but because she'd wanted him to make love to her.

No. He refused to be fooled. No doubt the old adage was true—blood was thicker than water. Look at how he felt about Effie. Three days ago he hadn't even known he had a daughter. Now she was already shaping his life, changing his future. There was certainly no way he would allow *her* to be treated the way Aristotle had treated Calista. No way would he let Effie be subjected to such cruel indignity. The very thought of emulating Aristotle Gianopoulous in any way turned his stomach.

Because little Effie had already won his heart.

With a stab of surprise Lukas realised there was nothing, absolutely nothing he wouldn't do for her—to protect her, to keep her safe. He intended to be a very permanent fixture in her life.

The question was, what the hell was he going to do about her mother?

CHAPTER SIX

'Wake up, sleepyhead.'

Calista opened her eyes to see her daughter clamber-ing into bed beside her. She was clutching a half-eaten *koulouri* in her hand—a ring-shaped bread roll, covered in sesame seeds that were now being scattered liberally over the bedclothes.

'You need to get up.'

Calista drew Effie towards her, breathing in her gor-geous little girl smell.

'Good morning, my darling. Did you sleep well?'

'Yes.' Effie squirmed impatiently in her arms. 'But you need to hurry up. We've got a busy day.'

Calista propped herself up on one elbow, pushing the hair out of her eyes. Checking her watch, she was surprised to see how long she had slept—a deep, drugging sort of sleep that had left her brain feeling slow to catch up. But the harsh reality of where she was kicked in soon enough.

She had spent the night in the largest bedroom in the villa, Dorcas having obviously decided to allocate it to the happy couple, filling it with fresh flowers and scented candles. She had even scattered rose petals over the bed—something which had produced a sardonic smile from Lukas when he had opened the door and ushered her in, suggesting she might like to make this room her own be-

fore turning to disappear down the corridor. She could still
see some of the crumpled petals caught in the bedding.

Now she was faced with the reality of what she had
agreed to—staying here on Thalassa with Effie, at least
for the foreseeable future. But what choice did she have?
She had no money, no contacts. She didn't doubt that Lukas
had plenty of both, and the memory of the smug, self-sat-
isfied way he had informed her of that still managed to
send her blood pressure skywards.

But then *everything* about Lukas Kalanos sent her blood
pressure rocketing skywards. And not just her blood pressure either. Her common sense, her self-control, her temper
and her sanity all seemed to cut loose from their moorings
when she was around him—not to mention her libido. Just
the sight of his lean, muscular body, the athletic way he
moved, the tilt of his head or the quirk of his dark brow
was enough to see her fighting to hang on to her composure, to counter the extraordinary effect he had on her.

'Come on, Mummy. We are going on my daddy's boat.'

Closing her eyes against an inward groan, Calista
opened them again to see her daughter's excited face.

A day on Lukas's boat—that was all she needed. Sailing
was Lukas's passion—something he had skilfully turned
from an indulgent hobby to an extremely successful business by investing in a fleet of luxury yachts and renting
them out. Most of his business was conducted from the
mainland, but at any one time there had always been a few
of his magnificent, sleek vessels anchored off the coast of
Thalassa. As a youngster Calista had loved to watch them
glittering in the sunshine, gently rocking on the azure sea.

She had loved to watch Lukas too, who had never been
happier than when he was clambering barefoot over the
deck of a boat or sailing into the wind, his dark curls blow-
ing madly in the breeze and the spray of the sea on his

face. She knew that he preferred sailing the smaller, more intimate yachts in favour of the floating gin palaces—remembered him telling her that it made him feel more at one with the sea, more alive.

'Quickly, Mummy. Get dressed!'

Taking in a deep breath, Calista pushed back the covers and swung her legs over the edge of the bed—but there she stopped. The image of Lukas, smiling and relaxed, his eyes dancing with the exhilaration of a day's hard sailing, had lodged in her mind and refused to be shifted. He had had such a zest for life back then—had been so spirited. So free.

And that freedom had been taken away from him.

She stretched her arms out to her sides to steady herself, bunching the sheets in her hands. For the first time she thought about what it must have been like for him—*really* thought. For Lukas, of all people, to have been deprived of the outside world, the sun and the sea, the rolling waves and the whistling wind. To lose his freedom for four and a half years...

It must have been torture for him—pure torture. Which would have been bad enough if he'd been guilty. But what if he *had* been wrongly convicted? What if all this time he had been innocent...?

Calista put her fist in her mouth, biting down on her knuckles. Ever since her world had exploded so dramatically she had been using Lukas's 'crime' as a shield to protect herself, to keep her strong. She couldn't help it that she had fallen in love with him. Fallen into a deeply painful, fathomless love that could never be cured. But Lukas was not the man she'd thought he was. He had been convicted of a heinous offence, as an accomplice in a shockingly immoral crime.

Finding out she was pregnant with his child might have

all but finished her—felled her on the spot—especially as she had been so young, so alone. But it hadn't. She had pulled through—more than pulled though. She had done a great job of raising her daughter single-handedly, as well as completing her nursing training and making sure there was always enough money to keep them both fed and clothed. Somehow she had drawn strength from Lukas's disgrace. From the knowledge that she was on her own. That she was totally responsible for both her own life and her daughter's.

And during her darkest hours—those miserable lonely nights when she had thought the dawn would never come—she had forced herself to remember what Lukas had done, the man he really was. Used his terrible crime as a prop to keep her upright.

But now that prop had gone—had been kicked away from under her. Now she was left sprawling on the floor by the shockingly painful truth. *Lukas was innocent.* She knew it in her heart—maybe she had always known it.

Which meant that her own father had been as guilty as sin.

'Mummy!' Effie slipped her hand into hers, attempting to tug her to her feet. 'Daddy is waiting for us.'

Heading to the bathroom, Calista felt as if her legs were made of lead. She would have to talk to Lukas—face up to the truth, no matter how painful it was. If nothing else, she owed him that.

Shading her eyes from the glare of the sun, Calista watched her daughter splashing about in the turquoise sea. Effie and Lukas were some distance from the boat, but instinctively Calista trusted Lukas to keep her safe. Effie couldn't yet swim—it was one of the things Calista had been meaning to teach her, but the thought of London's municipal swimming pools hadn't held much appeal. Now a couple of brightly coloured water wings were keeping her afloat as Lukas patiently explained to her how to kick her legs, holding her under the tummy and getting showered in the process.

'Well done—nearly there.' His voice carried clearly across the water. 'Now, see if you can swim across to me.'

Taking a few strokes away, he turned and waited for her to splash towards him, her little legs kicking wildly behind her.

'Yay, you did it!' Catching her up in his arms, he held her aloft to squeals of merriment, before safely tucking her beside him to swim back to the boat.

Calista quickly returned to her book.

'Did you see that, Mummy?'

The boat started to rock as first Effie and then Lukas climbed aboard.

'I was swimming all by myself.'

'That's brilliant, darling.' Calista made a show of closing her book and putting it down beside her, to prove that she was now in charge. She rose to her feet. 'Now, come on—let's get you dry.'

Moving in for a hug, Effie pressed her chilly wet body against Calista's sun-warmed skin, sending a rash of goose-bumps skittering all over her. She felt Lukas's merciless gaze travelling over every bare inch of her. Concentrating on pulling the water wings off Effie's skinny arms, she took hold of her hand and made her way towards the cabin.

But Lukas was in the way.

'Excuse me.' She tried to squeeze past him but still he refused to move, meaning she had no alternative but to raise her eyes to the magnificence of his body, to take in all his masculine glory. Just as he had planned she would.

Wearing an extremely snug pair of black trunks that

left little to the imagination, he stood before her, the epitome of glorious manhood, tall and bronzed, with sculpted muscles in all the right places. Droplets of water glittered on his skin and in his tightly curled chest hair, running in rivulets down his long, shapely legs and pooling at his feet on the varnished wood of the deck.

Calista swallowed. She had already sneaked a look at him when he had taken a graceful dive into the sea, before swimming round to the steps at the back of the boat to help Effie into the water. That had been more than enough to get her pulse racing. This blatant display of rampant masculinity was in danger of sending it into overdrive.

Mustering what little will-power she had left, she stepped deliberately round him, chin in the air, and led Effie down into the relative cool of the cabin.

'Next time I'm going to do it without the water wings.' Teeth chattering, Effie let herself be towelled dry. 'Daddy says I'm a fast learner.'

'I'm sure you are.' Rubbing at the dark curls, Calista kissed her daughter lightly on the nose. 'But you don't have to call him Daddy, you know. Not if you don't want to...not if it seems too soon. It's quite all right to call him Lukas.'

'That's okay, I like calling him Daddy. He says that the Greek children call their daddies Bampas. That's funny, isn't it?' She wrinkled her little nose happily. 'Is that what you called *your* daddy?'

No, Calista thought silently. She had never called Aristotle anything other than the formal word—Pateras. The more affectionate Bampas had seemed wrong when addressing the short-tempered, irascible, rather frightening figure that her father had been.

'And the word for yes is *nai*.' Effie was still chattering on as Calista tugged dry clothes onto her. 'That's funny too. Daddy said I must learn how to speak *all* the Greek words—then I can talk to anyone.'

'Well, we'll see.' Calista tried to disguise the tension in her voice. 'You won't need to speak Greek when we go back to London, will you?'

'S'pose not. I like it *here*, though.' Giving a yawn, Effie twisted a damp curl around her finger.

'Yes. Holidays are fun, aren't they?' Calista persisted. 'But going home will be good too. I bet Magda is missing us.'

'Hmm…' Effie nodded thoughtfully. 'P'raps she could come here too?'

'No, I don't think so darling. Now, d'you want to have a little nap?'

To her surprise Effie nodded and, lifting her arms, let Calista carry her through to one of the cabins, where she gently laid her down on the bed. Her eyes closed almost immediately.

Calista looked around her, tempted to stay down there rather than go back on deck and have to face Lukas again. But that would be cowardly—and she was not a coward. Reluctantly she climbed up into the sunshine.

Lukas had his back to her, squatting on the bow of the boat, doing something with some ropes.

Hearing her approach he turned. 'Effie okay?'

'Yes, she's fine. She's having a sleep. Must be all this fresh air.' She attempted a light-hearted laugh.

'A child can never have too much fresh air.'

Calista pursed her lips. So he was the expert now, was he? She watched with feigned indifference as he lithely rose to his feet and came towards her.

'Can I get you anything?' He bent to open the cool box that held the remains of their picnic. 'More food? A beer?'

'No, thanks.' She was already regretting the glass of

chilled white wine she had had earlier. What with that and the sun, her head was starting to swim a little. 'I think I'll just sit under the canopy here and read my book.'

'As you wish.'

Arranging herself on the comfortable cushions in the shade, Calista opened her novel. She heard the hiss of gas as Lukas took the cap off a bottle of beer, and raised her eyes to see him moving about with the bottle in one hand, checking on the winches of the rolled up sails, swinging under the beam to get to the back of the boat. The sea slapped gently on the sides. A seagull squawked overhead. She closed her eyes…

Lukas eased his tall frame onto the cushions beside Calista. She was sleeping peacefully, and a strand of red hair was caught on her slightly open lips, moving as she breathed. He let his eyes travel slowly over her body, lingering on the swell of her breasts under the small emerald-green triangles of her bikini top. Two strips of bare skin were just visible beneath, peeking out from where she had shifted and dislodged the fit of the bikini.

Lukas's throat moved. The temptation to run his finger over the exposed pale flesh was almost too much to resist. Or to run his tongue over it…then release the string ties around her neck and push the fabric away, so that his mouth could give her warm, full breasts the attention that they so blatantly deserved… He felt himself harden painfully beneath his trunks.

Tearing his eyes away, he looked out to sea to the hazy horizon way in the distance. He knew if he put his mind to it he could have pretty much any woman he wanted. So why was he torturing himself by lusting after this one? How had Calista got to him like this, so that his whole body thrummed for her…ached for her? Why was it that suddenly no other woman held the slightest interest for him?

He had been her first lover, of course. Could that explain this ludicrous obsession? He would never forget the moment they had both realised that there was no going back. That first exquisite moment of penetration when Calista had gasped for air, holding herself rigid as he had eased himself so carefully into her. The way she had clung to him, urging him in further, deeper, until she had taken all of him.

She had been so passionate, so aroused, so totally convincing. Over the years he had told himself that it must have been an act. But now… Now he wasn't so sure. Now when he looked into those remarkable green eyes of hers he saw lots of things—anger, hurt, fear, defiance. But not betrayal. And when he had laid bare Aristotle's guilt before her she had looked genuinely devastated. Broken.

Lukas raked a hand through his damp hair, narrowing his eyes as he watched the white sails of the boats in the distance. He wanted to move on, to stop agonising over the past and concentrate on the future. A future that would now most definitely involve his daughter.

Because Effie was the one truly miraculous thing to have come out of this mess. He still found it hard to believe that he had fathered a daughter. And one as undoubtedly special as Effie. He got a buzz every time he looked at her…every time he thought about her.

But there was something far less agreeable he was struggling to come to terms with. Something that had grown from an annoying niggle into a monster that refused to go away. He might have been Calista's first partner, but how many lovers had she had since? Five years had passed—ample time for her to have taken up with any number of suitors.

The very thought of her with another man—any man—boiled the blood in his veins, made his hands shake with impotent fury.

At least there didn't appear to be anyone on the scene at the moment. He'd had a quiet word with Effie, casually mentioning Mummy and her boyfriend in the same sentence, and had been mightily relieved when she had just looked at him in puzzlement.

That didn't mean there wasn't someone in the background, of course, but the way Calista had given herself to him on the day of the funeral—with such need, such greed, even, like a starving woman—suggested that there wasn't. Or if there had been he was now history. Or he damned soon would be. Because Calista was going to be his and his alone for as long as he deemed fit. To do with as he deemed fit.

Had he always intended this? Lukas wasn't sure. But the decision was made now. He wanted Calista. Not just once—clearly that had done nothing to slake his thirst—and not even for the occasional casual sex, albeit amazing. He wanted her in his bed every single night. And, more than that, he was going to make sure that she wanted *him*.

Hearing her stir, he turned back to look at her, watching as she moistened her lips with the tip of her tongue, moved back against the cushions. Leaning forward, he picked up the book that was resting on her stomach, the open pages sticking slightly to the suntan lotion on her skin. He had watched her applying it earlier on, rubbing it onto shoulders dusted with freckles, then her chest, down her arms and the flat of her stomach. He had been itching to take over, to smooth the lotion over her himself, to push aside the scraps of fabric and let his hot fingers slide across her breasts, her buttocks, to the places that were hidden from the sun...

But too late—or maybe just in time—she had finished. Snapping the cap of the bottle shut and shooting him a look of such haughty disdain it had made him smile despite himself.

Now she opened sleepy green eyes. He was close enough to see a split-second swirl of desire before alarm and then indignation took over.

'Lukas!' She scrabbled to push herself upright, sweeping her hair away from her face. 'You made me jump.'

'Guilty conscience?'

'No.' Immediately she was on the defensive. 'What are you doing, anyway? Why are you watching me?'

'Just admiring the view.'

'Well, don't.'

Calista didn't know which Lukas she found the more intimidating—the fiercely brutal and vengeful one she had been met with at her father's funeral, or the arrogantly sarcastic one who was deliberately letting his gaze rake over her now.

Neither of them represented the Lukas she had once known. The one she had fallen in love with. And yet she *had* caught a glimpse of that man. She had seen it in the way he was with Effie—so gentle, so patient. She had even seen it earlier on today, when he had been at the helm of the yacht, shooting her an unexpected smile as they had tacked fast into the wind, the pleasure of doing something he so clearly loved making him forget himself for a minute. Forget how much he hated her.

Calista felt her body begin to tingle beneath his scrutiny, the thrum of desire starting its traitorous beat. She needed to put a stop to it.

'Is there any water in the cool box?'

'Sure.'

Pushing himself to stand with one lithe movement, Lukas retrieved a bottle of mineral water and passed it to her. Calista took several deep gulps and looked down at herself. Even in the shade her skin was starting to turn pink— she burnt so easily it was ridiculous. She was glad that Effie wasn't going to have the same problem. She had inherited her father's colouring, albeit several shades lighter.

Feeling restored by the water, she started to get to her feet. 'I'm just going to check on Effie.'

'No need. I just did. She's still asleep.'

'Oh, right.' Calista sat back down.

There had been a cold inflexibility in Lukas's voice— as if he expected her to challenge him, or as if he was waiting for something. His eyes held hers for a couple of seconds before he stretched himself out on the cushions beside her, lying on his side with one arm under his head to prop him up.

He looked magnificent, even from the quick sideways glance that was all she would allow herself. She refused to give him the satisfaction of ogling that beautiful body, those tanned, honed muscles that screamed to be admired, to be touched. Because that was what he wanted. For some reason he seemed determined to taunt her with his perfect physique.

Calista pulled up her knees and hugged them to her chest. The more blatant his display, the more she was determined to cover herself up.

A couple of highly charged seconds ticked by, Lukas owned the silence by doing absolutely nothing. Calista drew in a breath. There was one sure way to counter the sexual tension that he was deliberately stoking between them. Much as she hated to fling herself into the pit of misery that had been caused by her father, she knew that she had to.

She cleared her throat. 'Lukas, I've been thinking.'

She shifted nervously on the sun lounger, forcing herself to meet his gaze. Lukas quirked a dark brow in response.

'What you were saying about my father...it's true, isn't it? He *was* responsible for the arms-smuggling.'

'Yes, Calista. It's true.' He stared at her, scanning her face with an intensity that stripped her bare—as if he could read her mind, see her more clearly than she could see herself.

'And Stavros, he had no part in it, did he?'

'None whatsoever.'

'And neither did you.'

With a very slight tilt of the head, his reply was given in the glittering blackness of his eyes.

An agonising second ticked by. The yacht rocked gently from the wake of a fishing boat heading out to sea. Calista wished that she was on it. That she could leap aboard and be chugged further and further away from this awful situation.

Instead she wrapped her arms around her knees more tightly, letting her hair fall over her face to cover her shame as she stared down at her painted toenails.

'I'm so sorry, Lukas.' It came out as barely more than a whisper.

'Sorry?' Lukas repeated the word, rolling it around his mouth as if it were made of stone. 'I hardly think "sorry" makes up for what happened.'

'Well, no, but...'

'Makes up for taking away my freedom, blackening my name, ruining my life.'

'No. I mean obviously nothing will make up for that.'

'For killing my father.'

That brought Calista's head up.

'That's not fair.' She lifted her hair from the nape of her

neck to try and cool herself down. 'Stavros had a weak heart—it said so in the autopsy report. He could have died at any time.'

'And yet he died after a furious row with Aristotle.'

'Even so...'

'Still defending him, Calista? That monster of a father of yours?'

'No—'

'Because if so I suggest you open your eyes and take a long, hard look at the man who sired you.'

'I don't want to. I don't need to.'

'Because if you did you would see exactly the sort of vile creature he was.'

'I know he did a terrible thing, Lukas.'

Close to tears, Calista covered her face with shaking hands. Admitting her father's guilt was excruciatingly painful but she knew she had to face up to it before she could move on. Face up to Lukas too, who shimmered quietly beside her like some sculpted bronze Greek god. But she wasn't responsible for Aristotle's crime. Despite what Lukas thought, *she* had done nothing wrong. She had to make him see that.

Taking a deep breath, she removed her hands from her face to see Lukas staring at her, his expression inscrutable. 'I swear to you, I had no idea what he was involved in. You *have* to believe me.'

'Okay.' There was a beat of silence before Lukas gave a small shrug. 'I believe you.'

'Good.' Calista felt her shoulders drop. 'Then you accept that I played no part in the conspiracy?'

'If you say so.'

'I do.' On a firmer footing now, Calista straightened up, pushing back her shoulders. This was the point when some sort of small apology from him might be called for.

Clearly that wasn't happening. 'Much as I regret what happened, I am not guilty of my father's crimes.'

'No.'

Lukas lifted the arm that was resting over his waist. For a moment Calista thought he was going to touch her, make some sort of conciliatory gesture, but instead he rubbed his hand around the back of his neck.

'But you are still guilty of betraying me.'

'No, I've told you—'

Lukas raised his hand to silence her.

'You accepted your father's version of events without question. You were prepared to believe that I was capable of such a heinous crime without even speaking to me. *That's* the betrayal I'm talking about.'

'I was wrong—I know that now.' She bit down on her lip. 'I'm so sorry I didn't trust you.'

'I don't want your wretched apologies!' Suddenly his voice was harsh, bitter. 'I don't give a damn what you think about me now.' He shifted the length of his body fractionally, his eyes boring into her. 'You still don't get it, do you?'

Calista stared back at him.

'Your father may have been responsible for getting me locked up, but in believing his lies you denied me the knowledge that I was a father. You stole from me the first four and a half years of Effie's life.' He shook his head in disgust. 'And if we hadn't met at the funeral—if I hadn't dragged it out of you—I still wouldn't know of her existence.'

'No, I *would* have told you. I was *going* to tell you.'

'Really? When, exactly? When she was eighteen? Twenty-one?'

'I had to think of Effie. To put her first...do what was best for her.'

'And what was "best for her" was to deprive her of her father?' His voice leached scorn. 'Thanks for that, Calista.'

Calsita cast about, desperately looking for a way to counter his contempt. 'For your information, life these past few years hasn't exactly been easy for me, you know.'

'Is that so?' He stared at her with obvious distaste. 'Have *you* been sharing a cell with an armed robber who would slit your throat for an ounce of tobacco?'

'Well, no, but…'

'Spent the one hour a day that you're allowed outside marching round a prison courtyard? Had your every movement recorded by security cameras?'

'No, of course I haven't.'

'Then don't you *dare* start telling me you have had it tough.'

'I can't undo the past, Lukas!' she cried out, her voice heavy with the weight of shame. 'I don't know what else I can say.'

'Nothing—there is *nothing* you can say.' There was a long beat of silence. 'But maybe there is something you can *do*.'

Reaching forward, he trailed a finger along her jawline, running it over her lips.

Calista felt her heart stutter, her eyes widening as his head lowered until his mouth was barely a centimetre from her own, his breath a whisper of soft promise.

'Maybe there is a way you can start making it up to me…'

And with one lithe movement he swung his magnificent body over hers.

CHAPTER SEVEN

HIS BODY HOVERED above her, braced by locked arms and toes that were pushed firmly into the padded lounger. Calista held herself very still, achingly aware of the corded muscles of his biceps, the hard-packed torso that was only inches away from her trembling body. She could feel the heat radiating off him, prickling over her, finding its way unerringly to her inner core. His breath fanned over her face, making her eyelashes flutter close until his lips touched hers and the familiar bolt of electricity made them shoot open again. One touch—that was all it took. One graze of his lips for her to shake with need. For her to fall apart.

Bending his elbows, Lukas lowered his body, adjusting the angle of his head very slightly until he deemed it just right and increased the pressure of his lips. It was a coaxing, persuasive kiss, gloriously sensual but leaving her in no doubt as to who was in control here—who had all the power.

For a split second Calista tried to fight against it, holding her facial muscles taut, her lips tight. But it was hopeless—and they both knew it. With a giddy rush of surrender she parted her mouth and immediately Lukas was there, giving a low growl of approval as his tongue found hers, tangling and stroking, hot and hard and heavy as he devoured her, stoking the familiar madness that gripped them both.

Calista thrust her hands into his hair, spreading her fingers so that she could hold him to her, seal them together. Sliding one arm under her back, Lukas flipped them so that she was on top of him, their mouths still fused by that burning, bruising kiss. The skin of their near naked bodies was erotically sealed all the way down—and then Lukas peeled them apart, his hand spanning her hips and moving her down until he had her where he wanted her: pressed firmly into his groin, where the length of his arousal welcomed her with its might and its power and its mind-numbing promise.

Calista heard herself moan, the wondrous feel of him shooting through every cell of her body, making her want him inside her so badly she had to stop herself from begging for it, right there and then. Instead she rocked against him, increasing the pressure, heightening the gloriously erotic sensation.

Lukas growled his approval.

The thin fabric of their swimwear was in danger of melding to their skin with the blistering heat they were generating. Raising herself up on one arm, Calista slid a hand between them, running it down the rippling muscles of his chest until she found the straining fabric of Lukas's trunks, where she traced the steel length of him. Lukas gave a primal shudder and suddenly his hands were all over her, pulling at the ties of her bikini behind her back and around her hips, the scraps of fabric falling apart in his hurry to possess her, his animal craving every bit as desperate as her own.

'God, Calista…' He ground the words into her shoulder. 'Look what you do to me.'

His mouth was on hers again, his hands skimming over

the warm skin of her naked buttocks, dipping into the valley between, his fingers sliding down to where she wanted him most.

'I can't get enough of you.' He groaned through the kiss. 'I will *never* get enough of you.'

Was that a threat or a promise? Calista didn't know—she didn't care. Her only conscious thought was that she wanted him so badly she feared she might explode with it.

But they had to find some control. Effie was asleep in the cabin below. They had to act responsibly.

As if Calista had somehow willed it to happen they both heard the sound at the same time. A sort of scuffling noise beneath them and then a clear little voice calling out.

'Mummeee!'

Hurriedly pushing herself away from Lukas's body, Calista looked down at herself—at the bikini top that hung loose around her neck, the bottoms that were just a scrap of fabric between her legs.

'I'm coming, darling. Just hang on one minute.'

After fumbling to retie all the fiddly strings she hastily adjusted the triangles of her bikini top to cover nipples stiff with longing, breasts still heavy with desire. Only then did she raise her eyes to Lukas, to see that he had been watching her every move. She caught the intensely dark gleam in his eyes—almost fierce, but with a hint of vulnerability—before he moved away, searching for a pair of board shorts to cover his considerable arousal.

And only just in time. A second later a tousled-haired head appeared at the top of the cabin steps, blinking into the sunshine.

'Here you are.' Effie looked curiously from one to the other, as if they were both being quietly assessed and found to be guilty. 'I didn't know where I was when I woke up.'

'Didn't you, darling?' Calista went to give her daughter a hug. 'It's okay. We're still on the boat.'

'I know that *now*!' She rolled her eyes before a broad grin spread across her pretty face. 'Can I go swimming again?'

'Um…yes, I don't see why not. I think I'll go in with you this time.' The idea of cooling water was suddenly very appealing.

'Yay! And Daddy too?'

'Maybe in a bit.' Lukas moved so that he was standing behind Calista, laying a hand on her shoulder and dipping his head so that he could whisper in her ear. 'To be continued, Ms Gianopoulous.' His breath fanned softly against her hair.

Calista swallowed. But with Effie tugging on her hand she was mercifully spared having to come up with any sort of reply.

Leaning back in his chair, Lukas stretched his arms behind his head. He had been working in his office all afternoon and he needed a break, but picking up the reins after being away for so long meant a lot of hard work and commitment.

His luxury yachting business, Blue Sky Charters, had been ticking over nicely in his absence. His staff had stayed loyal to him and, even though it hadn't grown the way it would have done had he been there in person to oversee it, it was a very thriving concern. He had been lucky, he supposed—though 'lucky' was hardly a word he would use—that the authorities had made no claim on his personal business. There was no connection between that and G&K Shipping, which had been decimated by the scandal.

But Lukas fully intended to see *that* concern succeed

again too, in honour of his father. He had already managed to buy back seven super-tankers. Nothing like the fleet of eighty they had had before Aristotle Gianapoulous had seen fit to blow the business sky-high, but it was a start. He also intended to clear his name—and, far more importantly, his father's name. He wanted the world to know just who had really been responsible for the vile trade in arms. Who the *real* guilty party had been.

Leaning forward, he closed the lid of his laptop. The villa was very quiet and still in the early evening sunshine. Too quiet, he realised. It was over a week since the three of them had arrived at Villa Helene, and Lukas had become used to having Calista and Effie around—to hearing the patter of Effie's feet running along the marble-tiled floors, her shrill little laugh echoing through the open-plan rooms. Even when he should have been relishing his solitude he found himself listening out for them. Just as he was doing now—waiting for sounds to indicate that they had returned from their trip to the beach.

Calista had stuck her head around the door after lunch, to announce that she was taking Effie down to the small sandy cove that was only a few hundred yards from the villa, approached by some rickety old wooden steps. By the tone of her voice it had been quite plain that he wasn't invited. Not that that would have stopped Lukas if he'd wanted to join them, but he had work to do. Besides, it appeared he and Calista were playing some sort of game. Over the past week she had seemed determined to hold him at arm's length, going out of her way to put distance between them whenever she could and finding excuses never to let them be alone together for any length of time.

Lukas had deliberately gone along with it, refusing to react. Being unreasonably reasonable just to wind her up. He'd decided he was prepared to play the long game. Well, long*ish*. In point of fact, watching that pertly rebellious body moving around the villa was driving him crazy—killing him. But in a perverse sort of way he was enjoying it. And knowing with increasing certainty that she was faking her casual indifference only added to the sexual tension that hummed steadily between them.

Lukas looked at his watch. Gone six o'clock. He had thought they would be back by now—although he knew that Effie always pleaded to stay longer when she was told it was time to leave the beach.

Seeing how much Effie obviously adored being here on Thalassa was a source of great satisfaction to Lukas—not least because of the way it made her mother squirm. On the one hand Calista was obviously happy that her daughter was having such a great time, but she also felt she had to keep reminding her—and him—that this was nothing more than a holiday, that they would shortly be returning to London.

Well, they would see about that. Lukas hadn't fully formulated his plans yet, but when he had he would be making quite sure that Calista abided by them. One thing was certain: now he had discovered Effie he had no intention of letting her go again.

Because he adored everything about this little girl. She had stolen his heart from the very first moment he had laid eyes on her, back in the kitchen of Calista's flat. She was a complete delight—the most unexpected joy to have come out of such terrible circumstances. Lukas would do anything to keep her close. And that included taming her flame haired mother.

Although 'taming' wasn't the right word. Lukas didn't want Calista tamed. He loved that wild, fiery streak of hers. The green eyes that flashed with fire as she glared at him, the way her hair whipped around her face, the nostrils that flared with contempt and the obstinate defiance that held her chin high. She was as maddening as hell, but somehow he kept coming back for more punishment.

And it *did* feel like punishment, the way she had got to him. Like a burr against his skin, she was impossible to ignore, to dismiss. For the sake of his own sanity Lukas had decided he would concentrate only on the sexual attraction between them. That was more understandable. And infinitely more pleasurable.

He would concentrate on the free spirit behind that feisty façade, the vibration between them whenever he took her in his arms, the abandoned, almost feral way she responded. As if overtaken by the force of nature. As if there was nothing she wouldn't do for him or let him do for her. That was what he would focus on. Because Lukas had never experienced a high like it before. No other sexual experience had come even close.

Not that he had been able to put his erotic theories into practice—not yet. They had only made love twice, with a four-and-a-half-year gap in between, and neither time had been perfect. The first time—thrilling though it had been—he had been too shocked, too caught up in the preciousness of the moment to make it last the way he should have. And the second time... Pushing Calista up against the wall and taking her like that had hardly been his finest hour—far from it. No matter how she had responded... how good it had felt.

No, the next time he and Calista made love—because there *was* going to be a next time, and soon—he was going to make sure the conditions were just right. He was going to see just what he and Calista could do together, just what intense sexual magic they were capable of.

Which was why he had spent some time carefully formulating a plan.

This morning a small batch of post had arrived for Calista—presumably forwarded on by the woman she shared her flat with. Petros had picked it up from the mainland and delivered it to the villa, along with a large flaxen-haired doll in a presentation box that he had proudly given to Effie as a gift from him and Dorcas. Effie had thanked him most politely, even though Lukas had seen her looking at it slightly askance. After he had gone she had set about divesting the doll of her fussy dress whilst Lukas had watched Calista flicking through the letters, only bothering to open one, reading it quickly and then stuffing it back in the envelope.

'Anything interesting?' Something about the pinched look on her face had begged the question.

'Not really.' Calista had taken a sip of her coffee. 'It's from my father's lawyer. They're reading the will on the twenty-eighth.'

'As in tomorrow?'

Looking at her phone, she'd checked the date. 'Um… yes.'

'Will you be going?'

'No. The office is in Athens. Besides, I want nothing to do with my father's legacy—not now I know the truth.'

Lukas had watched as she lowered her eyes, picking nervously at the corner of the embossed envelope. It had surprised him that he felt no sense of satisfaction that she had finally accepted the truth. Instead her obvious pain had arrowed to his heart.

'My half-brothers can share whatever meagre spoils there may be between them.'

'Not without you being there to sign them over, they can't.' Lukas had briskly switched to business mode. 'I suggest you go to Athens and take this opportunity to legally tie up the loose ends. Then perhaps you can move on.'

'And *I* suggest you drop the amateur psychology and mind your own business.'

Lukas had waited for the anger to kick in. Normally he didn't take kindly to being spoken to like that. Normally he would have made the perpetrator pay. But Calista's backlash had simply served to show him she still had plenty of fight left in her. It was almost a relief.

'Touched a nerve, have I?'

'No. I just don't need you to tell me what I should and shouldn't be doing, thank you very much.'

'Very well. But perhaps you might allow me to make a small suggestion. I also have business in Athens. We could go there tomorrow…maybe stay overnight in my apartment.'

'No,' Calista had replied firmly. 'It would be too disruptive for Effie.'

'Then perhaps Effie could stay here?' He had kept his voice deliberately light. 'I'm sure Dorcas and Petros would be happy to look after her.'

'Oh, *please*, Mummy.' Never one to miss a trick, Effie had looked up from where she had been walking the semi-clad doll across the table, turning her big green eyes on her mother. 'Can I stay with Dorcas and Petros? *Please?*'

'I don't know…' Calista had hurried to find an excuse. 'I mean, they might not want the bother of looking after you overnight.'

'Oh, they will. And, anyway, I won't be any bother. I can help Dorcas make some *kouloulou* biscuits.'

'*Koulourakia,*' Calista had prompted, repeating the name of the buttery biscuits that Effie loved so much.

'Yes, those. So *can* I, Mummy?'

'Well, maybe. We'll talk about it later.'

At which point Lukas had allowed himself a secret

smile. Thanks to his brilliantly wonderful daughter, step one of his plan had been successfully implemented.

Now he walked through the empty villa and out onto the terrace, shading his eyes against the glare of the swimming pool. In the distance he could hear the faint chatter of a small voice, coming closer, and then mother and daughter appeared at the top of the steps to his left. They both looked warm and windswept. Calista was wearing a sarong tied low around her hips and was weighed down by a beach bag and a cool box. Effie was struggling with an inflatable crocodile that was nearly twice her size, the breeze flapping it against her small body.

As Lukas started towards them he realised with a jolt of surprise just how pleased he was to see them.

'What the hell is *he* doing here?'

Calista's two half-brothers jumped to their feet as she and Lukas entered the lawyer's office. Behind her, Calista felt Lukas stiffen.

'He has no business being here.' Christos directed his venom at her. 'Get him out, Calista.'

'Sit down, Christos.' With a calm she didn't feel, Calista took a seat across the desk from the aged lawyer. 'Lukas is merely accompanying me.'

'To survey the damage he has caused, most likely.' Christos's eyes bulged in his head. 'To check that he has decimated our inheritance as much as he has his own. The cheating, lousy, lowlife—'

'Why would you want him here, Calista?' Yiannis cut across his brother when the sound of Lukas's intake of breath was enough tell him that Christos was in danger of getting himself into serious trouble.

Calista hadn't actually wanted Lukas to join them, but somehow she had ended up being cleverly outmanoeuvred by him. First he had insisted on delivering her to the revolving door of the office block, then on accompanying her in the lift to the correct floor, and before she had known it he had followed her right in.

'Why don't we all sit down?' From the other side of the desk Mr Petrides, the Gianopoulous family lawyer, who had to be at least eighty years old, showed that he had no time for family squabbles. 'The reading of the will shouldn't take too long. For Calista's benefit I will speak in English, if that is agreeable to you all?'

'Just get on with it.'

Christos returned to his seat, followed by Yiannis. Lukas drew up a chair to sit on the other side of Calista.

Clearing his throat, Mr Petrides began slowly reading through the legal jargon. Calista tried to concentrate, but it was difficult with Lukas beside her, sitting perfectly still but radiating enough suppressed hostility towards the Gianopoulous brothers to decimate a small country. Was he planning some sort of showdown? Was that why he was here? For the first time she wondered if she had been tricked into bringing them all together. But if so, did it matter?

Time ticked by. The office was cramped and stuffy, and before long Calista found her mind wandering. She hoped Effie was okay, although she didn't really have any doubt that she would be. Dorcas and Petros had been absolutely delighted by the idea of babysitting for twenty-four hours, and all three had waved them off gleefully. The couple were staying overnight at Villa Helene—presumably Lukas still didn't want his daughter anywhere near Aristotle's Villa Melina.

She, of course, had somehow found herself agreeing to stay the night at Lukas's Athens apartment. She had never been there before. As a teenager she had tried not to think about it, imagining all the women Lukas might have taken back there, picturing some sort of wild bachelor pad with black satin sheets and handcuffs hanging off the bedhead. Not that Lukas had ever given her reason to think that. He had been notoriously discreet about his private life. But that didn't mean he hadn't had one.

One thing was for sure: tonight she was going to have to be careful not to slip between those black satin sheets herself. All week long, ever since *that* kiss on the boat, she had been fighting the crippling effect he had on her. The seductive power that made her speech stilted, made her steps stumbling, made her insides turn to jelly.

So she had deliberately distanced herself from him, avoiding potentially intimate situations by ensuring that Effie was with her at all times. And in the evenings, after she'd had no alternative but to put Effie to bed, by burying her head in a book or deciding on an early night.

And, surprisingly, Lukas had put no pressure on her at all. In fact he had behaved like the perfect gentleman. Far from trying to persuade her to stay for a nightcap on the terrace, or go for a stroll under the starlit sky, he had seemed perfectly happy to see her disappear, politely wishing her goodnight before returning to his laptop and burying himself in work.

Calista had told herself that was a relief. He had obviously forgotten his whispered promise on the boat. He had decided to drop the whole seduction routine and give her some space. But as the days had gone on somehow her relief had turned to frustration and then doubt. His gentlemanly conduct had started to seem more like uninterest than respect. And despite herself Calista had found that she was lingering a few seconds longer than strictly necessary when she said goodnight, holding his dark hooded gaze when she should have looked away, threading her fingers through her hair in what might have been construed as a suggestive manner.

Not that it had made any difference. In return Lukas had simply given her one of his infuriating half-smiles, leaving her feeling flustered and stupid before heading for the safety of her room.

'So basically you are telling us that there is absolutely *nothing*!'

Christos's furious voice jolted her back to the present.

Mr Petrides surveyed him over the top of his glasses. 'I am saying that the small amount of assets your father had will need to be divided between his remaining creditors.'

'And Thalassa?' Yiannis leant forward. 'That has gone too?'

'There is no mention of the island of Thalassa.' Mr Petrides looked down at the papers before him. 'My understanding is that it was the property of your father's first wife and has recently been sold. To Mr Kalanos.'

'Why, you—'

Christos was on his feet again, but Yiannis intercepted, roughly shoving him back in his seat.

'So it is true?' Yiannis turned to Lukas, defeat etched into his face.

'Just as I said,' Lukas replied with icy calm, his fingers steepled beneath his chin, his gaze steady.

'So why the hell are we here?' Christos turned on Mr Petrides. 'Just to be humiliated? So that this man can gloat over the despicable way he has tricked us?'

'No, Christos.' The old man suddenly seemed to age before their eyes. 'The reason I have gathered you here today is because I have something to tell you. I believe it is time you learned the truth about your father.' He sat back, a shudder racking his body. 'These past few years I have kept quiet. At the time I thought it was out of loyalty to your father, but now I see it was just cowardice. However, now the situation has changed. I have been diagnosed with a terminal illness. And I feel the need to unburden myself before I die.'

'Oh, I am *so* sorry, Mr Petrides.' Calista reached forward to take hold of his hand, but he withdrew it, placing it in his lap.

'I don't deserve your sympathy, Calista. You see, I have been concealing information—from you and from the police. I am very sorry to have to tell you this…' He cast rheumy cyes over the three Gianopoulous siblings. 'But I am of the opinion that your father was responsible for the arms-smuggling. Not Stravros Kalanos.'

'*No!* You are lying.' Christos was on his feet again, spittle flying from his mouth. 'He's paying you to say that, isn't he?' He waved a finger at Lukas. 'This is all a filthy conspiracy.'

The old man sadly shook his head. 'I wasn't privy to the details of your father's dealings, but I have had my suspicions for some time. Suspicions that I should have mentioned to the authorities. That I now intend to share with them. Lukas…' He struggled to his feet. 'It is indeed fortuitous that you are here today, so that I can offer my apologies to you in person.' He beckoned Lukas closer. 'I won't ask for your forgiveness, because I know I don't deserve it, but I want to express my deepest regret for not coming forward before now. For the miscarriage of justice you have suffered and for the ruination of your father's name.'

Lukas stood up, his tall frame rigid with control. The air in the office was suddenly stiflingly hot. Mr Petrides held out a shaky hand, and for a second Lukas hesitated, before finally reaching to take it in his. Mr Petrides grasped it firmly, patting it with his other hand.

'Thank you, my son. That is more than I deserve. Rest assured I will do the right thing now—'

'Wait a minute,' Yiannis interrupted. 'You are only talking about *suspicions* here, Petrides. You need to think very carefully before making accusations you can't substantiate.'

'No one will believe the old fool, anyway.' Christos snarled.

'It's the truth.' Calista's voice rang out clearly. 'You need to know—both of you. Our father was the guilty party. Not Stavros, and not Lukas.'

'And *you'd* know, would you?'

'Yes, Lukas has told me everything and I believe him.'

'Well, more fool you.' Christos turned on her. 'We all know you've been simpering around your precious Lukas ever since you could walk. He could tell you black was white and you'd believe him.'

'That's enough.' Moving to stand beside Calista, Lukas rested his arm along the back of her chair. 'You need to learn some respect for your sister. Both of you.'

'*Respect?*' Christos sneered. 'D'you really think I'd respect *that*?' He waved a finger at Calista. 'That pathetic ginger creature who has never been anything but a worthless parasite.'

Calista felt Lukas go terrifyingly still.

'What did you just say?'

'Even her own mother didn't want her. Packing her off to Thalassa every summer before she eventually went and killed herself. Calista needs to watch out—that sort of madness is probably in the blood.'

'Christos!' Yiannis tugged at his brother's arm to pull him away.

But Lukas was already there, hauling Christos up by the scruff of the neck, his menacing face only inches from his sweating victim. For a second he held him there. Christos's legs kicked helplessly beneath him, and a look of blind panic came into his eyes as Calista shrieked Lukas's name and Yiannis stepped forward, wildly flapping his hands and tugging at his brother's jacket to try and release him.

'Leave him, Lukas!' Fearing for Christos's very life, Calista tried to get between them. 'He's not worth it.'

Lukas hesitated, letting out a low, savage snarl that curdled Calista's blood. But finally, slowly, he lowered Christos to the ground. Calista could see the effort it took for him to control his fury flaring in his nostrils, throbbing in the veins of his neck.

Hooking his fingers under the knot of Christos's tie, he held him at arm's length, giving him a look of utter disgust. 'Don't you ever, *ever* speak of Calista that way again.'

Christos attempted a grunt.

'Now, apologise.' Releasing his throat, Lukas took hold of his shoulders, roughly turning him to face Calista.

'It's okay. I don't care—'

'It is very much *not* okay!' Lukas's voice roared around the office. 'This creep is going to apologise, right now.'

'I'm sorry, okay?' Christos looked down at his feet.

'Not good enough. Look your sister in the eye, take back your filthy remarks and apologise properly.'

'I shouldn't have said those things.' Under Lukas's punishing gaze Christos did as he was told. 'I apologise.'

'Sit down.' Throwing him back into his chair, Lukas turned to Yiannis. 'You too.'

Yiannis did as he was told.

'It's time you two learnt a few home truths. Firstly, your father was an immoral, scheming villain who lied his way out of trouble by betraying my father and framing me. Secondly, if I ever hear either of you bad-mouthing

Calista again I won't be responsible for my actions. Do I make myself clear?'

The brothers nodded.

'Out of respect for Calista I won't pursue this any further. But that doesn't mean I don't want to.' He fixed Christos with a terrifying glare. 'Because, believe me, taking you outside would give me the greatest pleasure. You don't deserve a sister like Calista. She is brave and strong and honourable and she has more brains than you two idiots put together. Which brings me to my third point.' He paused, shooting a look at Calista. 'You might as well know: I am proud to say that Calista is also the mother of my child.'

Yiannis and Christos gaped in unison, rendered mute by this astonishing revelation.

'Yes, we have a daughter. And one day she will inherit my fortune, carry on my legacy. One day she will preside over the great Kalanos shipping empire. And believe me...' He levelled cold eyes at them. 'This time I intend to make sure that nothing and no one will ever have the power to bring us down.'

CHAPTER EIGHT

'NIGHTCAP?'

Lukas moved over the sideboard and picked up a bottle of brandy.

'Um…yes, why not?'

Calista accepted the glass from him and, taking a sip, felt the comforting burn slide down her throat.

They had returned from an evening meal at a small family-run restaurant, hidden in one of the many cobbled backstreets of this beautiful city. Sitting outside, sharing a table so small that their knees had touched and Lukas had been forced to stretch his long legs out to the side, she had felt blissfully relaxed after the drama of Mr Petrides's office.

The food had been delicious too and, combined with the warm night air, filled with the scent of jasmine and orange blossom, and the indigo sky dotted with stars overhead, she had found herself forgetting her problems for a while and just enjoying Lukas's company. Which was easy when he was being like this: charming, attentive, funny. The old Lukas. Neither of them had even mentioned the hateful scene earlier on—Mr Petrides's confession and the shocking behaviour of her brothers.

Now, however, Calista suspected that was about to change. Swilling the brandy around in her glass she looked about her, trying to delay the inevitable. 'Your apartment is beautiful.'

'Thank you.' Lukas came and stood by her side. 'Though I could do without the note of surprise.'

'Sorry!' Calista laughed. 'It's just not how I imagined it.'

'Dare I ask how that was?'

'No, probably best not to.'

'Let me guess—all black leather sofas and widescreen televisions?'

'Something like that.'

'And maybe a waterbed with satin sheets? A drawer full of sex toys.'

Calista felt herself flush. Could he read her mind? Or was she just guilty of dreadful stereotyping?

'You mean I've got that wrong too?' She tried to bat back a flippant quip to cover her embarrassment.

'Play your cards right and later on you might find out.'

Calista swallowed. She had walked right into that one.

She moved away from him into the centre of the open-plan room. 'I love all the artwork. Is that an original?' She pointed to a colourful portrait on the wall.

'It is indeed. Modern art is an interest of mine. It's a good investment too. But nothing in my collection really compares to this.' He pressed a switch and the curtains swished to one side and a wall of windows appeared. 'There. What do you think?'

Calista gasped. Before them twinkled the lights of the city of Athens, and in the distance, high above the city, was the Acropolis, glowing proudly against the night sky. 'That's incredible!'

'Even better from out here.' Crossing the room, Lukas took hold of her hand and, opening the glass doors, ushered her out onto the balcony. 'Quite something, isn't it?'

It certainly was. It was magical. Tipping back her head,

Calista let the soft night wrap itself around her, drinking in the majesty of the scene. It put life into perspective somehow, thinking about the thousands of years the ancient citadel had been standing there, watching over them, about generations of people gazing up at it, just as she did now, caught up in their own totally absorbing but all too fleeting worlds.

A small movement beside her made her turn. Lukas was studying her, his head on one side, as if she was some sort of fascinating puzzle. Boldly Calista returned his stare, and immediately the flame between them ignited. His dark, raw, intensely primal presence shuddered through her body, making her stomach contract and a heavy beat pulse in her core. Lukas raised his eyebrows fractionally… a small but infinitely telling gesture that weakened her knees.

God, she wanted him so much. She positively ached with it. If he were to kiss her now she knew exactly where it would lead.

But he didn't. Pulling his eyes away from hers, he gestured to a pair of stylish metal chairs. 'Shall we sit down?'

'Oh, yes—why not?' Desperate to hide her disappointment, Calista quickly did as she was told, all chirpy enthusiasm.

'So…' Lukas turned the dark force of his eyes back on her. 'It would seem that your dear brothers finally know the truth about your father.'

Calista pulled a face. 'They are not my "dear" brothers. I never want to see either of them ever again.'

'Well, that makes two of us.'

He stilled, eyes narrowed, suddenly deadly serious. 'If Christos ever dares to speak about you like that again, I swear I won't be answerable for my actions.'

Calista saw his fists clench.

'I'm still not sure how I stopped myself from killing him there and then.'

'You showed great restraint.' She risked a quick smile.

'I would cheerfully serve a life sentence for that.'

'No, you wouldn't.' Her smile immediately faded. 'He's not worth it.'

Lukas grunted. 'That's true.'

'Thanks for sticking up for me, by the way.' Calista hurried to move the conversation away from the toxic subject of prison sentences.

'That's okay.' His gaze sharpened. 'I meant what I said.'

'Well, thank you. I appreciate it.' Suddenly vulnerable, she looked away, searching for more solid ground. 'What you said about Effie inheriting the shipping business, though… Don't you think that was a bit premature?'

Lukas shrugged. 'No harm in letting them see that the Kalanos dynasty is set to thrive.'

'Hmm…' Calista was far from comfortable with that, but decided not to break the fragile ceasefire by challenging him now.

'I must admit I had always assumed that pair of clowns *knew* the truth about Aristotle,' Lukas continued. 'But judging by the look on their faces today I'm not so sure.'

'I think we were all taken in by our father's lies.' Calista gave him an anxious glance. 'I'm so sorry, Lukas.'

Lukas shook his head wearily. 'Let's call a truce—for tonight at least.'

She nodded. That was fine by her. Given the choice, she would never talk about it again. She would bury the whole wretched business so deep that it would take a nuclear explosion to bring it to light. But it wasn't as simple as that. Lukas had vowed to clear his name and his father's name. Presumably, thanks to Mr Petrides, he was now going to have the evidence to do it.

Aristotle would be exposed for the villain he had been. Which was only right. But that didn't mean the idea didn't fill her with dread. He had still been her father—Effie's grandfather.

Reluctantly she braced herself to ask the dreaded question. 'Can I ask you what you intend to do now?' She placed her glass down on the table between them. 'When will you go public about Aristotle?'

'When I am good and ready. What is it they say? Revenge is a dish best served cold?'

Calista shivered.

'Well, I would be grateful if you could give me some warning before you do…'

'Trying to cover your back, Calista?'

'No!' Indignation saw her temper flare, and she tossed back her head so her hair rippled over her shoulders. 'I'm just saying that if you give me some warning I can prepare myself and make sure Effie is shielded from any press intrusion.'

'Let me assure you that I will have Effie's best interests at heart at all times.'

'Oh, well…thanks…' Her voice tailed off. She had no idea what he meant by that—knew only that the statement held a dark possessiveness that thickened the blood in her veins.

'Speaking of Effie, there is something I have neglected to say to you.'

Now her heart leapt into her throat. If he was going to start talking about applying for custody again she was ready to fight. And fight she would. Tooth and nail and with any other body part she had.

'Yes?' Her green eyes flashed a powerful warning. 'And what's that?'

Lukas deliberately let a second pass. Far from being intimidated by her reaction, he seemed to be rather enjoying it. He picked up his glass and took a sip of brandy, clearly in no hurry to put her out of her misery.

'Just that I realise I have not given you the credit you deserve.'

'Credit for what?' Wrong-footed, Calista frowned back at him.

'For the excellent way you have raised our daughter.'

'Oh.' She finally let out a breath.

'Effie is obviously a happy, well-balanced and frankly exceptional child. You have done a great job.'

'Well, thank you.' Stupidly Calista felt herself flush.

'I can see she is highly intelligent too.' The smile in his voice raised her eyes again. 'Though I suspect she gets that from me.'

'Of course.' Calista played along. 'Along with her humility and modesty.'

Their eyes locked and the tension between them melted away—only to be replaced with something far more dangerous.

'Let's drink to that, then.' Lukas's glittering gaze held hers. 'To Effie, our very special little girl.'

They clinked glasses, and Calista swallowed down the lump in her throat with the swig of brandy. She could feel tears pricking the backs of her eyes, but she had no idea why.

'And to the future, of course.' Missing nothing, Lukas continued to hold her captive. 'Whatever it may hold.'

What, indeed? Trapped by the power of his eyes, Calista had lost the ability to think straight. She needed to get away. *Fast.*

'Well…' She gave an exaggerated stretch. 'It's getting late. I think I'll go to bed.'

She waited for Lukas to say something, to do something. In truth she was waiting for him to stop her. Instead he remained motionless, those mesmerising eyes still fixed on hers, burning into her, managing to awaken every cell in her body. She watched, tingling with anticipation, as he silently took another sip of brandy, his eyes never moving from her heated face.

'I'll say goodnight, then.' Rising to her feet, she made as if to go, but somehow her feet didn't get the message her brain was trying to transmit and she ended up in a sort of frozen pose, twisted away from him but not moving.

From behind her she heard Lukas laugh—a softly arrogant laugh that had her turning her head, ready to challenge him.

Except that didn't happen. Because suddenly Lukas was there, towering over her. His hands were everywhere—skimming across her shoulderblades, down her back, tracing the curve of her waist, cupping her bottom, pulling her against him. And finally plunging into her hair so that he could hold her steady for his kiss.

And what a kiss.

Hungry, possessive, masterful, it sent a white bolt of craving through Calista, pulsing deep, deep down inside her, throbbing hard and insistent with illicit need. Without a second thought she responded, moulding herself against his body, her mouth greedily crushing his as her lips parted to allow more of this gloriously forbidden pleasure. Her tongue sought his, tasting the hint of brandy on his breath, revelling in the raw, damp heat that mingled between them, tightening her breasts, weighting her core. Rendering her helpless with longing.

'Did you mention bed?'

Sweeping her up in his arms, Lukas moved them both inside, marching through the living area with her clinging to his neck until they were in his bedroom, where he laid her down almost reverentially on his enormous bed.

'Stay like that.'

His throatily sexy command shuddered through her, but the words were superfluous. Calista had no intention of going anywhere. She held her breath as he started to tear off his clothes, undoing a few top buttons of his shirt before giving up and impatiently tugging it over his head, leaving his hair deliciously ruffled. Next came his jeans and boxers and then he was naked before her. Gloriously, proudly naked. His magnificent body gleamed in the dim light of the room...the muscles of his chest were shadowed, hard and unyielding. Calista let her eyes travel south, feeling her mouth go dry as she took in the sculpted V-shape of his pelvis, the line of curling dark hair and then...the mighty swell of his arousal.

But she had no time to feast her eyes. Lukas was on the bed in a flash, kneeing astride her, his hands pushing the straps of her dress over her shoulders, his fingers feverishly working the zipper down her back as she arched up to allow him access. She raised her arms and together they pulled the dress over her head, Calista felt the hard swell of her breasts tugged upwards. Reaching behind her back, she undid her bra, and the hunger in Lukas's stare at the sight of her swollen breasts tightened her nipples to peaks of stone.

They crashed back down onto the bed together again, Lukas straddling her with the length of his body now, their mouths fused with blistering, scorching passion. She moved her hands to grip his jaw, trying to hold him steady so that she could drag in a breath, but he only allowed her one gasp of air before he commandeered her mouth again, continuing his wickedly relentless assault on her senses. Meanwhile his hands had found her panties, pushing them to one side so that he could find her swollen core.

Calista groaned against his mouth, throwing back her

head and writhing beneath his touch. *It felt so good. Too good.* It was ridiculous the way he could transport her to the realms of ecstasy just by the touch of his fingers. But she had no defences against this man. This was Lukas— the only man she had ever wanted. The only man she had ever loved.

She was teetering deliciously on the very edge when Lukas stopped, pushing himself back on his heels so that he could pull down her panties and discard them. Calista reached out her arms, desperate to bring him back to her, the small space between them feeling like a yawning chasm. But Lukas had other ideas. Moving her legs apart, he positioned himself between them, shooting Calista a look of dangerously dark promise. Then he lowered his head.

'Lukas…'

She didn't know what she had been going to say and it didn't matter anyway, because as soon as his tongue started to work its magic she was paralysed by the grip of some unknown euphoria. Shooting sensations spread out from her core, fanning through her body, reaching every nerve-ending and pinching them tight. Then tighter still.

'Nice?' Lukas looked up, a wickedly smug expression on his face.

Her only reply was to reach for his head, grasping his hair to push him back down on her again. He couldn't stop *now*.

'I'll take that as a yes.'

His words were muffled against her as he started his glorious assault again. Licking, tasting, nudging just the right spot, over and over again, somehow unerringly altering the pressure to her exact need until he finally quickened the pace and the pressure and she felt herself start to fall. Over and over an edge that wasn't there. To a place that didn't exist.

* * *

Moving his position, Lukas gazed down at Calista. She was lying on her back, sated, still reeling from the after-effects. Pride surged through him. *He had done that to her.* She looked so beautiful lying there, her eyes closed, her skin creamy white in the dim half-light of the room. Her hair rippled across the pillow in a tangle of gold. He wanted Calista with a possessiveness that shocked him with its power.

Leaning forward, he kissed her gently on the lips, watching as heavy eyelids slowly opened. Stretching out beside her, he slipped one arm under her body, pulling her on to his chest, catching the look in her eyes as they sparkled, stealing the breath from his lungs with their gloriously erotic promise.

Positioning her so that she was exactly where he wanted her—no, *needed* her—so that he could finally do the thing that seemed more imperative than life itself, Lukas thrust into her, and her ecstatic gasp of pleasure rang like music in his ears. Picking up speed, he felt her match his rhythm, thrust for thrust, taking him—all of him—and giving all of herself in return.

Her obvious confidence filled Lukas with inexplicable pride as she arched her body to take him deeper, her head thrown back so that the wild red curls tumbled down almost to her waist. With a few final delirious strokes they were there, both shattering into pieces, each screaming the other's name.

CHAPTER NINE

AS THE ISLAND of Thalassa came into view Calista felt her spirits soar. She couldn't wait to see Effie again. Even though they had only been apart for twenty-four hours she had missed her like mad. But it was more than that. Despite everything, Thalassa still held a special place in her heart.

That place had been well and truly buried the last time she had arrived here—for her father's funeral, less than two weeks ago. Then she had vowed that she would never return, that she would say goodbye to the island for ever. But things had changed. *Everything* had changed.

Lukas had happened.

The previous night had been just incredible. Never in her wildest dreams, her craziest fantasies, had she ever imagined a night like that. The intensity of their lovemaking, the blazing passion between them, had gone way beyond anything she had thought possible. It had been as if all the time they had been apart, all that had happened— the hurt, the anger and the secrets—had been distilled into pure, unadulterated desire. And that had been all it took for them to fall headlong into the madness that had consumed them both.

She had finally woken this morning to see Lukas staring down at her, his ebony eyes deeply serious. Then he had blinked the expression away, leaning forward to touch her lips with a gentle kiss and announcing that they really ought to get up.

But she had seen it—that closed, inscrutable look—and it had been then that it had struck her just how completely she had given herself to Lukas, how recklessly she had laid herself bare. And not just in the physical, earthly sense. By surrendering to such wild abandonment she had exposed her heart and her soul, her most fragile, deeply held emotions. Emotions that she knew Lukas would never share.

And that, she had realised with a stab of sorrow, had been a dangerously foolish thing to do.

They had gone to a small local café for breakfast. Over bowls of yogurt and honey topped with figs and walnuts Lukas had told her he had business to attend to in Athens that would take several days to complete, and had suggested she stay and keep him company. He had left her in no doubt as to what sort of 'company' he meant, and the look he had given her had arrowed straight to her loins, just as he had meant it to do.

With super-human effort she had declined. She had to get back for Effie. She wouldn't have felt comfortable being apart from her for another night, even though her daughter was most probably having the time of her life with Dorcas and Petros. And besides, she had already given far too much of herself to this man.

So Lukas had arranged for one of his charter yachts to take her back to Thalassa—one thing he was never short of was boats. It was crewed by a couple of young Greek gods—or at least that was what they thought they were. Bronzed and athletic, Nico and Tavi leapt about the yacht, winding in ropes and adjusting sails, all with rather more exhibitionism than Calista suspected was strictly necessary. Not that she minded. Even though they were probably about the same age as her, to Calista they seemed like boys. They couldn't hold a candle to Lukas. But that didn't mean she didn't enjoy their attentions. She felt young. She felt sexy. Right now she felt she could do anything.

'Miss Gianopoulous—over there!' Nico called down from his position halfway up a mast. 'Dolphins! And they are coming our way.'

Calista looked to where he was pointing and sure enough there was a large pod of dolphins, swimming towards them. Suddenly they were alongside the boat, all around them, joyfully leaping out of the water and rolling over in the wake behind them. It was such a wonderful sight, and strangely emotional too—as if the dolphins were escorting her home.

Fighting back the tears, Calista told herself to stop being stupid and get a grip. Thalassa was *not* her home. Nor would it ever be. She had to remember that. Last night had been completely wonderful, but in terms of their future nothing had changed between her and Lukas.

What was it he had said? *Let's call a truce—for tonight at least.* They were telling words. She would be very foolish indeed to ignore them.

Back at Villa Helene, just as Calista suspected, Effie had been having a wonderful time, being thoroughly spoiled by Dorcas and Petros. She was delighted to have her mother back, of course, but after her initial rapturous welcome seemed overly focussed on where Lukas was.

'So when *is* Daddy coming back?'

They were seated outside, at a long wooden table shaded by vines that were trained overhead to provide shade. Dorcas had prepared a delicious late lunch for them all—including Nico and Tavi, who ate with ravenous appetites. There was lots of chatter and laughter, but clearly Effie was missing her father.

'I told you, darling, he'll be back in a few days.'

'How many, *exactly*?' Effie's turned her huge green eyes on her mother, her forkful of food momentarily forgotten.

'I don't know exactly. Maybe a week.'

Effie stuck out her bottom lip.

'Ah, see how she misses her *baba*.' Nico leant across and ruffled Effie's hair, managing to extract a smile from her. 'I tell you what, little one, Tavi and I—we take you out on the boat and show you the dolphins. You like that?'

Effie nodded vigorously.

'That's settled, then. We are here for two more days. We have some fun.'

He shot Calista a cheeky glance which she pointedly ignored. Now they were on dry land the flirty banter she had enjoyed on the boat seemed misplaced. She certainly didn't want to give these young Adonises the wrong idea. But on the other hand they were only having a bit of harmless fun. What was wrong with spending a bit of time enjoying their company? Why did she always have to be so buttoned up?

Back in England, Calista's friends had despaired of her. Try as they might, they had never been able to prise her out for a night of revelry—seldom even persuaded her to join them for a girly night out. Student nurses knew how to party—that was a given—and Calista was letting the side down by refusing to join in. Sure, she had Effie to consider, but that didn't excuse her total inability to let her hair down at any time.

It also didn't excuse the way she rebuffed the advances of some of the teaching hospital's most attractive and eligible junior doctors. The ones who would have had many a young nurse vying for their bedside manner. But Calista seemed impervious to their charms. She had tried to explain that it was different for her—she had responsibilities. But in truth that was only part of the reason. A very small part. The real reason she had no interest in any other man could be summed up in one name: Lukas Kalanos.

But that didn't mean she couldn't enjoy a few Lukas-free days of relaxation on this beautiful island. She ought to make the most of the fact that his darkly dominating presence wasn't everywhere she looked. That she was being spared the penetrating hooded gaze that seemed to see right through her.

As the euphoria of the night before started wear off, and reality crept in, Calista knew it was time to bring herself down to earth. And keep herself there. So if Nico and Tavi wanted to entertain her and Effie over the next couple of days, why not?

'How many more days now?'

Calista glanced up from her phone, where she'd been looking at nursing jobs on the internet. She would need to start applying soon if she wanted to have a job lined up for September.

'How many days till what, darling?' She didn't really need to ask. She knew perfectly well what her daughter was talking about. She should too—she'd been fielding the same question for well over a week now.

'Till Daddy comes back.' Effie spelled out the question with impatient clarity.

'Um…I'm not sure.'

Calista looked down at her phone again, flipping from email to text. Nothing. That was nine days of silence from Lukas now…and counting… She tossed the phone onto the sofa beside her.

'Still, we're having a nice time here without him, aren't we?' Her voice sounded hollow even to her own ears. And it clearly didn't convince Effie, who wrinkled her small nose in reply.

'I suppose so. But it would be even nicer if Daddy was here.'

Calista drew in a breath. She was trying so hard to put on a brave face for Effie, but underneath she was a churning cauldron of hurt and anger. Two or three days—that was what Lukas had said when she had left him in Athens. Some business he had to attend to. It was unforgivable that he should abandon them like this, with no word of when he planned to return. *He* was the one who had insisted that she and Effie came to Thalassa and now he was ignoring them, leaving their lives suspended until such time as he deigned to honour them with his presence again.

With each day that crawled past, bringing still no word from him, Calista made up her mind that she and Effie should just go—pack up their stuff and return to London. But somehow she couldn't do it. One look at Effie's expectant little face and her resolve crumbled. She longed to see her daddy again. Somehow, in such a short space of time, Lukas had woven his magic spell around her and she adored him. To whisk her away now, with no real reason, would be just plain cruel. She couldn't punish her daughter for her own desperate heartache.

Because that was what it was. Her heart ached as if someone had reached in and crushed it, squeezing and squeezing with an unrelenting grip that would never loosen. And the worst thing was it was all her own fault. Despite denying it, even to herself, she had secretly taken the one night she and Lukas had shared and turned it into something it wasn't—and never would be. The start of a meaningful relationship. And she hated herself, *and* her wretched stupid heart, for being so utterly, blindly foolish.

Because this was *Lukas* they were talking about here.

The new Lukas. Cold and calculating and ruthless in the extreme. And how had she gone about protecting herself from this man? By falling into his arms, that was how. By urging him to make love to her, whispering his name against his skin and screaming it out as he brought her to orgasm. By betraying her feelings for him in the most obvious was possible.

Thinking back, she could see how he had manipulated her. The way he had drawn her in, let her come to him, waited like a wolf in his lair as she had come closer and closer. Only pouncing when he had been sure that she was his for the taking. Heat scorched her cheeks at the thought of how she had been used, how wantonly she had given herself to him. And now presumably she was being punished. By maintaining this silence Lukas was exerting his control, showing how little regard he had for her. How neatly she had fallen into his trap.

Well, she could nothing about what had happened that night, but at least she could pull her defences back into place now. And that meant not contacting him—treating his radio silence with the contempt it deserved. On the face of it at least.

She bitterly regretted the one text she had sent him, written on the boat when she'd been coming back to Thalassa, still glowing from the thrill of what they had shared. She had thanked him for a wonderful night. Actually *thanked* him. And there had been kisses. And a smiley face emoji. The thought of which now turned her stomach, even though the message had long since been deleted.

Somehow she had to put her stupidity behind her and move on. She needed to be strong now—banish all thoughts of a happy-ever-after and behave like the sensible adult she'd used to be. Before Lukas had decimated her heart. She would *not* run away. She would face up to him when he finally returned and do her best to convince him that what had happened between them had meant nothing to her. Clearly it hadn't to him.

'It's time for bed, my love.' Pulling Effie to her, Calista wrapped her arms around her daughter in a tight hug.

'Aw…not yet.' But her protestations were muffled by a big yawn. All the fresh air and sunshine of another day spent on the beach meant that sleep was not far away. 'I hope Daddy comes back tomorrow, then I can show him my shell collection.'

'Yes, well, I'm sure he'd love to see it. But Daddy is very busy, you know. He has a lot of work to do.'

'I know…he told me.' Effie yawned again. 'He's buying lots of big ships. *Really* big ships that cross the oceans full of things for other people.'

Was he? This was news to Calista. She'd had no idea that he was building up the shipping empire again. Not that she was surprised. She could see that restoring the family business—*his* family business, at least—would be a priority for Lukas. And at heart he was an entrepreneur, a highly successful businessman.

'Did he say anything else?' Calista asked the question lightly. She knew she shouldn't be grilling her daughter for information, but curiosity had got the better of her.

'Um…yes.' Effie snuggled into her side and tipped up her chin to meet her mother's eyes. 'But it's sort of a secret.'

'Oh. Well, in that case perhaps you had better not say.' Calista stroked Effie's hair, deliberately leaving a pause. In common with most four-year-olds, keeping secrets was not one of Effie's strong points. Calista knew she just had to wait.

'If I tell you, you must promise not to tell anyone else.'

'I promise.'

'Well…' Effie struggled to sit up so she could face her mother full-on, excitement shining in her eyes. 'The next big ship that Daddy buys—he's going to call it after *me*!'

'Really?'

'Yes. He's going to call it *Euphemia*. My proper name— not Effie.'

'Well, that is *very* exciting.'

'I know.' Effie felt for a lock of her mother's hair, twisting it around her fingers. 'I expect it must be hard to buy a big ship. That's why he's been away such a long time.'

'Maybe.' Calista pulled her close again for another hug. 'Come on then, you—bedtime.'

She carried Effie through to her bedroom, setting her down and sending her into the bathroom to brush her teeth. While she waited she sat down on the bed and a small cardboard box on Effie's bedside table caught her eye. She had never noticed it before. Picking it up, she lifted the lid and what she saw inside gave her a jolt.

'What's this, Effie?' She raised her voice over the running water and Effie's vigorous toothpaste-spitting.

Effie dutifully appeared in doorway, toothbrush in hand. 'Oh, that. It's a little bit of Daddy's hair.'

Calista stilled, a creeping feeling of unease spreading over her as she looked down at the small lock of hair. 'Why have you got a bit of Daddy's hair?'

'We did a swap. He cut a bit of *his* hair off to give to me, and I cut off a bit of mine to give to him. Daddy helped me because the scissors were sharp.'

Effie returned to the bathroom and replaced her toothbrush in the glass with a clatter.

'Oops!' Calista saw her troubled face reflected in the mirror. 'I've just remembered that was a secret too.'

'That's okay, darling.' Somehow Calista managed to keep her voice steady as Effie re-joined her. But a tremor was starting to ripple through her body, already making her hands shake as the realisation of what Lukas was up to took hold.

'Don't look so worried, Mummy.' Climbing into bed, Effie stopped to give her mother a reassuring kiss on the cheek.

Calista hastily tried to rearrange her frozen features.

'It was only a little bit of hair. I've got lots more.'

'Of course you have.'

Returning the kiss, Calista tucked her daughter up in bed, moved to close the shutters and then silently left the room, pulling the door almost closed behind her.

Walking through to the living room, she seated herself on the sofa and picked up one of the cushions, holding it against her mouth. Only then did she allow herself a muffled scream.

Lukas adjusted the microphone on his headset as he waited for clearance for take-off. He was certainly in no mood to be kept waiting today. As he flicked the switches on the dashboard clearance finally came through and, grasping the controls, he took the helicopter up into the air.

It had proved to be an exhausting couple of weeks. But now he was heading back to Thalassa with his plans for the future finally in place. Plans that would see Calista abiding by his rules. Rules that he would control meticulously, ruthlessly, but above all with his brain—not his traitorous body.

The night that he had spent with her...those hours of wild, uninhibited, mind-blowing sex...now seemed a lifetime ago. As if it had happened to a different man. Which in a way it had. Because Lukas was no longer the deranged lover who had reached repeatedly for Calista's soft body, murmuring her name into the darkness, crying it out on the wave of his release. Actions that had seen him laid dangerously bare.

He had wised up.

Not that he wouldn't still have to be on his guard at all times. Because where Calista was concerned his madness was never far away. Look at the way she had managed to get his granite heart pumping again, firing it with something dangerously close to feeling. *Almost.* And she was addictive, too. He had even asked her to stay on in Athens because he'd wanted more, had been greedy for another night of passion. And then another. But Calista had, of course, declined. Presumably she felt she had done enough already. Enough to bring him to heel.

He had been in a meeting the following day when the worm of doubt about her motives had crept in. Deep in negotiations to buy a multi-million-dollar freighter, he had been enjoying the bargaining, the high-powered cut and thrust. This vessel was another of the fleet that G&K Shipping had owned before their downfall and that Lukas was gradually buying back. And it was going to be named after his daughter. *Euphemia.*

When his phone had beeped with a text from Calista he had scanned it quickly, allowing himself a smile. He would phone later. When he could pass on the good news to Effie that he had her ship.

The deal had been successfully concluded and he'd been shaking hands with the CEO of the rival shipping company when the turn of their conversation had brought him up short.

'So it's true, then?' Georgios Papadakis had given him a quizzical look. 'You're intent on buying back the old fleet?'

Lukas had nodded his assent. He wasn't surprised that Papadakis knew the truth—that the secret was out. At this level the shipping industry was a small and tight-knit group of astute capitalists who made it their business to know everything.

'It is.'

'Well, I admire your tenacity, young man. But buying back the fleet is one thing—finding traders who have any confidence in the Kalanos name will be quite another. That was some scandal you and your father embroiled yourselves in.'

'For your information…' Lukas had fought to control the rage in his voice '…my father and I were entirely innocent of all charges. Aristotle Gianopolous was responsible for the arms-smuggling. Something I will prove to the world very shortly.'

'Is that so?' Lukas had noted that Papadakis didn't look entirely surprised. 'And just how do you intend to do that?'

'I have my ways. New evidence is coming to light all the time.'

That was certainly true. Apart from the old lawyer's testimony, that very morning a new line of enquiry had been opened up. A large South American drugs cartel had recently been busted, and during the police investigations it had come to light that *they* had been the intended recipients of the arms that had been illegally stowed on the G&K freight ship. The last fateful deal that Aristotle had struck.

Lukas was intending to fly to Bolivia that very afternoon to find out as much as he could. He didn't know how long it would take—only that he wouldn't be leaving until he had accomplished his mission. Until he finally had the evidence to expose Aristotle for the man he really was. For all the world to see.

'Interesting…' Papadakis had steepled his fingers. 'And taking up with the Gianopolous girl? Is that somehow part of the plan?'

'I have *not* taken up with Calista Gianopolous!'

'No? Well, that's not what I've heard,' Papadakis had replied. 'I must admit I was surprised. I would have thought she'd be a dangerous bedfellow—especially in view of what you've just told me. Keeping your enemies close. Is that what this is all about, Kalanos? Or is it something else?' The older man's eyes had twinkled mischievously. 'Have you fallen victim to her feminine charms?'

'No!'

'You wouldn't be the first to be taken in by such a siren, that's for sure. And the girl *is* a beauty—I'll give you that. But I would advise you to be careful. Trust any member of the Gianopolous family at your peril. If you are about to expose her father I dare say Calista is keen to save her own skin—and she won't much care how she goes about it.'

'I don't need your warnings, Papadakis.' Lukas's voice had been too loud, carried too much force. 'I've told you— there is nothing between me and Calista.'

'Except the small matter of a child, of course.'

Lukas stilled. So he knew about Effie too.

'Euphemia?' Papadakis indicated the paperwork on the desk between them, which showed the new name that Lukas had registered for his latest purchase. 'It doesn't take a genius to figure out the connection. So the Gianopoulous-Kalanos dynasty is set to rise from the ashes?'

'No.' Lukas's growl had echoed round the room. 'The Gianopoulous family will have no part in this. This will be a new dynasty, solely bearing the Kalanos name.'

Papadakis had given Lukas a knowing look. 'And yet you have just admitted that the child is Gianopoulous's granddaughter?'

'But she is *my* daughter!' Jumping to his feet, Lukas had glared down at the older man. 'That means she is a

Kalanos. That is all you need to know. That is all *anyone* needs to know.'

'If you say so.' Standing up, Papadakis had given him a friendly slap on the back. 'My advice to you would be to make sure you have everything legally tied up. And I mean *everything*. In my experience mixing business with pleasure can be a lethal combination.'

Lukas knew he was right. He had to stake his claim for the Kalanos family. And, although he hadn't fully known it until that moment, stake his claim for Effie as well.

Suddenly Calista's recent behaviour had come into sharp focus. Those subtle little references to Aristotle being Effie's grandfather. About lessening the impact of the truth on Effie. Well, Stavros Kalanos was Effie's grandfather too. Something Calista seemed to have conveniently forgotten. Had she been trying to manipulate him all this time to get him to keep quiet about her father's atrocities? Carry on taking the blame for them himself? Was that what their night together had been all about?

If so, she was going to be sorely disappointed. He might have wanted her in his bed that night—wanted her in his bed every night, come to that—but that was just sex. A basic physical attraction. She might have thought she could wheedle her way into his head, appeal to his better nature, but Lukas had news for her.

He didn't have a better nature. Only a darker, blacker version of himself that had been honed to lethal perfection by his spell in prison.

He had looked back down at the text she had sent him, suddenly filled with rage. All that thanking him for a wonderful night, the kisses, the smiley face emoji. What kind of fool did she take him for? He'd have had more respect for her if she'd begged.

Deleting the message there and then, he had felt in

his pocket for the small plastic bag containing a lock of Effie's hair, possessively closing his hand around it. If there had been any doubt before about what he was going to do, if he had felt any guilt, it had been washed away on a tide of cold realisation.

And, should he have needed any *more* convincing of Calista's betrayal, then this morning's distasteful little incident had thoughtfully provided it.

After an arduous ten days in Bolivia, Lukas had returned to Athens earlier today, having successfully secured all the information he needed. Before heading back to Thalassa he had decided to pay a quick, unannounced visit to Blue Sky Charters. He had been about to enter the office when voices from inside had jerked him to a halt.

'You don't stand a chance, man. A babe like Calista Gianopoulous wouldn't look at you twice.'

Lukas's hand had all but fused to the door handle.

'Oh, you think so, do you? I'm telling you—that day on the boat she was definitely giving me the come-on.'

'In your dreams!'

'Don't underestimate the Tavi charm, my friend. It never fails.'

'Yeah, right. If anything it was *me* she fancied. All that "Can you show me how to tie some knots?". I suspect it was more than my rope skills she was interested in.'

'Then perhaps we should settle this with a wager, Nico. First one to get a kiss out of Calista scoops the prize.'

Shaking with fury, Lukas had flung open the office door, crashing it against the wall. Nico and Tavi had scrambled to their feet, and Lukas had waited a beat for the red mist to settle, watching as they'd tried to arrange themselves before him, flushed-faced and sweating. Only then had he delivered his pronouncement—clearly and unequivocally.

'You're fired! Both of you! Get out!'

Now, as he flew the helicopter over the vivid blue Aegean Sea and the island of Thalassa came into view, Lukas could still feel that anger, that all-consuming rage. He could still taste its venom. But it had changed its form, had settled into solid, impenetrable rock that only served to strengthen his resolve.

Calista Gianopoulous had shown her true colours and the scales had fallen from his eyes. Now everything was in place. And she was about to find out the kind of the man he really was.

CHAPTER TEN

AT THE SOUND of the helicopter landing Calista felt her heart lurch. *He was back*. Putting down her book, she leapt to her feet, positioning herself in the middle of the room with her hands on her hips. But as the seconds dragged by and he still hadn't appeared she started to pace up and down, smoothing the fabric of her sundress with shaky hands, her blood pressure rising with every step.

'Kalispera.' Eventually he appeared, throwing her a casual glance before going into the kitchen and returning with a glass of water. 'Where's Effie?' He looked around him.

'She's not here.' Calista ground out her reply.

'I can see that.' Placing his glass down on a low table, he came and stood before her. 'Where is she?'

'It doesn't matter where she is. What's more to the point is where the hell have *you* been?'

'Missed me, have you?' He angled his broad shoulders in a deliberately casual pose. But the look in his eye was anything but casual. It was hard, ruthless, calculating.

'You flatter yourself, Lukas.' Calista averted her gaze from his face and took a couple of steps to the side. He was far too close. 'But it might have been nice if you had told us when you intended to return. Just out of common decency.'

'Common decency has never really been my thing.'

'No.' She met his eyes again, flashing an emerald-green warning. 'I should have realised that.'

He returned an infuriating smile, as if he was enjoying himself, playing with her. 'Well, I can see you are delighted to have me back now.' He looked around him. 'Where did you say Effie was?'

'I didn't.' Calista could feel her colour rising, staining the column of her neck. 'But, since you ask, she is over at Villa Melina. Dorcas is going to give her some tea and then Petros will bring her back.'

'Interesting…' Lukas closed the space between them with a single stride, looking down at her with heated, possessive intent. 'So we are alone.'

'We are. Which is just as well.'

'Even more interesting.' Reaching forward, he took hold of a curl of red hair, twisting it seductively around his finger, his eyes dancing over her face. 'What do you have in mind for us, Calista?'

'I'll tell you what I have in mind.' With a violent toss of her head Calista freed herself. 'Let's start by talking about what you have been doing for the last couple of weeks.'

'What I do with my time is none of your business, *agape*.'

'No? So nothing you have done is any of my business?'

'That's what I said.'

'Then you are a liar, Lukas Kalanos!'

'I beg your pardon?' Lukas's nostrils flared, the chill of his words freezing the air. 'What did you just call me?'

'A liar.' Fear stuttered in Calista's heart but she carried on regardless. She had gone too far to stop now. 'Because that's what you are.'

'I would take that back if I were you, Calista. You are treading on very dangerous ground.'

'No. I won't take it back.' She was riding the wave now, trying to ignore the crash that would inevitably follow.

'Then perhaps I need to put you straight about a few things.' Lukas fixed her with a brutally punishing stare. 'That you of all people should call me a liar is almost beyond belief. You, who have done nothing but deceive me by failing to tell me that I had a daughter for over four years, who would most likely never have told me if I hadn't forced the truth out of you. For you to have the bare-faced nerve to challenge my honesty is staggeringly hypocritical.'

'Not telling you about Effie is completely different. There is no comparison.'

'You lied by omission, Calista. And that is every bit as bad as lying to my face. Worse, in fact. It is even more cowardly. So don't even *think* about trying to defend yourself.'

'I am not interested in defending myself.'

'And, since we are on the subject of liars, why don't we talk about your father? The most heinous liar of all.'

'This is not about me or my father!' she hurled back, hitching her shoulders, wild-eyed with fury. 'This is about *you* sneaking behind my back and taking a sample of Effie's hair to be DNA-tested.'

Lukas remained silent, his eyes narrowing to lethal thick-lashed slits.

'Yes, you see, I know.' Triumphant now, Calista continued. 'So don't bother to deny it.'

'Why would I try and deny it?' Lukas folded his arms across his chest.

'So you admit it, then?'

'It is true that I have had a DNA test done to establish the paternity of my daughter. That's not an admission. It's a statement of fact.'

'A *fact* that you just happened to fail to tell me about?'

He shrugged his indifference.

'Lying by omission.' Calista threw his phrase back at him. 'I believe that was your expression.'

Lukas gave a low growl. 'Taking steps to establish a legal footing for my relationship with my own daughter hardly compares to the atrocities your family have inflicted on mine.'

'*A legal footing?*' Calista spat the words back at him. 'And what exactly does *that* mean? You weren't sure that she was yours—is that it?'

She fired the accusation at him like a missile, but deep down she hoped she was right. Because, insulting though that would be, it was far better than the alternative. The nightmare that had been tormenting her ever since she had discovered he'd taken a sample of Effie's hair.

'On the contrary.' Lukas's voice was as smooth as glass. 'I have never had any doubt that Effie is my daughter.'

Panic made her legs tremble, stealing the breath from her chest. 'So what, then? Why do a DNA test if you already knew the answer?'

A small but deadly smile touched Lukas's lips. 'You're a bright girl, Calista. I'm sure you can work it out. But if you want me to spell it out for you, I will. In order to have any legal control over my daughter I have to be able to prove paternity. Step one is to get my name on her birth certificate.'

Calista felt something shrivel inside her. She could have pointed out that she had hardly been in a position to ask him to sit beside her in the register office and put his name on the birth certificate, but that would only have strengthened his case. And besides, her terrified focus was elsewhere.

'And step two?' She tried to sound rational, but her heart was pounding at a terrifying rate.

'Step two?' Lukas ran a hand over his jaw, as if considering. 'Well, you might as well know. Step two is to apply for full custody of my daughter.'

'No!' The full horror enveloped her like a black shroud. Fists flying, she threw herself at Lukas, pounding at his chest. *'Never!'* The word was twisted into a strangled scream as she thrashed about, lashing out with wild but increasingly futile blows to the solid wall of his chest.

Lukas did absolutely nothing to stop her, taking the assault with a contemptuous calm that only made her more frantic, more desperate. With her hair flying around her face she raised her hand, ready to strike, but with lightning speed Lukas caught it, and along with the other one brought it down so that they were both trapped between them.

'Oh, no, you don't,' he growled. 'You have slapped my face once. You won't be doing that again.'

'Get off me! Let me go!' Calista tried to buck away but that only made Lukas tighten his hold. He looked down at her for a second, before pulling her towards him, releasing her wrists only to wrap his arms around her in a powerful embrace from which there was no escape.

Lowering his head, he whispered in her ear. 'I'll let you go when I am good and ready.'

Calista held herself rigid, her heart raging in her chest, the blood roaring in her ears. And there it was again—that febrile connection pulsing between them, hot and hard and impossible to ignore. *Desire.* Although that was too delicate a name for what she and Lukas felt for each other. It was hunger, craving, infatuation, a greedy obsession that tore at her soul, weakened her, at the same time as giving Lukas all the strength, all the power.

She could feel it now, rampaging through her as Lukas held her tightly against him. Feel the way it sapped her energy, melted her bones to liquid. She let out a breath, giving herself a moment, her body sagging with the sheer exhaustion of trying to fight this physical attraction. This all-consuming madness.

Above her, around her, almost a part of her, Lukas over-powered her—body and soul. Not by his physical strength, although that was undeniably a part of him, but simply by being the man he was. She swallowed against the pain of unshed tears blocking her throat as the reality of the ter-rible situation hit home.

She loved Lukas.

And right now that felt like the cruellest fate of all.

Loosening his hold, Lukas angled his head so that he could see her face, moving aside the thick twist of hair, the back of his hand brushing her cheek as he did so. Calista closed her eyes. She sensed his head coming closer, felt the soft whisper of his breath on her lips, felt them part slightly, provocatively, inviting his kiss.

With superhuman effort she controlled herself, rearing up and pushing him away. 'You may think you have all the power, Lukas—the wealth and the contacts to gain cus-tody of Effie.' She brushed away the hair that was stuck to her lips. 'But you are wrong. I will never let you take my daughter away from me. *Never.*' Her voice cracked with all the pain inside her, all the sadness and anger, the bitter-ness and regret. 'I would sooner die than give up my child.'

Taking several steps away, she glared at him, giving him the full force of her temper, fury glittering in her eyes. But inside she had never felt more scared, more vulnerable.

'Aren't we being a little melodramatic?'

Closing the gap, Lukas went to put a hand on her shoul-der, but she ducked beneath his arm, turning on her heel and marching from the room. She heard him following her down the corridor as she headed for her bedroom, but she refused to acknowledge the way he propped himself against the doorframe, watching her every move. Tugging open drawers, she dumped the contents on the bed before opening the wardrobe and pulling all the clothes off their hangers. Then, retrieving a suitcase, she unzipped the lid and started to stuff everything inside.

'Can I ask what you think you are doing?'

'Work it out for yourself, Lukas, you're a bright man.' She threw his words back at him before disappearing into the bathroom, collecting up an armful of toiletries and coming back to chuck them into the suitcase. 'I should have thought it was pretty obvious. I'm leaving.'

'Leaving?' Shouldering himself away from the door-frame, Lukas advanced towards her. 'Or running away?'

'Call it what you like.' Pointedly stepping past him, Calista headed for the adjoining room—Effie's bedroom—and began a repeat performance with her belongings. She couldn't stop to think—not now, not with Lukas hovering ever closer, his tall frame right beside her as she stuffed Effie's clothes into her little tiger-shaped suitcase. Glancing at her row of possessions on the windowsill—the collection of seashells, the doll that Dorcas and Petros had given her, the finely modelled sailing boat—a present from her father, which Effie adored—she made a split-second decision and snatched up the doll. The boat could stay there.

'Just in case you should be in any doubt, I am taking Effie with me.'

She had no idea what her plans were other than that she had to get away, right now, whilst her anger still had the capacity to propel her forward. Before real misery rendered her incapable of anything.

'Running away solves nothing, Calista. I would have thought you had learned that by now.'

'On the contrary.'

Brushing past him, she exited the room, pulling the tiger suitcase behind her, swinging the doll from her free hand. Back in her bedroom, she threw it on top of her own suitcase before attempting to zip up the lid. Her chaotic packing meant it refused to close. Opening it again, she saw the doll staring at her with glassy-eyed reproach before Callie turned her over, pressing her down firmly into the muddle of clothes.

'It gets me and Effie away from *you*. And there is nothing more important than that right now.'

'Really? And why do you suppose that is, Calista?'

He was beside her again, leaning over her, barring her way.

'Why are you so desperate to get away from me?'

'Because you are a deceitful, scheming bully—that's why. Because you are plotting to take my daughter away from me. Because—'

Her breathless tirade was silenced by Lukas taking hold of her chin, tipping her face so that she couldn't avoid the inky-black stare of his cruelly beautiful eyes. She felt her skin flare in response, her body straining with tension, but her darting gaze was steady as it was caught in his thrall.

'Because what, Calista? Go on—say it.'

'Because…because I *hate* you!' The words came out in a blind rush of emotion.

Calista took in a deep breath. She had said it before, of course, and it had always felt as if the only person she was punishing was herself. But at least she had come down on the right side of the dangerously thin line that separated the two most extreme of emotions. For she knew she could easily have fallen the other way—knew that as far as Lukas was concerned love and hate were inextricably linked in her neural pathways and always would be. Something he must never find out.

'Hate is a strong word, *agape*.'

Lukas ran a finger over her lips, resting it there as if to silence her. It was only a light pressure but it burned like fire, searing into her until she had to prise open her mouth to free herself from the sensation and take a gasp of air. Immediately Lukas's head lowered, until his mouth hovered over hers, just a hair's breadth away from possessing her with his kiss. A split second away from crashing through her defences...

'Hello!'

At the sound of their daughter's voice Calista sprang away, fleeing the bedroom as fast as her sandaled feet would take her. Lukas was left staring after her, exasperation, raging lust and impotent fury all surging through him in the cacophony of insanity that he had come to accept was part and parcel of his relationship with Calista. If you could call it a relationship.

'Hello, sweetheart.' He could hear her talking to Effie, her voice unnaturally high, false. 'Have you had a lovely afternoon?'

'Is Daddy here?' Effie cut to the chase. 'The helicopter's outside.'

'Well, yes, he is. But the thing is...'

'*Yassou*, Effie.' Lukas strode into the living room, spreading out his arms in time to catch his daughter as she launched herself at him.

'Yay! You're back.' Throwing her arms around his neck, she snuggled against him as Lukas settled her onto his hip. 'Why were you away so long?'

'I had a lot of work to do.'

'Did you buy my ship?'

'I did.'

'Cool. When can I see it?'

'Well, the thing is, darling—' Calista cut in.

'I'll see if I can arrange a visit very soon.'

'But it won't be that soon.'

Taking control, Calista advanced towards him, reaching out to take Effie from his arms then setting her on her feet and clasping her hand.

'Because there has been a change of plan, Effie. We are going back to England.'

'Aw…' Effie's expressive little face was furrowed with disappointment. 'Why?'

'Because we need to go home.'

'But *why*? I like it here.'

'I'm sure you do. But holidays can't last for ever.'

Effie stuck out her bottom lip. 'Will Daddy be coming with us?'

'No, he won't.'

Big green eyes gazed up at him and Lukas felt something twist inside him. 'Why not?'

'Because Daddy lives here, as you well know.' Calista looked down at her daughter, the patient reasoning in her voice starting to crack. 'Now, I've already packed our suitcases, so if Petros would be kind enough to give us a lift to the harbour…'

'I bet *Daddy* doesn't want us to go—do you, Daddy?'

Two pairs of green eyes swung in his direction, one beseeching, the other glistening with tension and anger and most of all warning.

'You must do as your mother says.' He had been silently watching the exchange between mother and daughter, but now Lukas gave his pronouncement with the full weight of his authority.

He saw the flash of surprise in Calista's eyes before she let out an audible breath.

He had to fight his every instinct, but Lukas knew this

was the right thing to do. The clever thing. He had no intention of getting into a slanging match with Calista now—not in front of Effie. If there was any moral high ground to be had he was going to take it. If Calista wanted to pack her bags and leave he wouldn't try and stop her. He could wait—at least a short while longer. And this was just the sort of unreasonable, unpredictable behaviour that would help him in the custody case. A case *he* was going to win.

Yes, very soon he would hold all the cards, and then he would see Calista come crawling back to him. It was an idea that already tightened the muscles of his groin. Once he held all the power he would have Calista just where he wanted her. And that, he knew with blinding certainty, was in his bed.

'Come on, now, little one.' Seeing Effie's bottom lip start to tremble, Lukas picked her up again and held her close. 'There's no need to be sad. I will be seeing you again very soon.'

'Promise?' The word was muffled against his chest.

'I promise. You must go with your mother now, but we'll be together again in no time.'

He put her down, giving her a little pat on the back to send her towards Calista, and their eyes clashed again. Sparks of fear and fight flew at him. She looked like a cornered animal, protecting her young. Which he supposed she was.

He chose to respond with nothing more than the faint quirk of a brow. 'Would you like me to take you back to the mainland in the helicopter?'

The more agitated he felt, the more reasonable he made himself sound. Whether he was trying to convince Calista or himself, or just limit Effie's distress, he wasn't sure. But he did know that the twisting pain in his gut had to be controlled at all costs.

'No, thank you.' Calista's brittle reply snapped between them. 'I am perfectly capable of sorting out my own travel arrangements.'

'As you wish.' But nevertheless he turned to address Petros, who stood in the doorway awaiting instructions, a worried look on his face. 'Petros, please see to it that there is a boat to transport Calista and my daughter back to the mainland.'

'Yes, sir.' Petros nodded solemnly.

'Come on, then, Effie.' With an arm around Effie's shoulder, Calista began to herd her out of the villa. 'Oh, the cases…' She looked behind her.

'Allow me.' Striding back into Calista's bedroom, Lukas picked up the two suitcases and followed them out to Petros's car, where he stowed the cases in the boot. He waited as Calista secured Effie's seatbelt, then leant to give his daughter another hug.

'Don't forget, *paidi mou*, I'll be seeing you again very soon.'

Effie nodded tearfully and, straightening up, Lukas turned to Calista who stood beside him, steadfastly avoiding his eye as she waited to close the car door.

'Calista.' He pronounced her name as a farewell.

'Goodbye, Lukas.' Proud and defiant, Calista returned his valediction.

For a moment they stared at one another, tension radiating between them like a palpable force.

'Until we meet again.' Leaning forward, Lukas spoke quietly against her ear. To a casual observer it might have looked like an affectionate gesture of parting, but it was far from that. The intent in his voice left no room for sentiment or ambiguity. 'I will be in touch very shortly to discuss arrangements.'

'Then you will be wasting your time.' Calista tossed

back her head, the rich red curls gleaming in the sunshine. 'There will be no arrangements. Effie is my daughter and she is staying with me.'

Moving past him, she went round to the other side of the car and opened the door.

Lukas was beside her in a flash, barring her way. 'Then you had better get yourself a good lawyer, Calista. You're going to need one.'

Calista glared back at him, eyes ablaze as she waited for him to get out of her way. Lukas watched as she seated herself inside the car, tugging her short dress down over her thighs before reaching across to take hold of Effie's hand.

'Oh, just so you know…' He ducked his head inside for one last parting shot. 'I will shortly be going public about your father. You might want to mention *that* to your lawyer as well.'

And with that he closed the door and banged on the roof as a signal for Petros to leave.

Standing with his hands on his hips, Lukas watched as the car took off, throwing up a cloud of dust as it bumped over the dry single-track road. He was staring at the rear window, at the back of Calista's head, when Effie's little face appeared. With her fingertips pressed to her lips she blew him a series of quick kisses before Calista's arm reached out to turn her to face the front again.

Walking back into the villa, Lukas closed the door behind him and looked around. Strangely enough, he had never felt more alone in his life.

CHAPTER ELEVEN

'PUT IT ON, Mummy.' Effie pointed to the mortarboard resting on Calista's lap.

They were on their way to her graduation ceremony in the grand university hall—something that Effie was looking forward to far more than her. Calista hesitated.

'Go on,' Effie prompted. 'Then everyone can see that this is your special day.'

'Okay!' Giving her daughter a smile, Calista did as she was told and positioned the silly hat on her head, waggling the tassel at her. 'There. Happy now?'

Effie nodded and turned to look out of the taxi window again. Calista stared at her profile. Effie being happy meant more to her than anything else in the world, and it tore at her heart to see how much quieter she had been these past few weeks, how withdrawn. She would have worn a clown outfit to the graduation ceremony if she'd thought it would cheer her up, complete with flappy shoes and red nose. But she knew there was only one thing that would light up Effie's life again, and that was to be reunited with her father.

It had been three weeks since they had returned to London, and Effie's persistent pestering about when she was going to see her daddy again had eventually settled into a gloomy acceptance that she wasn't. And that had only made Calista feel worse.

But she had fought against it—adopting a relentlessly upbeat and positive attitude, determined that she was going to make up for Lukas's absence. They'd had trips to the zoo and the park, picnics and ice creams. Effie had even been allowed to stay up long past her bedtime, snuggled against her on the sofa. Although in truth this last had been more for her own benefit. Because anything was better than being alone…being left to stare at the whole hideous mess of her life.

Every day she expected it to happen—she would hear on the news that her father's heinous acts had been exposed or a solicitor's letter would come saying that Lukas had filed for custody of Effie. Or both. Every morning she woke with the sick dread of what the day might bring, only to find that it brought nothing. No word from Lukas at all. And, far from finding any sense of relief, all she felt was pain. A tangible, physical pain—as if someone had reached in and ripped out her heart. Because that was what loving Lukas did to her. It tortured her.

The sudden screech of brakes brought her back to the present, followed by the thud of an impact that jerked them both forward against their seat belts.

'What's happened, Mummy?'

'I'm not sure, darling.' Calista looked anxiously at her daughter. 'Are you okay?'

'Yes, I'm fine.' Effie peered out of the taxi window. 'But I think that man is dead.'

Following her gaze, Calista saw a young man sprawled across the road. Quickly she unbuckled her seatbelt. She could deal with this. She was, after all, a qualified nurse.

'I'm sure he's not dead. You stay here, Effie, I'm going to see what I can do to help him.'

Effie nodded obediently and Calista leapt out of the cab to where the casualty lay. He was unconscious, still wearing a crash helmet, and his head was twisted sideways. Blood poured from a serious wound to his leg. A few feet away was the mangled wreck of his motorbike. She knelt down beside him to feel for the pulse in his neck. It was scarily weak.

'I didn't see him!' Beside her the taxi driver was choking with panic. 'He came out of nowhere. I couldn't have avoided him.'

'Call an ambulance!' Calista said firmly. This was not the time for apportioning blame.

A small group of onlookers had started to gather around them—pedestrians and people getting out of their cars as the traffic backed up behind them, horns tooting impatiently already.

'Does anyone here have any first aid experience?' There was an ominous silence.

'You.' She pointed to an intelligent-looking young man on the edge of the crowd. 'Come and help me.'

He obediently stepped forward. 'Are…are you some sort of doctor, miss?'

Standing upright, she realised she must look a bit odd, dressed in her flowing black and red graduation gown, complete with mortarboard.

'I'm a nurse.' Tossing the mortarboard to one side, she took off the gown and thrust it at the young man. 'Rip this up. We need to make a tourniquet to stop the blood.'

She bent over the casualty again, just in time to see his eyes roll back in his head. *No!* She wouldn't allow him to die. She simply wouldn't.

Grabbing the strip of fabric offered by her helper, she tied it tightly around the casualty's thigh and then, unzipping his leather jacket, started CPR, pumping at his chest with her linked hands as hard as she could, totally focussed on what she had to do.

Minutes passed and still she worked, blotting every-thing else out, refusing to give up no matter how much her arms ached, how heavily her breath rasped in her throat. She could hear the wail of an ambulance siren in the dis-tance, coming closer. *Hurry up, hurry up.* She could do this. She was going to keep this young man alive.

Lukas held his finger against the buzzer for Calista's flat. Irritation clenched his jaw. She was either ignoring him or she was out. Or, worse still—he felt the irritation turn to something much darker—she and Effie had upped sticks and left.

He should have told them he was coming, of course. That would have been the sensible thing to do. But all sense went out of the window as far as Calista was concerned. Besides, he was looking forward to surprising Effie. And her mother too—but in a very different way.

He had spent the intervening weeks in Athens, working all hours, pushing himself harder and harder to achieve his goals. And he had succeeded, leaving the staff of Kalanos Shipping reeling from the full force of his formidable de-mands and expectations. As for Blue Sky Charters—the sacking of Nico and Tavi had sent shock waves through that company. The sheer ruthlessness of their boss meant they were now all on high alert to make sure the same thing didn't happen to them.

Aside from business, Lukas had instructed his lawyers to start custody proceedings for his daughter and had col-lated more than enough information to expose Aristotle Gianopoulous for the monstrous villain that he was.

He should have been feeling pleased with himself, sat-isfied with all he had accomplished. Instead he just felt knotted up with tension. Far from feeling any sort of tri-umph, he couldn't shake off the feeling that he had somehow overstepped the boundaries—mistreated Calista right from the start. *Somehow she had made him feel bad.* And that was despite everything he knew, all that she had done. It didn't make any sense.

He missed Effie, of course. Villa Helene felt horribly empty without her there, without her cheery little face opposite him at the breakfast table, without hearing her asking him what they were going to do that day. He had hoped that relocating to his apartment in Athens would improve his frame of mind, but he had found no relief from his gloom there either. Quite the reverse.

Throwing himself into his work had only darkened his mood, made him more irritable, more unreasonable. And the fleeting thought that maybe he should go out, seek some entertainment in one of Athens's many exclusive clubs, had been so repugnant that he'd wondered if he was ill—if there was something physically wrong with him.

But he wasn't ill—at least not in the accepted sense of the word. Deep down he knew all too well where the source of his malaise came from. *Calista Gianopoulous,* that was where. She had crept under his skin, peeled back the protective layers, made him question everything about himself—his motives and his morals. *She had got to him.* His hollow yearning for something undefined had gradually given shape to the certainty that he had to have her in his life. Permanently.

It was a deeply shocking realisation.

And he didn't just mean in his bed at night—although the recollection of what they had done still mercilessly ripped into him. The image of Calista…beautiful Calista… her hair wildly cascading down her back, was seared onto his retina, appearing without his permission whenever he tried to close his eyes. The memory of the way she had looked when he had brought her to orgasm, the way she had felt, tasted, smelled, filled his mind, blocked his sleep and stole his sanity. Try as he might, he simply couldn't get her out of his head.

Which was why last night he had finally given up and made the decision to come to London and sort out this infuriating state of affairs once and for all. How he was going to do it, Lukas no longer had any idea.

But first he had to find her.

The front door opened and Magda appeared.

'I'm looking for Calista. Is she in? Is my daughter here?'

'No. She and Effie have already left.'

'Left?' The word struck fear into his heart and mentally he was already tracking them down, bringing them back, doing whatever it took to return them to where they belonged. With him.

'Yes, for our graduation ceremony.'

Magda held up the gown that Lukas had failed to notice was draped over her arm. Then she pointed over at a taxi idling on the other side of the road.

'That's my taxi, there. Calista went ahead of me because she wanted to—'

'It doesn't matter why.' Rudely interrupting, he ushered Magda towards the waiting taxi and all but bundled her in, following behind her and slamming the door. Leaning forward, he went to speak the taxi driver before realising he had no idea where they were going. 'Wherever *she* says.' He indicated the astonished Magda. 'And make it fast.'

But it wasn't fast. They had been travelling for less than ten minutes when the traffic ground to a halt. There was a queue of vehicles backed up as far as the eye could see.

'There's been an accident, mate.' The taxi driver slid back the glass partition to speak them. 'You might find it quicker to go on foot.'

Hell and damnation. Thrusting some money at him, Lukas took hold of Magda's hand and pulled her out after him.

'You know the way?' He raised his voice over the sound of the ambulance that was fighting its way through the traffic on the other side of the road.

'I should do.' Magda straightened her skirt. 'I've studied there for three years.'

'Then what are we waiting for? Lead the way.'

'How is he, Dr Lorton?' Calista leapt up as the A&E doctor came towards her.

'Out of danger.' The doctor put an arm around her shoulders. 'You did a great job, Nurse Gianopoulous.'

'And the leg?'

'They've taken him up for surgery now. Mr Dewsnap is pretty certain he can save it.'

'Oh, thank God for that.'

'Seriously, though, Calista, I mean it. You saved that young man's life. Your mummy...' he bent down to speak to Effie, who was busy colouring in some complicated anatomical drawings that someone had found to keep her occupied '...is a proper hero!'

Effie beamed back at him.

'Shame you had to miss your graduation ceremony, though.' Straightening up, Dr Lorton eyed Calista.

'Oh, I'm not bothered about that. At least the gown was put to good use!'

'And this was far more exciting.' Effie joined in the conversation. 'I had a ride in the front of an ambulance and everything.'

'So I heard!'

Calista scooped up her daughter and gave her a big hug. She hoped this incident hadn't been too traumatic for her.

The ambulance that had arrived at the scene had come from the hospital where she'd done her nursing practice and she'd known the paramedics on board. Reluctant to leave her patient, she had accepted their suggestion that she accompany them back to the hospital. There was no way she could have gone on to the ceremony looking as she did anyway—all wild and bloodied. Plus the fact that in all the confusion she'd left her handbag in the taxi, which meant that as well as missing her purse and her phone she didn't have the keys to get into her flat.

She'd called the taxi firm, who had promised to return her bag to the hospital, but in the meanwhile she'd had a shower and found a change of clothes in her locker while various members of staff had fussed over Effie. Judging by the look on her face, Effie had had the time of her life.

'I think I'm going to be a nurse when I grow up.' Wriggling to be put down, Effie went back to her colouring. 'Either that or a shipping *magnet* person.'

'Wow!' Dr Lorton gave Calista an astonished grin.

Calista tried to smile back but her lips had frozen on her face.

'Just like my daddy.'

Lukas's patience was wearing dangerously thin. It felt as if he had been here for hours, seated at the back of this echoing hall of hallowed learning, watching an endless parade of students filing onto the stage to collect their scrolls of achievement, shaking hands, smiling, moving on. What was worse was that there was no sign of Calista. Now he could see Magda, lining up at the bottom of the steps, waiting to be called. This had to be Calista's class. Where the hell *was* she?

'Calista Gianopoulous!'

Suddenly her name echoed around the hall, only to be

met with silence, followed by whisperings and some shuffling of papers before they moved on to the next student.

Lukas rose to his feet and moved to the edge of the hall, then made his way towards the front, waiting in the wings. Had Calista found out that he was here? Was that why she had done a disappearing act?

He looked around him, scanning the assembled audience as if half expecting her to have donned some disguise or to be hiding under a seat. Though he had no idea why. Calista never shied away from confrontation. If she were here now she'd be more likely to be laying into him, eyes flashing, breasts heaving, that wild red hair being tossed around her heart-shaped face. Lukas sucked in a breath. God, how he had missed her.

'Magda Jedynak.'

He positioned himself at the bottom of the steps as Magda descended, deftly ushering her to one side as the applause rang out for the next student.

'Where is she, Magda?'

'I don't know!' Moving them into a small chamber off the main hall, Magda looked at him with genuine concern. 'I can't understand it. She and Effie left well before me… us, I mean. I've tried texting her—but nothing.'

'Then try again.' He omitted to say that he himself had already left countless unanswered messages on her phone.

Fumbling beneath her robe, Magda produced her phone and flicked on the screen. 'One message, but it's not from Calista.'

Lukas scowled. He had no intention of standing there watching her read a message from her boyfriend.

'Oh, it *is* Cal—she's using someone else's phone. There's been an accident…she and Effie are at the hospital.'

'Which hospital?' A wave of black panic washed over

him, consumed him, and his words sounded as if they'd been spoken by someone else.

'Um… St George's. But she says not to worry. They are both—'

Before Magda had the chance to finish her sentence Lukas was gone, his footsteps thundering down the central aisle between the rows of seats, every head turning in his direction as he wrenched open the ancient wooden doors and flung himself out into the street.

'How much longer do we have to stay here?'

'Not long. As soon as the taxi company bring my bag we can go. Now, come away from the doors.'

Clearly the novelty of being at the hospital had worn off for Effie, and she was entertaining herself by activating the automatic doors at Reception. Calista threw the well-thumbed magazine back down on the table in front of her and yawned. All she wanted to do was to go home.

'He's here!'

Looking up at Effie's yelp of pleasure, Calista saw her jumping up and down, waving madly.

'All right, calm down!' A taxi had pulled up outside, but it hardly merited Effie's ecstatic welcome. She was obviously emotionally overwrought.

'Look, look. It's Daddy! He's *here*!'

Calista felt the world do a giddy spin. *Lukas?* No, he couldn't be! But suddenly there he was, powering through the doors towards them, so commanding, so strikingly handsome that all eyes were on him.

As if watching in slow motion Calista saw him scoop up an overjoyed Effie, quickly casting his eyes over her, and saw the look of grim determination on his face soften as he bent to kiss her on the forehead. Then he turned and straightened up, and suddenly the full force of his attention was on her.

Calista swallowed. Eyes as black as midnight tore into her, immediately shredding the paper-thin patches she had tried to put in place to protect her heart. It was as if he could destroy her with just one look. Tear her apart. This man could control the pumping of her heart, the breath in her chest, the blood in her veins.

He was everything to her, and the more she tried to fight it the more entangled she became. Like a fish caught in a net, the more she thrashed about trying to escape, the worse it was for her.

'Calista.' He was right in front of her now, swallowing her space, with Effie clamped to his side like a limpet. 'What's happened? Are you okay?'

Calista realised that she was standing up, one hand gripping the back of the seat. *No!* she wanted to scream at him. *I am not okay. Every fibre of my being yearns for you... every molecule aches because of you. Loving you has undone me, destroyed me. And I will never, ever recover.*

But none of those words could be said. So, straightening her spine, she pulled in a breath. 'Yes, I'm fine.'

'And Effie?'

'She's fine too. We are both…fine.'

'Then what are you doing here?' Setting Effie down on her feet, he bore down on Calista, placing possessive hands on her shoulders.

'I could ask *you* the same question.'

'For God's sake, Calista.' He frantically searched her face. 'What's going on? Magda said there had been some kind of accident.'

'A man on a motorbike,' Effie helpfully chipped in. 'Mummy saved his life.'

'But neither of you was injured?'

Calista shook her head.

'Thank God!' Lukas's shoulders visibly dropped.

'We were in the taxi that hit him, that's all. Did you say you'd seen Magda?' Calista furrowed her brow, struggling to understand.

'Yes. At the graduation ceremony.'

'You've been to Magda's graduation ceremony?' Her brain seemed to have turned to pulp, like a ball of newspaper left out in the rain. Nothing was making any sense.

'No—well, yes...'

'What were you doing there?'

'I went looking for *you*, of course.'

'Right...' Calista made herself breathe through the fog. There was something about his phrase—*looking for you*—that sent a chill down her stiffened spine. He hadn't come to *see* her, He had come to *find* her. And that had a very different connotation.

She stared into his face, so beautiful but so brutally punishing. A rogue muscle twitched in his cheek and she knew she had read him right.

'Can I ask why?' Her voice held a thread of steel but as she waited the dread of his reply wound around her, tightening its grip. She held her head very still, as if afraid it might part company from the rest of her body.

Silence fell between them. The voices of the people around them were reduced to a soft babble. Lukas shifted his weight from one leg to the other, staring at her with a dark intensity that seemed to be searching her soul.

Or was it his own soul?

For the first time Calista caught the flash of vulnerability in his eyes. Could it be that he was actually battling with himself? Fighting some internal conflict?

His eyes never leaving her face, he took the black

leather document case from under his arm and after a moment's pause chucked it onto a nearby seat.

'To do this.'

With a rapid movement he wrapped his arms around her, pressing her against him, one hand moving to the small of her back, where it branded her with its possessive heat.

'And then this.'

Lifting her chin, he took a second to gaze at her startled face before lowering his head and claiming her lips in a blisteringly passionate kiss.

And Calista surrendered to it, melting against him, because there had never been any question of her doing anything else.

She was dimly aware of a ripple of applause, a whistle of appreciation. And then the gleefully shocked voice of her daughter, saying, 'Ew, *yuck*!'

CHAPTER TWELVE

'SHE'S ALREADY SOUND ASLEEP.' Coming through from Effie's bedroom, Calista accepted the glass of champagne that Lukas proffered and sank down onto the sofa. 'She was obviously worn out.'

'I'm not surprised.' Magda came and sat beside her. 'From the sound of it she has had quite a day!'

Calista laughed. Effie had certainly made the most of the day's events, explaining them first to Lukas and then to Magda, and then to the florist who had delivered an enormous bouquet of flowers sent by the patient's family. She had gone into graphic detail over just how her mummy had saved this man's life because he had actually been totally, properly dead, and how she was the biggest hero ever because everybody said so.

'Mmm…yum.' Magda took a sip from her glass. 'Thank you for this, Lukas.' She looked up at him with a mixture of curiosity and blatant admiration.

'My pleasure.'

Calista followed her gaze. Standing with his back to the window, Lukas stood tall and imposing, owning the space even though this was supposed to be *her* domain. She tried to look at him dispassionately—the way Magda would see him. But that only set her heart racing, the way it always did. The way it always would.

Wearing dark grey suit trousers and a fine pinstriped grey and white shirt with the sleeves rolled up, he epitomised the billionaire businessman at ease. Except there was something tense about the set of his shoulders, the angle of his lightly stubbled jaw. His hair had grown since that day she had glimpsed him on the other side of her father's grave—the day that had so dramatically impacted on her life. The severe style he had worn in prison was now softened by loose dark curls at the nape of his neck and starting to fall over his forehead before they were raked back by his impatient hand.

But if his hairstyle was softer it was the only thing about him that was. As she stared at him now, still exuding that chillingly austere authority, Calista felt a knife plunge into her soul. Because she knew why he was here. Despite the urbane courteousness, despite the very public kiss they had shared in the hospital, he was here to try and take Effie from her. It was written all over his treacherous face.

'I would like to propose a toast.' His rich, dark voice resonated around the small room.

'Oh, yes—good idea.' Magda sat upright, her glass raised.

'To the two newly qualified nurses. May you both have long and distinguished careers.'

'Thank you. I'll drink to that.' Magda smiled and Lukas stepped forward so that the three of them could clink glasses.

'And, of course, to Calista.'

'Yay! Callie! Our very own hero!'

They clinked glasses again, and Magda leant in to give Calista a big hug. But as Magda pulled away she caught the look on Lukas's face, saw the way his eyes had settled on Calista and she gave a little cough.

'You know what?' She tugged theatrically at the neck of her blouse. 'I think I might make myself scarce.'

'No, don't do that.' Calista reached for her hand, clutching at it in desperation.

'Actually, Magda,' Lukas cut in, 'I want to ask you a favour. Would you mind babysitting this evening, so that I can take Calista out for a meal?'

'Of course.' Magda grinned helpfully. 'Gladly. You go.'

'Oh, no, Magda.' Calista looked at her friend with beseeching eyes. 'I'm sure you must have plans of your own for this evening.'

'No, no plans at all—other than polishing off the rest of that bottle of champagne. You go. And don't hurry back.'

Calista looked daggers at her. Was Magda doing this deliberately? Wasn't she making it perfectly obvious that the thought of being left alone with Lukas filled her with a sickening dread?

'Good, that's settled, then.' Putting his glass down on the table, Lukas picked up his jacket and hooked it over his shoulder with one finger. 'I have a couple of things to do, so I'll pick you up in an hour. Oh…'

He turned, and Calista saw the hard light glittering in his eyes. 'You might want to dress up. After all, this evening is something of a celebration.'

Lukas's dark brows drew together as he watched Calista's mouth close around her forkful of lobster mousse, seeing her swallow, licking her lips with the tip of her tongue to savour the last morsel. They were seated in an exclusive French restaurant in the heart of Mayfair, chosen by Lukas in the hope that the intimate atmosphere would be conducive to conversation. To them starting to sort out their differences. But there had been precious little of that so far.

Polite on the surface, Calista seemed to be paying great attention to her meal. But her body language was stiff, bordering on hostile, as if she was poised, ready to strike back at anything he might say. He, in turn, was still wrestling with the internal struggle that had been plaguing him ever since he had arrived in London, so intent on achieving his aims.

Aims that now floated dead in the water.

The custody case would be dropped. He could never take Effie away from Calista. The idea was preposterous—it always had been. He had been fooling himself from the start. He had been so angry, so hell-bent on making Calista pay for the past, on making up for the years he had lost with his daughter that he had allowed a red mist to cloud his vision, bitterness and vitriol to twist his logic.

Seeing them together in the hospital had forcibly changed his mind. The fact that they were safe, unharmed, had brought such a massive rush of relief it had left him winded, unbalanced. How else could he explain what he'd done—kissing Calista like that, in front of everyone?

No, he could never separate them. Calista and Effie came as a package—a warm, loving, funny, devoted package. He didn't want to tear them apart. He wanted them both. With *him*. Permanently. The question was, just how did he achieve that?

Lukas looked down, fighting to try and order his thoughts. It was hellishly difficult. Seeing Calista again in the flesh, that beautiful porcelain-pale flesh so smooth and warm and incredibly inviting, messed with his head to the point where he thought it might explode. It messed with other parts of his body too.

Suggesting that she dress up this evening had not been such a clever idea. The short gold-coloured cocktail dress shimmered over her curves, catching the light as she turned. With a fitted bust, square neckline and wide shoulder straps it was not particularly revealing—more classy and sexy, a little bit quirky…just like Calista herself. She had swept her hair up into a loose bun at the nape of her neck, the stray curls of hair falling softly around her face giving her a Renaissance, ethereal look.

She looked enchanting, eminently tempting, but most of all *deadly*.

Because Calista was like a drug to him—dangerous and addictive. She made him act in ways that were totally out of character. Firstly his brutish behaviour on the day of her father's funeral—something that he now looked back on with shame—and, even worse than that, the way she was making him feel right now. Raw, hollow, vulnerable. Like no other woman ever had made him feel. Not even close. Hungry with something that wasn't just lust.

Lukas had always known that he craved Calista's body. After all, hadn't he spent years in his prison cell plotting how he would claim her, repeat the sexual experience they had shared, only this time on *his* terms? It had been one of his few pleasures in that echoing temple of misery—something to keep him sane.

Oh, he had dressed it up as revenge, or maybe some sort of sexual infatuation that he needed to get out of his system, but now he knew it was neither of those things. It wasn't just sexual possession he craved—he wanted all of her…body and soul. This wasn't an animal urge. This went deeper—much deeper. To a dark and unknown place where feelings lurked that he didn't want to acknowledge, where emotions that had lain dormant had suddenly started to shift, to rise up, become real. Sentiments that had no part in his life.

The word *love* floated unbidden into his mind, refusing to be batted away. Was it possible that he was in love with Calista? It was an idea so alien, so ridiculous, that he refused to give it countenance. Instead he turned it around to make it more palatable. He wanted Calista to love *him*—

that was what it was. The way she said she once had. *That* he could deal with.

He picked up his glass and took a swallow of red wine.

'Well, you have certainly made our daughter proud today.'

'Yes.' Calista allowed herself a small smile. 'But I hope seeing all that drama hasn't been too much for her—you know, gives her nightmares or something.' She glanced at the watch on her wrist. 'I probably shouldn't be too late back.'

'Effie will be just fine.' He spoke firmly, taking control. He wasn't going to let her slip away from him like that. 'First there are things we need to discuss.'

'Very well.' She sat back as the waiter cleared away their plates, folding her arms across her chest. 'Say whatever it is you have to say. But I warn you, Lukas, if it's about taking Effie away from me—'

'It's not.'

His words brought her up short and he saw the look of hope in her eyes as she raised her hand to her mouth in a gesture so charming, so beguiling, that it twisted something inside him. For all her bravado he could see she was afraid of what he might do to her. Once he would have gained satisfaction from that—now it just made him feel like a heel.

'I have decided not to file for custody of Effie.'

'You have?' Relief lit up her eyes and she leant forward to clasp his hand. But almost immediately doubt set in and she let go again, tightly linking her hands in front of her. 'What made you change your mind?'

'I have come up with a better solution.' He concentrated on making his voice even, as flat and smooth as a becalmed sea. 'You and Effie will come and live with me in Greece.'

Calista's shoulders sagged, her eyes clouding over for

a moment before her head went back and the fire returned with a vengeance. 'No, Lukas!'

'I think Athens would be the preferred location.'

Lukas continued as if she hadn't spoken. If he stopped to consider her insulting automatic refusal he feared his self-restraint, already tested to the limit, might well shatter completely.

'Though I am prepared to consider other areas, as long as they are not too far from Thalassa.'

'You are not listening to me. Effie and I are going nowhere. We are staying here—in the UK.'

'You may choose the property—more than one, if you so wish, as large and as grand as you like. We will find the very best school for Effie.'

Still he persevered, ignoring the roaring in his ears, his nails digging into his palms as he fought to control the frustration that was surging inside him. The overwhelming urge to sling her over his shoulder and carry her off to his cave there and then.

'I said no.'

'You will want for nothing.' He made one last almighty effort.

A current of electricity crackled between them, waiting to be touched, to do its harm.

'Nothing except my freedom.'

Calista reached for it, whispering the words under her breath.

For a long moment they stared at one another, bitterness and anger holding them both taut, silent. And something else—always that something else that neither of them could control, try as they might.

'I hardly think *you* are in a position to talk about loss of freedom.' The words trickled out insidiously, like a ribbon of poison.

'No. And you are never, *ever* going to let me forget it, are you?' Calista snatched up her napkin, balling it in her fist. 'That's what all this is really about, isn't it, Lukas? You are still trying to make me pay for the sins of my father by threatening to take Effie away from me.'

'Dammit, Calista!' His raised voice turned the heads of other diners and he took a moment, forcing himself to find some control. 'This is nothing to do with your wretched father. This is about Effie being a part of my life. *My life.*' He almost hissed the words at her. 'Not just yours—no matter how much you would like it to be that way. Can't you see? I'm *trying* to find a workable solution!'

'By insisting that we move to Greece?' Still she pushed. 'By putting me and Effie in a golden cage and throwing away the key?'

'Did I *say* it would be like that?'

'No?' She tossed back her head. 'Then tell me what it *would* be like.'

Lukas dragged in a breath, searching for the very last shreds of his patience. 'You would have your own life, your own friends. If you wanted to pursue your nursing career I wouldn't have a problem with that.'

'Oh, how very gracious of you.'

Lukas ground down hard on his jaw. She was really pushing him now.

Reaching forward, he covered her fidgeting hands with his own and fixed her with a merciless stare. 'If I were you, *agapi mou*, I would drop the attitude.'

'Or what?' She fired the shot back at him.

What, indeed? *Or I will make you pay.* The words remained unspoken in his head. Along with the image of how he would do it. With her naked beneath him, on top of him, in front of him. With her screaming his name in ecstasy, begging for more. He could have happily taken her right there and then—swept aside the silver cutlery, the fine china plates and crystal glasses and really given the other diners something to stare at. So strong were his feelings for her. Such was the power she had over him.

He let his eyes close for a second, reining in the crazy madness that was threatening to drag him under.

'Or you may regret it.'

It was a poor substitute for what he wanted to say, what he wanted to do, but as the waiter arrived with their next course he let go of her hands and sat back.

Minutes passed. Lukas began eating his steak. Calista nudged her sea bass with her fork.

'So, how would you see it working?' Her voice was quiet, brittle.

'Working?'

'Well…' She pushed her plate away from her. 'You say that I would have my own friends. Would that be *men* friends?'

Instantly every muscle in Lukas's body tightened, the veins in his neck throbbing with suppressed rage at the very thought.

'No, I thought as much.' Calista gave a hollow laugh of victory. 'Whereas *you*, presumably, would be free to see who you wanted, whenever you wanted. A pretty parade of women on your arm, in your bed.'

'And that would bother you?' He tried to cover his body's betrayal with a deliberately flippant reply.

Calista twitched. 'It wouldn't bother *me*.' She was lying through her pretty white teeth. 'But it would be very damaging for Effie.'

'And if I were to promise that there would be no women?'

'Don't make promises you can't keep, Lukas.'

'Oh, believe me, I don't.' He paused, choosing his words

with care. 'If we live together there will be no women in my bed.'

'Yeah, right.'

'Other than you, of course.'

'Me?' Pure shock flushed her cheeks.

'Yes—you, Calista. I have every confidence that you will be enough to satisfy my sexual needs.'

'Then your arrogance has taken over your senses.' Green eyes flashed back at him, twists of flame-coloured curls dancing around her heated face. 'Whatever makes you think that I would agree to share your bed?'

'Because I have seen the way you come apart in my arms, felt your nails clawing my back, heard your voice scream my name.' He was going to spare her no mercy. 'You can deny it all you want—do the whole ice maiden routine if it makes you feel better. But you and I both know the truth. You want me every bit as much as I want you. The attraction between us is mutual. And, more than that, it is beyond our control.'

'You flatter yourself. I can control it any time I like.'

'The way you did after your father's funeral? In my apartment in Athens? Even at the hospital today when I kissed you? If that is your definition of control I look forward to being there when you lose it.'

'You know what, Lukas?' Throwing down her napkin, Calista started to get up from the table. 'I'm leaving.'

'No, you are not.'

The booming power of his voice saw Calista glance around her, then sit down again. Picking up his glass, Lukas took a deep swallow of wine, taking a moment to steady himself.

'You can leave when you've heard what I have to say.'

'I've heard enough, thank you.'

'No, you haven't.' He looked down at his wine glass,

twisting the stem between his fingers, rotating it once, twice. 'Not so long ago you told me that you once loved me.'

'So?'

'That has led me to a surprising conclusion.' He raised his eyes, deliberately spearing her with their lethal intensity.

Calista stared back at him. Her brow was furrowed but there was a softness there, a tenderness that clutched at his chest.

'I put it to you, Calista Gianopoulous…' he swallowed firmly '…that you still do.'

CHAPTER THIRTEEN

CALISTA FELT HER face crumple, her cheeks burn with humiliation. Stupid woman that she was. *Stupid, stupid woman.* Instinctively she raised her hands to try and cover her mortified expression, but it was too late. He had seen it. She had caught his complacent look before she had shamefully lowered her eyes to the floor.

He knew.

She might has well have had the words pinned to her back on a piece of paper, the way children did in the school playground. *Calista loves Lukas. Spread it.*

She had spent so long trying to cover it up—from him, from herself, from the whole damned world—that now, when it came to the crunch, when she really should have had her defences shored up, Lukas had brought them crashing down with a simple, elegant theory. But worse than that—far worse…and she could hardly believe her own idiocy here…for one moment of pathetic lunacy she had thought he was going to tell her that *he* loved *her.*

She was obviously losing it. The balance of her mind was clearly disturbed. She was ill.

Reaching down, she felt for her bag. She really was leaving now, and nothing Lukas could say or do would stop her. Scraping back her chair, she pushed herself shakily to her feet and automatically Lukas did the same. She could feel his eyes all over her, spreading goosebumps across her skin as if he had reached out to stop her. But he didn't.

She started to move, weaving her way between the tables and past the *maître d'* at the entrance, convinced that at any moment she would feel Lukas's strong grasp on her arm, bringing her to a halt. But, no. Now she was through the main door and outside, racing up the steps and onto the pavement. She paused for a split second, unsure which way to go, listening to her heart thudding in her chest.

A soft rain was falling, dampening the London streets, picked out by the orange glow of the streetlights. Calista turned right, with no clear idea of where she was going other than that it had to be far away from Lukas. She had embarrassed herself enough for one evening. Now she wanted to hide away and lick her wounds. She walked at a brisk pace, dodging past other pedestrians: laughing groups of young people dressed in their glad rags, foreign tourists putting up their umbrellas, a few late-night shoppers.

Every now and then she glanced over her shoulder to see if Lukas was following her. Her relief was tinged with absurd disappointment when she realised he was not. She strode on through St James's Park, where people were walking their dogs, lovers strolling arm in arm, until she reached the Embankment, where finally she slowed to a stop, leaning against the wall and dragging in a painful breath.

The River Thames flowed lazily before her, lights dancing on the black water, illuminated pleasure boats gliding by, smaller craft going about their business. All totally oblivious to her misery.

Lukas watched her from his position against a tree, twenty or so yards away. She had been easy enough to follow, her red hair bobbing up and down as she had marched through the streets, that golden dress of hers shimmering beneath the streetlights before disappearing again into the shadows.

No matter how dark it was, how much she tried to blend in with the crowd, he could always have picked her out. Even blindfolded, with a hood tied over his head. Because Calista shone like a bright light for him. And like a moth he was drawn to her, hypnotised by her. He was under her spell...

Calista shivered, the fine rain settling on her bare skin, running in rivulets between her breasts. She should hail a taxi and go home.

For the first time it occurred to her that maybe that was where Lukas had gone. Why would he chase through the streets of London after her when he could simply park his elegant self down on her shabby couch and wait for her to return? Or maybe he had done neither of these things but returned to the executive suite of his exclusive hotel to gloat over his victory—the fact that he had won her heart.

'Calista?'

With a gasp of shock she spun around, straight into the solid wall of Lukas's body. Strong arms encircled her, pressing her against him. He felt so good. So right.

'You are soaking wet.' Moving them apart, Lukas shrugged off his jacket and wrapped it around her shoulders, pulling the lapels together under her chin. Then, taking hold of her face, he gazed into her eyes.

'Why are you following me?' She made a weak attempt to confront him, but in truth she was tired of fighting. So very tired.

Lukas gave a short laugh. 'You didn't think I would let you go, did you?' Releasing one hand, he smoothed it over the damp curls of her hair, tucking the stray locks behind her ear. 'I will *never* let you go.' His voice was terrifyingly calm.

Calista stared back at him. Like a deadly promise his words permeated her skin and her bones, squeezing past her internal organs until they found her very core, where they pulsed low and hard and unforgiving.

'And I have no say in the matter?'

'None whatsoever.' He lowered his head, and his breath was a warm caress against her face before his lips brushed hers with a soft, feather-light touch. 'From now on you do as I say.'

'Oh, you think so, do you?' Calista whispered hoarsely.

'Yes, I do.' He pulled back a fraction. 'Firstly I want a proper answer to the question that saw you bolt from the restaurant.' Ebony-black eyes searched her face. '*Do* you love me, Calista?'

Calista waited a beat before finally giving in. 'Yes.'

One hushed word said it all.

'Then say it.' It seemed he was determined to torture her.

'I love you, Lukas.' There was no point in denying it now. She was already stripped bare. 'I wish I didn't, but I do.'

'Hmm…I'm liking the first part of that confession. The second part less so.' He traced his fingertip across her mouth as if to erase it.

'This isn't funny, Lukas.'

'I'm not laughing. In fact when it comes to you and me I have never been more serious about anything in my life.'

'There *is* no "you and me".'

'Oh, but there is.' His eyes shone black. 'I must admit I was afraid that there might never be. I knew I had the power to force you to share custody of Effie, to come and live with me in Greece or the UK or wherever. That didn't really matter. But the one thing I couldn't do was force you to love me.'

'You didn't need to force me.'

'I know that now. And I thank the gods that have intervened on my behalf to make this happen.'

'Lukas…'

'No, hear me out, Calista. There is nothing standing in our way now. We can be a couple—a *real* couple, in every sense of the word. In fact…' He paused, suddenly deadly serious. 'I want us to be man and wife.'

With a gasp Calista freed herself from him arms. 'You're asking me to *marry* you?'

'Is that so shocking?'

'Yes!' She wobbled on her feet as if she had stepped off the highest rung of a ladder. 'Shocking and impossible. It can *never* happen.'

'Why? You have admitted that you love me. We both love Effie. What is there to stop us?'

Calista looked down, unshed tears blocking her throat. 'To make a relationship work…a marriage work…both parties need to love each other.' Her voice was very small. 'Not just one.'

Lukas let his eyes travel slowly over her dejected but still defiant figure. Her head was bent, her torso swamped by the jacket that hung over her shoulders. Raindrops sparkled in her hair and as he reached for her, bringing her close and tipping her head, he could see the glitter of tears in her eyes.

And the shackles of his pride fell away.

Suddenly, miraculously, he was able to say what he thought—accept what he had always known. He was free to face up to the truth and express the one thing that mattered—the only thing that mattered. He was in love with

Calista. He had never said it before, even to himself, but it was a simple incontrovertible fact.

He sounded out the words in his head. *I love you, Calista.* They seemed surprisingly natural—as if they had always been there waiting to be spoken. But there was also a strange sense of loss. Because by giving his heart to Calista he was losing a part of himself. The bitter and resentful part...the hostile, vengeful part. It had been with him so long, knew him so well, that he had thought it made up the man he was.

But now he knew differently. Without even trying, without even knowing it, Calista had slain that vicious monster and set him free. Free to love her.

And yet she had no idea what she had done.

Taking her face in his hands, he turned it towards him and caught the pain in her eyes, the hurt. He wanted to take it away with a blistering kiss. He longed to show his love for her, right there and then, and not by using mere words. But that would have to come later. Right now words would have to do. If only he could find them.

'If love is the issue then there is no impediment to our marriage.'

Calista stared back at him, uncomprehending. Which wasn't surprising, considering he'd sounded like a jumped-up lawyer or a jerk—or both.

'What I'm trying to say is...' He rubbed the pads of his thumbs along her jaw. 'What I'm trying to tell you...'

'Yes?'

Oh, for God's sake, man.

'Calista.' He pulled in a breath. 'You are the most obstinate, infuriating, maddeningly wonderful woman that I have ever had the good fortune to come across.' Calista blinked back at him. 'And I love you with all my heart.'

There was a stunned silence.

'No.' Calista pulled away. 'You can't.'

'Yes, Calista, I do.'

'You're just saying that.' She cast about as if looking for an answer, her eyes following the inky-black river. 'This is just some plan you have come up with to try and trick me. Or you think it's what I want to hear. Or maybe it's some sort of aberration.'

'You mean I would have to be suffering some sort of mental illness to be in love with you?' The corner of his mouth quirked.

'Yes—no. I don't know.' Looking back at him, she frowned solemnly. 'Maybe…'

'Then I am indeed afflicted.'

He smiled at her now…an open, guileless smile that was rewarded with a small twitch of her lips. But that wasn't enough—he wanted much more. So he waited, his head on one side, his eyebrows raised, his eyes holding hers. And finally he was rewarded with a real smile, so dazzling, so heartfelt that it threatened to undo him completely.

He pulled her back into his arms, burying his face in her wet hair, inhaling her uniquely wonderful scent mixed with the dampness of a London night.

'I love you, Calista. Whether you believe it or not. Whether you want me to or not. If that makes me crazy in the head…' he pulled back to look into her face again '… Then I'm guilty as charged.'

'Oh, Lukas!'

'And I want to marry you more than anything in the world.' Dropping down onto one knee, Lukas took hold of her hands and clasped them to his chest. 'Calista Gianopoulous, would you do me the greatest honour of becoming my wife?'

Calista looked down at him, her eyes shining with love and tears and with what Lukas desperately hoped was the most important 'yes' of his life. From somewhere behind them Big Ben began pealing the hour. He counted three, four, five agonising chimes before Calista finally spoke.

'Yes, Lukas Kalanos.' Her voice cracked and tears started to run down her cheeks. Hysteria was not far away. 'My answer is yes. I *will* marry you!'

Relief and elation and pure, fathomless love sprang Lukas to his feet and he held out his arms for Calista to fall into, wrapping her in a crushing embrace.

Big Ben's final toll rang out unheard. Because as their eyes closed and their lips met for this most precious, tender kiss time for Calista and Lukas stood perfectly still.

'Does this look okay?' Calista stood before Lukas wearing one of his pristine shirts over the gold cocktail dress, artfully tied around her waist, sleeves rolled up. 'I don't want to go back looking like a dirty stop-out.'

'But that's exactly what you are, *agape*.' Lukas pulled her towards him, linking his arms around her waist. 'And a very sexy one at that.'

Pressed so closely against him, Calista felt the stirrings of his arousal.

'How about we ring Magda and say we will be another hour or so?'

'No!' With a laugh she pushed him away.

Having spent the night at Lukas's hotel, they had only just managed to get themselves up and showered and dressed—all of those things repeatedly interrupted by more carnal matters. And this after a night of such passion, such intense emotional and physical joy, that it didn't seem possible that they could still crave more of one another. But of course they did. And always would.

'We can't impose on Magda any more.' She gave him

a quick kiss. 'And, besides, Effie will be waiting for us. I can't wait to tell her we're getting married!'

'You think she will be pleased?'

'Pleased? She'll be *ecstatic*! She adores you, Lukas, surely you know that? Just like her mother does.' Her eyes shone with love. 'Plus, of course, she'll get to be bridesmaid.'

'Whatever did I do to deserve you two?' Suddenly serious, Lukas pulled back to look into her eyes. 'I've been such a fool, Calista—such an idiot, trying to control you rather than letting myself love you, mistaking the intensity of my feelings for anger and revenge when all the time I was just madly in love with you.'

'You had every right to be filled with fury after what my father did to you. What *I* did.'

'No, not you, Calista. You were completely blameless. I concocted that story because I couldn't believe you'd come to me that night simply because you wanted me.'

'Not just wanted you, Lukas—*loved* you. Even then. But I couldn't tell you. I let my pride get in the way of admitting the truth.'

'I love your pride. And your smile and your scowl and your temper and your big heart. Especially your big heart.' He gave her a lopsided smile. 'Even when it means I end up having to reinstate members of my own staff.'

Calista grinned. 'Thanks for agreeing to do that. I'm sure Nico and Tavi have learnt their lesson, and you said yourself they're good workers. It was just a bit of silly chest-beating, you know that.'

'I do now.'

For a second they gazed at one another in silence. Then Calista bit down on her lip.

'Come on—spill.' Lukas searched her face. 'What's troubling you now?'

'I was just thinking about my father.'

'Ah.' The hollow sound rang with bitterness. 'I'd rather not think about him.'

'But we have to.' Calista felt the familiar feeling of torture start to seep into her happiness. 'I'm assuming you still intend to expose what he did?'

Lukas shook his head and, reaching for her hands, held them against his chest. 'No, not now. Not knowing how it would impact on you.'

He moved over to the table and pulled a sheaf of papers from the document case Calista remembered he had been holding when he had arrived at the hospital.

'Here. These are for you.'

'What are they?' Nervously she reached to take them from his outstretched hand.

'Evidence of Aristotle's involvement in the arms-smuggling. How he wrongly implicated my father and me. It's all in there.'

'Oh, God...' Calista's free hand flew to cover her mouth. 'I'm so sorry, Lukas.'

'No more apologies, Calista. Please. Let's put the past behind us. I don't care about any of it any more. You can chuck it on the fire, shred it—do whatever you want with it. The future is all that matters now. You, me and Effie. The most wonderful future I could ever wish for.'

Calista looked down at the hateful papers in her hand. There was nothing she would like to do more than destroy them. But she knew with depressing certainty that she couldn't. Destroying evidence didn't destroy the past. Her father's evil deeds couldn't be eradicated. And the damage he had inflicted along the way to Stavros and to Lukas...

No, she couldn't keep the burden of that secret. She wouldn't be able to live with herself.

'I'm going to take these to the police.' She held up the papers with a shaky hand.

Lukas stared at her in alarm. 'No, Calista, you don't have to.'

'Yes—yes, I do.'

'Please think very carefully before you do anything rash. The fall-out could be pretty nasty.'

'I know that. But you and your father have taken the blame for Aristotle's crimes for far too long. It's time the truth came out.'

'And you're sure about this?'

'Yes, quite sure. My loyalties are to *you* now—you and Stavros, the Kalanos family. Very soon I will bear the Kalanos name, and Effie too, once the paperwork is sorted. I will no longer be a Gianopoulous and neither will she. Maybe when the truth is out I will be able to move on, put my traitorous bloodline behind me. Free myself of the ties of my father.'

'Calista Kalanos. I can't tell you how good that sounds.'

'Mmm…for me too.'

They kissed again.

'You are extraordinarily brave, Calista—you know that, don't you?'

'Not brave. Just doing what has to be done.'

'Then I will be right there beside you to support you. No one will lay any blame at *your* door. I will make sure of that. If they try they will have me to answer to.'

'You and me against the world, eh?'

'No, not against it. Owning it—making it ours. You and Effie are my world. All I could ever want and all I could ever ask for. Except maybe…'

'Yes, go on—what?'

'Maybe a little brother or sister for Effie. Or both. Or a couple of each… In fact maybe we should start now.'

Laughing, Calista pushed herself back from his embrace to gaze into his midnight eyes. 'I love you, Lukas. So, *so* much.'

'I love you too, Calista, more than words can say. And I can't wait to spend the rest of my life with you.'

'Me too, Lukas,' Calista whispered softly against his lips. 'Me too.'

* * * * *

If you enjoyed
THE GREEK'S PLEASURABLE REVENGE
why not read these other
SECRET HEIRS OF BILLIONAIRES *stories?*

THE SECRET TO MARRYING MARCHESI
by Amanda Cinelli
DEMETRIOUS DEMANDS HIS CHILD
by Kate Hewitt
THE DESERT KING'S SECRET HEIR
by Annie West
THE SHEIKH'S SECRET SON
by Maggie Cox
THE INNOCENT'S SHAMEFUL SECRET
by Sara Craven

Available now!

MILLS & BOON®

MODERN™

POWER, PASSION AND IRRESISTIBLE TEMPTATION

A sneak peek at next month's titles...

In stores from 15th June 2017:

- **The Pregnant Kavakos Bride** – Sharon Kendrick *and*
  The Secret Kept from the Greek – Susan Stephens
- **Sicilian's Baby of Shame** – Carol Marinelli *and*
  Salazar's One-Night Heir – Jennifer Hayward

In stores from 29th June 2017:

- **The Billionaire's Secret Princess** – Caitlin Crews *and*
  Claiming His Convenient Fiancée – Natalie Anderson
- **A Ring to Secure His Crown** – Kim Lawrence *and*
  Wedding Night with Her Enemy – Melanie Milburne

Just can't wait?
Buy our books online before they hit the shops!
www.millsandboon.co.uk

Also available as eBooks.

MILLS & BOON®

EXCLUSIVE EXTRACT

Ariston Kavakos makes impoverished Keeley Turner a proposition: a month's employment on his island, at his command. Soon her resistance to their sizzling chemistry weakens! But when there's a consequence, Ariston makes one thing clear: Keeley *will* become his bride…

Read on for a sneak preview of
THE PREGNANT KAVAKOS BRIDE

'You're offering to *buy* my baby? Are you out of your mind?'

'I'm giving you the opportunity to make a fresh start.'

'Without my *baby*?'

'A baby will tie you down. I can give this child everything it needs,' Ariston said, deliberately allowing his gaze to drift around the dingy little room. 'You cannot.'

'Oh, but that's where you're wrong, Ariston,' Keeley said, her hands clenching. 'You might have all the houses and yachts and servants in the world, but you have a great big hole where your heart should be—and therefore you're incapable of giving this child the thing it needs more than anything else!'

'Which is?'

'Love!'

Ariston felt his body stiffen. He loved his brother and once he'd loved his mother, but he was aware of his limitations. No, he didn't do the big showy emotion he suspected she was talking about and why should he, when he knew the brutal heartache it could cause? Yet something told him that trying to defend his own position was pointless. She would fight for this child, he realised. She would fight with all the strength she possessed, and that was going to complicate things. Did she imagine he was going to accept what she'd just told him and play no part in it? Politely dole out payments and have sporadic weekend meetings with his own flesh and blood? Or worse, no meetings at all. He met the green blaze of her eyes.

'So you won't give this baby up and neither will I,' he said softly. 'Which means that the only solution is for me to marry you.'

He saw the shock and horror on her face.

'But I don't want to marry you! It wouldn't work, Ariston—on so many levels. You must realise that. Me, as the wife of an autocratic control freak who doesn't even like me? I don't think so.'

'It wasn't a question,' he said silkily. 'It was a statement. It's not a case of *if* you will marry me, Keeley—just when.'

'You're mad,' she breathed.

He shook his head. 'Just determined to get what is rightfully mine. So why not consider what I've said, and sleep on it and I'll return tomorrow at noon for your answer—when you've calmed down. But I'm warning you now, Keeley—that if you are wilful enough to try to refuse me, or if you make some foolish attempt to run away and escape...' he paused and looked straight into her eyes '...I will find you and drag you through every court in the land to get what is rightfully mine.'

Don't miss
THE PREGNANT KAVAKOS BRIDE
by Sharon Kendrick

Available July 2017
www.millsandboon.co.uk